PENGUIN

RED CAVALRY AND OTHER STORIES

ISAAC BABEL was born in Odessa in 1894, the son of a dealer in agricultural machinery, and he grew up in a typically assimilated Jewish
family amid the flourishing Hebrew and Yiddish intellectual life of
this cosmopolitan seaport. His first story was published in Kiev in
1913. In Petrograd (St Petersburg), in 1915, he won the encourage-
ment and life-long patronage of Maxim Gorky. Gorky published
Babel's stories and sketches in his *Letopis'* and, after the revolution, in
his anti-Bolshevik newspaper *Novaya zhizn'*, closed down by Lenin
in July 1918. Babel spent the revolutionary years writing erotic tales
for his unpublished collection *Petersburg 1918*. In 1920, however, he
joined the Red Cossacks in the short war against Poland and used his
experiences in his unforgettable *Red Cavalry* (1926). When excerpts
from *Red Cavalry* and *Odessa Stories* appeared in Moscow in 1923,
Babel rose to instant fame but also controversy. The 'autobiographical'
Childhood series and more Odessa and Red Cavalry stories followed,
as well as an attempt at a book exposing the cruelty of forced collectivization, *Velikaya krinitsa*. He also tried his hand at plays and wrote
film scripts to try and withstand the increasing demands for political
conformism. Declaring himself the 'master of the genre of silence',
Babel survived the Stalinist Terror until he was arrested suddenly in
1939. He was secretly tried on trumped-up charges of espionage and
treason and executed on 27 January 1940.

DAVID MCDUFF was born in 1945 and was educated at the University
of Edinburgh. His publications comprise a large number of translations of foreign prose and verse, including contemporary Scandinavian
work. His first book of verse, *Words in Nature*, appeared in 1972. He
has translated a number of nineteenth-century Russian prose works for
the Penguin Classics series. These include Dostoyevsky's *The Brothers
Karamazov*, *Crime and Punishment*, *The Idiot* (2004), *The House of the
Dead*, *Poor Folk and Other Stories*, Tolstoy's *The Kreutzer Sonata and
Other Stories* and *The Sebastopol Sketches*, and Nikolai Leskov's *Lady
Macbeth of Mtsensk*. He has also translated Andrei Bely's novel *Petersburg*
for Penguin.

ISAAC BABEL

Red Cavalry and Other Stories

Edited with Notes by EFRAIM SICHER
Translated with an Introduction by
DAVID McDUFF

PENGUIN BOOKS

PENGUIN BOOKS

Published by the Penguin Group
Penguin Books Ltd, 80 Strand, London WC2R ORL, England
Penguin Group (USA) Inc., 375 Hudson Street, New York, New York 10014, USA
Penguin Group (Canada), 10 Alcorn Avenue, Toronto, Ontario, Canada M4V 3B2
(a division of Pearson Penguin Canada Inc.)
Penguin Ireland, 25 St Stephen's Green, Dublin 2, Ireland
(a division of Penguin Books Ltd)
Penguin Group (Australia), 250 Camberwell Road,
Camberwell, Victoria 3124, Australia (a division of Pearson Australia Group Pty Ltd)
Penguin Books India Pvt Ltd, 11 Community Centre, Panchsheel Park, New Delhi – 110 017, India
Penguin Group (NZ), cnr Airborne and Rosedale Roads, Albany,
Auckland 1310, New Zealand (a division of Pearson New Zealand Ltd)
Penguin Books (South Africa) (Pty) Ltd, 24 Sturdee Avenue, Rosebank 2196, South Africa

Penguin Books Ltd, Registered Offices: 80 Strand, London WC2R ORL, England

www.penguin.com

First published 1994
Reprinted with revisions 1998
Published in Penguin Classics 2005
4

Translated by David McDuff from an annotated edition by Efraim Sicher

Printed in the United States of America

ISBN-13: 978-0-14-044997-6

Contents

INTRODUCTION   ix

EARLY STORIES

Old Shloyme   3
Ilya Isaakovich and Margarita Prokofyevna   7
Shabbos Nakhamu   II

'AUTOBIOGRAPHICAL' STORIES

Childhood. At Grandmother's   21
The Story of My Dovecot   27
First Love   41
In the Basement   49
Awakening   59
Di Grasso   67
Guy de Maupassant   71
The Journey   80

RED CAVALRY

Crossing the Zbrucz   91
The Catholic Church in Novograd   93
A Letter   96
The *Konzapas* Commander   101
Pan Apolek   103
The Sun of Italy   112
Gedali   116
My First Goose   119
The Rebbe   123
The Way to Brody   126
The Theory of the *Tachanka*   128

The Death of Dolgushov   131
Kombrig 2   136
Sashka Christ   138
The Life Story of Pavlichenko, Matvey Rodionych   144
The Cemetery in Kozin   150
Prishchepa   150
The Story of a Horse   152
Konkin   156
Beresteczko   160
Salt   163
Evening   167
Afonka Bida   170
At St Valentine's   177
Squadron Commander Trunov   182
The Ivans   190
A Sequel to the Story of a Horse   198
The Widow   199
Zamość   204
Treason   208
Czesniki   213
After the Battle   218
The Song   222
The Rebbe's Son   225
Argamak   227

ODESSA STORIES

The King   237
How It was Done in Odessa   244
Justice in Brackets   254
Lyubka Kózak   260
The Father   267
Sunset   277
The End of the Almshouse   289
Karl-Yankel   299

CONTENTS

NOTES   311

TEXTUAL NOTES   327

APPENDIX   Lionel Trilling's introduction to the
first English translation (1955) of Isaac Babel's
Collected Stories   340

Introduction

Few twentieth-century writers present the literary biographer with quite such an enigma as Isaac Emmanuilovich Babel (1894–1940). His shadowy, for the most part undocumented life ended obscurely, with his arrest by the Stalinist secret police. The volumes of reminiscences by those who knew him, such as that published in Moscow in 1989,[1] have done little to increase our knowledge of the circumstances of his life and death. Viktor Shklovsky, in an account of a visit he made as a young man with Babel to Tolstoy's estate at Yasnaya Polyana, provides what is perhaps the most vivid portrait to be found in the book – yet his characterization of Babel as 'the man with the quiet voice' also leads us away from the writer's individual personality and destiny towards a region of self-effacement and self-abandonment that ends in disappearance: 'After that quiet day I never saw Babel again.'

Even those who might have been thought to be closest to Babel have found it difficult to retain a clear, complete picture of him as he was in life. Nathalie Babel, the writer's daughter, who was ten years old and in France when her father was arrested by the Soviet secret police, says that she grew up

> wishing that some day, somewhere, a door would open and my father would come in. We would recognize each other immediately, and without seeming surprised, without letting him catch his breath, I would say, 'Well, here you are at last. We've been puzzled about you for so long; although you left behind much love and devotion, you bequeathed us very few facts. It's so good to have you here. Do sit down and tell us what happened.'[2]

Nathalie Babel also describes a visit she made in 1961 to Moscow –

where one can still meet people who loved him and continue to speak of him with nostalgia. There, thousands of miles from my own home in Paris, sitting in his living-room, in his own chair, drinking from his glass, I felt utterly baffled. Though in a sense I had tracked him down, he still eluded me. The void remained; I knew so little about him.[3]

And she alludes to a trait in her father's character that compounded this problem: 'although he appeared to be jovial and talkative, he was, in reality, not very communicative. Moreover, he loved to confuse and mystify people.'[4]

The numerous myths, false rumours and stories about Babel that circulated after his disappearance and death – among them that he managed a stud farm, had a love affair with the sister of Yagoda (the ex-chief of the political police), was a Trotskyite, a spy, and that he engaged in black-market activities – are in part, one realizes, the result of Stalinist denigration and disinformation, but may also owe something to Babel's own strange and fantastic sense of humour, which was often turned against himself. In trying to understand the complexity of his life and its relation to his fiction, it may be best to begin with one of Babel's own autobiographical statements, in this case the one that is included in the 1979 Aliya edition of his stories[5] and is a 1932 archival version of the more widely published autobiography of 1924:

Was born in Odessa, in the Moldavanka,[6] the son of a Jewish shopkeeper. At my father's insistence studied Hebrew, the Bible and the Talmud until I was sixteen. At home was made to study a large number of subjects from morning to night. I took my rest at school. The school was called the Emperor Nicholas II Commercial College of Odessa. This was a cheerful, undisciplined, noisy and multilingual college. There the sons of foreign merchants, the children of Jewish brokers, Poles of noble descent, Old Believers and many overgrown billiards players were taught. In the intervals between classes we went off to the port, to the pier or to the Greek coffee-houses to play billiards, or to the Moldavanka to drink cheap Bessarabian wine in the cellars.

French was taught better than the other subjects. The teacher was a Breton and possessed a literary gift, like all Frenchmen. I learned the classics by heart with him, got on to close terms with the French colony in Odessa and from the age of fifteen began to write stories in French.

After graduating from the college I was sent to Kiev; in 1915 I found myself in St Petersburg. In St Petersburg things were tough, I had no 'right of residence',[7] I kept out of the way of the police and lodged in a cellar on Pushkin Street which was the home of a tormented, drunken waiter. In 1916 I began to take my literary works around the editorial offices; I was driven from every quarter, the editors (the late Izmaylov, Posse[8] and others) all tried to persuade me to get a job as a shop assistant, I did not listen to them and at the end of 1916 found myself at Gorky's. To this encounter I owe everything. Gorky published my first stories in the November 1916 issue of *Chronicle* (I was made answerable for these stories under Article 1001),[9] he taught me the important things and then – when it had become clear that my two or three tolerable youthful experiments were no more than an accidental success, and that I was going to get nowhere with literature and that I wrote extremely badly – Aleksey Maksimovich sent me among people. For seven years – from 1917 to 1924 – I had occasion to learn many things. I was a soldier on the Romanian front, then served in the Cheka, in Narkompros,[10] in the food-supply expeditions of 1918, in the Northern Army against Yudenich,[11] in the First Cavalry, in the Odessa Gubkom, was a reporter in St Petersburg and Tbilisi, was production manager at the 7th Soviet Printing House in Odessa, et cetera. And only in 1923 did I learn how to express my thoughts clearly and not at too great length. For this reason I date the beginning of my literary work from 1924, when my stories 'Salt', 'A Letter', 'The Death of Dolgushov', 'The King' and others appeared in the journal *Lef*.[12] Over two years *Red Cavalry* and *Odessa Stories* were written. Then there began for me a new time of travelling, silence and gathering of strength. I now stand at the beginning of new work.

This account of Babel's life is only partly true. Nathalie Babel has pointed out that in it, apart from the stress laid on his meeting with Gorky, her father 'does not differentiate between important and trivial details. Apparently, Babel's intention was to present an appropriate past for a young Soviet writer who was not a member of the Communist Party.' There are a number of fabrications in the 'autobiography', including the occupation of Babel's father (he was in reality not a shopkeeper but a salesman of agricultural machinery). The matter is made no easier if we turn to Babel's so-called 'Autobiographical Stories' in search of the facts about his life. Here we find a complex interweaving of fact, fiction and fantasy. Several of the key events, characters and statements in the stories are the result of pure invention. Babel did not, for example, come 'from a destitute and muddle-headed family', as he asserts in 'In the Basement', but from a fairly well-to-do and orderly one. The average Odessa Jewish family was not as Babel describes it in his stories, clinging to the traditions of the past, but was instead rather like its North American counterpart, one in which a considerable degree of 'assimilation' had taken place. While it is true that Moldavanka, Odessa's slum district, was an infamous haunt of prostitutes and gangsters, including Misha 'The Jap' Vinnitsky, prototype of Benya Krik, Babel did not spend the first years of his life there: soon after his birth his parents moved to the Black Sea port of Nikolayev, and it was there that he went to primary school and began his study of English, French and German. If Babel did witness an anti-Jewish pogrom, neither he nor the rest of the Babel family were physically harmed in it. Nathalie Babel has provided the following cautionary information for readers of 'The Story of My Dovecot' and 'First Love':

Nor would his father have had to kneel at a Cossack's feet and beg that his store be spared, for the simple reason that Babel's father did not own a store. He owned a warehouse, which was neither broken into nor plundered during the pogrom. I must add (and this may be a disillusionment to readers of 'First Love') that no member of the Babel family was red-headed, that my grandmother's name was Fanny, not Rachel, nor would she ever have thought of addressing her husband in the terms used by the woman in the story; she was a modest, sensitive woman. It is, of course, not impossible that there was a charming girl named Galina who wore a Chinese peignoir, and who excited the passions of my father at the age of ten. But if she did exist, my father was the only member of the family who had the privilege of knowing her.[13]

The actual course of Babel's life appears to have been roughly as follows: born on 13 July 1894 (30 June Old Style) in the Moldavanka, a suburb of Odessa, Babel was taken by his family to Nikolayev, on the Black Sea coast, where he spent the first nine years of his life, and where in 1899 his sister was born. In early 1905, he began his studies at the Nicholas II Commercial College in Odessa, living with his two aunts and his maternal grandmother in a house on Tiraspolskaya Street, and later in the same year his father, Emmanuil Isaakovich, also returned to Odessa with his wife. After a few months during which the family stayed with the aunts, the Babels moved to an apartment at 17 Richelieu Street, one of the most attractive streets in the city. Babel's father dealt in agricultural machinery, and had an office on Politseyskaya Street, where many shipping and import–export firms had their premises. He wanted to give his children, particularly his son, the best education he could, and Babel had to study modern languages, music (he took lessons with the virtuoso teacher Stolyarsky, though he did not make much progress as an instrumentalist), and Ancient Hebrew. The young Babel's consciousness of his Jewish past and roots is well-evidenced in his earliest known short story, 'Old Shloyme', published in 1913 as a contribution to the 'Jewish Question' against the background of anti-Jewish edicts and pressure to assimilate.

The *numerus clausus*, which restricted the number of Jewish students who could attend any given educational institution, prevented Babel from entering the University of Odessa. At first, Babel followed in his father's footsteps and enrolled at the Kiev Institute of Financial and Business Studies, which was evacuated to Saratov on the outbreak of war in 1914. There, the following year, he wrote the story 'Childhood. At Grandmother's', apparently the seed of the later childhood stories, which shares their theme of breaking away from the Jewish home. In 1915 Babel enrolled in the Psycho-Neurological Institute in Petrograd (as St Petersburg was now called), a liberal arts college which admitted Jews and was well known for its students' political activism. Far from living in a cellar pursued by police, Babel obtained the residence permit required for Jews and boarded with the Slonim family, until he was conscripted to the Romanian front (and was therefore absent from the scene of the Bolshevik coup the following month). During his time in St Petersburg he wrote several stories, including 'Ilya Isaakovich and Margarita Prokofyevna', which Gorky published in his journal *Chronicle*.

On Babel's recuperation from malaria and return to the Revolutionary capital, he wrote critical sketches and stories for Gorky's Menshevik newspaper *New Life*, closed down by Lenin in July 1918, when much of the opposition press was suppressed. Babel seems to have avoided starvation in Petrograd by working as a translator for the infamous Cheka secret police (though this is denied by Nathalie Babel) and, as a protegé of Gorky, for the People's Commissariat of Education. He also wrote some risqué stories about prostitutes and experimented with modernist prose (the series *Petersburg 1918* and *Etchings*). In 1919 he married Yevgeniya Borisovna Gronfeyn, a talented artist and daughter of his father's business friend. By all accounts the marriage was not a happy one. In 1920, the Soviet–Polish War now under way, Babel joined Budyonny's cavalry as a war correspondent for ROSTA, the Soviet news agency, reporting on the action at the Soviet–Polish front in Budyonny's propaganda newspaper *Red Trooper*. This experience completely exhausted him, and he returned to Odessa suffering from lice and acute asthma. Doctors advised that he try to live for a time in a warmer climate. After a short period working in a state publishing house, he moved with his wife to a house taken by the Gronfeyns near Batum in the Caucasus, where it was thought his health might improve. During this time, from 1921, Babel began to work on the stories of *Red Cavalry*. In 1924 Babel and his wife moved to Moscow. The *Red Cavalry* stories, and some of the *Odessa Stories*, about Jewish gangsters in the days before the Revolution, that had been appearing in the Odessa press, were republished in the Moscow journals *Red Virgin Soil* and *Lef* (the latter edited by Mayakovsky), and he acquired almost immediate fame as a writer. The *Red Cavalry* stories aroused Budyonny's wrath – he saw them as a slander on his troops. By 1925, following the death of Lenin, the internal political situation had begun to grow more ominous, and the writer began to think about following his mother and sister abroad. His wife lived in France from 1925 until 1957, the year of her death. The separation from his family caused the writer much anxiety, and things were not made any easier by the fact that there was no Soviet embassy in Brussels, where his mother and sister lived, and the difficulty of obtaining visas for them to visit Russia was a source of great worry to him. His wife had to try to obtain the visas for herself and the other members of the family from the embassy in Paris, but she dreaded visiting it, and as a result the family's papers were very seldom kept in valid order.

In 1925 Babel began to turn away from the 'Odessa' and 'Red Cavalry' tales towards childhood themes in search of a sparser prose style. 'The Story of My Dovecot' and 'First Love' were both published in the same year. These stories were intended eventually to form a book, which was also to contain 'In the Basement' (1929), 'Awakening' (1930) and, probably, 'Di Grasso' (published in 1937). Also in 1925, Babel began to write film scripts in order to support himself and his family financially. This led to problems, as Babel tended to over-commit himself with journalistic and film work, accepting advances and then being unable to meet the required deadlines, thus involving himself in debt. Anxieties of this kind, coupled with anxieties about his dispersed émigré family, made the writing of his own stories increasingly difficult for him. His extremely high personal artistic standards also tended to bring him into conflict with practical reality. To the editor of a journal who demanded new material he wrote that he would rather be flogged in public than send in a manuscript one moment sooner than he believed it to be ready. This pattern of stress and overwork continued into the 1930s, and when Babel had finally managed to write enough stories for a new volume, the political climate had grown so repressive that he could not publish them.

Before the birth of his daughter Nathalie in Paris in 1929, Babel had already returned from a year in Paris to settle his late father-in-law's affairs, but faced changing circumstances inside the Soviet Union. The end of the 1920s saw the beginning of Stalinism and the first Five Year Plan, the attacks on Zamyatin and Pilnyak, the rise of the personality cult and the dragooning of writers to serve the cause of socialism. Why Babel remained in the Soviet Union at this time when he could have lived abroad (though he didn't fancy becoming a taxi driver or émigré writer like Nabokov), has never been adequately explained. His daughter Nathalie has ascribed it to a mixture of patriotism and personal honour:

Babel was convinced that a writer mutilates himself and his work when he leaves his native country. He always refused to emigrate and never once thought of his trips abroad as a means of escape. Moreover, his sense of honour demanded that he stay among his own people.

We know that Babel was well aware of the cruelty of the Stalinist regime, for he talked about it with intimate friends on his trips abroad. Nothing, however, could shatter his feeling that he belonged to Russia and that he had to share the fate of his countrymen. What in so many people would have produced only fear and terror, awakened in him a sense of duty and a kind of blind heroism.[14]

Whatever his reasons for staying in Russia, Babel began increasingly to seek a place as a member of the established order. In 1930 he observed at first hand the collectivization of the rural economy of the Ukraine, and in June that year moved to Molodyonovo, near Moscow, where he became the secretary of the village soviet. In 1932 he was allocated an apartment in Moscow, a rare privilege reserved for Party workers and the cultural–political élite. The apartment was in a house occupied by foreigners: this was something almost unheard of in those days, since contact with foreigners was strictly forbidden for most Russians, and could lead to suspicion and even arrest. From the middle of April until the end of May 1933 Babel was Gorky's guest in Sorrento. Throughout this period, Babel was 'silent' as a writer. Silence was regarded with as much hostility by the authorities as outright dissidence, and every so often the writer was called upon to explain why he had written no new works in praise of the existing order and the building of socialism. He would respond in terms that were ambiguous and evasive. Like several other Soviet writers, Babel could not adapt his style to the portrayal of life in factories and collective farms (though he made some attempts to write about them). Perhaps because of his connections with highly placed officials, he managed to ward off the worst of the criticism for some time. In 1935, however, his fortunes changed. His play *Mariya* – not, in any case, one of his most successful works – was violently criticized by the Party establishment and withdrawn by the Moscow theatre that had already begun rehearsals of it. In 1936 critics were marking the tenth anniversary of Babel's silence since his last book, *Red Cavalry*. From 1932 Babel lived with an engineer on the Moscow metro construction, Antonina Nikolayevna Pirozhkova, who bore him a daughter, Lidia. But the last few years of his life were spent in uncertainty and fear of arrest, though he managed to complete some important projects, including a collaboration with Sergey Eisenstein on the film of Turgenev's story *Bezhin Meadow* (1936), for which he wrote the script – the second version of the film displeased the authorities, and the director was made to recant in public. A letter Babel wrote to his mother, quoted by Nathalie Babel, gives an idea of the writer's state of mind:

My nice Mama, if I write seldom it is not because my life is hard – compared with millions of people's, my life is easy, happy and privileged – but because it is uncertain, and this uncertainty derives entirely from changes and doubts connected with my work. In a country as united as ours, it is quite inevitable that a certain amount of thinking in clichés should appear and I want to overcome this standardized way of thinking and introduce into our literature new ideas, new feeling and rhythms. This is what interests me and nothing else. And so I work and think with great intensity, but I haven't any results to show yet. And, inasmuch as I myself do not see clearly how and by what methods I will reach these results (I do see my inner paths clearly, though), I am not sure myself where and in what kind of environment I ought to live if I am to achieve my goal, and this is what causes my reluctance to drag anyone along behind me and makes me an insecure and wavering man who causes you so much trouble.[15]

Gorky's death in 1936 meant the end of any hopes Babel might have had of remaining safe from arrest. Even though he had friends in high places whom he knew from the days of the Civil War, and was able to intercede on behalf of friends, more and more of whom were disappearing into the hands of the authorities, he knew it was only a matter of time before he too suffered their fate. Yet, paradoxically, the insecurity of his position was accompanied by an elevation of his social status. Increasingly isolated, from 1937 onwards he lived a strangely privileged and comfortable life as a distinguished Soviet writer. An anti-fascist congress in Paris in 1935, to which he accompanied the reluctant and sick Pasternak, was his last opportunity to visit abroad and he was already under surveillance. At this time he began to frequent the homes of some of the most feared men in the country, the heads of the secret police, Yezhov and Yagoda. Nadezhda Mandelstam wrote of him:

Babel told us that he associated only with policemen and drank only with them. The day before he had been drinking with one of the principal policemen in Moscow, and the latter had explained while drunk that he who lives by the sword dies by the sword. The leaders of the militia really did die one after the other . . . Yesterday this one was arrested, a week ago that one . . . 'Today you're alive, but tomorrow the devil only knows where you may end up . . .'
The word 'policeman' was, of course, a euphemism. We knew that Babel was talking about Chekists, but among his boon companions I think there were also genuine police officials.
O.M. [Osip Mandelstam] wanted to know why Babel felt drawn to 'policemen'. The distributor where death was issued. To put his fingers on it? 'No,' Babel replied, 'I won't touch it with my fingers, but just take a sniff to find out what it smells like.'
It is no secret that among the 'policemen' whom Babel visited was Yezhov. After Babel's arrest, Katayev and Shklovsky used to sigh that Babel had been so afraid that he had even gone to Yezhov, but it had not helped, and it was precisely for that that Beria had had him arrested . . . I am certain that Babel went to him not out of cowardice but out of curiosity – in order to take a sniff and find out what he smelt like.[16]

By 1939 Babel was deputy chairman of the editorial board of the State Literary Publishing House, Goslitizdat. He had a dacha in Peredelkino, and was working on new stories, which were still very much in his own style, making few or no concessions to the demands for political conformism that were being made on him. A volume of these new stories was advertised by the publishing house Soviet Writer (*Sovetskiy pisatel*) for publication that same year. Quite suddenly, on 15 May, Babel was arrested at Peredelkino, and all the furniture and written materials in his Moscow apartment and his dacha were seized and taken away by the secret police. The dwellings were then sealed. None of the manuscripts and papers were seen again, and there were rumours that they were destroyed during the German advance on Moscow. Babel was taken by car to Moscow's Lubyanka prison, smiling and apparently unafraid. His last known words before he disappeared were: '*Ne dali mne zakonchit*' – 'They did not let me finish.'

We now know the precise nature and time of Babel's death. He was charged with pro-Trotsky activities and with being a foreign spy as part of a writers' anti-Soviet conspiracy (which the secret police were trying to invent for a show-trial). Babel was tried on 26 January 1940 and shot the next day. Babel's first wife, who remained in Paris, appears to have believed until the late 1950s that Babel survived the war, having been assured by Ilya Ehrenburg in 1946 that he was under house arrest somewhere in Russia. But the writer's second wife, Antonina Pirozhkova, was informed in 1940 that Babel had been given ten years' hard labour 'without right of correspondence' (i.e. to write or receive letters) by a military tribunal. In 1954 the sentence was revoked, and the official death certificate stated merely that the writer had died on 17 March 1941, not specifying where or how.

The shadowy, unclear nature of Babel's life stands in marked contrast to his personality, which from his writings alone emerges as clearly focused in its humour, intelligence and lyrical depth. That this should be so seems to indicate that the conventional biographical method may not be the best one for understanding Babel's complex artistic nature. Perhaps what is needed instead is an approach that cuts across the several and apparently conflicting realities he inhabited, showing how his personality adapted to each of them. The structuralist-based study by the Babel scholar Efraim Sicher, *Style and Structure in the Prose of Isaac Babel* (1985), represents one such approach, constituting an analysis of Babel's creative personality through the special features of his work and the ways in which these relate to the conditions under which it was born. Another method, which bears similar results, and has been extensively applied by the literary critic Simon Markish, principally in his afterword to the Aliya edition of Babel's short stories, (*Russko-yevreyskaya literatura i Isaak Babel* – 'Russian Jewish literature and Isaac Babel')[17] is to concentrate on the central fact of Babel's biography and career as a writer – that although he wrote in Russian, he was first and foremost a Jewish writer, with roots deep in Hebrew and Yiddish literary culture.

As Markish points out, Babel fits in very well with the general picture of Soviet writing in the 1920s. The story cycle *Red Cavalry* bears many similarities to other works by Soviet writers about the Civil War, like Furmanov's *Chapayev*, Fadeyev's *The Rout* and the short stories of Vsevolod Ivanov. Its experimentalism is in some ways related to that of the Serapion Brothers group of writers, and its pictorial vividness has a counterpart in Sholokhov's *Quiet Flows the Don*. Likewise, the evocation of the gangster underworld in Babel's *Odessa Stories* is linked to the general preoccupation with criminal matters that was expressed, for example, in a work like Leonid Leonov's novel *The Thief*. Markish even sees a common feature in Babel's inability to create under Stalinism:

Even Babel's notorious silence, his disastrously small output after 'Sunset' (1928) and the relative weakness of this meagre output compared with the works of the 1920s, are only an extreme form of the sickness and crisis of the whole of Soviet literature that were revealed during the transition to the 1930s.

Yet Babel differed from most of the other writers of the early Soviet period in one special circumstance – that he belonged not to Russian, but to Russian-Jewish literature. And unlike many other Jewish writers, he did not need to choose a Jewish language in the manner of Chaim Bialik, for example, who while at Talmudic academy decided to write in Hebrew, rather than Yiddish or Russian.

The tradition that Babel belonged to was a comparatively young one. During the nineteenth century the movement of Jewish secular enlightenment called the *Haskala*, which took its origins in Germany, gave rise to a Hebrew and Yiddish literary culture in the Russian Empire, with centres in Warsaw, Vilna and Odessa. One aim of the enlightenment was to bring about a degree of assimilation to European, non-Jewish culture. In Germany this process went much faster than in Russia, facilitated both by the relative civil liberties and by the relative prosperity of German Jews compared to their Russian counterparts. In Russia Jews had to contend with a much harsher attitude on the part of the authorities, particularly in the last decade of the century, yet even so they managed to develop a Russian-language culture that ran parallel to the Yiddish and Hebrew ones, and Russian became another of the languages of the Jewish diaspora. From the early 1860s onwards, Russian-Jewish journals and newspapers began to appear, like the famous *Dawn*, which was published in Odessa. At the turn of the century the rise of Zionism, which had been impelled by the increasing hostility towards the Jews of Russia under the reign of Alexander III, reinforced the establishment of Russian as a language of literature and journalism: the Zionists, while advocating a return to Hebrew as the authentic Jewish language, temporarily promoted Russian as a 'progressive' alternative to Yiddish. Writers like Vladimir Jabotinsky and the Jewish nationalist poet Semyon Frug expressed in Russian the hopes, sufferings and aspirations of those who sought a new life in the United States or Palestine, then an Ottoman protectorate.

In 1914, with the outbreak of the First World War, the

territories of Russia that lay within the Jewish Pale became the battleground on which the rival armies fought out the conflict, and the result was an exodus of Jews to the south of Russia, particularly to Odessa. It was in Odessa that the flowering of Hebrew and Yiddish literature took place. Babel was personally acquainted with some of the great figures of Jewish writing who lived there from an older generation; in particular Mendele Moykher-Sforim, whose work Babel later translated into Russian. He was also familiar with the writing of Sholom Aleykhem, whom he translated. Of the newer generation, he had read books by Klausner, Ravnitsky and Akhad Haam. None the less, it was as a writer of Russian that Babel began his career: the story 'Childhood. At Grandmother's' affirms his Russian-Jewish origins in terms of language and artistic style, and also in terms of attitude and philosophical outlook. Above all, the story displays a strong element of conflict – between a loathing of the constricting atmosphere of the Jewish home and an attraction to and sense of belonging to the Russian-Jewish world from which it arises. In his study of Babel, Simon Markish sees in this characteristic the roots of Babel's literary art:

The house itself, its way of life and its mistress give rise within the boy to the following response: 'All of it at that moment seemed extraordinary to me and made me want to flee from it all and yet remain for ever' ... The familiar way of life and atmosphere are suddenly transformed, acquiring a gripping keenness of novelty and inspiring, at once, both horror (or, perhaps, revulsion), and a sense of 'one's own', of the kindred, the inseparable, the inescapable. In essence, here is the whole of the Jewish Babel, the root of his social and emotional judgements, the foundation of his aesthetics. Jewishness, whether it be of the unshakeably traditional, *shtetl*-Hassidic kind, or of the urban, enlightened and emancipated kind, is perceived dually, the heritage is both accepted and rejected simultaneously. And this excludes the everyday scene-painting, the apologetics and the denunciations that are characteristic of the old Russian-Jewish literature, and gives a fresh and wonder-struck view from the side. Precisely from here come the exoticism of the commonplace and the brutish, the fantastic sharpness of lines, the hysterical whoop of colours. But from here, too, come the loneliness, the inevitable ill-definedness, the impossibility of attaining any shore, the doom of being for always and for everyone 'other'. A position that gives inestimable artistic advantages (which Babel utilized with great success, to the end) and anticipates by a long way the position of the finest masters of American-Jewish literature, from Henry Roth to Saul Bellow and Philip Roth.

In the course of his long and thorough study, Markish shows how this dual perspective, of acceptance and rejection of Jewish tradition, helped Babel to break away from the narrowly 'Jewish' style and subject-matter of 'Old Shloyme' and 'Ilya Isaakovich and Margarita Prokofyevna', through the expanded, though still basically Jewish, plot and character medium of *Odessa Stories*, to the relatively non-Jewish world of *Red Cavalry*. *Red Cavalry* marks the pinnacle of Babel's literary achievement – it is the work that demonstrates his dualism most forcefully and vividly, and in it his personality splits in two. Without it being immediately obvious, the stories have two narrators: one is the Jewish war correspond-ent, Kirill Vasilyevich Lyutov, bespectacled, bookish and sensitive, and the other is the person whom Lyutov would like to become, and constantly strives to be – a true revolution-ary and Bolshevik soldier with no fear of blood and killing. This dichotomy accounts for the extreme physical violence that is manifested in many of the stories: it is as though Babel were trying to overcome his own horror at what he has seen and witnessed, and to turn it into a kind of vivid, surreal poetry. At the opposite end of the spectrum is the character of the Jew Gedali, who believes in 'the International of good men' and with whom Lyutov vainly remonstrates, more than half-convinced that the old man is right:

'... The International, *panie* comrade, one does not know what to eat it with ...'

'One eats it with gunpowder,' I replied to the old man. 'And seasons it with the finest blood ...'

The conflict is also sharply delineated in the character of the Red Army soldier Bratslavsky, the son of the Zhitomir Rebbe Motale Bratslavsky, in the story 'The Rebbe's Son'. Bratslavsky's life, as he dies of typhoid on the floor of the editorial train, demonstrates its chaotic fragmentation in the contents of his trunk:

Here everything was dumped together – the warrants of the agitator and the commemorative booklets of the Jewish poet. Portraits of Lenin and Maimonides lay side by side. Lenin's nodulous skull and the tarnished silk of the portraits of Maimonides. A strand of female hair had been placed in a book of the resolutions of the Sixth Party Congress, and in the margins of communist leaflets swarmed crooked lines of Ancient Hebrew verse. In a sad and meagre rain they fell on me – pages of the Song of Songs and revolver cartridges.

Bratslavsky is in a sense Lyutov's double, manifesting in an extreme form the latter's uncertainty about his personal, social and historical identity. To the theme, common enough in 'revolutionary' literature, of the wavering intellectual, detached from the 'masses', Babel adds the new theme of the intellectual Jew, unable to reconcile himself to the brutality and slaughter involved in the creation of the 'radiant future'. The story 'My First Goose' is, of course, the most famous example of this dilemma, with its attendant sense of helplessness and despair, in Babel's writings. But there are others, such as the scene depicted in 'Beresteczko', of a group of Bolshevik-led Cossacks executing an aged Jew:

Directly under my window several Cossacks were shooting an old Jew with a silvery beard for espionage. The old man was screaming and trying to tear himself free. Then Kudrya from the machine-gun detachment took the old man's head and put it under his arm. The Jew calmed down and stood with his legs apart. With his right hand Kudrya pulled out his dagger and carefully cut the old man's throat, without splashing any blood on himself. Then he knocked on the closed window frame.

'If anyone's interested,' he said, 'they can come and get him. He's all yours . . .'

Why, given such evident antipathy to the methods of revolution, did Babel none the less support the Bolsheviks and strive to serve them as a writer? In the absence of detailed biographical material relating to his life, we are at a loss to explain this in any concrete, definitive way. Even his letters, published in French and English translation, are to say the least opaque, and bear the mark of both a fear of official censorship and what one senses to be an inner, personal reticence. Nathalie Babel describes the letters dating from the period 1936–9 as being 'gradually drained of substance; they resemble more and more the reports an employee makes to his superiors about his work and health . . . He did not even mention things that the censor would very likely have passed . . .' Nathalie Babel also writes of her father's 'terrible anxiety', of 'his certainty that he would eventually be destroyed like the others'.[18]

Yet fear alone could not explain away a lifetime's reticence. In reading Babel, whether it is his stories, his correspondence or his diaries, one has very little sense that he ever really had much genuine sympathy for the aims and aspirations of Bolshevism, even though he supported it in practice. If one is to look for his motivation, the driving force that impelled him along the road of his destiny as a 'Soviet writer', one must above all, I believe, examine an area of his early development that throws at least some light on his complex personality. It is, directly or indirectly, linked to his consciousness of his Jewish identity, and to his desire, so poignantly analysed by Markish, both to remain faithful to his Jewish roots and to be free of them.

In the story 'Awakening' Babel describes a feature of life in the Odessa of his childhood which, almost against his will, left a deep mark on him. This was the remarkable proliferation in that city of performing musicians, in particular violinists, most of them from Russian-Jewish families. From Odessa came Mischa Elman and Jascha Heifetz, and the great violin teacher Stolyarsky, who later taught David Oistrakh. In the story, Stolyarsky becomes 'Mr Zagursky', though 'Auer' is of course the real, and famous, violin virtuoso and teacher Leopold Auer:

When a boy was four or five, his mother took the tiny, puny creature to Mr Zagursky. Zagursky ran a *Wunderkind* factory, a factory of Jewish dwarfs in lace collars and patent-leather shoes. He sought them out in the slums of the Moldavanka, in the evil-smelling courtyards of the Old Market. Zagursky gave them a first push in the right direction, and then the children were sent to Professor Auer in St Petersburg.

Babel's father decided that his son should keep up with the rest, and become a child prodigy, and the boy was sent for lessons with Stolyarsky at an early age. Babel describes his dislike of playing the violin in no uncertain terms: 'the sounds crawled out of my violin like iron filings'. And he tells us: 'During my violin practice I placed on my music stand books by Turgenev or Dumas and, scraping out heaven only knows what, devoured page after page.'

Thus the vicarious musical ambition of his parents became supplanted by a genuine ambition of his own – to become a writer. Yet somehow the connection between writing and music as a performing art – a connection possibly unconscious, since instilled at an early age – seems to have lingered on in Babel's psyche for most of his life. One has a sense that for Babel his writing career was really something akin to a career as a concert artist, to be pursued regardless of social change and outer circumstances, with stoicism and dedication to an art that demanded self-effacement, hard work, discipline and love. From one point of view, his passionate advocacy of Maupassant and Dumas may be seen as equivalent to the commitment a classical instrumentalist brings to the works of the nineteenth-century concert repertoire: in his own writing he continued to interpret that European tradition and to sound its clear, distinctive note against the turbulence of history. Here, perhaps, we have a key to the apparent enigma of his situation. For in Babel we are presented with an extreme paradox: that of a practitioner of 'art for art's sake' who tried to put himself and his writing at the service of a social and political revolution. Just what that revolution meant to him is not clear; yet at some level in his consciousness it seems to have been associated with his Jewish patrimony, and with the aspiration of generations of Jews for a better society and a better world. That the dream turned sour, threatening and bloodily destructive was merely one more twist of history that must be faced with stoicism and courage. His adherence to the artist's moral duty to stay with his art to the end was what made Babel remain in the Soviet Union – for he had identified his art with the life and the destiny of his own people, and to uproot that art from its soil would be to desert them. And so, to the end, he continued to write of the Kriks and the Moldavanka, of the world that had died with the Revolution and which the Revolution was somehow, perhaps almost mystically, expected to transform and replace.

After Babel's death, his work fell into neglect in the Soviet Union. There was no room for his brand of stoical individualism in the Stalinist Russia of the 1940s and early 1950s. Not until the late fifties and early sixties did his stories become available again, though only in selected, censored editions. With the repressive climate of the Brezhnev years and the pressure against Jewish activism that continued right until

Gorbachov, little new material was published. Even recent editions of the stories, published in the early nineties, are not complete. In the West, Babel has been known through a series of translations that have appeared sporadically since the 1930s. Nearly all of these, including the *Collected Stories* of 1955 (reprinted in 1983), have been made from the censored versions that were published in the Soviet Union both during and after Babel's lifetime. Not until 1979 did a Russian edition of the best-known stories, in their original, uncensored form, appear in the Aliya Library series published in Israel, under the editorship of the Babel scholar E. Sicher. This edition reconstitutes the three major cycles of Babel's corpus – 'Autobiographical Stories' (the childhood series Babel intended to publish as 'Story of my Dovecot'), *Red Cavalry* and *Odessa Tales* – and forms the basis for the present volume.

NOTES

1. *Vospominaniya o Babele 1938–1939–1940*, Moscow, 1989.
2. *Isaac Babel, The Lonely Years. Unpublished Stories and Private Correspondence*, translated from Russian by A.R. MacAndrew and Max Hayward, edited and with an introduction by Nathalie Babel, New York, 1964, p. ix.
3. ibid., p. ix.
4. ibid., p. xiv.
5. Isaak Babel, *Detstvo i drugie rasskazy*, Tel-Aviv, 1979.
6. A district of Odessa where before the Revolution many Jews lived in poverty. The Moldavanka was famous as a hideout for gangsters and criminals.
7. This is an invention: in fact Babel lodged with the engineer L.I. Slonim and his wife A.G. Slonim, with whom he corresponded for many years. Babel did have the residence permit required of Jews in the Russian capital.
8. A.A. Izmaylov (1873–1921) was a scholar and editor. V.A. Posse was a former editor of the journal *Life*.
9. An article of the penal code that prohibited the publication of

works detrimental to good morals. The charge was one of porno-
graphy.
10. The People's Commissariat of Education.
11. The White Army general who tried to take Petrograd in 1919.
12. The journal of the 'Left Front of Art', edited by the poet Mayakovsky.
13. op. cit., p. xv.
14. ibid., pp. xxi–xxii.
15. ibid., p. xxii.
16. Nadezhda Mandelstam, *Vospominaniya*, New York, 1970, p. 341.
17. op. cit., pp. 319–45.
18. op. cit., p. xxv.

EARLY STORIES

Old Shloyme

Although our little town is not large, although its inhabitants are few, although Shloyme has lived for sixty years in the town without a break, even so, not everyone would be able to tell you who Shloyme is, or what he is like. That is because he has simply been forgotten, in the way that an unneeded, inconspicuous object is forgotten. Old Shloyme was such an object. He was eighty-six years old. His eyes were watery; his face, a small, dirty, wrinkled face, was covered by a yellowish, never-combed beard and a mane of thick, tangled hair. Shloyme almost never washed, seldom changed his clothes, and he had a bad smell: his son and daughter-in-law, in whose home he lived, had given him up as a bad job, concealed him in a warm corner and forgotten him. A warm corner and food – that was what remained to Shloyme, and, it seemed, it was enough for him. To warm his old, broken bones, to eat a good piece of fat, juicy meat – those were for him the highest enjoyment. He would arrive first at table, greedily follow each piece with unblinking eyes, convulsively stuff the food into his mouth with long, bony fingers and eat, eat, eat until he was refused any more, even one more little piece. It was revolting to watch Shloyme as he ate: the whole of his small, emaciated figure trembled, his fingers were covered in grease, his face pitiful, full of a terrible fear lest a wrong be done to him, lest he be forgotten. Sometimes the daughter-in-law played practical jokes on Shloyme: at table she would, as if accidentally, leave him out: the old man would begin to grow agitated, look helplessly about him, try to smile with his crooked, toothless mouth; he wanted to show that the food was not important to him, that he was all right as he was, but in the depths of his eyes, in the fold of his mouth, in

3

his extended imploring arms could be felt such pleading, this smile, produced with such difficulty, was so pitiful, that the jokes were forgotten and Old Shloyme received his portion.

Thus did he live in his corner – ate and slept, and in summer also warmed himself in the blaze of the sun. He had, it appeared, long ago lost the ability to understand anything. His son's business activities, the events of the household, did not interest him. Indifferently he gazed at all that occurred, and there merely stirred within him the fear that his grandson might see that he had a dried-up piece of gingerbread hidden under his pillow. Never did anyone speak to Shloyme, seek his advice, ask him to help them. And Shloyme was very pleased when, after supper one day, his son came over to him and loudly shouted in his ear, 'Papasha, we're being evicted from here, evicted, do you hear, kicked out!' The son's voice trembled, his face was contorted as by pain. Shloyme slowly raised his faded eyes, looked about him, took something in with difficulty, wrapped himself more tightly in his grease-stained frock-coat, made no reply and plodded off to bed.

From that day on Shloyme began to notice that something was wrong in the house. His son was downcast, neglected his business, sometimes wept and looked furtively at his chewing father. His grandson stopped attending the grammar school. His daughter-in-law shouted in a shrill voice, wrung her hands, pressed her boy to her and wept, wept bitterly, hysterically.

Now Shloyme had an occupation – he looked and tried to understand what was happening. Troubled thoughts stirred within his long-inactive brain. 'They're being kicked out of here!' Shloyme knew why they were being kicked out. But why, he couldn't leave! He was eighty-six, he wanted to keep warm. Outside it was cold, damp . . . No, Shloyme was not going anywhere. He had nowhere to go, nowhere at all. Shloyme hid in his corner and he wanted to embrace the shaky wooden bed, stroke the stove, the dear, warm stove that was as old as he was. He had grown up here, lived his poor, cheerless life here and wanted his old bones to rest in the small home cemetery. In the moments when he had such thoughts, Shloyme grew unnaturally animated, went to his son, tried to tell him many things, excitedly, to tender some advice, but ... it was so long since he had talked to anyone, or given advice to anyone about anything. And the words would freeze in his toothless mouth, the hand which he had raised would fall, helplessly. Shloyme shrivelled up, as if ashamed of his outburst, went back morosely to his corner and listened to what his son and daughter-in-law were talking about. His hearing was poor, but he picked up some of it, picked it up with fear, with horror. At such moments his son would sense fixed upon him the wild and heavy gaze of the old man who was being driven out of his mind and the pair of small eyes which with a cursed question were constantly guessing at something, trying to fathom something. On one occasion a word was spoken too loudly: the daughter-in-law had forgotten that Shloyme was not yet dead. And after this word a quiet, as-if-stifled wail was heard. It came from Old Shloyme. With faltering steps, dirty and tousled, he slowly crept over to his son, seized him by the hands, stroked them, kissed them, without removing his inflamed gaze from his son, shook his head several times and for the first time in many, many years a tear rolled from his eyes. He said nothing more. With difficulty he got up off his knees, wiped the tears away with a bony hand, for some reason shook the dust off his frock-coat and made his way back to his corner, where the warm stove was ... Shloyme wanted to warm himself. He was cold.

From that time on, Shloyme did not think of anything else. He knew one thing: his son wanted to go away from his people, to a new God. The old, forgotten faith stirred within him. Shloyme had never been religious, seldom prayed and had earlier even been considered godless. But to go away, completely, to go away from one's God, the God of a humiliated and suffering people – that he did not understand. Heavily the thoughts tossed and turned inside his head, slowly he pondered, but these words stood immutably, firmly, menacingly before him: 'This must not be, must not be!' And when Shloyme had grasped that the disaster was inevitable, that his son would not be able to endure, he said to himself, 'Shloyme, Old Shloyme, what can you do now?' Helplessly the old man looked around him, puckered his mouth sorrowfully, as children do, and tried to weep an old man's bitter tears. They were not there, the relieving tears. And then, at that moment, when his heart had begun to sicken, when his mind had grasped the limitlessness of the disaster, then Shloyme cast a loving glance into his warm corner for the last time and decided that he was not going to be kicked out of here, never would he be kicked out. They would not let Old Shloyme eat the piece of dried-up gingerbread that was lying under his pillow. Well, so what? Shloyme would tell God of the wrong that was done to him here. After all, God existed, God would take him in. Of that Shloyme was convinced.

At night, trembling with cold, he got up out of his bed. Quietly, so as not to wake anyone, he lit a small kerosene lamp. Slowly, like the old man he was, moaning and shivering, he began to pull on his dirty clothes. Then he took a stool, a rope, which he had placed in readiness the evening before, and, faltering with weakness, clutching at the walls, went out into the street. Immediately he felt so cold . . . He trembled in all his body. Shloyme quickly secured the rope on a hook, stood up beside the door, put the stool in place, climbed up on to it, wound the rope around his thin, shaking neck, with a final effort pushed the stool away, had time with his dimmed eyes to survey the little town in which he had lived for sixty years without a break, and hung . . .

There was a strong wind, and soon the feeble body of Old

Shloyme began to sway before the door of the house in which he had left a warm stove and the grease-stained Torah of his fathers.

Ilya Isaakovich
and Margarita Prokofyevna

Gershkovich came out of the police inspector's office with a heavy heart. He had been told that if he did not leave Oryol on the first train he would be deported under guard. And to leave meant to lose business.

Briefcase in hand, thin and unhurried, he walked along the dark street. On the corner he was hailed by a tall female figure:

'Want to come with me, dear?'

Gershkovich raised his eyebrows, looked at her through flashing spectacles, thought for a moment and answered reticently, 'Yes.'

The woman took him by the arm. They walked round the corner.

'Where will we go? To a hotel?'

'I want to stay all night,' replied Gershkovich, 'at your place.'

'That will cost you three roubles, Papasha.'

'Two,' said Gershkovich.

'It's not worth my while, Papasha . . .'

After some argument, they settled on two and a half. They walked on.

The prostitute's room was small, clean, with torn curtains and a pink lamp.

When they arrived, the woman took off her coat, unbuttoned her blouse . . . and winked.

7

'Ugh,' Gershkovich said with a wry face, 'what foolishness.'
'You're angry, Papasha.'
She sat on his knees.
'Touch wood,' said Gershkovich. 'I suppose you weigh about five *poods*?'*
'Four thirty.'
She gave him a long-drawn-out kiss on his greying cheek.

'Ugh,' Gershkovich said again, making a wry face, 'I'm tired, I want to go to sleep.'
The prostitute stood up. Her face had become unpleasant.
'Are you a Jew?'
He looked at her through his spectacles and replied: 'No.'
'Papasha,' said the prostitute slowly, 'this is going to cost you ten.'
He got up and walked to the door.
'Five,' said the woman.
Gershkovich turned back.
'Make the bed for me,' the Jew said wearily, took off his jacket and looked round for somewhere to hang it. 'What's your name?'
'Margarita.'
'Change the sheet, Margarita.'
The bed was a wide one, with a soft feather mattress.
Gershkovich slowly began to undress, took off his white socks, stretched his sweaty toes, locked the door, put the key under the pillow and lay down. Margarita, yawning a little, unhurriedly took off her clothes, squinting, squeezed out a pimple on her shoulder and began to plait her thin hair for the night.
'What's your name, Papasha?'
'Eli. Elya Isaakovich.'
'Are you in commerce?'

* Indicates an explanatory note, pages 317-30.

'Our commerce . . .' Gershkovich replied, vaguely.

Margarita blew out the night lamp and lay down . . .

'Touch wood,' said Gershkovich. 'She's been fattened up.'

Soon they fell asleep.

Next morning the sun's bright light bathed the room. Gershkovich woke up, got dressed, went over to the window.

'We have the sea, you have the fields,' he said. 'That's good.'

'Where are you from?' asked Margarita.

'Odessa,' replied Gershkovich. 'A first-rate town, a good town,' and he smiled craftily.

'I can see you find everywhere good,' said Margarita.

'That's true,' said Gershkovich. 'It's good wherever there are people.'

'What a fool you are,' said Margarita, sitting up a little in bed. 'People are wicked.'

'No,' said Gershkovich, 'people are good. They have been taught to think that they are wicked, and they have come to believe it.'

Margarita thought, then smiled.

'You're a funny one,' she said slowly, and attentively she looked him over.

'Turn away. I'm going to get dressed.'

After that they had breakfast, tea with ring-shaped rolls. Gershkovich taught Margarita how to spread butter on her bread and to put the sausage on top in a special way.

'Try it, but I have to be off now.'

On his way out, Gershkovich said:

'Take three roubles, Margarita. Believe me, there's nowhere one can earn a copeck.'

'You're a miser, a miser. All right, give me three, then. Will you come back this evening?'

'Yes.'

In the evening Gershkovich brought supper – herring, a bottle of beer, sausage, apples. Margarita was wearing a dark, shapeless dress. As they ate they talked.

'One can't get by on fifty roubles a month,' said Margarita. 'It's such a lousy trade that one has to dress in cheap rags – and go without food. I pay fifteen for this room, remember that . . .'

'With us in Odessa,' Gershkovich replied after a moment's thought, cutting the herring with effort into equal portions, 'in the Moldavanka, you can have a room fit for a tsar for ten roubles.'

'Remember that people push around in my room, one can't avoid the drunks . . .'

'Every person has his troubles,' said Gershkovich, and he told her about his family, his unsteady business affairs, his son who had been called up for military service.

Margarita listened, her head on the table, and her face was attentive, quiet and thoughtful.

After supper, having taken off his jacket and wiped his spectacles thoroughly with a piece of cloth, he sat down at the little table and, moving the lamp towards him, began to write business letters. Margarita washed her hair.

Gershkovich wrote unhurriedly, attentively, raising his eyebrows, pondering from time to time, and, when he dipped his pen, never once forgot to shake off the excess ink.

His writing at an end, he made Margarita sit down on the copying book.

'You are, touch wood, a lady of weight. Sit there for a bit, Margarita Prokofyevna, if you please.'

Gershkovich smiled, his spectacles flashed, and his eyes became brilliant, small, laughing.

The next day he left town. As he walked up and down the platform, a few minutes before the train was due to depart, Gershkovich observed Margarita coming quickly towards him with a little bundle in her hands. The bundle contained pies, and greasy stains from them had seeped through the paper.

Margarita's face was red, pitiful, her bosom was agitated from quick walking.

'Greetings to Odessa,' she said, 'greetings . . .'

'Thank you,' replied Gershkovich; he took the pies, raised his eyebrows, reflected on something for a moment and hunched his shoulders.

The third bell sounded. They stretched out their arms to each other.

'Until we meet again, Margarita Prokofyevna.'

'Until we meet again, Elya Isaakovich.'

Gershkovich got into the carriage. The train moved off.

Shabbos Nakhamu*

A story from the 'Hershele' cycle*

And the morning and the evening were the fifth day. And the morning and the evening were the sixth day.* On the sixth day – Friday evening – it is necessary to pray: having prayed, to stroll about the town in one's Sabbath hat and come home in time for supper. At home the Jew drinks a glass of vodka – neither God nor the Talmud forbid him to drink two – eats his *gefilte* fish and his raisin *kugel*. After supper he becomes cheerful. He tells his wife stories, then sleeps, having closed one eye and opened his mouth. He sleeps, and Gapka in the kitchen hears music – as though from the town a blind fiddler has arrived, standing under the window and playing.

Thus it is with every Jew. But Hershele is not every Jew. Not for nothing has his fame spread over all Ostropol, all Berdichev, all Vilyuysk.*

11

Of six Fridays Hershele celebrated one. On the other evenings he and his family sat in darkness and cold. The children cried. His wife hurled reproaches. Each one of those reproaches was as heavy as a cobblestone. Hershele would reply in verse.

One day – we are told of such an incident – Hershele wanted to be provident. On a Wednesday he set off for the fair, in order to make some money for the Friday. Wherever there is a fair, there is a *Pan*.* Wherever there is a *Pan*, there ten Jews will be hanging about. From ten Jews you will not make three groschen. They all listened to Hershele's jokes, but there was no one at home when it came to the reckoning.

His stomach as empty as a wind instrument, Hershele trudged home.

'What have you earned?' his wife asked him.

'I have earned a life beyond the grave,' he replied. 'Both rich man and poor man promised me it.'

Hershele's wife had only ten fingers. She bent each one of them in turn. Her voice rumbled like thunder in the mountains.

'For every wife her husband is a man. Only mine thinks he can feed a wife on words. God grant that by New Year he should lose his tongue, his hands and his feet.'*

'Amen,' replied Hershele.

'In every window candles are burning as though oak trees have been lighted in the houses. But in our house the candles are thin as matches, and the smoke from them is such that heaven itself feels sick. Everyone is baking white bread but my man has brought me firewood as wet as a pigtail that has just been washed . . .'

Hershele did not venture a single word in reply. Why throw logs on the fire when it is already burning brightly? That was the first thing. And what can one say in reply to a quarrelsome wife, when she is right? That was the second.

The time went by, and his wife grew tired of shouting.

Hershele left the room, lay down on the bed and began to think.

'Should I not go to Rebbe Boruchl?'* he asked himself. (Everyone knew that Rebbe Boruchl suffered from black melancholy, and there was no better medicine for him than the words of Hershele.)

'Should I not go to Rebbe Boruchl? The *tsadik*'s* beadles give me the bones, and keep the flesh for themselves. That is true. Flesh is better than bones, bones are better than air. Let us go to Rebbe Boruchl.'

Hershele rose and went to harness his horse. It looked at him sternly and sadly.

'See here, Hershele,' its eyes said, 'you did not give me any oats yesterday, you did not give me any oats the day before yesterday, and today I have received nothing. If you do not give me oats tomorrow, I must start to think about my life.'

Hershele could not withstand the attentive look; he lowered his eyes and stroked the soft, horsey lips. Then he sighed so loudly that the horse grasped everything and he decided: 'I will go on foot to Rebbe Boruchl.'

When Hershele set off, the sun stood high in the sky. A hot road ran away ahead. White oxen slowly pulled carts of fragrant hay. Muzhiks, dangling their legs, sat on the high loads and waved their long knouts. The sky was blue, and the knouts were black.

When he had gone a part of the way – some five versts – Hershele drew near to a forest. The sun was by now leaving its post. Gentle fires were kindling in the sky. Barefooted girls were driving cows in from pasture. Each of the cows had a swaying, rosy udder filled with milk.

In the forest Hershele was met by coolness, quiet twilight. The green leaves inclined towards one another, stroked one another with flat hands and, having whispered quietly in the heights, returned to their places, rustling and quivering.

Hershele did not heed their whispering. Playing inside his

stomach was an orchestra as big as the ones at the balls in the house of Count Potocki.* A long road lay ahead of him. From the flanks of the earth a light darkness came hurrying, closed above Hershele's head and fluttered about the earth. Immovable lanterns lit up in the heavens. The earth fell silent.

Night had fallen when Hershele walked up to the inn. There was a light in the small window. By the window in the dark room sat the proprietress Zelda, sewing swaddling clothes. Her belly was so big that she looked as though she were about to give birth to a team of three horses. Hershele looked at her small, red face with its blue eyes and greeted her.

'May I rest at your inn for a bit, proprietress?'

'You may.'

Hershele sat down. His nostrils swelled like a bellows. Hot fire flashed in the stove. In a large cauldron water boiled, splashing some snow-white curd dumplings with foam. In the golden bouillon rocked a plump chicken. From the oven came the smell of raisin cake.

Hershele sat on the bench, writhing like a woman in childbirth. In a single minute more plans had been born within his head than King Solomon had wives.

In the room it was quiet, the water boiled and the chicken rocked on the golden waves.

'Where is your man, then, proprietress?' asked Hershele.

'My man has gone to see the *Pan* to pay him the money for the rent.' The proprietress fell silent. Her childish eyes stared, open wide. Suddenly she said, 'I sit here here at the window thinking. And I want to ask you a question, Mr Jew. I expect you travel much about the world, have studied with the rebbe and know about life. I have not studied with anyone. Tell me, Mr Jew, will Shabbos Nakhamu come to us soon?

'Eh-heh,' thought Hershele. 'A nice little question. Every potato grows in God's kitchen garden . . .'

'I ask you, because my man promised, "When Shabbos

Nakhamu comes we'll go and stay with Mamasha. And I'll buy you a dress and a new wig, and we'll go and ask Rebbe Motale for a son to be born to us, and not a daughter" – all this when Shabbos Nakhamu comes. And I thought – is this a person from the other world?'

'You are not mistaken, proprietress,' Hershele replied. 'God himself put those words on to your lips ... You will have both a son and a daughter. I am Shabbos Nakhamu, proprietress.'

The swaddling clothes slipped down from Zelda's knees. She got to her feet, and her little head bumped against the crossbeam, for Zelda was tall and plump, red and young. Her high breasts were like two small, tight sacks stuffed with grain. Her blue eyes were open wide, like a child's.

'I am Shabbos Nakhamu,' Hershele confirmed. 'I have been walking for two months already, proprietress, walking in order to help people. It is a long journey – from heaven to earth. My boots are worn to shreds. I have brought you a greeting from all your family.'

'From Auntie Pesya, too?' the proprietress cried, 'from Papasha, too, and Auntie Golda, do you know them?'

'Who doesn't know them?' replied Hershele. 'I have spoken to them as I am speaking to you now.'

'How do they live there?' asked the proprietress, folding her trembling fingers on her belly.

'They live badly,' Hershele said dolefully. 'How can a dead person live? They don't give balls there ...'

The proprietress's eyes filled with tears.

'It's cold there,' Hershele went on, 'cold and there isn't much to eat. They eat as the angels do. No one in the other world has the right to eat any more than the angels do. What does an angel need? He snatches a sip of water, and that suffices him. You will not see a glass of vodka there once in a hundred years ...'

'Poor Papasha ...' whispered the proprietress, shocked.

'At Passover he will have one potato pancake. The pancake lasts him a day and a night.'

'Poor Auntie Pesya,' the proprietress shivered.

'I myself go hungry,' Hershele said, his head inclined to one side, and a tear rolled down his nose and vanished in his beard. 'I cannot say a word, you see there I am considered one of their company . . .'

Hershele did not finish his words.

Clumping her heavy feet, the proprietress impetuously rushed towards him bearing plates, bowls, glasses, bottles. Hershele began to eat, and then the woman understood that he really was a person from the other world.

For a beginning, Hershele had jellied minced liver with fine-chopped onion. Then he drank a glass of manorial vodka (there was orange peel floating in it). Then he had fish, mixing the aromatic fish soup with mashed potatoes and pouring half a jar of red horseradish sauce on the edge of his plate, sauce that would have brought tears to the eyes of five Polish landowners with forelocks and caftans.

After the fish Hershele did justice to the chicken and sipped the hot bouillon with droplets of fat floating in it. The curd dumplings, bathing in melted butter, leapt into Hershele's mouth as the hare leaps away from the hunter. It is not necessary to say what happened to the pie – what else could have happened to it, if normally Hershele never saw a pie from one year's end to the other? . . .

After supper the proprietress got together the things which she had decided to send to the other world by means of Hershele – to Papasha, Auntie Golda and Auntie Pesya. To her father she had assigned a new prayer-shawl, a large bottle of cherry liqueur, a jar of raspberry jam and a pouch of tobacco. For Auntie Pesya a pair of warm grey socks had been provided. To Auntie Golda went the old wig, a large comb and a prayer-book. In addition, she furnished Hershele with boots, a round loaf, some crackling and a silver coin.

'Give them my greetings, Mr Shabbos Nakhamu, give my greetings to them all,' she said in taking leave of Hershele, who was carrying off a heavy bundle with him. 'Or wait a little, my husband will soon be here.'

'No,' Hershele replied. 'I must hurry. Do you suppose that you are the only one I must visit?'

In the dark forest the trees were asleep, the birds were asleep, the green leaves were asleep. The pale stars that watch over us were drowsing in the heavens.

When he had gone a verst, Hershele stopped, out of breath, threw the bundle from his back, sat down on it and began to think to himself.

'You ought to know, Hershele,' he said to himself, 'that there are many fools in the world. The proprietress of the inn was a fool. Her man may be a clever fellow, with large fists, fat cheeks and a long knout. If he comes home and catches up with you in the forest, then . . .'

Hershele did not make any effort to find the answer. He at once buried the bundle in the ground and left a mark so that the hidden spot could be easily found.

Then he ran to the other side of the forest, stripped naked, embraced the trunk of a tree and began to wait. His wait was not a long one. At daybreak Hershele heard the crack of a knout, the smacking of lips and the thud of hooves. This was the innkeeper coming, having set off in pursuit of Mr Shabbos Nakhamu.

On drawing level with the naked Hershele, who was embracing the tree, the innkeeper stopped his horse, and his face became as stupid as that of a monk who has met the Devil.

'What are you doing here?' he asked in a halting voice.

'I am a person from the other world,' Hershele replied dolefully. 'I have been robbed, and the important papers I was taking to Rebbe Boruchl have been taken away from me . . .'

'I know who robbed you,' the innkeeper howled. 'I too have an account to settle with him. Which way did he go?'

'I cannot say which way,' Hershele whispered bitterly. 'If you like, give me your horse, and I will catch him up in the twinkling of an eye. Meanwhile you wait here. Take your clothes off, stand by the tree, hold it up, and do not stray one step from it until I return. This tree is a holy one, and many things in our world are supported by it . . .'

Hershele did not have to study a man long in order to know what made him tick. From the first glance he had realized that there was not much difference between the husband and the wife.

And indeed, the innkeeper took off his clothes and stood beside the tree. Hershele got into the cart and galloped off. He dug up his things, loaded them into the cart and drove to the edge of the forest.

Here Hershele lifted the bundle on to his shoulders again and, leaving the horse, began to stride off along the road that led straight to the house of the Holy Rebbe Boruchl.

It was already morning. The birds were singing with their eyes closed. The innkeeper's horse dejectedly hauled the empty cart to the place where it had left its master.

He was waiting for it, pressed against the tree, naked under the beams of the rising sun. The innkeeper was cold. He shifted from one foot to the other.

'AUTOBIOGRAPHICAL'
STORIES

Childhood. At Grandmother's

On Saturdays I returned home late, after six lessons. Walking along the street did not seem to me an idle occupation. As I walked I had remarkably good dreams and everything, everything was native and familiar. I knew the signboards, the stones of the houses, the windows of the shops. I knew them individually, only for myself I was firmly convinced that in them I could see the principal thing, the secret thing, what we grown-ups call the essence of things. Everything impressed itself vigorously on my soul. If people talked in my presence about a shop, I remembered the signboard, the shabby gold lettering, the scratch on its left corner, the young woman cashier with her tall hairdo, and I remembered the atmosphere that lived around that shop and did not live near any other. And from the shops, the people, the air, the theatre playbills, I created a city of my own. To this day I remember it, feel it and love it; feel it as we feel the scent of our mother, the scent of her kindness, her words and smile; I love it because in it I grew, was happy, sad and dreamy, passionately and uniquely dreamy.

I always walked along the main street – there were the most people there.

The Saturday I want to describe occurred at the beginning of spring. At that time of year our air does not have the quiet softness that is so sweet in central Russia, above the peaceful brook, the modest valley. What we have is a light and brilliant freshness, a shallow and chill-breathing passion. I was a complete child at that time and understood nothing, but I felt the spring and bloomed and reddened from the chill.

The walking took up a lot of my time. I examined at length the diamonds in the window of the jeweller's, read the theatre playbills from A to Z, and one day inspected in the shop of Madame Rosalie the pale pink corsets with their long, wavy suspenders. Then, as I was preparing to go farther, I bumped into a tall student with a large black moustache. He smiled and asked me: 'Are you studying?' I was confused. Then he solemnly clapped me on the shoulder and said patronizingly, 'Carry on in the same spirit, colleague. My compliments. I wish you every happiness!' He began to roar with laughter, turned and went. I was very embarrassed and trudged off home, no longer lost in contemplation of Madame Rosalie's display windows.

This Sabbath afternoon was supposed to be spent at Grandmother's. She had a separate room right at the back of the flat, behind the kitchen. In a corner of the room stood a stove: Grandmother always suffered from cold. The room was hot and stuffy, and this always made me depressed and feel I wanted to escape to freedom.

Through to Grandmother's room I dragged my stuff, my books, my music stand and my violin. The table was already set for me. Grandmother sat down in the corner. I ate. We said nothing. The door was closed. We were alone. For dinner there was *gefilte* fish with horseradish sauce (for which it is worth becoming a Jew), a rich, tasty soup, roast meat with onions, salad, compote, coffee, pie and apples. I ate it all. I was a dreamer, that was true, but a dreamer with a big appetite. Grandmother cleared away the crockery. The room was now tidy. In the window stood wilted flowers. Of all living creation, Grandmother loved her son, her grandson, the dog Mimka and flowers. And Mimka arrived too, curled up on the sofa and fell asleep at once. She was a terrible sleepy-head, but a wonderful dog, good-hearted, sensible, small and pretty. Mimka was a pug-dog. Her coat was light in colour. Even in old age she never grew fat or flabby, never put on weight, but remained shapely and slender. She lived with us a long time, from birth to death, the whole of her fifteen years' doggy life, and loved us – quite plainly, and most of all Grandmother, who was stern and without mercy to anyone. What friends they were, silent and secretive, I shall tell another time. It is a very good, touching and tender story.

And so, we were three – Grandmother, Mimi and I. Mimi slept. Grandmother, in a good mood, wearing her best silk dress, sat in the corner, and I was supposed to do my homework. That day was a hard one for me. I had had six lessons at the grammar school, and Mr Sorokin, my music teacher, was supposed to be coming, as was Mr L., the Hebrew teacher, to give me a lesson I had missed, and then perhaps also Monsieur Peysson, the French teacher, and the lessons had to be prepared. With L. I could cope, we were old friends, but the music and the scales – what misery! First I got down to my homework. I laid out my exercise books, began carefully to work out the problems. Grandmother did not interrupt me, God forbid. Her tension, her reverence for my work gave her face a stupid look. Her eyes, round, yellow, transparent, never left me. Whenever I turned a page they would slowly follow my hand. Anyone else would have found her persistently observing, ceaseless gaze very hard to put up with, but I was used to it.

Then Grandmother heard my lessons. Russian, it should be said, she spoke badly, distorting the words in her own peculiar way, mixing Russian ones with Polish and Hebrew. She could not read or write Russian, of course, and held the book upside down. But this did not prevent me from reciting the lesson to her from beginning to end. Grandmother listened, understood none of it, but the music of the words was sweet to her, she went in awe of learning, believed me, believed in me and wanted me to become a *bogatyr* (a hero in Russian folklore) – such was her name for a man who was rich (*bogaty*). I finished the lessons and proceeded to read a book – I was reading Turgenev's *First Love* at the time. I liked everything in it, the clear words, the descriptions, the conversations, but trembled at the scene where Vladimir's father strikes Zinaida on the cheek with his horsewhip. I heard the whistle of the whip, the supple leather dug into me keenly, painfully, instantaneously. I was seized by an inexplicable excitement. At that point I had to stop reading, walk about the room. Meanwhile, Grandmother sat immovable, and even the hot, heavy air did not stir, as though it knew I was studying and must not be disturbed. The heat in the room kept increasing. Mimka began to snore. And earlier it had been quiet, ghostly quiet, not a sound had been heard. At that moment it all seemed extraordinary to me and made me want to flee from it and yet remain for ever. The darkening room, Grandmother's yellow eyes, her small figure, wrapped in a shawl, doubled up and silent in the corner, the hot air, the closed door, and the smack of the whip and that penetrating whistle – only now do I understand how strange it was, how much it meant to me. From this troubled state I was delivered by the doorbell. Sorokin had arrived. At that moment I hated him, hated the scales, that incomprehensible, superfluous, shrill music. It must be admitted that this Sorokin was a good fellow, wore his black hair in a crew cut, had large red hands and full red lips. That day under Grandmother's eye he was to work for a whole hour, even more, was to exert himself to the utmost. All this got not the slightest recognition. Grandmother's eyes followed his movements coldly and tenaciously, remaining indifferent and alien to him. Grandmother took no interest in people from outside. She required that they fulfil their obliga- tions to us, and that was all. We began the lesson. It was not that I was afraid of Grandmother, but for a solid hour I had to experience upon my person the immoderate zeal of poor Sorokin. He felt very out of place in this remote room, in front of a peacefully sleeping dog and a hostile, coldly watching old woman. At last he began to take his leave. Grandmother indifferently gave him her large, firm, wrinkled hand without even moving it. As he went out, he caught hold of a chair.

I endured the following hour as well – Mr L.'s lesson, and awaited the moment when the door would close behind him, too.

Evening came. Distant, golden points caught fire in the heavens. Our courtyard – a deep cage – was blinded by the moon. In the neighbours' house a female voice had begun to sing the romance 'Why Do I Madly Love?'. My family had gone to the theatre. I grew sad. I was tired. I had read so much, studied so much, seen so much. Grandmother lit a lamp. Her room at once became quiet: the dark, heavy furniture was gently illumined. Mimi woke up, padded about the rooms, came back again and began to wait for supper. The maid brought the samovar. Grandmother was very fond of tea. For me, there was gingerbread. We drank in great quantity. In Grandmother's deep, sharp wrinkles sweat began to gleam. 'Are you sleepy?' she asked. 'No,' I answered. We began to talk. And again I heard Grandmother's stories. Long ago, many years past, a certain Jew had run an inn. He was poor, married, burdened with children and traded in illicit vodka. The police commissioner came and harassed him. He began to find life difficult. He went to see the *tsadik* and said, 'Rebbe, the police commissioner is vexing me to death. Intercede for me with God.' 'Go in peace,' the *tsadik* said to him. 'The police commissioner will settle down.' The Jew went away. In the doorway of his inn he found the police commissioner. The latter lay dead with a purple, swollen face.

Grandmother fell silent. The samovar hissed. The woman next door went on singing. The moon went on dazzling. Mimi wagged her tail. She was hungry.

'In the old days people had faith,' said Grandmother. 'Life was simpler then. When I was a girl the Poles rose up in rebellion. Near us there was a Polish count's manor. The tsar himself came to see the count. For seven days and nights there was carousing there. At night I ran to the count's castle and looked in through the lighted windows. The count had a daughter and the finest pearls in the world. Then there was the uprising.* Soldiers came and dragged him out to the square. We all stood around and wept. The soldiers dug a pit. They wanted to blindfold the old man. He said, 'I don't need one,' stood facing the soldiers and ordered, 'Fire!' The count was a tall, grey-haired man. The muzhiks loved him.

As they were beginning to bury him, a messenger arrived in haste. He had brought a reprieve from the tsar.

The samovar had gone out. Grandmother poured a final, cold glass of tea, and sucked a piece of sugar in her toothless mouth.

'Your grandfather,' she began, 'knew a lot of stories, but he didn't have faith in anything, all he had faith in was human beings. He lent all his money to friends, and when he went to see them they threw him downstairs, and his mind became touched.' And Grandmother told me about my grandfather, a tall, sarcastic, passionate and despotic man. He played the violin, wrote at nights and knew all the languages. He was possessed by an unquenchable thirst for knowledge and life. A general's daughter fell in love with their eldest son, he saw a great deal of the world, played cards and died in Canada at the age of thirty-seven. Grandmother had only one son left, and me. It was all over. Day inclines towards evening, and death approaches slowly. Grandmother falls silent, inclines her head and weeps. 'Study,' she says with force, 'study, you will attain everything – wealth and fame. You must know everything. Everyone will fall down and abase themselves before you. Everyone must envy you. Don't have faith in human beings. Don't have friends. Don't lend them money. Don't lend them your heart.'

Grandmother does not say any more. Silence. Grandmother thinks of the years and sorrows that are past, thinks about my fate, and her stern precept is heavily – for ever – laid upon my weak child's shoulders. In the dark corner the incandescent cast-iron stove gives out an intense heat. I cannot breathe, there is nothing to breathe, I must run outside to fresh air, to freedom, but I have no strength to raise my drooping head.

In the kitchen there is a clatter of crockery. Grandmother goes there. We are getting ready to have supper. Soon I hear her metallic, angry voice. She is shouting at the maid. I feel strange and hurt. After all just now she was breathing peace and sadness. The maid snarls back. 'Get out of here, hireling,' the intolerably high voice rings out with uncontainable fury. 'I am the mistress here. You are destroying our property. Out.' I cannot endure this deafening, iron shout. Through the half-open door I can see Grandmother, her face strained, her lower lip quivering finely and mercilessly, her throat distended as though it were swollen. The maid makes some retort. 'Go,' said Grandmother. It has grown quiet. The maid has bowed and, inaudibly, as though afraid of offending the silence, crept out of the room.

We eat our supper in silence. We eat well, abundantly and at length. Grandmother's transparent eyes are immobile and* where they are looking, I do not know. After supper she . . .

More than that I do not see, for I sleep very soundly, sleep a youthful sleep behind seven seals in Grandmother's hot room.

The Story of My Dovecot

To M. Gorky

In my childhood I very much wanted to have a dovecot. Never in all my life have I desired anything more intensely. I was nine years old when Father promised to give me the money to buy wood and three pairs of doves. That was in 1904. I was getting ready to take the entrance exam for the preparatory form of the Nikolayev grammar school. My family lived in the town of Nikolayev in the province of Kherson. That province no longer exists, our town is now part of the Odessa Administrative District. I was only nine, and I was afraid of the exams. Now, after two decades, it is very hard to say how horribly I was afraid of them. In both subjects – Russian and arithmetic – I had to get not less than five. The percentage quota at our gymnasium was a tough one, only 5 per cent. Out of forty boys only two who were Jewish could enter the preparatory form. The teachers put tricky questions to those boys: none of the others was given such difficult questions as we were. It was for this reason that Father, in promising to buy me some doves, demanded two five-pluses. He had completely worried me to death. I fell into a strange, interminable daydream, a long, childish dream of despair, and took the exam in that dream and yet none the less passed it with better marks than the rest.

I had an aptitude for learning. The teachers, though they were cunning, were unable to take my intelligence and my avid memory from me. I had an aptitude for learning and received two fives. Then, however, everything altered. Khariton Efrussi, a grain merchant who exported wheat to Marseilles, offered a bribe of five hundred roubles, I was given a five-minus instead of a five, and then, in accordance with the regulations, young Efrussi was admitted. My father was greatly grieved at the time. Ever since I was six he had taught me all the subjects one could think of. The incident with the minus brought him to the point of despair. He wanted to give Efrussi a beating, or send two men from the market to give Efrussi a beating, but Mother dissuaded him from his evil thoughts, and I began to get ready for the second exam, the following year, for the first form. Behind my back my family persuaded the teacher to take me through the course for the preparatory form and the first form in a single year and, as we were in complete despair, I learned three books off by heart. Those books were Smirnovsky's grammar, Yevtush-evsky's arithmetical problems and Putsykovich's primer of elementary Russian history. Children do not use those books any more, but I learned them off by heart, line by line, and the following year at the exam in the Russian language I received from the teacher Karavayev the unattainable five-pluses. Our little town whispered for a long time about my extraordinary success, and Father was so pitifully proud of it that I could not bear to think about his restless instability and about how he submitted so helplessly to any change and was either gladdened or depressed by it.

The teacher Karavayev was better than a father to me. Karavayev was a rubicund, indignant man from the Moscow studentry. He was barely thirty years old. On his manly cheeks the colour bloomed as it does on the cheeks of peasant children who do not engage in heavy work, a not repulsive mole sat on one of those cheeks, and from it grew a tuft of ash-grey feline hair. Present at the exam, in addition to Karavayev, was the assistant administrator, Pyatnitsky, who was considered an important person in the gymnasium and in the province as a whole. At the exam the assistant administrator asked me questions about Peter the Great; I experienced then a sense of oblivion, a sense of the nearness of the end and the abyss, an arid abyss lined with rapture and despair.

I knew by heart the section about Peter the Great from Putsykovich's book and the poem by Pushkin. I recited that poem in a violent sob; florid human faces suddenly rolled into my eyes and shifted about there like the cards from a new pack. They were shuffled at the bottom of my eyes, and in these moments, trembling, straightening up, in haste, I shouted Pushkin's stanzas with all my might. I shouted them for a long time, no one interrupted my crazy squealing, choking, muttering. Through a crimson blindness, through the violent freedom that had taken possession of me, all I could see was the old, inclined face of Pyatnitsky with its silvered beard. He did not interrupt me and merely said to Karavayev, who was exulting for me and for Pushkin:

'What a nation,' the old man whispered, 'your Yids, the Devil is in them . . .'

And when I fell silent, he said:

'All right, now off you go, my little friend.'

I went out of the classroom into the corridor and there, in the corridor, leaning against the brown, unwhitewashed wall, began to awaken from the convulsion of my exhausted dreams. Russian boys were playing around me, the school bell hung not far away above the well of the main staircase, the little caretaker was dozing on a broken chair; I looked at the caretaker and woke up. Children were stealthily approaching me from all sides. They wanted to give me a flick on the nose or simply have a bit of a game, but Pyatnitsky suddenly appeared in the corridor. As he passed, he stopped for a moment, and the frock-coat moved over his back in a slow, arduous wave. I saw confusion in that spacious, fleshy, lordly back and advanced towards the old man.

'Boys,' he said to the little schoolboys, 'leave this boy alone,' and placed a fat, soft hand upon my shoulder.

'My little friend,' said Pyatnitsky, the assistant administrator, swinging round, 'tell your father that you have been admitted to the first form.'

A magnificent star flashed on his chest, medals clinked near his lapel, and his large, black, uniformed body began to walk away on straight legs. It was constricted by the gloomy walls; it moved between them as a wooden barge moves in a deep canal, and vanished through the doorway of the headmaster's study. The little servitor took tea in to him with solemn commotion, and I ran home to the shop.

In our shop, a muzhik client, full of doubt, sat scratching himself. At the sight of me, Father deserted the muzhik and at once believed my story. He shouted to his apprentice to close the shop and rushed off to Sobornaya Street to buy me a cap with a badge. Poor Mother was scarcely able to tear me away from that madman. Mother was pale at that moment and was looking into my future. She kept caressing me and then pushing me away with revulsion. She said that the newspapers published a list of all the boys who had been admitted to the gymnasium and that God would visit retribution on us and people laugh at us if we bought a school uniform ahead of time. Mother was pale, she was scanning the destiny in my eyes and looking at me with bitter compassion, as at a cripple, because she knew how unlucky our family was.

All the men in our family were trusting and quick to take unconsidered actions, we had no luck in anything. My grandfather was once a rabbi in Belaya Tserkov, but he was banished from there for blasphemy and, with much fuss and in great poverty, lived another forty years, studied modern languages and began to go mad in the eightieth year of his life. My Uncle Lev, my father's brother, studied at the Volozhin Yeshivah;* in 1892 he evaded military conscription and abducted the daughter of a quartermaster serving in the Kiev Military District. Uncle Lev took this woman to California, to Los Angeles, deserted her there and died in a house of ill-repute among Negroes and Malays. After his death the American police sent us his inheritance from Los Angeles – a large trunk, bound around with brown iron hoops. In this trunk there were dumb-bells, locks of female hair, Uncle's prayer-shawl, horsewhips with gilt knobs and flower tea in boxes decorated with cheap pearls. Of the whole family there remained only crazy Uncle Simon, who lived in Odessa, my father and I. But my father was unbelievably trusting in other people, he insulted them with the raptures of his first love. People did not forgive him for this and deceived him. For this reason, my father believed that his life was governed by a malicious destiny, an inexplicable being that hounded him and was unlike him in every way. And so, of all our family, I was the only one my mother had left. Like all Jews I was small of stature, puny and suffered headaches from too much study. All this was seen by Rakhil, my mother, who was never blinded by her husband's destitute pride and incomprehensible belief that our ancient family would one day become stronger and more sublime than the other people on the earth. She did not expect success for us, she did not want the new school blazer and only allowed me to have my photograph taken by a photographer for the big portrait. Yet all the same we had to buy a cap with a badge.

On 20 September 1905 the list of those who had entered the first form was posted up in the grammar school. My name was on the list. All our relatives went to look at that piece of paper, and even Shoyl, my grand-uncle, came to the school. I loved that vainglorious old man because he sold fish at the market. His fat hands were always moist, covered with fish-scales, and stank of cold, beautiful worlds. Because of this, Shoyl differed from ordinary people, and also by virtue of the mendacious stories he used to tell about the Polish uprising of 1861. In the old days Shoyl had been an innkeeper in Skvira; he had seen Nicholas I's soldiers shoot Count Godlewski and the other Polish insurgents. On the other hand, perhaps he had not. Nowadays I know that Shoyl was merely an old ignoramus and a naïve liar, but I have not forgotten his stories for they were very good. And so even foolish Shoyl came to the school to read the list with my name on it and in the evening, not afraid of anyone, not afraid of the fact that he was loved by no one in the world, danced and stamped his feet at our miserable ball.

Father arranged a ball in celebration and invited his colleagues – grain merchants, brokers for the sale of country properties and travelling salesmen who sold agricultural machines in our region. Those salesmen would sell machines to anyone. The muzhiks and landowners were afraid of them, it was impossible to get away from them without buying something. Of all Jews the travelling salesmen are the most worldly-wise and cheerful. At our soirée they sang Hassidic songs that consisted of only three words* but went on for a very long time, with many amusing intonations. The touching charm of those intonations can be appreciated only by those who have had occasion to celebrate the Passover among the Hassidim, or have been to Volhynia and visited their noisy synagogues there. In addition to the travelling salesmen, old Liberman, who had taught me the Torah and Ancient Hebrew, came. In our town he was called *Monsieur* Liberman. He drank a little more of the Bessarabian wine than was good for him, the traditional silk tassels of the *tsitsit** crept out from under his red waistcoat and he toasted me in Ancient Hebrew. The old man congratulated my parents in this toast and said that at the exam I had vanquished all my enemies, had vanquished the Russian boys with fat cheeks and the sons of our coarse men of wealth. Thus in ancient times had David, King of Judah, vanquished Goliath, and just as I had triumphed over Goliath, so would our stalwart people vanquish by the power of their intellect the enemies who had surrounded us and were waiting for our blood. Having said this, Monsieur Liberman began to weep and, weeping, drank yet more wine and began to shout '*Vivat!*' The guests took him into the circle and began to lead him in an old-fashioned quadrille as at a wedding in a Jewish *shtetl.** Everyone was merry at our ball, even mother got drunk, though she did not like vodka and could not understand how it was possible to like it – for this reason she considered all Russians mad and could not understand how women could live with Russian husbands.

But our happy days came later. They came for Mother when she began to enjoy the happiness of making sandwiches for me before I left for the gymnasium and when she went from shop to shop, buying my New Year's presents – pencil-box, money-box, satchel, new books in paper bindings and exercise books in shiny covers. No one in the world feels new things more intensely than children. Children start at that smell like a dog at the scent of a hare, and experience a madness which later, when we become grown-ups, is called inspiration. And this pure childish sense of ownership over things that smell of a tender dampness and the coolness of new things was communicated to Mother. It took us a month to get used to the pencil-box and the unforgettable morning twilight, when I drank tea at the large, illuminated table and gathered my books into my satchel; it took us a month to get used to our happy life, and only after the first term did I remember about the doves.

I had everything prepared for them – one rouble fifty and a dovecot made out of a box by Grand-uncle Shoyl. The dovecot had been painted brown. It had nests for twelve pairs of doves, fretted slats on the roof and a special grille that I had invented to make it easier to lure in strangers. Everything was ready. On Sunday 20 October I prepared to set off for the hunters' market, but sudden disasters blocked my path.

The story I am relating, that of my entrance to the first form of the gymnasium, took place in the autumn of 1905. At that time Tsar Nicholas I was giving the Russian people a constitution, orators in tattered coats were clambering up on to pedestals outside the building of the town parliament and delivering speeches to the people. At night there was the sound of shooting in the streets, and Mother did not want to let me go to the hunters' market. Since early morning on 20 October the boys who lived next door had been flying a kite right opposite the police station, and our water carrier, having abandoned all his tasks, was walking down Rybnaya Street pomaded, with a red face. Then we saw the sons of the baker Kalistov haul a leather vaulting horse into the street and begin to do gymnastics in the middle of the roadway. No one tried to stop them; Semernikov the policeman was even egging them on to jump a bit higher. Semernikov was wearing a home-woven silk sash, and his boots had been more highly polished that day than they had ever been before. My mother was frightened, more than by anyone else, by a policeman not wearing his uniform; it was because of him that she would not let me go out, but I stole out through the backyard and ran all the way to the hunters' market, which was situated a long way behind the station.

At the hunters' market, in his regular place, sat Ivan Nikodimych, the dove fancier. In addition to doves, he was also selling rabbits, and a peacock. The peacock, its shining tail unfolded, sat on a perch, moving its small impassive head this way and that. One of its feet was tied round with a length of twisted string, the other end of the string was trapped by Ivan Nikodimych's wicker chair. As soon as I got there I bought from the old man a pair of cherry-coloured doves with dirty, luxuriant tails and a pair of crested ones, and put them away in a small sack which I kept at my front, next to my skin. I still had forty copecks left after my purchase, but the old man was unwilling to let me have a male and female dove of the Kryukov breed. The thing I liked about Kryukov doves was their beaks – short, granular, friendly. Forty copecks was the right price for them, but the huntsman was asking too much and turned away his yellow face, which had been incinerated by the lonely passions of the birdcatcher. Towards the end of the market, seeing that there were no other customers, Nikodim Nikodimych called me over to him. Everything turned out my way, everything turned out badly. At twelve noon or a little later a man in felt boots came across the square. He walked lightly, on swollen feet, but animated eyes burned in his worn-out face.

'Ivan Nikodimych,' he said, as he walked past the huntsman, 'put your instrument away; in town the Jerusalem gentlefolk are receiving a constitution. On Rybnaya they have entertained the Babels' grandfather to death . . .'

He said this walking lightly between the cages like a barefoot ploughman walking along a boundary path.

'It's wrong,' Ivan Nikodimych muttered after him, 'it's wrong,' he shouted more sternly, gathering together the rabbits and the peacock, and shoving the Kryukov doves towards me for forty copecks. I put them away in my sack and started to watch the people scattering away from the hunters' market. The peacock on Ivan Nikodimych's shoulder was the last to go. It sat like the sun in a damp, autumn sky, it sat the way July sits on the pink shore of a river, a scorching July in long, cold grass. I watched them go, the old man, his cobbler's chair and the beloved cages wrapped up in coloured rags. There was no one at the market now, and shots rang out not far away. Then I ran towards the station, cut across a square that had suddenly capsized, and flew into a deserted lane that had been pounded with yellow earth. At the end of the lane, in a wheelchair, sat the one-legged Makarenko, who rode around the town in a wheelchair selling cigarettes from a tray. The boys from our street bought cigarettes from him and children loved him; I rushed towards him along the lane.

'Makarenko,' I said, out of breath from running, and patted the one-legged man's shoulder, 'have you seen my Grand-uncle Shoyl?'

But the cripple did not answer. His coarse face, composed of red fat, of fists, of iron, was translucent. In terrible agitation he moved restlessly in the wheelchair and his wife Katyusha, with her padded posterior towards us, was sorting out some things that lay scattered on the earth.

'Where have you got to in your counting?' asked the one-legged man, recoiling from the woman with his whole body, as though he knew that her answer would be intolerable to him.

'Fourteen pairs of gaiters,' said Katyusha, without straightening up, 'six quilt covers, now I'm counting the bonnets . . .'

'Bonnets!' Makarenko shouted, choked, and made a sound as though he were sobbing. 'It's plain, Katerina, that God has picked me out to answer for all the rest . . . People are carrying off whole rolls of cloth, people have what people ought to have, but what we have is bonnets . . .'

And indeed, a woman with a fine, burning-hot face was running along the lane. She was holding an armful of fezzes in one arm and a piece of cloth in the other. In a happy, desperate voice she was calling her children, who had disappeared; a silk dress and a blue jacket trailed after her flying body, and she did not seem to hear Makarenko, who was trundling after her in his chair. The one-legged man could not catch her up; his wheels clattered, he turned the handles but he still could not make it in time.

'*Madamochka*,' he shouted deafeningly, 'in the name of God, *madamochka*, where did you get that printed calico?'

But the woman with the flying dress was no longer there. From round the corner in the same direction a wobbly cart swung out. A peasant lad stood in the cart.

'Where's everyone gone running off to?' asked the lad, raising a red rein above his nags, which were frisking in their collars.

'They're all on Sobornaya,' Makarenko said beseechingly, 'that's where they all are, my friend; whatever you can get, bring it to me, and I'll buy the lot . . .'

But the lad, hearing about Sobornaya, did not waste any time hanging about. Bending over the front of the cart, he lashed the piebald nags. The horses, like calves, bounced their dirty croups and rushed off at a gallop. The yellow lane was again left yellow and deserted, and then the one-legged man looked at me with his faded eyes.

'Has God picked me out, or what?' he said lifelessly. 'Am I the Son of Man to you, or what . . . ?'

And Makarenko stretched out to me a hand that was tainted with apoplectic leprosy.

'What have you got in your bag?' he said and took the sack that warmed my heart.

With a fat hand the cripple turned the doves upside down

and pulled out a cherry-coloured female. Its feet thrown back, the bird lay in the palm of his hand.

'Doves,' said Makarenko and, his wheels squeaking, approached me. 'Doves,' he repeated, like an inevitable echo, and struck me on the cheek.

He struck me a swinging blow, his hand now clenched; the dove cracked on my temple, Katyusha's wadded posterior swayed before my eyes and I fell to the earth in my new overcoat.

'Their seed ought to be destroyed,' Katyusha said then, and she straightened up, away from the bonnets. 'I cannot abide their seed and their stinking men . . .'

She said something else about our seed, but I heard nothing more. I lay on the earth, and the entrails of the crushed bird trickled from my temple. They flowed down my cheeks, coiling, splashing and blinding me. Soft dove guts crept over my forehead, and I closed a last unstuck eye so as not to see the world that was spreading about before me. That world was small and horrible. A stone lay in front of my eyes, a stone that was dented like the face of an old woman with a large jaw, a fragment of string lay not far off and a tuft of feathers that was still breathing. My world was small and horrible. I closed my eyes so as not to see it, and I pressed myself against the earth that lay beneath me in calming dumbness. That pounded earth in no way resembled our life and the anticipation of exams in our life. Somewhere far away across it rode disaster on a lame and lively horse, but the sound of its hooves grew faint, died, and silence, the bitter silence that sometimes afflicts children in misfortune, suddenly annihilated the boundary between my trembling body and the earth that was moving nowhere. My earth smelt of moist entrails, of the the grave and of flowers. I smelt its odour and began to weep without any fear. I walked along an alien street crammed with white boxes, I walked in an attire of bloodstained feathers, alone in the middle of pavements that were swept as clean as on a Sunday, and wept more bitterly, completely and happily than I ever wept again in all my life. White wires hummed above my head, a mongrel ran ahead of me and in a lane to one side a young muzhik in a waistcoat was smashing a window frame in the house of Khariton Efrussi. He was smashing it with a wooden mallet, threatening it with his whole body and, sighing, smiling in all directions the good-natured smile of inebriation, sweat and mental energy. The whole street was full of the crunching, cracking and singing of shattering wood. The muzhik was hammering only so he could lean over, sweat and shout extraordinary words in a mysterious, non-Russian language. He shouted them and sang, tearing his blue eyes inside out until in the street there appeared a religious procession with cross and gonfalons, coming from the town parliament. Old men with dyed beards bore in their hands the portrait of the neatly combed tsar, gonfalons with sepulchral saints waved above the procession, and inflamed old women swept irrepressibly forward. The muzhik in the waistcoat, when he saw the procession, pressed his mallet to his chest and ran off behind the banners, while I, waiting for the procession to pass, stole away home to our house. Its white doors were wide open, the grass by the dovecot trampled down. Only Kuzma had not left. Kuzma, the yardkeeper, sat in the shed on Shoyl's corpse laying out the dead man.

'The wind carries you like a bad wood chip,' said the old man, when he saw me. 'You've been away for ages . . . Look how the people have given our grandad the chop . . .'

Kuzma began to snuffle, turned away and started to take a pike-perch out of the flies of grand-uncle's trousers. Two pike-perch had been stuffed into grand-uncle: one into the flies of his trousers, the other into his mouth, and though grand-uncle was dead, one of the pike-perch was still alive and shuddering.

'They gave our grandad the chop, no one else,' said Kuzma,

throwing the pike-perch to the cat. 'He cursed the people from one end to the other, cursed the lot of them clean to blazes, he did, the brave old fellow ... You ought to put a couple of five-copeck pieces on his eyes ...'

But at that time, ten years old, I did not know why dead people needed five-copeck pieces on their eyes.

'Kuzma,' I said in a whisper, 'save us ...'

And I went over to the yardkeeper, embraced his old crooked back with its one raised shoulder and saw grand-uncle from behind that dear back. Shoyl lay in the sawdust, his chest crushed, his beard turned up, in rough clogs worn on bare feet. His legs, placed apart, were dirty, mauve, dead. Kuzma fussed around them, then he bound the jaws, looking all the while to see what else he needed to do with the dead man. He fussed as though he had some new acquisition in his house, and cooled down a bit only when he had combed the dead man's beard.

'Cursed them all to blazes, he did,' he said, smiling, survey-ing the corpse with love. 'If Tartars had come across him, he'd have sent the Tartar packing, but it was Russians who came, and women with them, Cossack women; Cossacks think it's an insult to forgive a man, I know those Cos-sacks ...'

The yardkeeper put some more sawdust under the dead man, threw off his carpenter's apron and took me by the hand.

'Let's go and see your father,' he muttered, pressing me tighter and tighter. 'Your father's been looking for you since early this morning, thought you were dead ...'

And I went with Kuzma to the house of the tax assessor, where my parents had taken refuge in their flight from the pogrom.

First Love

When I was ten years old I fell in love with a woman called Galina Apollonovna. Her last name was Rubtsova. Her husband, an officer, went off to the Japanese war* and returned in the October of 1905. He brought many trunks back with him. These trunks contained Chinese objects: screens, precious weapons, thirty *poods* in all. Kuzma told us that Rubtsov had bought these objects with the money he had made in military service in the directorate of the Engineering Corps of the Manchurian Army. Not only Kuzma, but other people said the same thing. People found it hard not to gossip about the Rubtsovs, for the Rubtsovs were happy. Their house was adjacent to our property, their glass veranda usurped a part of our land, but Father had not quarrelled with them on that account. Rubtsov, the tax assessor, had a reputation in our town as a fair man who maintained friendly relations with Jews. And when the officer, the old man's son, arrived back from the Japanese war, we all saw how well and happily they settled down together. Galina Apollonovna held her husband's hands for whole days on end. She could not take her eyes off him, because she had not seen her husband for one and a half years, but I felt horror at her gaze, turned away and trembled. In her exultant eyes I saw the wonderful, shameful life of all people upon earth, I wanted to fall asleep in an extraordinary slumber, in order to forget about that life that exceeded all my dreams. Galina Apollonovna used to stroll about the rooms with her hair down, wearing red shoes and a Chinese peignoir. Under the lace of her low-cut chemise one could see the deepening and beginning of her white, swelling, downwards-crushed breasts, and on her robe there were embroidered pink silk dragons, birds, hollow trees.

41

All day she lounged about with a vacant smile on her moist lips, bumping into the trunks that had not yet been unpacked and the gymnastic rope ladders that were littered about the floor. If she had bruised herself, she would lift her peignoir above her knees and say to her husband:

'Give baby a kiss . . .'

And the officer, flexing his long legs in their narrow dragoon's trousers, their spurs, their close-fitting, kidskin boots, would get down on the dirty floor and, smiling, moving his legs and crawling across on his knees, kiss the hurt place, the place where there was a swollen crease from the garter. I saw those kisses from my window. They caused me suffering. Unbridled fantasies tormented me, but this is not worth talking about, for the love and jealousy of ten-year-old boys are in every respect similar to the love and jealousy of grown men, except that in boys these feelings are more secret, more exalted, more ardent. For two weeks I did not go to the window and avoided Galina until a chance incident brought us together. This chance incident was the anti-Jewish pogrom that in 1905 broke out in Nikolayev and other towns within the Jewish pale. Crowds of hired murderers ransacked my father's shop and killed my Grand-uncle Shoyl. All this happened in my absence, on the sad morning when I was buying doves from Ivan Nikodimych the hunter. For five years out of the ten I had lived, I had dreamed about doves with all the power of my soul, and then, when I had bought them, Makarenko the cripple had smashed the doves on my temple. Then Kuzma took me to the Rubtsovs. On the gate of the Rubtsovs' house a cross had been drawn in chalk, they were left alone, they hid my parents in their house. Kuzma took me to the glass veranda. There in the green rotunda sat Mother and Galina.

'We must wash,' said Galina, 'we must wash, little rabbi . . . Our whole face is covered in feathers, and the feathers have blood on them . . .'

She embraced me and led me along a passage that had a sharp odour. My head lay on Galina's hip, her hip moved and breathed. We arrived at the kitchen, and Rubtsova put me under the tap. A tall goose was simmering on a tiled stove, gleaming kitchen utensils hung along the walls, and beside the utensils, in the cook's corner, hung Tsar Nicholas, adorned with paper flowers. Galina washed off the remains of the dove that had dried on my cheeks.

'You shall be a bridegroom, my little snub-nose,' she said, kissing me on the lips with her pouting mouth and looking round.

'Little rabbi,' she whispered suddenly, 'look, your papa is upset just now, he walks about the streets all day doing nothing. Why don't you call your papa home . . .?'

And through the window I saw the deserted street with an enormous sky above it and my red-haired father walking along the roadway. He had no hat covering his lightly ruffled red hair; his cotton shirt-front was turned askew and fastened by some button or other, but not the one it ought to have been fastened by. Vlasov, an emaciated workman in wadded soldier's rags, was following my father relentlessly.

'Babel,' he was saying in a hoarse, earnest voice, touching my father affectionately with both hands, 'we don't need freedom so that the Yids can be free to haggle . . . Give light to the life of a working man for his labour, for this terrible great labour . . . Give it to him, friend, do you hear, give it to him . . .'

The workman was begging Father for something and touching him; flashes of pure, drunken inspiration alternated in his face with dejection and sleepiness.

'Our lives ought to be like those of the Milk-drinkers,'* he muttered, tottering on his unsteady legs, 'our lives ought to be like the Milk-drinkers', only without that Old Believers'* God. It's the Jews who profit from him, no one else . . .'

And Vlasov, with wild despair, began to shout about the

43

Old Believers' God, who took pity only on the Jews. Vlasov cried out, stumbled and tried to catch up with his unknown God, but at that moment a Cossack mounted patrol crossed his path. An officer in trousers with stripes down the seams and a silver parade belt rode at the head of the detachment, a tall peaked cap on his head. The officer rode slowly and without looking to either side. He rode as though he were in a ravine, where one can only look ahead.

'Captain,' whispered Father, when the Cossack drew level with him, 'captain,' said Father, gripping his head, and he got down on his knees in the mud.

'What can I do for you?' replied the officer, looking ahead of him as before, and he brought his hand in its lemon suede glove up to his peaked cap.

Ahead, on the corner of Rybnaya Street, ruffians were smashing our shop and throwing out boxes of nails, the machines and the new portrait of me in school uniform.

'There,' said Father without getting up off his knees, 'they are smashing the things that are vital to me, captain, and why . . .'

'Yes, sir!' the officer muttered, put his lemon glove to his cap and touched the reins, but his horse did not move. Father crawled in front of it on his knees, rubbing against its short, good-natured, slightly ruffled legs and its thick, patient, hairy muzzle.

'Yes, sir!' repeated the captain; he jerked the reins and rode away, the Cossacks moving off after him. They sat dispassionately in their high saddles, they rode through their imaginary ravine and disappeared from view at the turning into Sobornaya Street.

Then Galina again pushed me to the window.

'Call your papa home,' she said, 'he hasn't had anything to eat since early morning.'

And I stuck my head out of the window.

'Papa,' I said.

Father turned round when he heard my voice.

'My little son,' he mouthed with inexpressible tenderness, and began to tremble with love for me.

And together we went to the Rubtsovs' veranda, where Mother lay in the green rotunda. Beside her bed lay dumb-bells and gymnastic equipment.

'Lousy copecks,' Mother said to us in greeting, 'human life and children and our unlucky fortune – you gave them everything . . . Lousy copecks,' she shouted in a deep, hoarse voice that was not her own, jerked on the bed and grew quiet.

And then, in the silence, I hiccupped. I stood by the wall with my cap pulled down over my eyes and could not stop hiccupping.

'For shame, my little snub-nose.' Galina smiled with her disdainful smile and flicked me with her stiff peignoir. She walked over to the window in her red shoes and began to hang Chinese curtains on the unusual window ledge. Her exposed arms drowned in the silk, the living tress of her hair moved on her hip and I looked at her with rapture.

A bookish, nervous boy, I looked at her as if she were a remote stage lit by many lights. And at the same time I imagined I was Miron, the son of the charcoal-dealer who traded on our corner. I imagined myself in the Jewish Self-Defence League and there I am, like Miron, walking in tattered shoes that are tied with string. On my shoulder, on a green cord, hangs a worthless rifle; I am kneeling by an old wooden fence, shooting back at the murderers. Behind my fence stretches a vacant lot, and in it there are piles of dusty charcoal. The useless rifle shoots badly, the assassins in beards, with white teeth, are coming closer and closer to me; I experience a proud sense of imminent death and see, high up, in the blueness of the world, Galina. I see an embrasure cut in the wall of a gigantic house that is built of myriads of bricks. This purple house defies the lane in which the grey earth has been badly flattened; at its topmost embrasure stands Galina, flushed with a merciless winter gaiety, like a rich girl at a skating rink. With her disdainful smile she is smiling from the inaccessible window; her officer husband, half-dressed, is standing behind her, kissing her on the neck . . .

As I tried to stop hiccupping I imagined all this so as to love Rubtsova more bitterly, more ardently, more hopelessly, and, perhaps, because the bounds of sorrow are not great for one who is ten years old. The foolish dreams helped me to forget the doves and the death of Shoyl, I might even have forgotten about these murders had not Kuzma come on to the veranda at that moment with that terrible Jew Aba.

It was dusk when they arrived. On the veranda burned a meagre lamp, somehow lopsided at one end, a blinking lamp, the spasmodic travelling companion of misfortunes.

'I've got grandad all dressed up nice,' said Kuzma, as he came in, 'he lies there very handsome now. And look, I've brought someone from the synagogue, let him say something over the old man . . .'

And Kuzma pointed to the bored beadle, Aba.

'Let him whimper for a bit,' said the yardkeeper, amicably. 'If the beadle stuffs his gut, he will bother God all night . . .'

He stood on the threshold – Kuzma – with his good-natured, broken nose turned in all directions, and was about to describe with as much emotion as possible how he had bound the dead man's jaws, but Father interrupted the old man:

'If you please, Reb Aba,' said Father, 'say a prayer or two over the deceased. I will pay you . . .'

'But I fear you will not pay,' Aba replied in a bored voice, putting his bearded, fastidious face on the tablecloth, 'I fear you will take my money and go away with it to Argentina, to Buenos Aires, and open there a wholesale business with my money . . . A wholesale business,' said Aba, giving his contemptuous lips a chew and pulling towards him the *Son of the*

Fatherland newspaper that lay on the table. In this newspaper there was a report about the tsar's manifesto of 17 October and about freedom.

'. . . Citizens of Free Russia,' Aba spelled out, chewing his beard which he had stuffed into his mouth, 'citizens of Free Russia, a bright Sunday of Christ's Resurrection to you . . .'

The newspaper was sideways before the old beadle, swaying: he read it sleepily, singsong-fashion, and pronouncing the Russian words he did not know with extraordinary stresses. Aba's stresses were like the indistinct speech of a Negro who has just arrived in a Russian port from his native land. They made even my mother laugh.

'I am committing a sin,' she cried, leaning out from the rotunda. 'I am laughing, Aba . . . Say, better, how do you live and how is your family?'

'Ask me about something else,' Aba muttered, without releasing his beard from his teeth, and continuing to read the newspaper.

'Ask him about something else,' Father said after Aba, and he went out into the middle of the room. His eyes, smiling at us through tears, suddenly turned in their orbits and fixed themselves on a point that was visible to no one else.

'*Oy*, Shoyl,' Father articulated in a level, false, preparatory voice, '*oy*, Shoyl, dear man . . .'

Father's face, which had tightened into a spasm, was rent by exultation, and he was preparing to bawl as Jewish widows bawl at funerals or like old women in Morocco, old women who have landed in misfortune. We saw that he was going to bawl horribly, and Mother gave us advance warning.

'Manus,' she cried, growing instantly distraught, and beginning to tear at her husband's breast, 'look how our child suffers. Why do you not hear his little hiccups, why is this, Manus?'

And Father fell silent. His dying eyes were surrounded by tears

'Rakhil,' he said fearfully, 'I cannot tell you, Rakhil, how sad I am about Shoyl . . .'

He went into the kitchen and returned from it with a glass of water.

'Drink, *artiste*,' said Aba, coming over to me, 'drink this water, which will help you just as a censer helps a dead man . . .'

And, true enough, the water did not help me. I hiccupped all the more fiercely. A snarl escaped from my breast. A swelling, pleasant to the touch, rose up on my throat. The swelling breathed, filled out, covered my gullet and tumbled out of my collar. Within it bubbled my lacerated breath. It bubbled like boiling water. And when towards night I was no longer the lop-eared boy I had been throughout all of my previous life, and became a writhing ball, rolling in my own green vomit, Mother, wrapping herself in her shawl and gown, taller and more shapely, approached the rigid Rubtsova.

'Dear Galina,' said Mother in a loud, singing voice, 'how we are troubling you and dear Nadezhda Ivanovna, and all your family . . . how ashamed I am, dear Galina . . .'

With flaming cheeks Mother pushed Galina towards the door, then she rushed up to me and stuffed her shawl into my mouth to suppress my groans.

'Be brave, dear son,' she whispered, 'be brave, my poor Babel, be brave for Mama . . .'

But even if I had been able to put up with it, I would not have done so, because I no longer had any feeling of shame. I tossed about on the bed and, falling to the floor, did not take my eyes off Galina. Fear was shaking the woman and making her writhe; I snarled in her face, so as to prolong my power over her; I snarled in triumph, in exhaustion, with the ultimate exertions of love.

Thus did my illness begin. I was ten at the time. In the morning I was taken to see the doctor. The pogrom continued, but we were left alone. The doctor, a fat man, found that I had a nervous illness.

'This illness,' he said, 'occurs only in Jews and among Jews it occurs only in women.'

So the doctor was surprised to find I had such a strange illness. He told us to go to Odessa and the professors as soon as possible, and there await the warm weather and the sea bathing.

And so we did. A few days later I travelled with Mother to Odessa to stay with Grandfather Levi-Itskhok and Uncle Simon. We sailed in the morning by steamer, and by midday the brown waters of the Bug gave way to the heavy green swell of the sea. Before me opened life in the home of crazy Uncle Levi-Itskhok, and I said farewell for ever to Nikolayev, where ten years of my childhood had passed. And now, when I remember those sad years, I find in them the beginning of the ailments that torment me, and the causes of my premature and dreadful decline.

In the Basement

I was a deceitful boy. This was the result of reading. My imagination was always inflamed. I read during lessons, in the recesses, on my way home, at night under the table, hidden by the tablecloth that hung down to the floor. Behind a book I let slip all the matters of this world – playing truant from school at the port, starting to play billiards in the coffee-houses on Grecheskaya Street, going swimming at Langeron.* I had no schoolfriends. Who would have wanted to consort with such a fellow? . . .

One day I saw a book about Spinoza in the hands of our top boy Mark Borgman. He had just read it and could not wait to tell the boys who surrounded him about the Spanish

Inquisition. What he was telling them was just a learned muttering. There was no poetry in Borgman's words. I could not hold out, and intervened. To those who were willing to listen to me, I described old Amsterdam, the twilight of the ghetto, the philosophers who were diamond-cutters. To what I had read in books I added much that was my own. I could not do otherwise. My imagination heightened the dramatic scenes, modified the endings, made the beginnings more mysterious. Spinoza's death, his free, lonely death, appeared in my imagination like a battle. The Sanhedrin* was trying to force him to repent, but he did not break. I brought Rubens into the same story. In my version, Rubens stood by the head of Spinoza's bed making the dead man's death-mask.

My school-fellows, their mouths wide open, listened to this fantastic tale. It was told with fervour. When the bell rang we reluctantly dispersed. At the next recess Borgman came over to me, took me by the arm, and we began to stroll about together. After a short time had passed, we came to an agreement. Borgman was not a bad specimen of the top boy variety. To his powerful brains schoolboy wisdom was a mere scrawl in the margins of the book proper. That book he sought with avidity. Silly little twelve-year-olds though we were, we already knew that there lay ahead of him a life that was learned and out of the ordinary. He did not even do any homework, merely attended class. This sober and reserved boy grew attached to me because of the peculiar way I had of muddling up all the things in the world, things more simple than which it would have been impossible to conceive.

That year we moved up to the third form. My report was covered in three-minuses. So strange was I with all my nonsense that the teachers, after some thought, decided not to give me twos. At the beginning of the summer Borgman invited me to his dacha. His father was director of the Russian Bank for Foreign Trade. This man was one of those who were making Odessa into a Marseilles or Naples. Within him lived the mettle of the old Odessa wholesale merchant. He belonged to the company of sceptical and urbane idlers. Borgman's father avoided speaking Russian: he expressed himself in the coarsish, abrupt language of Liverpool captains. When in April the Italian Opera visited our city, a dinner was held for the company at Borgman's flat. The puffy banker – the last of the Odessa wholesale merchants – struck up a little two-month intrigue with the big-bosomed prima donna. She took away with her memories that did not burden her conscience, and a necklace that had been chosen with taste and had not cost too much.

The old man was the Argentine consul and the president of the Stock Exchange Committee. He was very clever. It was to his house that I had been invited. My aunt, Bobka by name, trumpeted this around the whole courtyard. I took the steam tram to the 16th Bolshoy Fontan* stop. The dacha stood on a low red precipice right by the seashore. On the precipice a flower garden had been laid out with fuchsias and clipped globes of thuya.

I came from a destitute and muddled family. I was filled with admiration for the furnishings of the Borgman dacha. In leafy avenues white wicker chairs gleamed. The dining-table was covered in flowers, the windows were fitted with green casings. In front of the house a low wooden colonnade stretched spaciously.

In the evening the bank director arrived home. After dinner he placed a wicker armchair right at the edge of the precipice, facing the moving plain of the sea, pulled up his white trousers, lit a cigar and began to read the *Manchester Guardian*. The guests – ladies from Odessa – played poker on the veranda. At one corner of the table hissed a slender samovar with ivory handles.

Card-gamblers and gourmandes, slatternly women of fash-ion, secretly loose, with scented lingerie and large thighs, they flapped black fans and staked gold coins. The sun penetrated to them through a screen of wild vines. Its fiery orb was enormous. Reflections of bronze made heavy the women's black hair. The sparks of the sunset entered their diamonds, diamonds hung everywhere – in the hollows between breasts slipped apart, in tinted ears and on blueish, tumescent female fingers.

Evening fell. A bat rustled past. The sea rolled more blackly on to the red rock. My twelve-year-old heart swelled with the gaiety and ease of others' wealth. Joining hands, my chum and I walked down a long avenue. Borgman told me he was going to be an aeronautical engineer. There was a rumour that his father was going to be appointed London representative of the Russian Bank for Foreign Trade – Mark would be able to receive his education in England.

In our house, the house of Aunt Bobka, no one talked of such things. I had nothing with which to repay this boundless magnificence. Then I told Mark that even though everything in our house was different, Grandfather Levi-Itskhok and my uncle had travelled the whole world and had thousands of adventures. I described these adventures in order. My consciousness of the impossible instantly left me, I took Uncle Wolf through the Russo-Turkish War to Alexandria, to Egypt . . .

Night straightened up in the poplars, the stars leaned on the bending leaves. As I talked, I swung my arms. The fingers of the future aeronautical engineer trembled in my hand. Waking with difficulty from the hallucination, he promised to come and see me the following Sunday. Armed with this promise, I took the steam tram home to Bobka's.

For a whole week after my visit I imagined I was a bank director. I pulled off operations worth millions of roubles with Singapore and Port Said. I acquired a yacht and sailed alone on it. When Saturday came round it was time to wake up. The following day little Borgman was coming. Nothing of what I had told him existed. What existed was something else, something far more astonishing than what I had thought up, but at twelve years of age I had as yet absolutely no idea of how to get along with truth in this world. Grandfather Levi-Itskhok, the rabbi who had been driven out of his *shtetl* for having forged Count Branitsky's* signature on promissory notes, was, in the view of our neighbours and the boys in the neighbourhood, a madman. As for my Uncle Simon-Wolf, I could not stand him because of his noisy eccentricity, full of senseless fire, shouting and bullying. Only with Bobka was it possible to come to some arrangement. Bobka was proud of the fact that the son of a bank director was on friendly terms with me. She saw this friendship as the beginning of a career and baked a jam strudel and a poppy-seed flan for the guest. The whole heart of our tribe, which held out so well in struggle, was contained in those flans. Grandfather, with his lacerated top hat and the rags on his swollen feet, we hid with our neighbours the Apelkhots, and I implored him not to show himself until the guest had left. Simon-Wolf was also found something to do. He went off with his horse-dealer friends to drink tea at the Bear Inn. At this inn the tea was served with vodka, and it was a safe assumption that Simon-Wolf would be delayed. Here it must be said that the family from which I come did not resemble other Jewish families. There were drunkards in our stock, there were men who seduced generals' daughters and threw them over before they had taken them to the limit, and Grandfather forged signatures and wrote blackmail letters for deserted wives.

I put all my efforts into keeping Simon-Wolf away for the whole day. I gave him the three roubles I had saved. It takes a while to run through three roubles. Simon-Wolf would come home late, and the bank director's son would never find out that the story about my uncle's kindness and strength was a false one. To be honest, if one considered with one's heart, it was a truth, not a lie, but on first view of the dirty and noisy Simon-Wolf this incomprehensible truth could not be perceived.

On Sunday morning Bobka dressed up in a brown woollen dress. Her fat, kindly bosom lay everywhere. She put on a kerchief with a black floral print, the kerchief that is worn in the synagogue at Yom Kippur and Rosh Hashana.* Bobka placed tarts, jam, pretzels on the table and began to wait. We lived in the basement. Borgman raised his eyebrows as he passed along the hump-backed floor of the corridor. In the outside passage stood a water-butt. As soon as Borgman got inside, I began to entertain him with all sorts of wonders. I showed him the alarm clock which Grandfather had made with his own hands, right down to the last small screw. The clock had a lamp attached to it; when the clock counted off the half-hour or the hour, the lamp lit up. I also showed him the keg of shoe polish. The recipe for this polish was the invention of Levi-Itskhok; he would give this secret away to no one. Then Borgman and I read a few pages of Grandfather's manuscript. He wrote in Yiddish, on rectangular, yellow sheets as enormous as geographical charts. The manuscript was entitled 'Man with No Head'. In it were described all the neighbours Levi-Itskhok had had during the seventy years of his life: first in Skvira and Belaya Tserkov, and then in Odessa. Undertakers, cantors, Jewish drunkards, female cooks at circumcisions and the rogues who carried out the ritual operation – these were Levi-Itskhok's heroes. They were all cantankerous people, inarticulate, with knobbly noses, pimples and squint backsides.

As we read, Bobka appeared in her brown dress. She floated in with a samovar on a tray, surrounded by her fat, kindly bosom. I introduced them. Bobka said, 'Pleased to meet you,' held out her sweaty, motionless fingers and shuffled her feet. It was all going brilliantly, could not have been better. The Apelkhots did not let Grandfather go. I brought out his treasures one by one – grammars in every language and sixty-six volumes of the Talmud. Mark was dazzled by the keg of shoe polish, the ingenious alarm clock and the mountain of Talmud, all of them things that could not be seen in any other house.

We each drank two glasses of tea with the strudel. Bobka, nodding her head and backing away, disappeared. I attained a happy state of mind, struck a pose and began to declaim the lines of poetry I loved more than anything else in life. Antony, bending over Caesar's corpse, addresses the Roman people:

> Friends, Romans, countrymen, lend me your ears;
> I come to bury Caesar, not to praise him . . .

Thus does Antony begin his performance. I choked and pressed my hands to my breast.

> He was my friend, faithful and just to me;
> But Brutus says he was ambitious;
> And Brutus is an honourable man.
> He hath brought many captives home to Rome,
> Whose ransoms did the general coffers fill:
> Did this in Caesar seem ambitious?
> When that the poor have cried, Caesar hath wept:
> Ambition should be made of sterner stuff:
> Yet Brutus says he was ambitious,
> And Brutus is an honourable man.
> You all did see that on the Lupercal
> I thrice presented him a kingly crown,
> Which he did thrice refuse. Was this ambition?
> Yet Brutus says he was ambitious,
> And sure he is an honourable man . . .

Before my eyes – in the mist of the universe – hung the face of Brutus. It grew whiter than chalk. The Roman people, growling, advanced towards me. I raised my arm – Borgman's eyes obediently moved after it – my clenched fist trembled, I raised my arm . . . and saw through the window Uncle Simon-Wolf walking across the courtyard accompanied by Leykakh the second-hand dealer. They were carrying a clothes-rack made of deer antlers and a red trunk with brackets in the form of lions' jaws. Bobka also saw them from the window. Forgetting about the guest, she flew into the room and seized me with trembling hands.

'My dear heart, he's been buying furniture again! . . .'

Borgman, in his school blazer, began to get up and bowed to Bobka in bewilderment. The door was being forced. In the corridor there resounded a crash of boots, the noise of a trunk being moved. The voices of Simon-Wolf and the red-haired Leykakh thundered deafeningly. Both were one over the eight.

'Bobka,' shouted Simon-Wolf, 'try to guess how much I paid for these horns . . .'

He blared like a trumpet, but in his voice there was uncertainty. Even though he was drunk, Simon-Wolf knew how we hated the red-haired Leykakh, who egged him on to all his purchases and flooded us with unnecessary, silly furniture.

Bobka said nothing. Leykakh squeaked something to Simon-Wolf. In order to muffle his snake-like hissing, in order to suppress my anxiety, I began to shout in Antony's words:

> But yesterday the word of Caesar might
> Have stood against the world; now lies he there,
> And none so poor to do him reverence.
> O masters! If I were disposed to stir
> Your hearts and minds to mutiny and rage,
> I should do Brutus wrong, and Cassius wrong,
> Who, you all know, are honourable men . . .

At this point there was a thud. Bobka had fallen, knocked off her feet by a blow from her husband. She had probably made some bitter remark about deer's antlers. The daily performance began. Simon-Wolf's brazen voice caulked up all the holes in the universe. He was shouting what he always shouted:

'You are pulling out of me the glue,' my uncle complained in a thunderous voice, 'you are pulling out of me the glue in order that you should stuff your dog-mouths. A stone you have put on my neck, a stone hangs on my neck . . .'

Cursing Bobka and me with Yiddish curses, he promised us that our eyes would fall out, that our children would begin to rot and decompose while yet in their mother's womb, that we would not be able to bury each other and that we would be dragged by the hair to a common grave . . .

Little Borgman got up from his seat. He was pale, and he was looking around him. The locutions of Yiddish blasphemy were incomprehensible to him, but he was familiar with Russian cursing. Simon-Wolf did not mince his words either. The bank director's son kneaded his little peaked cap in his hand. I saw him in a double image as I did my utmost to shout down all the evil in the world. My mortal despair and the death of Caesar which had just been accomplished fused into one. I was dead, and I was shouting. A wheezing rose up from the bottom of my existence:

> If you have tears, prepare to shed them now.
> You all do know this mantle. I remember
> The first time ever Caesar put it on;
> 'Twas on a summer's evening in his tent,
> That day he overcame the Nervii.
> Look! In this place ran Cassius' dagger through;
> See what a rent the envious Casca made;
> Through this the well-beloved Brutus stabbed,
> And as he pluck'd his cursed steel away,
> Mark how the blood of Caesar followed it . . .

Nothing could silence Simon-Wolf. Bobka, who was sitting on the floor, sobbed and blew her nose. The imperturbable Leykakh continued to move the trunk about behind the partition. And now my crazy grandfather conceived a desire to come to my assistance. He broke loose from the Apelkhots, crept up to the window and began to saw away on his violin, probably so that Simon-Wolf's foul language should not be audible to passers-by. Borgman looked out of the window, which was cut at ground level, and moved back in horror. My poor grandfather was pulling faces with his blue, stiffened mouth. He was wearing his bent top hat, a black oriental cloak with bone buttons, and ragged boots on his elephant feet. His smoke-sodden beard hung in wisps, moving to and fro in the window. Mark ran for it.

'It's all right,' he muttered, as he made his escape to freedom, 'it's really quite all right . . .'

His little blazer and peaked cap flickered in the courtyard.

At his departure my agitation vanished. Resolve and calm took hold of me. When Grandfather, having covered his rectangular sheet with Hebrew characters (he was describing the Apelkhots, in whose home, by my good offices, he had spent the entire day), lay down on his bunk-bed and fell asleep, I went out into the corridor. The floor there was made of earth. I moved along in the darkness, barefoot, in my long, patched shirt. Through the chinks in the boards the cobbles shimmered like blades of light. In the corner, as always, stood the water-butt. I lowered myself into it. The water cut me in two. I let my head go under, choked, came to the surface again. From above, on a shelf, a cat looked at me sleepily. The second time I held out longer, the water squelched around me, my groaning sank into it like a screw. I opened my eyes and saw at the bottom of the barrel the sail of my shirt and a pair of small feet pressed together. Again I did not have enough strength, I came to the surface. Beside the barrel stood Grandfather in his bed-jacket. His only tooth rang out.

'My grandson.' He spoke the words contemptuously and distinctly. 'I go to take castor oil,* that I should have something to put on your grave . . .'

I began to shout, beside myself, and lowered myself into the water with all my might. I was hauled out by Grandfather's feeble hand. Then for the first time that day I began to cry, and the world of tears was so enormous and beautiful that everything except tears sank away from my eyes.

I regained consciousness on my bed, swathed in blankets. Grandfather was pacing about the room, whistling. Fat Bobka was warming my hands on her bosom. I gave them up to it.

'How he shivers, our little fool, our child,' said Bobka. 'Where does he get the strength to shiver so . . .'

Grandfather gave his beard a tug, whistled and began to pace about again. Behind the wall Simon-Wolf was snoring with painful exhalations. Having had his fill of fighting for a day, he never woke up at night.

Awakening

All the people of our circle – brokers, shopkeepers, bank and steamship office employees – taught their children music. Our fathers, seeing no chance of success for themselves, devised a lottery. They established it on the bones of little children. Odessa was seized by this madness worse than other towns. For decades our town put *Wunderkinder* on the concert platforms of the world. From Odessa came Mischa Elman, Zimbalist, Gabrilowich; Jascha Heifetz* began among us.

When a boy was four or five, his mother took the tiny, puny creature to Mr Zagursky.* Zagursky ran a *Wunderkind* factory, a factory of Jewish dwarfs in lace collars and patent-leather shoes. He sought them out in the slums of the Molda-vanka, in the evil-smelling courtyards of the Old Market.

Zagursky gave them a first push in the right direction, and then the children were sent to Professor Auer* in St Petersburg.

In the souls of these starvelings with blue, swollen heads dwelt the mighty power of harmony. They became renowned virtuosi. And so my father decided to hold his own with Heifetz and Mischa Elman. Though I had passed *Wunderkind* age – I was in my fourteenth year – my short stature and puny physique made it possible for me to be mistaken for an eight-year-old. In this lay all their hopes.

I was taken to see Zagursky. Out of respect for my grandfather he agreed to charge a rouble a lesson – a low fee. My grandfather Levi-Itskhok was the laughing-stock of the town, and its adornment. He stalked about the streets in his top hat and ragged boots resolving doubts on the obscurest of matters. He was asked what a Gobelin was, why the Jacobins betrayed Robespierre, how artificial silk was made, what a Caesarean section was. My grandfather was able to answer these questions. Out of respect for his learning and madness Zagursky charged us a rouble a lesson. Also, he spent time on me because he feared Grandfather, for there was no point in spending time on me. The sounds crawled out of my violin like iron filings. I myself was cut to the heart by those sounds, but Father kept up the pace. At home there was no talk of anything but Mischa Elman, who had been exempted from military service by the tsar himself; Zimbalist, according to my father's information, had been presented to the king of England and had played at Buckingham Palace; Gabrilowich's parents bought two houses in St Petersburg. *Wunderkinder* brought their parents wealth. My father could have reconciled himself to poverty, but he needed fame.

'It's impossible,' people who had dined at our expense said, to stir up gossip, 'it's impossible that the grandson of such a man . . .'

But my thoughts were elsewhere. During my violin practice I placed on my music stand books by Turgenev or Dumas and, scraping out heaven only knows what, devoured page after page. By day I told tall stories to the neighbours' urchins, by night I transferred them on to paper. Writing was a hereditary occupation in our family. Levi-Itskhok, whose mind became touched as he approached old age, had spent the whole of his life writing 'Man with No Head'. I took after him.

Three times a week, laden with violin-case and music, I trailed off to Witte Street, formerly Dvoryanskaya Street, to Zagursky's. There, along the walls, waiting their turn, sat Jewish girls, hysterically aflame. They pressed to their weak knees violins that were larger than those who were to play at Buckingham Palace.

The door of the inner sanctum would open. From Zagursky's study, reeling, emerged large-headed, freckled children with thin necks like the stalks of flowers, and a paroxysmic flush upon their cheeks. The door would bang shut, having swallowed the next dwarf. On the other side of the wall the teacher in bow-tie and red curls, with weedy legs, exerted himself to the utmost, sang, conducted. The director of a monstrous lottery, he was inspired, peopling the Moldavanka and the black cul-de-sacs of the Old Market with the ghosts of pizzicato and cantilena. This chant was later brought to a devilish height of brilliance by old Professor Auer . . .

In this sect I had no place. A dwarf, as they were, I discerned a different kind of inspiration in the voices of my ancestors.

I found the first step difficult. One day I left the house loaded up with case, violin, music and twelve roubles in cash – payment for a month's tuition. I walked along Nezhinskaya Street. In order to reach Zagursky's I should have turned into Dvoryanskaya, but instead I went up Tiraspolskaya and found myself at the port. The time of my lesson flew by in Prak-ticheskaya Harbour. Thus did my liberation begin. Zagursky's waiting-room saw me no more. My schoolmate Nemanov and I got into the habit of going aboard the steamship *Kensington* to see a certain old seaman, Mr Trottyburn by name. Nemanov was a year younger than I, but had since the age of eight engaged in the most intricate commerce one could imagine. He was a genius at commercial deals and always delivered what he promised. Now he is a millionaire in New York, the director of General Motors, a company as powerful as Ford. Nemanov dragged me along with him because I obeyed him without a word. From Mr Trottyburn he bought smuggled tobacco-pipes. These pipes were carved in Lincoln by the old seaman's brother.

'Gentlemen,' Mr Trottyburn would say to us, 'mark my words, children must be made by one's own hand ... To smoke a factory-made pipe is like putting an enema tube in your mouth. Do you know who Benvenuto Cellini* was? ... He was a master. My brother in Lincoln could tell you a thing or two about him. My brother doesn't get in anybody's way. He's just convinced that children must be made by one's own hand, and not by somebody else's ... We cannot but agree with him, gentlemen ...'

Nemanov sold Trottyburn's pipes to bank managers, foreign consuls, wealthy Greeks. He made a 100 per cent profit.

The pipes of the Lincoln master breathed poetry. Into each one of them had been inserted an idea, a drop of eternity. In their mouthpieces gleamed a yellow eye, their cases were lined with satin. I tried to imagine the life in Old England of Matthew Trottyburn, the last master of the pipe, resisting change.

'We cannot but agree with him, gentlemen, that children must be made by one's own hand ...'

The heavy waves by the sea wall distanced me further and further from our house, which was steeped in the smell of onions and Jewish destiny. From Prakticheskaya Harbour I moved on to the breakwater. There, on a stretch of the sand bar, the boys from Primorskaya Street spent their days. From morning to night they did not pull on their trousers; they dived under the barges, stole coconuts for dinner and awaited the time when the steamerfuls of water-melon would drift slowly in from Kherson and Kamenka, and those water-melons could be split open on the moorings of the port.

It became my dream to learn to swim. I was ashamed to confess to these bronzed boys that, born in Odessa, I had not seen the sea until the age of ten, and at fourteen did not know how to swim.

How late I had to learn the essential things! In my child-hood, nailed to the Gemara,* I led the life of a sage, and when I was grown older began to climb trees.

The ability to swim proved to be beyond my reach. The fear of water that had haunted all my ancestors – Spanish rabbis and Frankfurt money-changers – pulled me to the bottom. The water would not support me. Exhausted, satu-rated with salt water, I would return shoreward to my violin and music. I was attached to the instruments of my crime and dragged them about with me. The struggle of the rabbis with the sea continued until pity was shown me by the water god of those parts, the proofreader of the *Odessa News*, Yefim Nikitich Smolich. Within this man's athletic breast dwelt compassion for Jewish children. He lorded it over throngs of rachitic starvelings. Nikitich gathered them in the bedbug-infested rooms of the Moldavanka, took them to the sea, dug in the sand with them, did gymnastics with them, dived with them, taught them songs and, getting thoroughly fried in the vertical rays of the sun, told them stories about fish and animals. To grown-ups Nikitich would explain that he was a natural philosopher. Nikitich's stories made the Jewish chil-dren die with laughter; they squealed and fawned upon him like puppies. The sun besprinkled them with creeping freckles, freckles the colour of lizards.

*

The old man had watched my single-handed combat with the waves out of the corner of his eye without saying anything. Having seen that there was no hope and that I was never going to learn to swim, he included me among the tenants of his heart. It was always with us here, his merry heart, it never put on any airs, was never mean, never troubled. With his copper shoulders, with his head of a gladiator grown old, with his bandy, bronzed legs he lay among us behind the breakwater, among the last dregs of a tribe that did not know how to die, like the ruler of these water-meloned, kerosened waters. I loved that man as only a boy who is sick with hysteria and headaches can love an athlete. I never left his side and tried to oblige him.

He said to me:

'Don't you worry . . . Strengthen your nerves. The swimming will come by itself . . . What do you mean, the water won't support you? . . . Why shouldn't it?'

When he saw how I was reaching out to him, Nikitich made an exception for me alone of all his disciples, invited me as a guest to his clean, spacious attic covered in mats, showed me his dogs, hedgehog, tortoise and pigeons. In exchange for these riches I brought him a tragedy of my own composition.

'I *thought* you scribbled,' said Nikitich, 'you have that kind of a look . . . You no longer look anywhere else . . .'

He read my writings through, shrugged one shoulder, ran his hand through his abrupt grey curls, walked to and fro about the attic.

'I suppose,' he articulated in a drawl, falling silent after each word, 'that within you there is a spark of the divine . . .'

We went down to the street. The old man stopped, banged his stick forcefully against the pavement and fixed his eyes on me.

'What is it you lack? . . . Your youth is no problem, it will pass with the years . . . What you lack is a feeling for nature.'

With his stick he pointed out to me a tree that had a reddish trunk and a low crown.

'What kind of tree is that?'

I did not know.

'What's growing on this bush?'

I did not know that, either. He and I walked through the small square on Aleksandrovsky Prospect. The old man poked his stick at every tree, he clutched me by the shoulder whenever a bird flew past and made me listen to the different calls.

'What kind of bird is that singing?'

I was unable to reply. The names of trees and birds, their division into species, the places birds fly to, which direction the sun rises in, when the dew is heaviest – all that was unknown to me.

'And you presume to write? ... A man who does not live in nature as a bird or an animal lives in it will never write two worthwhile lines in all his life ... Your landscapes are like descriptions of stage scenery. The devil take me, what have your parents been thinking of for fourteen years?'

'What have they been thinking of? Protested promissory notes, the private residences of Mischa Elman.' I said nothing of this to Nikitich, I kept quiet.

Back home, at dinner, I did not touch my food. It would not go down.

'A feeling for nature,' I thought. 'My God, why did I never think of that before? Where am I going to find someone who can explain the calls of the birds and the names of the trees to me? What do I know about them? I might be able to recognize lilacs, when they're in bloom, anyway, lilacs and acacias. There are lilacs and acacias on Deribasovskaya and Grecheskaya Streets.'

While we were having dinner Father told a new story about Jascha Heifetz. Near Robin's he had encountered Men-delssohn, Jascha's uncle. The boy, it turned out, was getting eight hundred roubles a performance. Work out how much that made at a rate of fifteen concerts a month.

I worked it out, it came to twelve thousand a month. Doing the multiplication and carrying four in my head, I looked out of the window. Across the cement yard, in a gently billowing cloak and cape, with reddish ringlets showing from under his soft hat, leaning on his cane, stalked Mr Zagursky, my music teacher. It could not be said that he had noted my absence before time. More than three months had already passed since my violin had sunk down to the sand off the breakwater.

Zagursky was coming up to the front door. I rushed to the back door – it had been boarded up the day before to keep out thieves. There was no salvation. I locked myself in the lavatory. Half an hour later the family had gathered outside the door. The women were crying. Bobka, my aunt, was rubbing a fat shoulder against the door and going off into fits of sobs. Father said nothing. Then he began to speak more quietly and distinctly than he had ever spoken in his life.

'I am an officer,' said my father. 'I have an estate. I ride out hunting. The muzhiks pay me rent. I have put my son in the Cadet Corps.* I have no reason to worry about my son . . .'

He fell silent. The women breathed heavily through their noses. Then a terrible blow fell upon the lavatory door, Father was beating against it with his whole body, he was hurling himself against it at a run.

'I am an officer,' he howled, 'I ride out hunting . . . I'll kill him . . . His number's up . . .'

The hook sprang off the door, but there was still the bolt, held by a single nail. The women, squealing, rushed across the floor and seized Father by the legs; out of his mind, he tore himself loose. In the nick of time Father's old mother arrived.

'My child,' she said to him in Yiddish, 'our grief is great. It has no bounds. Only blood was lacking in our house. I do not want to see blood in our house . . .'

Father began to groan. I heard his shuffling, retreating footsteps. The bolt hung by a final nail.

I sat in my fortress until night-time. When everyone had gone to bed, Aunt Bobka took me to Grandmother's. We had a long way to go. The moonlight froze on unknown bushes, on trees that had no name. An invisible bird gave a peep and was silent — perhaps it had fallen asleep. What kind of bird was it? What was its name? Is there dew in the evening? Where is the constellation of Great Bear situated? In what direction does the sun rise?

We walked along Pochtovaya Street. Bobka held me tightly by the hand, so that I should not run away. She was right. I was thinking of escape.

Di Grasso

I was fourteen years old. I belonged to the fearless army of theatre-ticket touts. My boss was a swindler with one eye that was always screwed up and an enormous silky moustache. His name was Kolya Shvarts. I drifted into his orbit that unhappy year when the Italian Opera in Odessa went bankrupt. Following the advice of the newspaper reviewers, the impresario did not send for Anselmi and Titto-Ruffo,* and decided to make do with a good ensemble. For this he was punished; he went bankrupt, and we with him. To put things right again we were promised Chaliapin, but Chaliapin wanted three thousand for a performance. In his place, the Sicilian tragic actor Di Grasso* arrived with his company. They were brought to the hotel in wagons stuffed with children, cats, cages in which Italian birds hopped. Surveying this gypsy encampment, Kolya Shvarts said, 'Boys, this is not merchandise . . .'

After his arrival the tragic actor set off for the market with a purse. In the evening – with another purse – he presented himself at the theatre. For the first performance there were barely fifty people in the audience. We let the tickets go at half price, but there were no takers.

That evening they performed a Sicilian folk drama, a story as ordinary as the alternation of night and day. The daughter of a wealthy peasant got engaged to a herdsman. She stayed faithful to him until one day a young swell from the town arrived dressed in a velvet waistcoat. As she talked to the visitor, the girl giggled at the wrong time and fell silent at the wrong time. Listening to them, the herdsman kept moving his head like a startled bird. For the whole of the first act he pressed himself against walls, went off somewhere in his flapping trousers and came back again, looking around him.

'Dead as a doornail,' said Kolya Shvarts at the interval. 'This is merchandise for Kremenchug.'*

An entr'acte was made to give the girl time to ripen for betrayal. In the second act we did not recognize her – she was intolerant, absent-minded and, being in a hurry, gave the herdsman back his engagement ring. Then he led her up to a cheap, painted statue of the Holy Virgin and in his Sicilian dialect said: 'Signora,' he said in his low voice and turned away, 'the Holy Virgin wants you to hear what I have to say . . . To Giovanni, who has arrived from the town, the Holy Virgin will give as many women as he wants; but I need none but you, Signora . . . The Virgin Mary, our Immaculate Protectress, will tell you the same thing, if you ask her, Signora . . .'

The girl stood with her back to the painted wooden statue. As she listened to the herdsman, she stamped her foot impatiently. On this earth – oh, woe to us! – there is no woman who is not reckless at those moments when her fate is being decided . . . She remains alone at those moments, alone, without the Virgin Mary, and asks no questions of her . . .

In the third act Giovanni from the town met his fate. He

was being shaved by the village barber, his strong, manly legs
thrown about all over the proscenium; under the sun of Sicily
the creases of his waistcoat shone. The stage represented a
Sicilian fair. In a remote corner stood the herdsman. He stood
in silence, amidst a carefree throng. His head was lowered,
then he raised it, and under the weight of his burning,
attentive gaze Giovanni started to move, began shifting restlessly in his chair and, pushing the barber away, leapt to his
feet. In a strained voice he demanded of the policeman that
the latter should remove any gloomy and suspicious people
from the square. The herdsman – played by Di Grasso –
stood pondering, then he smiled, rose into the air, flew across
the stage of the municipal theatre, landed on Giovanni's
shoulders and, biting his throat right through, growling and
looking from side to side, began to suck the blood from the
wound. Giovanni came crashing to the floor, and the curtain
– closing with noiseless menace – hid from us both murdered
man and murderer. Expecting nothing further, we rushed to
the box-office in Theatre Lane, which was to open the
following day. Running at the head of us all was Kolya
Shvarts. At dawn the *Odessa News* informed those few people
who had been in the theatre that they had seen the most
remarkable actor of the century.

On this visit to our town Di Grasso played *King Lear*,
Othello, *La Mort Civile*, Turgenev's *The Sponge*, asserting with
each word and movement that in the frenzy of noble passion
there is more justice and hope than in the joyless principles of
the world.

The tickets for these plays went at five times their asking
price. In their hunt for ticket touts, the buyers would find
them at an inn – bawling, purple-faced, disgorging harmless
blasphemy.

A current of dusty, rosy heat was admitted to Theatre Lane.
Delicatessen owners in felt bedroom slippers brought green
bottles of wine and kegs of olives out into the street. In vats in

front of the shops macaroni boiled in foaming water, and the steam from it condensed in the far-off heavens. Old women in men's lace-up boots sold mussels and souvenirs, running after hesitant customers and shouting. Wealthy Jews with forked, combed beards drove up in carriages to the Northern Hotel and knocked quietly at the rooms of stout, black-haired women with moustaches – the actresses of Di Grasso's company. Everyone in Theatre Lane was happy, except for one person, and that person was I. At that time disaster was approaching me. At any moment Father might notice the absence of the watch I had taken from him without his permission and had pawned with Kolya Shvarts. Having had time to grow accustomed to the gold watch and being a man who drank Bessarabian wine of a morning instead of tea, Kolya, his money now returned to him, was none the less unable to bring himself to give me the watch back. That was his temperament. Just like my father. Squeezed between these two men, I watched the hoops of other people's happiness scudding past me. There was nothing left for me but to flee to Constantinople. It had all been arranged with the second engineer of the steamship *The Duke of Kent*, but before putting to sea I decided to take my leave of Di Grasso. He was playing, for the last time, the herdsman who is detached from the earth by an unfathomable force. To the theatre had come the Italian colony led by their bald and shapely consul, fidgeting Greeks, bearded external students, staring fanatically at a point visible to none, and the long-armed Utochkin.* Kolya Shvarts had brought his wife in a violet shawl with a fringe, a woman fit to be a grenadier and as long as a steppe, with a crumpled, sleepy little face at its outer edge. It was drenched in tears when the curtain was lowered.

'Down-and-out,' she said to Kolya as they left the theatre, 'now you see what love is . . .'

Stepping heavily, Madame Shvarts walked along Lanzheronovskaya Street; tears flowed from her fishy eyes, the fringed shawl on her fat shoulders shuddered. Shuffling with mannish steps, her head quivering, she enumerated deafeningly, to the whole street, the women who got along well with their husbands.

'"Little chicken", those husbands call their wives, "Little goldie", "Little child" . . .'

The subdued Kolya walked beside his wife, quietly blowing out his silky moustache. Out of habit, I went after them, sobbing. Growing quiet for a moment, Madame Shvarts heard my weeping and turned round.

'Down-and-out,' she said to her husband, her fishy eyes goggling, 'let me not live my appointed days unless you give that boy his watch back . . .'

Kolya froze, his mouth open wide, then recovered himself and, giving me a painful tweak, shoved the watch at me sideways.

'What do I get from him,' the coarse, weeping voice of Madame Shvarts lamented, as it drew away, 'brutish tricks today, brutish tricks tomorrow . . . I ask you, down-and-out, how long can a woman wait? . . .'

They reached the corner and turned into Pushkin Street. Clutching the watch, I remained alone and suddenly, with a clarity such as I had never experienced until then, I saw the columns of the Town Parliament stretching aloft, the illumined leaves of the boulevard, the bronze head of Pushkin with the dim reflection of the moon on it: for the first time I saw the things that surrounded me as they really were – lulled into calm and inexpressibly beautiful.

Guy de Maupassant

In the winter of 1916 I found myself in St Petersburg with a forged passport and without a copeck. I was given shelter by a teacher of Russian philology,* Aleksey Kazantsev.

He lived in Peski,* in a frozen, yellow, foul-smelling street. In order to eke out his meagre salary he did translations from Spanish; Blasco Ibáñez* was becoming famous at that time.

Kazantsev had never been in Spain, even passing through, but a love for that country filled his being – he knew every castle, garden and river in Spain. In addition to myself there pressed close to Kazantsev a large number of people who had been kicked out of the regular pattern of life. We lived in want. Now and again the gutter newspapers printed, in small type, our notes on current events.

In the mornings I lounged about the morgues and the police stations.

Happier than any of us, however, was Kazantsev. He had a motherland – Spain.

In November I was offered the post of clerk at the Obukhov steelworks, not a bad job, which carried with it exemption from military service.

I declined to become a clerk.

Even at that time – twenty years old – I said to myself: better to go hungry, to go to prison, to be a tramp, than to sit at an office desk ten hours a day. There is no particular daring in this vow, but I have not broken it and shall not do so. The wisdom of my grandfathers sat in my head: we are born for the pleasure of work, fighting, love, we are born for that and for nothing else.

As he listened to my lectures, Kazantsev ruffled the short yellow down on his head. The horror in his gaze was intermingled with admiration.

At Christmas fortune smiled on us. The barrister Bendersky, owner of the Halcyon publishing house, planned to bring out a new edition of the works of Maupassant. Raisa, the barrister's wife, undertook the translation. But nothing had yet come of the grand venture.

Kazantsev, who translated from Spanish, was asked if he knew anyone who could help Raisa Mikhaylovna. Kazantsev suggested me.

The following day, wearing a jacket that belonged to someone else, I set off for the Benderskys'. They lived on the corner of Nevsky and the Moyka, in a house that had been built from Finnish granite and decorated with pink columns, embrasures and stone coats of arms. Bankers without family or breeding, converts to the Christian faith who had got rich in the supply business, they had built a large number of these vulgar, pseudo-majestic castles in St Petersburg before the war.

A red carpet ran up the staircase. On the landings, raised on their hind legs, stood plush velvet bears.

In their gaping jaws burned crystal lamps.

The Benderskys' lived on the third floor. A chambermaid with a head-dress and high breasts opened the door. She led me into a drawing-room that was decorated in ancient Slavonic style. On the walls hung blue paintings by Roerich* – prehistoric stones and monsters. About the corners – on the china cupboards – ancient icons were arranged. The chambermaid with the high breasts moved majestically about the room. She was shapely, myopic, haughty. In her grey, wide-open eyes there was a hardened licentiousness. The girl moved slowly. I reflected that in love-making she must twist and turn with violent swiftness. The brocade curtain that hung above the door began to sway. A black-haired woman with pink eyes and a large bosom came into the drawing-room. It did not take much time to recognize in Benderskaya the ravishing type of Jewess that comes from Kiev and Poltava, from the replete towns of the steppes, planted with chestnuts and acacias. These women let their resourceful husbands' money overflow into the rosy fat on their bellies, the backs of their necks, their round shoulders. Their sleepy, delicately ironic smiles drive the garrison officers out of their minds.

'Maupassant is the only passion of my life,' Raisa said to me.

Trying to restrain the swaying of her large hips, she went

out of the room and returned with a translation of 'Miss Harriet'. In her translation there remained not even a vestige of Maupassant's phrasing – free, flowing, with the long breathing of passion. Benderskaya wrote with wearisome correctness, lifelessly and casually – the way Jews used to write the Russian language in earlier days.

I took the manuscript home with me, and there, in Kazantsev's attic – among the sleepers – cut clearings in someone else's translation. This is not such unpleasant work as it might seem. A phrase is born into the world good and bad at the same time. The secret rests in a barely perceptible turn. The lever must lie in one's hand and get warm. It must be turned once, and no more.

In the morning I took back the corrected manuscript. Raisa had not been lying when she had spoken of her passion for Maupassant. She sat immobile during the reading, her hands clasped: those satin hands flowed to the floor, her forehead was pale, the lace between her downwards-crushed breasts moved aside and trembled.

'How did you do it?'

Then I began to speak of style, of the army of words, an army in which all kinds of weapons are on the move. No iron can enter the human heart as chillingly as a full stop placed at the right time. She listened, her head inclined, her painted lips slightly open. A black gleam shone in her lacquered hair, smoothly drawn back and divided by a parting. Her legs, with strong, soft calves, in shiny stockings, were placed apart over the carpet.

The chambermaid, turning her hardened, licentious eyes away to the side, brought in breakfast on a tray.

A glassy St Petersburg sun lay on the faded, uneven carpet. Twenty-nine books by Maupassant stood above the table on a little shelf. With melting fingers the sun touched the morocco leather bindings of the books – the beautiful tomb of a human heart.

We were served coffee in small blue cups and we began to translate 'Idyll'. Everyone recalls the story of how the hungry young carpenter sucks the overflowing milk of the fat wet-nurse. It happens on a train going from Nice to Marseilles, one intensely hot midday in the land of roses, the motherland of roses, there, where plantations of flowers descend to the shore of the sea . . .

I left the Benderskys' with a twenty-five rouble advance. That evening our commune at Peski was as drunk as a flock of intoxicated geese. We scooped up the unpressed caviar in spoons and followed it down with liver sausage. Tight, I began to rail against Tolstoy.

'He got frightened, your count, he got cold feet . . . His religion is fear . . . Frightened by cold, old age, death, the count made himself a woolly jumper out of faith . . .'

'Go on,' Kazantsev kept saying, shaking his bird-like head.

We fell asleep beside our own beds. I dreamed about Katya, the forty-year-old washerwoman who lived below us. In the mornings we got boiling water from her. I had never even seen her face clearly, but in my dream Katya and I did God only knows what. We exhausted each other with kisses. I could not restrain myself from going to ask her for boiling water the following morning.

I was met by a faded, shawl-crossed woman with loosened ash-grey curls and damp hands.

From that day on I had breakfast at the Benderskys' every morning. Our attic acquired a new stove, herring, chocolate. Twice Raisa drove me out to the islands in her carriage. I lost my inhibitions and told her about my childhood. The story sounded dismal, to my own surprise. From under the moleskin cap, shining, frightened eyes looked at me. The reddish fur of their eyelashes quivered dolefully.

I made the acquaintance of Raisa's husband – a sallow-faced Jew with a bald head and a flat, strong body that was turned slantwise for the purpose of flight. Rumour had it that

he was close to Rasputin. The profits he made out of the
military supply business had given him the look of a man
possessed. His eyes wandered, the fabric of reality had broken
for him. Raisa was embarrassed when introducing new people
to her husband. Because of my youth I noticed this a week
later than I should have done.

After New Year Raisa had a visit from her two sisters in
Kiev. One day I brought the mansucript of 'The Confession'
and, not finding Raisa at home, came back again in the
evening. Dinner was in progress in the dining-room. From
there came the silvery neighing of mares and the boom of
men's voices, outrageously exultant. In wealthy houses that
have no traditions, dinner is a noisy affair. It was a Jewish
noise, with thunderous peals and melodious endings. Raisa
came out to me wearing a ball gown with a bare back. Her
feet, in unsteady little patent-leather shoes, stepped awk-
wardly.

'I'm drunk, darling' – and she stretched out to me arms that
were covered with platinum chains and emerald stars. Her body
swayed like the body of a snake rising towards the ceiling to the
accompaniment of music. She shook her frizzled hair, jangled
her rings, and suddenly fell into an armchair with ancient
Russian carving. On her powdered back smouldered scars.

Through the wall there was another explosion of female
laughter. From the dining-room emerged the sisters with
their little moustaches, just as strapping and full-busted as
Raisa. Their busts were pushed forward, their black hair
flowed loose. Both were married to Benderskys of their own.
Incoherent female gaiety filled the room, the gaiety of mature
women. The husbands wrapped the sisters in sealskin mantles,
in Orenburg shawls, shod them in little black overshoes;
beneath the snowy visors of their shawls remained only
rouged and burning cheeks, marble noses and eyes with a
myopic, semitic sheen. After a bit of noise they left for the
theatre, where Chaliapin was singing in *Judith.*

'I want to work,' Raisa babbled, stretching out her bare arms, 'we have lost a whole week . . .'

From the dining-room she brought a bottle and two wine-glasses. Her breasts moved freely in the loose silk of her gown, the nipples erect under the silk.

'A sacred vintage,' said Raisa, as she poured out the wine, 'Muscadet '83, my husband will murder me when he finds out . . .'

I had never had any dealings with Muscadet '83 before and had no hesitation in drinking down three glasses, one after the other. They at once carried me off to side-lanes where orange flame wafted and music was heard.

'I'm drunk, darling . . . What are we working on today . . .'

'Today it's "L'aveu".'

'So, "The Confession", then. The sun is the hero of this story, le soleil de France. Melted drops of sun, falling on the red-haired Céleste, were turned into freckles. The sun polished with its vertical rays, wine and apple cider, the phiz of the coachman Polyte. Twice a week Céleste took cream, eggs and chickens to sell in the town. For fare she paid Polyte ten sous for herself and four sous for the basket. And on each journey Polyte, winking, would ask the red-haired Céleste: 'But when are we going to have a bit of fun, ma belle?'

' "What is your meaning, Monsieur Polyte?"

'As he bobbed up and down on the driver's seat, the coachman explained: "To have a bit of fun means to have a bit of fun, the devil take me . . . A lad and a girl — and no music needed . . ."

' "I do not like such jokes, Monsieur Polyte," replied Céleste, moving away from the lad with her skirts that hung over her mighty calves in their red stockings.

'But that devil Polyte kept roaring with laughter, and coughing — "One day we shall have a bit of fun, ma belle," — and tears of merriment rolled down his face, which was the colour of brick-blood and wine.'

I drank down another glass of the sacred Muscadet. Raisa clinked glasses with me.

The chambermaid with the hard eyes walked through the room and disappeared.

'*Ce diable de Polyte* . . . In two years Céleste had paid him forty-eight francs. That was two francs short of fifty. At the end of the second year, when they were alone in the coach and Polyte, who had had a few ciders before leaving, asked, as was his wont, "Aren't we going to have a bit of fun, Mademoiselle Céleste?" – she replied, lowering her eyes, "I am at your service, Monsieur Polyte . . ."'

Raisa collapsed on to the table with a roar of laughter. *Ce diable de Polyte* . . .

'The coach was harnessed to a white nag. The white nag, its mouth pink with age, went slowly. The merry sunlight of France surrounded the large coach that was shut off from the world by a rusty hood. A lad and a girl need no music . . .'

Raisa handed me a glass. This was my fifth.

'*Mon vieux*, to Maupassant . . .'

'Aren't we going have a bit of fun today, *ma belle* . . .' I stretched over to Raisa and kissed her on the lips. They began to tremble and swell.

'You're a funny one,' Raisa muttered through her teeth, staggering backwards. She pressed herself against the wall, spreading her exposed arms. On her hands and shoulder spots began to burn. Of all the gods ever crucified on a cross, this was the most seductive.

'Please sit down, Monsieur Polyte.'

She directed me to a sloping blue armchair made in Slavonic style. Its back was of carved wood with a design of interlaced tails. I made my way to it, stumbling.

The night had placed under my hungry youth a bottle of Muscadet '83 and twenty-nine books, twenty-nine petards filled with pity, genius, passion . . . I leapt up, knocked over the chair, bumped into the shelf. The twenty-nine volumes came crashing to the carpet, their pages flew asunder, they stood on their sides . . . and the white nag of my fate moved slowly on.

'You're a funny one,' Raisa growled.

I left the granite house on the Moyka before midnight, when the sisters and husband would return from the theatre. I was sober and could have walked on a single board, but it was much better to stagger, and I swayed from side to side, singing loudly in a language I had only just invented. Down the tunnels of the streets, lined by a chain of street lamps, in waves, passed the vapours of the fog. Monsters roared behind seething walls. The wooden pavements cut off the legs of those who walked on them.

At home, Kazantsev was asleep. He slept sitting up, his thin legs stretched out in their felt boots. The canary fluff was standing up on his head. He had fallen asleep by the stove, leaning over *Don Quixote* in an edition of 1624. On the title page of this book there was a dedication to the Duc de Broglio. I got into bed silently, so as not to wake Kazantsev, moved the lamp towards me and began to read a book by Édouard de Maynial – *La Vie et l'oeuvre de Guy de Maupassant.*

Kazantsev's lips were moving, his head kept slumping down.

And that night I discovered from Édouard de Maynial that Maupassant was born in 1850 to a Normandy nobleman and Laure Lepoitevin, Flaubert's cousin. At the age of twenty-five he experienced his first attack of hereditary syphilis. With his energy and high spirits he tried to put up a fight against the disease. At first he suffered from headaches and fits of hypochondria. Then the spectre of blindness arose before him. His eyesight deteriorated. He became paranoic, unsociable, litigious. He struggled fiercely, tossed about the Mediterranean in a yacht, fled to Tunis, to Morocco, to central Africa – and wrote incessantly. Having achieved fame, in his fortieth year he cut his throat and nearly bled to death. He was locked up in a lunatic asylum. There he crawled about on all fours and ate his own excrement. The last entry in his medical report reads: '*Monsieur de Maupassant va s'animaliser*'. He died at the age of forty-two. His mother outlived him.

I read the book to its end and got out of bed. The fog had come up to the window, obscuring the universe. My heart was constricted. I was brushed by a foreboding of truth.

The Journey

I walked away from the collapsed front in November 1917. At home Mother kitted me out with linen and dry rusks. I reached Kiev the day before Muravyov* began shelling the city. My aim was to get to St Petersburg. For twelve days and nights we sat it out in the basement of Khaim Tsiryulnik's hotel in the Bessarabka. I received an exit permit from the commandant of Soviet Kiev.

There is in the world no spectacle more cheerless than Kiev railway station. Its temporary wooden huts have for many years now disfigured the approaches to the town. On the wet boards lice chirred. Deserters, black-market speculators, gypsies lay all together in a huddle. Old Galician women urinated standing on the platform. The low sky was furrowed by clouds, sodden with murk and rain.

Seventy-two hours passed before the first train left. At first it stopped every verst, then it got going in earnest; the wheels began to rattle more excitedly, to sing a powerful song. In our heated goods van this made everyone happy. Speedy travel made people happy in 1918. At night the train gave a jolt and stopped. The door of the goods van slid open and the green radiance of the snows was revealed to us. Into the goods van came a station telegraphist in a fur-lined fur coat tied with a thin leather belt and soft Caucasian boots. The telegraphist stretched out his hand and tapped a finger on his open palm.

'Documents for this destination . . .'

Nearest to the door lay curled up on bales, an inaudible old woman. She was going to Lyuban to see her son who worked on the railway. Beside me drowsed, sitting up, the school-master Yehuda Veynberg and his wife. The schoolmaster had got married a few days ago and was taking his young wife to St Petersburg. All the way they had been whispering to each other about the composite method of teaching. Their hands were joined even in sleep, placed one in the other.

The telegraphist read their warrant, which was signed by Lunacharsky,* pulled from under his fur coat a Mauser with a narrow and dirty muzzle and shot the schoolmaster in the face. At the telegraphist's back stood a big, round-shouldered muzhik in a fur cap with unfastened ear flaps and back flap. The superior winked to the muzhik, the latter put his lamp on the floor, undid the dead man's flies, cut off his sexual organs with a small knife and began to stuff them into his wife's mouth.

'You wouldn't touch *tref*,'* said the telegraphist, 'so eat something kosher.'

The woman's soft throat swelled. She said nothing. The train was standing in the steppe. The corrugated snow gleamed with a polar brilliance. Jews were being thrown out of the carriages on to the rails. Shots rang out unevenly, like exclamations. The muzhik in the unfastened fur cap led me off behind a stack of firewood and began to search me. We were lit by a moon that kept going behind clouds. The lilac wall of the forest smoked. Rigid, stubby, frozen fingers crawled over my body. The telegraphist shouted from the platform of the carriage:

'Is he a Yid or a Russian?'

'A Russian,' the muzhik muttered as he rummaged about my person, 'but he'd make a good rabbi . . .'

He brought his crumpled, worried face close to mine – ripped from my underpants the four gold ten-rouble pieces my mother had sewn into them for the journey, took off my boots and overcoat and then, turning his back, clapped the palm of his hand edgewise along the nape of my neck and said in Yiddish:

'*Antloyf, Khaim . . .*'*

I went in the snow, in my bare feet. A target was burned into my back, the centre of the target passed through my ribs. The muzhik did not shoot. Amidst the columns of the pine trees, amidst the closed-in cavern of the forest swayed a light wreathed in crimson smoke. I ran to the forest warden's hut. It reeked with the smoke of pressed dung. The forest warden gave a groan when I burst into his hut. Swathed in strips cut from fur coats and greatcoats, he sat in a bamboo chair, crumbling tobacco on his knees. Stretched in smoke, the forest warden groaned; then, getting up, he bowed to me from the waist:

'Go away, dear father. Go away, dear citizen . . .'

He led me out to the path and gave me rags to wrap my feet in. By late morning I reached a *shtetl*. At the hospital there was no doctor to amputate my frost-bitten feet: the ward was being run by the doctor's assistant. Each morning he swooped up to the hospital on a short black stallion, tethered it to the horse-rail and came in to see us aflame, with a bright lustre in his eyes.

'Friedrich Engels,' said the doctor's assistant, his pupils shining like coals, as he bent down at the head of my bed, 'tells us that nations must not exist, but we say on the contrary – the nation must exist . . .'

Tearing the bandages from my feet, he would straighten up and, gritting his teeth, ask softly:

'Where? Where is it taking you . . . Why does it move

about, your nation . . .? Why does it stir up trouble, foment unrest . . .?'

The Soviet got us out by night, in a wagon – patients who had not got on with the doctor's assistant and old Jewesses in wigs, the mothers of the *shtetl*'s commissars.

My feet healed. I moved further along the destitute road to Zhlobin, Orsha, Vitebsk.

The muzzle of a howitzer served as cover on the stretch of the way from Novo-Sokolniki to Loknya. We rode on the open gun platform. Fedyukha, chance travelling companion, who had made the great journey of the deserters, was a storyteller, wise-cracker, joker. We slept under the short, mighty, upturned muzzle and warmed each other with ourselves in a canvas pit spread with straw, like the lair of a wild animal. After Loknya, Fedyukha stole my suitcase and disappeared. The suitcase had been issued to me by the *shtetl*'s Soviet, and contained two sets of soldier's linen, rusks and some money. Two days and nights – we were getting close to St Petersburg – went by without food. At Tsarskoye Selo Station I witnessed the last of the shooting. An anti-profiteer detachment fired into the air as it greeted the approaching train. The speculators were taken out on to the platform, and their clothing was stripped from them. On to the asphalt, beside the real people, flopped rubber ones, filled with alcohol. At the ninth hour of the evening the station hurled me out of its wailing prison on to Zagorodny Prospect. On the wall across the street, outside a boarded-up chemist's shop, the thermometer showed twenty-four degrees of frost. The wind was thundering in the tunnel of Gorokhovaya; above the canal a gas light was on the wane. This frozen, basalt Venice was motionless. I entered Gorokhovaya as though it were an ice-covered field obstructed by rocks.

In house number two, the former governor's office, were the quarters of the Cheka.* Two machine-guns, two iron dogs with raised muzzles, stood in the vestibule. I showed the commandant the letters of Vanya Kalugin, my sergeant in the Shuysky Regiment. Kalugin had since become an investigator in the Cheka; in his letters he asked me to come and see him.

'Go to Anichkov,' said the commandant, 'he's there now . . .'

'I'll never make it' – and I smiled in reply.

Nevsky Prospect flowed into the distance like the Milky Way. It was marked off by the carcasses of horses as by so many milestones. With their legs in the air the horses supported a sky that had fallen low. Their gaping bellies were clean, and glistened. An old man who looked like a guardsman pulled past me a carved toy sledge. Exerting himself, he drove his leather feet into the ice; on the back of his head was a Tyrolean hat, his beard was tied together with string and stuck into a shawl.

'I'll never make it,' I said to the old man.

He stopped. His leonine, pock-marked face was completely calm. He thought about himself and went on pulling the sledge.

'Thus does the need to conquer St Petersburg pass,' I thought, trying to remember the name of the man who was trampled to death by the hooves of Arab chargers at the very end of his journey. It was Yehuda Halevi.*

Two Chinese in bowler hats with loaves of bread under their arms stood on the corner of Sadovaya. With cold-sensitive fingernails they marked off segments on the bread and showed them to the prostitutes who approached them. The women walked past them in a silent parade.

By Anichkov Bridge, near Klodt's* horses, I squatted down on the ledge of the statue.

In the cranberry-coloured side-wing, the door was open. A blue gaslight gleamed above a lackey who had fallen asleep in an armchair. In the wrinkled, deathly inked face the lower lip sagged; a soldier's blouse, bathed in light, covered the court trousers, which were sewn with gold braid. A shaggy, inky arrow pointed the way to the commandant. I went up the staircase and passed through some empty, low-ceilinged rooms. Women, painted in dark, gloomy colours, sang and danced in rings on the ceilings and the walls. Wire mesh covered the windows, on their frames hung the broken upright bolts. At the end of the suite of rooms, illumined as though on a stage, at a table in a circle of straw-like muzhik's hair, sat – Kalugin. Before him on the table lay a pile of children's toys, rag dolls of various colours, tattered picture books.

'Here you are,' said Kalugin, raising his head, 'hello . . . You're needed here . . .'

I moved aside with my hand the toys that were scattered about the table, lay down on its shining wood surface and . . . woke up – moments or hours had gone by – on a low sofa. The rays of the chandelier played above me in a glassy waterfall. The rags that had been cut from me lay on the floor in a puddle that had accumulated there.

'Take a bath,' said Kalugin, who was standing over the sofa; he picked me up and carried me to the bath-tub. It was an old-fashioned bath-tub, with low sides. No water came from the taps. Instead, Kalugin filled it for me from a pail. On pale yellow, satin pouffes, on wicker seats without backs, clothes were spread about – a dressing-gown, with buttons, a shirt and socks made of woven double silk. I disappeared up to my head in the underpants, the dressing-gown had been made for a giant, I tripped on the sleeves with my feet.

'What's this, are you making fun of Aleksandr Aleksandrovich,'* said Kalugin, as he rolled up my sleeves. 'The fellow weighed about nine *poods* . . .'

Somehow we managed to tie up the dressing-gown of Emperor Alexander III and returned to the room from which we had come. This had been Maria Fyodorovna's library, a scented box with gilded bookcases against the walls, full of crimson stripes.

I told Kalugin which of us in the Shuysky Regiment had been killed, which of us had been elected commissars, which of us had gone to the Kuban. We drank tea, stars ran in the crystal walls of the glasses. We swallowed them down with horse-meat sausage, black and on the raw side. We were divided from the world by the thick, light silk of the curtains; the sun that was fixed to the ceiling refracted and shone, a suffocating heat came from the pipes of the steam central heating.

'Here goes,' said Kalugin, when we were done with the horse-flesh. He went off somewhere and came back with two boxes – a gift from Sultan Abdul-Hamid to the Russian tsar. One of the boxes was made of zinc, the other was a cigar box with bands and paper medallions. '*A sa majesté, l'Empereur de toutes les Russies*' was engraved on the zinc lid – 'from a well-wishing cousin . . .'

Maria Fyodorovna's library was filled by the aroma that had been familiar to her a quarter of a century earlier. The cigarettes, twenty centimetres in length and as thick as a finger, were wrapped in pink paper; I do not know if such cigarettes were smoked by anyone in the world except the Emperor of all the Russias, but I opted for a cigar. Kalugin smiled as he looked at me.

'Here goes,' he said, 'with any luck they've not been counted . . . The lackeys told me that Alexander III was a confirmed smoker; he liked tobacco, kvass and champagne . . . Yet there are five-copeck clay ashtrays on his table and patches on his trousers . . .'

And true enough, the dressing-gown in which I had been arrayed was grease-stained and shiny, and had been mended many times.

We passed the remainder of the night going through the toys of Nicholas II, his drums and toy trains, his christening clothes and his exercise-books with their childish scrawl. Photographs of great princes who had died in their infancy, locks of their hair, the diaries of the Danish Princess Dagmar, the letters of her sister, the Queen of England, exuding scent and decay, crumbled under our fingers. On the title-pages of the Gospels and Lamartine, friends and Fräuleins – the daughters of burgomasters and state councillors – said farewell in slanting, assiduous lines to the princess who was going away to Russia. Queen Louise,* her mother, a small landowner, concerned herself with making arrangements for the children: she married one of her daughters to Edward VII, Emperor of India and King of England, the other to a Romanov, while her son George was made the King of Greece. In Russia Princess Dagmar became Princess Maria. Far away now were the canals of Copenhagen and King Christian's chocolate-coloured sideburns. Giving birth to the last of the royal family, the little woman had rushed about with vixen-like malice in the palisade of the Preobrazhensky Grenadiers, but her maternal blood had been spilt on the implacable, vengeful granite earth . . .

We could not tear ourselves away from this obscure and fatal chronicle until dawn. Abdul-Hamid's cigar was finished. In the morning Kalugin took me to the Cheka at No. 2 Gorokhovaya. He had a word with Uritsky.* I stood behind the hangings that fell to the floor in heavy folds. Fragments of words reached my ears.

'The lad's one of us,' Kalugin was saying, 'his father's a shopkeeper, engaged in commerce, but he's turned his back on them . . . He knows several languages . . .'

The Commissar of the Interior for the Communes of the Northern Region came out of his study with his swaying gait. Behind the lenses of his pince-nez his loosened, swollen eyelids, scorched by insomnia, were falling out.

They made me a translator in the Foreign Department. I was given a soldier's uniform and dinner coupons. In the corner of the former St Petersburg Borough Hall that was allotted to me I undertook the translation of statements that had been made by diplomats, *agents provocateurs* and spies.

A day had not passed, and I had everything – clothes, food, work and comrades faithful in friendship and death, comrades the like of which are not to be found anywhere in the world except in our land.

Thus, thirteen years ago, did my wonderful new life begin, a life full of thought and gaiety.

RED CAVALRY

Crossing the Zbrucz

Nachdiv 6* has reported that Novograd-Volynsk was taken at dawn today. The staff has moved out of Krapivno, and our transport is strung like a noisy rearguard along the high road, along the unfading high road that goes from Brest to Warsaw and was built on the bones of muzhiks by Nicholas I.

Fields of purple poppies flower around us, the noonday wind is playing in the yellowing rye, the virginal buckwheat rises on the horizon like the wall of a distant monastery. The quiet Volyn is curving. The Volyn is withdrawing from us into a pearly mist of birch groves, it is creeping away into flowery knolls and entangling itself with enfeebled arms in thickets of hops. An orange sun is rolling across the sky like a severed head, a gentle radiance glows in the ravines of the thunderclouds and the standards of the sunset float above our heads. The odour of yesterday's blood and of slain horses drips into the evening coolness. The Zbrucz, now turned black, roars and pulls tight the foamy knots of the rapids. The bridges have been destroyed, and we ford the river on horseback. A majestic moon lies on the waves. The horses sink into the water up to their backs, the sonorous currents ooze between hundreds of horses' legs. Someone sinks, and resonantly defames the Mother of God. The river is littered with the black rectangles of carts, it is filled with a rumbling, whistling and singing that clamour above the serpents of the moon and the shining chasms.

Late at night we arrive in Novograd. In the billet that has been assigned to me I find a pregnant woman and two redhaired Jews with thin necks: a third is already asleep, covered up to the top of his head and pressed against the wall. In the room that has been allotted to me I find ransacked wardrobes, on the floor scraps of women's fur coats, pieces of human excrement and broken shards of the sacred vessels used by the Jews once a year, at Passover.

'Clear up,' I say to the woman. 'What a dirty life you live, landlords . . .'

The two Jews get up from their chairs. They hop about on felt soles, clearing the detritus off the floor, they hop about in silence, monkey-like, like Japanese in a circus; their necks swell and revolve. They spread a torn feather mattress for me, and I lie down facing the wall, alongside the third, sleeping, Jew. A timid destitution immediately closes over my place of rest.

All has been murdered by silence, and only the moon, clasping her round, shining, carefree head in blue hands, plays the vagrant under the window.

I stretch my numbed legs, I lie on the torn mattress and fall asleep. I dream of *nachdiv* 6. He is pursuing the *kombrig** on a heavy stallion, and puts two bullets in his eyes. The bullets penetrate the *kombrig's* head, and both his eyes fall to the ground.

'Why did you turn the brigade about?' Savitsky – *nachdiv* 6 – cries to the wounded man, and at that point I wake up because the pregnant woman is fumbling with her fingers in my face.

'*Panie*,'* she says, 'you are shouting in your sleep, and you're throwing yourself about. I'm going to make your bed up in the other corner, because you're pushing my Papasha . . .'*

She raises thin legs and a round belly from the floor and removes the blanket from the man who has fallen asleep. An old man is lying there, on his back, dead. His gullet has been torn out, his face has been cleft in two, dark blue blood clings in his beard like pieces of lead.

'*Panie*,' the Jewess says, as she shakes up the feather mattress, 'the Poles were murdering him, and he begged them: "Kill me out in the backyard so that my daughter doesn't see me die." But they did what suited them. He died in this room, thinking about me. And now tell me,' the woman said suddenly with terrible force, 'tell me where else in all the world you would find a father like my father . . .'

Novograd-Volynsk, July 1920

The Catholic Church in Novograd

I set off yesterday with a report to the military commissar, who had put up at the house of the absconded Catholic priest. In the kitchen I was greeted by Pani* Eliza, the Jesuit's housekeeper. She gave me amber tea and sponge fingers. Her sponge fingers smelt like a crucifixion. A cunning sap was contained within them, and the odorous fury of the Vatican.

In the church next door to the house the bells were roaring, pulled by a crazed ringer. The evening was teeming with the stars of July. Pani Eliza, shaking her attentive grey locks, filled my plate with biscuits, and I revelled in the food of the Jesuits.

The old Polish woman called me *pan*, by the threshold grey-haired old men with ears turned to bone stood to attention, and somewhere in the serpentine gloom coiled the soutane of a monk. The *pater* might have fled, but he had left his assistant – Pan Romuald.

A snuffling eunuch with the body of a giant, Romuald bestowed upon us the honoured title of 'comrades'. He passed a yellow finger over the map, indicating the areas of the Polish rout. Gripped by a hoarse rapture, he counted off the wounds of his motherland. Let meek oblivion swallow up the memory of Romuald, who betrayed us without pity and was shot by a stray bullet. But that evening his tight soutane rustled at every door curtain, furiously swept every corridor and smiled knowingly at anyone who wished to drink vodka. That evening the monk's shadow slunk after me relentlessly. He would have become a bishop, Pan Romuald, had he not been a spy.

I drank rum with him; the breathing of a mysterious way of life could still be sensed in the ruins of the priest's house, and its insinuating temptations rendered me powerless. Oh, the crucifixes, as tiny as the talismans of courtesans, the parchment of Papal Bulls and the satin of women's letters that had rotted in the blue silk of waistcoats! . . .

I see you from here, faithless monk in your lilac cassock, the intumescence of your hands, I see your soul, soft and without mercy, like the soul of a cat, I see the wounds of your God, exuding seed like a fragrant poison that intoxicates virgins.

We drank rum as we waited for the commissar, but he still did not return from headquarters. Romuald collapsed in a corner and fell asleep. He is still asleep, quivering from time to time, and outside the window in the orchard the avenue of trees changes colour under the black passion of the sky. Thirsting roses sway in the darkness. Green lightnings flame in the cupolas. A naked corpse lies at the foot of the slope. And a lunar brilliance streams over the dead legs stuck out apart.

Here is Poland, here is the haughty sorrow of the Republic! An unwilling intruder, I spread out a louse-ridden mattress in the seat of worship that has been abandoned by its holy minister, place beneath my head a folio in which is printed a poem to his excellency, the illustrious leader of the Polish nobility, Josef Pilsudski.

Destitute hordes are trundling towards your ancient cities, O Poland, the song of the union of all the serfs rings out above them, and woe to thee, Republic, woe to thee, Prince

Radziwill, and to thee, Prince Sapieha,* prominent for an hour! . . .

Still there is no sign of my commissar. I seek him at headquarters, in the orchard, in the church. The gates of the church are open, I go inside and am greeted by two glowing silver skulls on the lid of a broken coffin. In fear I rush down a flight of stairs, into a dungeon. An oak staircase leads from there to the altar. And indeed, I can see a great number of lights moving about rapidly on high, right up in the cupola itself. I can see the commissar, the Commander of the Special Section, and Cossacks holding candles. They respond to my feeble cry and lead me up out of the cellar.

The skulls, which have turned out to be carvings on a catafalque, no longer instil me with fear, and all together we continue the search – for that is what it was – begun when piles of military uniforms were found in the priest's rooms.

With a flashing of the embroidered equine muzzles of our cuffs, with an exchange of whispers and a jangling of spurs, we wheel around the resonant building, wax melting over our hands. Holy Virgins encrusted with precious stones follow our progress with their eyes, as pink as those of mice; flame throbs in our fingers and rectangular shadows writhe on the statues of St Peter, St Francis, St Vincent, on their sweet rosy cheeks and curly beards picked out in carmine.

We wheel and search. Bone push-buttons respond to our fingers, icons that have been made in two sections move apart to reveal dark dungeons and caves that blossom with mould. This church is ancient and full of mystery. Within its shiny walls it conceals secret passages, niches and double doors that open soundlessly.

O stupid priest, who hung the bodices of his female parishioners upon the nails of the Saviour! Behind the Holy Doors we found a trunk containing gold coins, a morocco leather bag with banknotes in it and cases from Parisian jewellers containing emerald rings.

Afterwards we counted the money in the commissar's room. Columns of gold, carpets made of money, a fitful wind that blew on the flames of the candles, the crow-like madness in the eyes of Pani Eliza, the thunderous laughter of Romuald and the never-ceasing roar of the bells being swung by Pan Robacki, the crazed bell-ringer.

'I must get out of here,' I said to myself, 'out of here and away from these winking madonnas who have been deceived by soldiers . . .'

A Letter

Here is a letter home to the motherland that was dictated to me by Kurdyukov, a young lad in our special detachment. It does not deserve oblivion. I copied it without any embellishments, and give it here word for word, just as it is:

DEAR MAMA YEVDOKIA FYODOROVNA,

In the first lines of this letter I hasten to inform you that, thank the Lord, I am alive and well, and hope to hear the same from you. And also I bow to you deeply from the white of my face to the damp earth . . . [There follows a list of relatives, godfathers, godmothers. This we shall omit. Let us pass to the second paragraph.]

Dear Mama Yevdokia Fyodorovna Kurdyukova, I hasten to write you that I am in the Red Cavalry Army of Comrade Budyonny,* and here too is your son's godfather, Nikon Vasilyich, who is at present a Red Hero. They have taken me on, and I am in the special political detachment, where we deliver literature and newspapers around the positions – the Moscow *Izvestia*, of the Central Executive Committee, the Moscow *Pravda* and our own merciless newspaper, the *Red Trooper*, which every man at the front desires to read, after which he goes out to cut down the villainous Polish nobs with his sabre, and I am living in Nikon Vasilyich's very splendid quarters.

Dear Mama Yevdokia Fyodorovna, please send me what you can according to the best of your ability. Please kill the little spotted hog and make up a parcel for me addressed to Vasily Kurdyukov, political section under Comrade Budyonny. Every night I lie down to rest without any food in my belly and without any clothes either, so it is damned cold. Write me a letter about my Styopa, telling me if he is alive or dead, please have a look at him and tell me if he still overreaches himself or has stopped, and also about the mange on his forelegs, and whether he has been shod or not. Please, dear Mama Yevdokia Fyodorovna, be sure to wash his forelegs with the soap I left behind the icons, and if Papasha has used up all the soap then buy some more in Krasnodar and God will look after you. I can also write to you that the land here is very poor, the muzhiks hide from our Red eagles out in the woods with their horses, there is not much wheat to be seen and what there is is terrible thin, we laugh at it. Our landlords sow rye, and oats as well. The hops grow on sticks here, so they come up very tidy; they use them to make *samogon*.*

In the second bit of this letter I hasten to tell you about Papasha, that he killed my brother Fyodor Timofeich Kurdyukov with his sabre about a year ago. Our Red brigade of Comrade Pavlichenko was advancing on the town of Rostov, when there was a treason within our ranks. And at that time Papasha was with Denikin* as commander of a company. The people that saw him said that he wore medals on his front, like under the old regime. And because of this treason we were all taken prisoner and my brother Fyodor Timofeich met Papasha's eye. And Papasha began to slash Fyodor with his sabre, saying: 'Mercenary, Red dog, bitch's brood,' and various other things and he went on slashing him until it was dark, and then my brother Fyodor Timofeich died. That day

I wrote you a letter, about how Fedya lies without a cross. But Papasha caught me with the letter and said, 'You are your mother's child, you are of her stock, a trollop's brat. I have made her belly great and will make it great again, my life is ruined, I will destroy my seed for justice,' and various other things. I accepted suffering from him, like Our Saviour Jesus Christ. Except that soon I ran away from Papasha and managed to get to my unit under Comrade Pavlichenko. And our brigade got an order to go to the town of Voronezh to get reinforcements and we got reinforcements there, and also horses, cartridge pouches, revolvers and all the things we are supposed to have. Of Voronezh I can report to you, dear Mama Yevdokia Fyodorovna, that it is a very splendid little town, probably slightly bigger than Krasnodar, the people in it are very handsome, you can bathe in the river. We were each given two pounds of bread a day, half a pound of meat and the proper amount of sugar, so we had sweet tea in the morning when we got up, and the same in the evening and forgot we were hungry, and for the main meal I went to my brother's Semyon Timofeich's for goose or blinis and then after that lay down and had a rest. At that time the whole regiment wanted Semyon Timofeich for commander because he is such a desperado and an order came from Comrade Budyonny saying it was all right, and he got two horses, good clothes, a separate cart for his odds and ends and the Order of the Red Banner, and I was counted in as his brother. From now on if any of the neighbours start making your life hell, Semyon Timofeich is quite empowered to cut them into little pieces. After that we started to chase General Denikin, killed thousands of them and hounded them into the Black Sea, only there was no sign of Papasha anywhere and Semyon Timofeich looked for him all over the positions, because he was really missing our brother Fedya. But, dear Mama, you know Papasha and his stubborn nature, what do you suppose he'd gone and done? Dyed his beard real cheeky-like from red to raven and gone to live in the town of Maykop wearing his own clothes so that none of the inhabitants knew he'd been a country constable under the old regime. But the truth cannot be hid for long, and your son's godfather Nikon Vasilyich happened to catch sight of him in the hut of an inhabitant and wrote Semyon Timofeich a letter. We mounted our horses and covered two hundred versts – me, brother Senka* and the lads from the Cossack settlement who volunteered to ride along.

And what did we see in the town of Maykop? We saw that the rear was in no way in sympathy with the front and that everywhere there was treason and the place was full of Jews, like under the old regime. And Semyon Timofeich had a right old argy-bargy with the Jews, who would not let Papasha go and had locked him up in the prison, saying that an order had come from Comrade Trotsky saying that prisoners were not to be executed, and that they would put him on trial themselves – 'Don't worry, he'll get what's coming to him.' But Semyon Timofeich took what was coming to him and proved that he was the commander of a regiment and had had all the Orders of the Red Banner from Comrade Budyonny, and he threatened to execute everyone who was arguing about Papasha and would not hand him over, and the lads from the Cossack settlement did some threatening, too. Well, then Semyon Timofeich got Papa, and he began to flog Papasha and lined all the men up and down the yard, like they are supposed to do according to military discipline. And then Senka splashed some water on Timofey Rodionych's beard, and the dye ran out of his beard. And Senka asked Timofey Rodionych:

'Is it good for you, Papasha, to be in my hands?'

'No,' Papasha said. 'It's bad for me.'

Then Senka asked:

'And what about Fedya, when you were laying into him with your sabre, was it good for him to be in your hands?'

'No,' said Papasha, 'it was bad for Fedya.'

'And did you ever think, Papasha, that it would be bad for you, too?'

'No,' said Papasha, 'I never thought it would be bad for me, too.'

Then Senka turned round to the crowd and said:

'Well, the way I see it is that if I end up with your lot, there won't be no mercy for me. So now, Papasha, we are going to put an end to you . . .'

And Timofey Rodionych began to swear insolently at Senka by his mother and the Mother of God and beat Senka about the gob, and then Semyon Timofeich sent me away, so you see, dear Mama Yevdokia Fyodorovna, I am not able to describe to you how they put an end to Papa, as I was sent away.

After that we got a stop in the town of Novorossisk. Of that town I can tell you that on the other side of it there is no more land, but only water, the Black Sea, and we stayed there right up until May, when we advanced to the Polish front and are knocking the Poles about for all we are worth . . .

I remain your loving son Vasily Timofeich Kurdyukov. Dear Mama, please take a look at Styopka and God will look after you . . .

This is Kurdyukov's letter, of which not one word has been altered. When I had finished he took back the closely written sheet of notepaper and hid it in his shirt, next to his bare skin.

'Kurdyukov,' I asked the boy, 'was your father a bad lot?'

'My father was a dog,' he replied surlily.

'And is your mother better?'

'Mother is as she should be. If you want to see – here's our family . . .'

He held out to me a broken photograph. It showed

Timofey Kurdyukov, a broad-shouldered country constable in a uniform peaked cap and a beard with a parting; immobile, high cheek-boned, with a glazed stare in his colourless vacant eyes. Beside him in a little bamboo easy chair glimmered a tiny peasant woman in a house-jacket that had been let out at the seams, with highly coloured, consumptive and shy features. And against the wall, against that shabby provincial photographic background of flowers and doves, towered two lads – monstrously huge, slow-witted, broad-faced, goggle-eyed, frozen as if on drill parade, Kurdyukov's two brothers – Fyodor and Semyon.

The Konzapas* Commander

There is a moaning in the village. The cavalry is ruining the crops and changing horses. To replace their allotted nags the troopers are seizing working horses. There is no point in rebuking anyone for it. Without horses there can be no cavalry.

But awareness of this does not make the peasants feel any easier. The peasants crowd around the headquarters building and will not go away.

They drag along their jibbing old nags, whose legs are skittering with weakness. Deprived of their breadwinners, the muzhiks – feeling an access of bitter bravery and aware that bravery does not last for long – are making haste, without any hope, to cheek the authorities, God, and their own wretched fates.

Zh—, the staff commander, is standing on the porch of the building in full dress uniform. Shading his inflamed eyelids, he is obviously listening attentively to the muzhiks' complaints. But his attention is no more than a ploy. Like any disciplined and overtired executive, he knows how to switch off all brainwork completely during the empty moments of existence. In these few moments of blissful, cow-like vacancy the commander of our headquarters kicks new life into his worn-out engine.

So it is on this occasion with the muzhiks.

To the soothing accompaniment of their desperate and incoherent din, Zh— keeps a watch from the wings on that gentle crush within his brain that heralds purity and energy of thought. The necessary intermission having arrived, he intercepts a final muzhik's tear, snarls in true commanderly fashion and retreats to his room in the building in order to work.

On this occasion not even snarling was necessary. Dyakov came up to the porch at the gallop on his fiery Anglo-Arabian – Dyakov was formerly a circus athlete and is now the *konzapas* commander – red-faced, grey-moustached, in a black cloak and with silver stripes down the legs of his red oriental trousers.

'A blessing from the Father Superior on honest stinkers,' he shouted, reining in his steed at full gallop, and at that very moment his mangy little horse, one of those that had been requisitioned by the Cossacks, collapsed beneath him.

'There, comrade commander,' a muzhik began to wail, slapping the seams of his trousers. 'There, that is what your lot are giving our lot . . . Have you seen what they are giving us? How can a man run a farm with a beast like that . . .'

'Ah, but for that horse,' Dyakov began, speaking clearly and weightily, 'for that horse, my venerable friend, you are fully entitled to receive at *konzapas* the sum of fifteen thousand roubles, and if that horse were a little rosier about the gills you might, my dear friend, receive at *konzapas* the sum of twenty thousand roubles. However, that horse has fallen – but wait. If a horse falls and gets up again, it is a mount, but if it does not, then it is not a mount. But this neat little filly is undoubtedly going to get up for me . . .'

'O, Lord, O Mighty Merciful Mother of mine,' said the

muzhik, waving his arms aloft, 'how is it to get up, the poor creature . . . The poor thing will die . . .'

'You insult the horse, my good man,' Dyakov replied with deep conviction.'Quite simply, you . blaspheme, my good man.' And he deftly removed his fine athlete's body from the saddle. Straightening his magnificent legs, each of which was gripped by a thong at the knee, splendid and agile, as though on the stage, he moved towards the expiring beast. Mournfully she stared at Dyakov with a deep, stern eye; she licked from his crimson palm some kind of invisible command and at once the enfeebled horse felt the power that flowed from this grey-haired, sprightly and vigorous Romeo. Moving her muzzle, her tottering legs slipping as she felt the impatient and authoritative tickling of the whip under her belly, the nag slowly and carefully rose on to her legs. And we all saw a slender hand in a fluttering sleeve pat the dirty mane and the whip cling with a moan to the bleeding flanks. Trembling in all her body, the nag stood on her four legs, never taking her dog-like, fearful, lovelorn eyes from Dyakov.

'There you are, it's a mount,' Dyakov said to the muzhik, adding gently, 'and you were making all that fuss, my long-lost friend . . .'

Throwing the reins to his orderly, the *konzapas* commander took the four steps at one leap and, with a flap of his opera cloak, vanished into the headquarters building.

Belyov, July 1920

Pan Apolek

The charming and wise story of Pan Apolek went straight to my head like old wine. In Novograd-Volynsk, that hastily overrun town, among huddled ruins, fate threw at my feet a gospel that had been sheltered from the world. Surrounded by the guileless radiance of haloes, I took a vow that day that I would follow the example of Pan Apolek. And sweetness of dreamy spite, bitter contempt for the dogs and pigs of mankind, fire of taciturn and intoxicating revenge – I brought these in sacrifice to my new vow.

In the quarters of the absconded Novograd priest there hung an icon high upon the wall. On it was the inscription: 'The Death of John the Baptist'. I immediately recognized in John the portrait of a man I had once seen somewhere.

I remember: between walls straight and bright there stood the gossamer silence of a summer morning. At the foot of the picture the sun had placed a straight ray of light. Glittering dust swarmed in it. Straight towards me, descending from the blue depths of the niche, came the long figure of John. A black cloak hung solemnly about that inexorable body, so repulsively emaciated. Drops of blood gleamed in the cloak's round fastenings. John's head had been obliquely severed from his ragged neck. It lay upon a clay dish, tightly gripped by the large, yellow fingers of a soldier. I thought I knew the corpse's face. The portent of a secret brushed against me. On the clay dish lay a head that had been copied from the head of Pan Romuald, the helpmeet of the absconded priest. From the grinning mouth hung the tiny body of a snake with highly coloured shiny scales. Its head, small, soft pink and full of animation, stood out in strong contrast to the dark backdrop of the cloak.

I marvelled at the painter's art, his dark invention. On the following day I saw the even more remarkable red-cheeked Holy Virgin that hung above the matrimonial bed of Pani Eliza, the old priest's housekeeper. On both canvases lay the mark of a single brush. The fleshy face of the Virgin – it was a portrait of Pani Eliza. And then I drew near to solving the mystery of the Novograd icons. It was a trail that led me to the kitchen of Pani Eliza, where on scented evenings the shades of old feudal Poland gathered together, with a painter who was a holy fool at their head. But was he a holy fool, Pan Apolek, who had peopled the outlying villages with angels and installed the lame convert Janek among the saints?

He had come here with blind Gottfried thirty years before, one unremarkable summer's day. The friends — Apolek and Gottfried — had reached Shmerel's pothouse, which stands on the Rowno high road, two versts from the town line. In Apolek's right hand was a box of paints, with his left he led the blind accordionist. The melodious tread of their German shoes, studded with nails, rang with peace and hope. From Apolek's scraggy neck hung a canary-yellow scarf, and on the blind man's Tyrolean hat swayed three chocolate-brown feathers.

Inside the pothouse the new arrivals laid out their paints and accordion on the windowsill. The artist unwound his scarf, interminable as the ribbon of a conjuror at a country fair. Then he went out into the courtyard, took all his clothes off and sluiced his pale, thin, sickly body with icy water. Shmerel's wife brought the guests raisin vodka and a bowl of fragrant Polish pies. His hunger satisfied, Gottfried placed his accordion on his bony knees. He gave a sigh, threw his head back and moved his thin fingers. The sounds of Heidelberg's songs filled the smoke-cured walls of the Jewish tavern. Apolek joined in with the blind man in a rattling voice. It all looked as though someone had brought to Shmerel's the organ from the church of St Indeghilda, and the Muses had settled down on the organ in a row, dressed in gaily coloured, wadded scarves and iron-studded German shoes.

The guests sang until sunset, then they put the accordion and the paints into canvas bags, and with a deep bow Pan Apolek handed a sheet of paper to Brajna, the the pothouse keeper's wife.

'Dear Pani Brajna,' he said, 'please accept from a roaming

artist, baptized with the Christian name of Apollinarius, this, your portrait — as a sign of our humble gratitude, as a testimony to your lavish hospitality. If the Lord Jesus will prolong my days and improve my art, I shall return in order to paint this portrait in colour. Pearls will suit your hair, and on your bosom we shall paint an emerald necklace . . .'

On the small sheet of paper in red pencil, pencil as red and soft as clay, the laughing face of Pani Brajna was depicted, surrounded by copper curls.

'My money!' Shmerel exclaimed, when he saw the portrait of his wife. He grabbed his stick and set off in pursuit of his guests. But on the road Shmerel recalled the pale body of Apolek, sluiced with water, and the sun in his little courtyard and the quiet chime of the accordion. The pothouse keeper was troubled and, setting his stick aside, returned home.

On the following morning Apolek presented the Novograd priest with the diploma that proved he had graduated from the Munich Academy, and laid out before him twelve paintings on themes from Holy Scripture. These paintings had been done in oils on thin sheets of cypress wood. The *pater* saw upon his table the burning purple of robes, the lustre of emerald fields and flowery veils thrown over the plains of Palestine.

The saints of Pan Apolek, all this assortment of rejoicing and simple-minded elders, grey-bearded, ruddy-faced, had been crammed into floods of silk and mighty evenings.

That very same day Pan Apolek received a commission to decorate the new church. And over the Benedictine the *pater* said to the artist:

'*Sancta Maria*,' he said, 'my dear Pan Apollinarius, from what realms of wonder has your joyous blessing descended upon us? . . .'

Apolek worked diligently, and already after only a month the new church was full of the bleating of flocks, the dusty gold of sunsets and straw-coloured cows' teats. Buffaloes with worn hides strained in harness, pink-muzzled dogs ran before the flock, and in their cradles, hung against the palms' straight trunks, chubby infants rocked. One cradle was surrounded by the brown and tattered robes of Franciscan monks. The crowd of the Magi was slashed by glittering pates and by wrinkles as crimson as wounds. In the crowd of the Magi the little, old-womanish face of Leo XIII* was lit by a foxy smile and the Novograd priest himself told the beads of a carved Chinese rosary with one hand, and with the other, free, hand blessed the new-born Jesus.

For five months Apolek crawled, imprisoned in his wooden seat, along the walls, around the cupola and along the gallery.

'You have a predilection for familiar faces, my dear Pan Apolek,' the priest said one day, having recognized himself in one of the Magi and Pan Romuald in the severed head of John the Baptist. He smiled, the old *pater*, and sent a goblet of brandy to the artist who was working under the cupola.

In the time that followed, Apolek completed a Last Supper and a stoning of Mary Magdalene. On one Sunday he unveiled the decorated walls. The distinguished citizens who had been invited by the priest were able to identify in St Paul the lame convert Janek, and in Mary Magdalene the Jewish girl Elka, daughter of parents unknown and mother of many a wayside babe. The distinguished citizens ordered that the blasphemous images be painted over. The priest brought down threats upon the head of the blasphemer. But Apolek did not paint over the decorated walls.

Thus there began an unprecedented war between the mighty body of the Catholic Church, on the one hand, and an insouciant icon dauber, on the other. It lasted for three decades – a war as merciless as the passion of a Jesuit. Thus, by chance, the meek and gentle idler very nearly became the founder of a new heresy. But he would have been the trickiest and most comical antagonist of all that the devious and stormy history of the Roman Church has known. An antagonist who went around the world in blissful inebriety, with two white mice under his shirt and a set of the most delicate brushes in his pocket.

'Fifteen zlotys for a Holy Virgin, twenty-five zlotys for a Holy Family and fifty zlotys for a Last Supper with portraits of all the client's male relatives. The client's enemy may be portrayed in the figure of Judas Iscariot, and this costs ten zlotys extra.' Thus did Apolek announce his services to the local peasants after he had been driven out of the church that was being built.

There was no shortage of commissions. And when, a year later, summoned by the urgent letters of the Novograd priest, a commission of inquiry from the Bishop of Zhitomir arrived, it found these monstrous family portraits, sacrilegious, naïve and picturesque as the blooms of a tropical garden, even in the poorest and most evil-smelling huts. Josephs with grey hair centre-parted, Christs smeared with pomatum, rural Marys who had had many children, sitting with their knees wide apart – these icons hung in the front corners, surrounded by garlands of paper flowers.

'He has installed you among the saints in your own life-times,' exclaimed the Apostolic Vicar of Dubno and Novokon-stantinov, replying to the multitude that was defending Apolek, 'he has surrounded you with the unspoken accoutre-ments of holiness, you, the thrice-fallen into the sin of disobedi-ence, the secret distillers, the pitiless moneylenders, the cheats, the sellers of your own daughters' innocence.'

'Your Holiness,' said the hobbling Witold, receiver of stolen goods and cemetery attendant, 'in what does the most merciful Pan God see truth, and who will tell the dark folk what the truth is? And is there not more genuine truth in the paintings of Pan Apolek, who has gratified our pride, than in your words, which are full of railing and scorn . . .'

The cries of the multitude put the apostolic vicar to flight. A consensus in the town's outlying districts threatened the security of the church's servants. The artist who was commissioned in place of Apolek did not dare to paint over Elka and lame Janek. They may be seen even now in the side chapel of the Novograd church: Janek – the Apostle Paul – a timorous cripple with the black, wispy beard of the rural apostate, and she, the fornicatress from Magdala, sickly and crazed, with dancing body and hollow cheeks.

The struggle with the priest had lasted three decades. Then the Cossack horde had driven the old monk from his odorous nest of stone, and Apolek – oh, the vicissitudes of fortune – had settled into Pani Eliza's kitchen. And here I, a passing guest, drink of an evening the wine of his discourse.

Discourse – on what? On the romantic days of the Polish nobility, on the fanaticism of women's fury, on the artist Luca della Robbia* and on the family of the carpenter from Bethlehem.

'There is something I wish to tell you, Mr Writer . . .'* Apolek confides to me mysteriously before supper.

'Yes,' I reply, 'yes, Apolek, I am listening . . .'

But the church's lay-brother, Pan Robacki, austere and grey, bony and big-eared, is sitting too near us. He hangs out before us the faded canvases of silence and hostility.

'I wish to tell you,' Apolek whispers, leading me to one side, 'that Jesus, the son of Mary, was married to Deborah, a maiden of Jerusalem, and of common birth . . .'

'O, ten .czlowiek,'* Pan Robacki shouts in despair, 'ten czlowiek will not die in his own bed . . . Ten czlowiek will be killed by other folk.'

'After supper,' Apolek murmurs in a disappointed voice, 'after supper, if it may please you, Mr Writer . . .'

It pleases me. Stirred by the beginning of Apolek's story, I walk about the kitchen, waiting for the cherished hour. Meanwhile, outside the window is the night, like a black column. Outside the window the dark and living orchard has grown stiff. Like a gleaming, milky flood, the road flows under the moon towards the church. The earth is enveloped in a gloomy radiance, necklaces of glowing fruits hang from the bushes. The scent of lilies is pure and strong, like spirit. This fresh poison is sucked in by the deep seething respiration of the kitchen range, deadening the resinous odour of the fir logs that are scattered about the kitchen.

Apolek, in pink bow and threadbare pink trousers, is pottering about in his corner like a graceful animal. His table is smeared with glue and paint. The old man works with small and frequent movements, and the quietest of melodic tattoos is coming from his corner.

Old Gottfried is beating it out with his trembling fingers. The blind man sits unmoving in the oily yellow sheen of the lamp. Inclining his bald forehead, he listens to the interminable music of his blindness and to the muttering of Apolek, his eternal friend.

'. . . And what the priests and Mark the Evangelist and Matthew the Evangelist tell you, that is not the truth . . . But the truth may be revealed to you, Mr Writer, and in exchange for fifty marks I am ready to paint a portrait of you in the aspect of the Blessed Francis against a background of greenery and sky. He was a very simple saint, Pan Francis. And if you, Mr Writer, have a girl in Russia to whom you are betrothed . . . Women love the Blessed Francis, though not all women, pan . . .'

Thus, in a corner pungent with fir wood, did the story of the marriage of Jesus and Deborah begin. This girl had, according to Apolek, had a bridegroom. Her bridegroom had been a young Israelite whose business was the selling of elephant tusks. But Deborah's wedding night had ended in bewilderment and tears. The woman was seized by terror when she saw her husband approaching her nuptial bed. An unendurable hiccup swelled her gullet. She spewed out all that she had eaten at the wedding feast. Shame fell upon Deborah, her father, her mother and the whole of her family.

Her bridegroom left her, mocking, and gathered all the guests together. Then Jesus, seeing the extraordinary torment of the woman who yearned for her husband and feared him, assumed the bridegroom's clothing and, full of compassion, united himself with Deborah as she lay in her vomit. Then she came out to the guests, loud with rejoicing and slyly turning away her gaze like a woman who is proud of her fall. And only Jesus stood to one side. A deathly perspiration broke out on his body, and the bee of sorrow stung him in the heart. Observed by no one, he left the feasting chamber and withdrew to a deserted region east of Judaea, where John was awaiting him. And Deborah bore her firstling boy . . .

'And where is he?' I exclaimed, laughing and horrified.

'The priests concealed him,' Apolek pronounced with solemnity, bringing a slight, delicate finger close to his toper's nose.

'Mr Artist,' Robacki exclaimed suddenly, rising out of the darkness, and his grey ears began to move. 'What are you saying? It is impossible . . .'

'Yes, yes,' Apolek said, shrinking away and seizing hold of Gottfried. 'Yes, yes, *panie* . . .'

He pulled the blind man towards the exit, but in the doorway tarried for a moment and beckoned to me with his finger.

'A Blessed Francis,' he whispered, winking, 'with a bird on his sleeve, a dove or a goldfinch, as Mr Writer pleases . . .'

And he disappeared with his blind and eternal friend.

'Oh what foolishness,' said the lay brother, Robacki. 'That man will not die in his own bed . . .'

Pan Robacki opened wide his mouth and yawned like a cat. I took my leave and went home to my plundered Jews, to sleep.

A homeless moon was loitering about the town. And I strolled together with it, keeping warm within me unfulfillable dreams and out-of-tune songs.

The Sun of Italy

Yesterday I sat in Pani Eliza's kitchen again, under a heated garland of green fir branches. I sat by the warm, living, querulous stove, and then returned to my quarters in deep night. Down there against the precipice the soundless Zbrucz rolled its dark and glassy wave.* My soul, filled with the tormenting intoxication of a dream, smiled at persons unknown, and my imagination, a blind and happy old hag, swirled before me like a July mist.

The charred town – fractured columns and the hooks of cruel old women's little fingers dug into the earth – seemed to me raised into the air, convenient and unreal as a dream. The naked brilliance of the moon poured down on it with inexhaustible force. The damp mould of the ruins blossomed like the marble of an opera seat. And I waited with troubled soul for Romeo to emerge from behind the clouds, a satin Romeo, singing of love, while behind the scenes a depressed electrical technician was keeping his finger on the switch that would put out the moon.

Past me flowed the blue roads, like jets of milk that had spurted from many breasts. As I returned home I felt a sense of dread at the prospect of encountering Sidorov, my neighbour, who brought down on me at nights the hairy paw of his depression. By good fortune, on this particular night, torn to pieces as it was by the milk of the moon, Sidorov ventured not a word. Surrounded by books, he was writing. On the table a hunchbacked candle smoked – the ominous camp-fire of dreamers. I sat to one side, dozing, and the dreams hopped around me like kittens. And only late at night was I woken by an orderly who had come to summon Sidorov to headquarters. They left together. Then I went quickly over to the table at which Sidorov had been writing, and looked through his books. There was a teach-yourself Italian course, a picture of the Forum and a plan of the city of Rome. The plan was covered all over with small crosses and dots. The vague intoxication fell from me. I bent over the densely filled sheet of paper and with a sinking heart, clenching my fingers, read someone else's letter. Sidorov, the depressed killer, tore to shreds the pink cotton wool of my imagination and hauled me off into the corridors of his sober-minded insanity. The letter was open at the second page – and I did not dare to look for the beginning:

. . . One of his lungs has been pierced and he has gone slightly demented or, as Sergey says, has 'flown out of his mind'. Indeed, merely going out of it would not be good enough for him, the fool. Anyway, tails sideways and joking apart . . . Let us address the order of the day, my dear Victoria . . .

I did three months' campaign with Makhno* – a wearisome swindle and nothing more . . . And only Volin is still there. Volin is arraying himself in apostolic vestments and clambering up from anarchism among the Lenins. Terrible. And the leader listens to him, strokes the dusty barbed wire of his curls and passes out through his rotten teeth the long snake of his muzhik's grin. And now I am not sure that there is not in all of this the pestiferous seed of anarchism and that we are not going to wipe your prosperous noses for you, home-made Tsekists* from a home-made Central Committee 'made in Kharkov', your home-made capital. Your plain chaps don't like remembering now the sins of their anarchist youth and laugh at us from the elevation of their state wisdom – the devil take them . . .

And then I landed up in Moscow. How did I land up in Moscow? The lads caused offence to someone about requisitioning and other things. I, ditherer that I am, intervened. They set on me – and it served me right. The wound was not worth speaking of, but in Moscow, ah, Victoria, in Moscow I grew speechless from misfortune. Every evening the hospital nurses would bring me a tiny peck of buckwheat porridge. They bridled with reverence, they hauled it along on a big tray, and I hated that top-priority porridge, those extra rations and that planned Moscow. In the Soviet I later ran into a little handful of anarchists. They are fops or half-crazy old men. Stuck my nose in at the Kremlin with a plan of real work. They patted me on the head and promised to make me a deputy chief if I mended my ways. I did not mend my ways. What happened after that? After that there was the front, the Red cavalry and the men smelling of damp blood and human remains.

Rescue me, Victoria. The state wisdom is driving me out of my mind, the boredom is making me drunk. If you do not help me, I shall expire without any plan at all. And who would want a worker to snuff it in such an unorganized manner – not you, after all, Victoria, betrothed who will never be wife. There, sentimentality, well, let it go to the accursed mother of so-and-so . . .

Now let us talk business. I am bored in the cavalry. I cannot ride because of my wound, and that means that I cannot fight. Please use your influence, Victoria – get them to send me to Italy. I am studying the language and in two months' time I shall be able to speak it. In Italy the land is smouldering. Much is ripe already. All that is needed is a couple of shots. I shall provide one of them. What's needed there is to send the king to join his ancestors. That is very important. Their king is a good old chap who plays for popularity and has photographs taken of himself with tame socialists for reproduction in family journals.

Do not say anything at the Central Committee or Commissariat of Foreign Affairs about shots or kings. They will pat you on the head and mumble, 'a romantic'. Just say, 'He is ill, bad-tempered, drunk with depression, he wants bananas and the sun of Italy.' I have deserved it, after all, or have I not? Just in order to recuperate until I am better – and then *basta*. But if they refuse, then let them send me to the Odessa Cheka ... It's a very sensible one, and ...

... What stupid things, what unfairly stupid things I am writing to you, my friend Victoria ...

Italy – it has entered my heart like an evil obsession. The thought of that land which I have never seen is as sweet to me as the name of a woman, as your name, Victoria ...

I read the letter through and began to lay myself down on my crushed-through, unclean bed, but sleep did not come. Through the wall the pregnant Jewess was sincerely weeping, and she was answered by the sighs and muttering of her lanky husband. They were remembering the items of property of which they had been robbed and were blaming each other for their ill luck. Then, before daybreak, Sidorov came back. On the table the burnt-down candle was expiring. Sidorov took another stub of candle from his boot and, unusually pensive, used it to crush the sputtering wick. Our room was dark, gloomy, everything in it breathed a damp, nocturnal fetor, and only the window, filled with the moonlight, shone like a deliverance.

He came and put the letter away, my tiresome neighbour. Stooping, he sat down at the table and opened an album of photographs of the city of Rome. The sumptuous volume with its gilt-edged pages lay before his olive-green, inexpressive face. Over his round back gleamed the crenellated ruins of the Capitol and the arena of the Colosseum glowing in the sunset. A photograph of the royal family had been placed here too, between the large, shiny pages. On a scrap of paper torn from a calendar there was a picture of the frail, affable King Vittorio Emmanuele with his black-haired wife, Crown Prince Umberto and an entire litter of princesses.

And now the night, full of distant, painful bell sounds, a

rectangle of light in the damp and darkness, and inside it the deathly face of Sidorov, a lifeless mask suspended over the candle's yellow flame.

Gedali

On the eve of the Sabbath I am tormented by a dense sadness of memories. On these evenings, long ago, the yellow beard of my grandfather would stroke from time to time the volumes of Ibn-Ezra.* With her gnarled fingers my old grandmother in her lace head-dress told fortunes over the Sabbath candle, sobbing sweetly. The heart of a child was rocked to and fro on those evenings like a small ship on enchanted waves. Oh, Talmuds of my childhood, turned to dust! Oh, dense sadness of memories!

I wander around Zhitomir in search of the shy star.* Outside the ancient synagogue, beside its yellow and indifferent walls, old Jews sell whitening, blueing, wicks – Jews with the beards of prophets, with passionate rags on their sunken chests . . .

Here before me is the bazaar and the death of the bazaar. Slain is the rich soul of abundance. Mute padlocks hang on the stalls and the granite of the paving is as clean as the bald pate of a dead man. It blinks and fades – the shy star . . .

Success came to me later, success came just before the setting of the sun. Gedali's shop had hidden itself away in the rows of tightly closed shops. Dickens, where was your kindly shade on that day? You would have seen in that old curiosity shop gilded slippers and ship's cables, an antique compass and a stuffed eagle, a Winchester hunting rifle with the date 1810 engraved on it, and a broken saucepan.

Old Gedali is walking round his treasures in the rosy emptiness of the evening – a diminutive shop owner in smoked glasses and a green frock-coat that touches the floor. He is rubbing his slender white hands, tweaking his greyish-blue beard and, his head inclined, listening to the invisible voices that have floated down to him.

This is a shop like the specimen box of a solemn and inquisitive boy who will one day be a professor of botany. In this shop there are both buttons and a dead butterfly, and its little owner is called Gedali. Everyone has left the market, Gedali has remained. And he hovers in a labyrinth of globes, skulls and dead flowers, waves a multicoloured feather duster and blows the dust off the dead flowers.

And now we are sitting on beer barrels. Gedali coils and uncoils his narrow beard. His top hat sways above us like a small black tower. Warm air is flowing past us. The sky is changing colour. Soft blood is pouring from an overturned bottle up there above, and I am enveloped in a gentle odour of decay.

'The revolution – we will say yes to her, but will we say no to the Sabbath?' Thus begins Gedali, entwining me in the silken thongs of his smoked eyes. 'Yes, I hail the revolution, yes, I hail her, but it hides from Gedali and sends ahead of it nought but shooting . . .'

'The sun does not enter eyes that are closed,' I reply to the old man, 'but we shall rip open those closed eyes . . .'

'The Pole closed my eyes,' the old man whispers, barely audibly, 'the Pole, the vicious dog. He takes a Jew and tears out his beard, ugh, the dog! And now he is being beaten, the vicious dog. That is wonderful, that is the revolution. And then he that has beaten the Pole says to me; 'Hand in your gramophone to be registered, Gedali . . .' 'I love music, pani,' I reply to the revolution. 'You do not know what you love, Gedali, I will shoot at you, and then you will find out, I cannot do otherwise than shoot, because I am the revolution . . .'

'She cannot do otherwise than shoot, Gedali,' I say to the old man, 'because she is the revolution.'

'But the Pole shot, my gentle *pan*, because he was the counter-revolution: you shoot because you are the revolution. But the revolution – that is pleasure. And pleasure loves not orphans in the house. Good deeds are done by a good man. The revolution is the good deed of good men. But good men do not kill. That means the revolution is being made by bad men. But the Poles are also bad men. So who will tell Gedali where is the revolution and where is the counter-revolution? Once upon a time I studied the Talmud, I love the commentaries of Rashi* and the books of Maimonides.* And there are also other men of understanding in Zhitomir. And so we all, we learned men, fall upon our faces and cry aloud, 'Woe to us, where is the sweet revolution? . . .'

The old man fell silent. And we saw the first star, shining through in the Milky Way.

'The Sabbath is coming in,' Gedali pronounced with solemnity. 'The Jews must go to the synagogue . . . *Panie* comrade,' he said, getting up, and the top hat, like a small black tower, swayed upon his head. 'Bring a few good men to Zhitomir. *Ai*, in our town there is a shortage, *ai*, a shortage! Bring good men, and we will give them all our gramophones. We are not know-nothings. The International – we know what is the International. I too want the International of good men, I want each soul to be taken and registered and given first-grade rations. Here, soul, eat, please, and have from life your pleasure. The International, *panie* comrade, one does not know what to eat it with . . .'

'One eats it with gunpowder,' I replied to the old man. 'And seasons it with the finest blood . . .'

And now out of the blue darkness she has ascended her throne, the youthful Sabbath.*

'Gedali,' I say, 'today is Friday, and it is already evening. Where may one obtain a Jewish shortcake, a Jewish glass of tea and a little of that superannuated God in one's glass of tea? . . .'

'There is none to be had,' Gedali replies to me, hanging the padlock on his specimen box, 'none to be had. Next door there is a cook-shop, and good men worked in it, but no one eats there now, they weep instead . . .'

He fastened three bone buttons of his green frock-coat, flicked himself with the cockerel feathers, splashed a little water on the soft palms of his hands, and moved away – tiny, solitary, pensive, in a black top hat and with a large prayer-book under his arm.

The Sabbath is coming in. Gedali – the founder of an unrealizable International – has gone to the synagogue to pray.

My First Goose

Savitsky, *nachdiv* 6, stood up at the sight of me, and I was astonished at the beauty of his gigantic body. He stood up and with the purple of his breeches, with his little raspberry-coloured cap flicked over to one side, with the medals stuck on his chest, cut the *izba** in two as a standard cuts the sky. He smelt of unobtainable scent and the sickly sweet coolness of soap. His long legs were like girls clad to the shoulders in shining jackboots.

He smiled at me, smacked his riding-switch against the table and pulled towards him an order that had just been dictated by the chief of staff. It was an order to Ivan Chesnokov to advance with the regiment that had been entrusted to him in the direction of Chugunov-Dobryvodka and, on making contact with the enemy, to destroy the same . . .

'. . . Which destruction,' the *nachdiv* began to write, using up the whole sheet, 'I charge to the responsibility of the same Chesnokov, right up to the supreme sanction, which I shall administer on the spot, which you, Comrade Chesnokov, for this is not the first month you have been working with me at the front, cannot be in any doubt about . . .'

Nachdiv 6 signed the order with a flourish, threw it to the orderlies and turned his grey eyes, dancing with merriment, towards me.

'I say!' he cried, and cut the air with his switch. Then he read the document concerning my attachment to divisional staff.

'Make this an order,' said the *nachdiv*, 'make it an order and enrol him for any delight except service at the front. Can you read and write?'

'Yes,' I replied, envying the iron and flowers of his youthfulness. 'I'm a law graduate from St Petersburg University . . .'

'Ah, so you're a milksop, are you?' he shouted, laughing. 'And with glasses on your nose, too, what a wretched little . . . They send you without making any inquiries, and they'll kill a man for glasses here. Think you can get along with us, eh?'

'Yes, I can get along with you,' I replied, and walked to the village with the billeting officer to find a place where I could sleep the night. The billeting officer carried my trunk on his shoulder, the village street lay before us and in the sky, round and yellow as a pumpkin, the dying sun breathed its rosy last.

We walked up to a hut with painted garlands on it. The billeting officer stopped and suddenly said with a guilty smile:

'Our lads here have a stupid thing about glasses, and there's nothing to be done about it. Your man of distinction – he's not to be found here. But lay a finger on a lady, the properest lady that ever there was, and our fighting lads will give you a fond caress . . .'

With my trunk upon his shoulders, he hesitated, came right up to me, then jumped away again in despair, and ran into the front yard. The Cossacks were sitting there on some hay, shaving one another.

'Right, lads,' the billeting officer said, putting my trunk down on the ground. 'Following an order issued by Comrade Savitsky you're to give this fellow a billet, and no funny business, because this fellow has suffered in the line of learning . . .'

The billeting officer turned crimson and walked off without turning round. I touched the peak of my cap and saluted the Cossacks. A young lad with long, flaxen hair and a beautiful Ryazan face walked over to my trunk and hurled it out of the gate. Then he turned his posterior to me and, with a special knack, began to emit some disreputable sounds.

'Artilleryman number double zero,' a Cossack who was somewhat older shouted to him, and began to laugh, 'rapid fire! . . .'

The lad exhausted the resources of his simple knack and walked off. Then, crawling about on the ground, I began to gather up the manuscripts and the torn cast-offs that had fallen out of my trunk. I gathered them up and took them away to the other end of the yard. Outside the hut on some bricks stood a mess tin; pork was being cooked in it, its smoke was like the smoke that rises in the village of one's childhood home, and it aroused within me mingled hunger and a loneliness without parallel. I covered my broken trunk with hay, made a pillow of it, and lay down on the ground in order to read in *Pravda* Lenin's speech at the Second Congress of the Comintern.* The sun fell on me now and then from behind the crenellated knolls, the Cossacks tripped over my legs, the lad mocked at me tirelessly, and the welcome lines of print approached me by a thorny road and were unable to get to me. Then I put down the newspaper and went to see the mistress of the house, who was spinning yarn on the front steps.

'Ma'am,' I said, 'I need to eat.'

The old woman raised the overflowing whites of her semi-blind eyes towards me and lowered them again.

'Comrade,' she said after a pause. 'all this business makes me want to hang myself.'

'Mother of the Lord God and my soul,' I grumbled in vexation then, and gave the old woman a shove in the chest with my fist. 'Do I have to discuss it with you . . .'

And turning away I caught sight of someone else's sword lying on the ground not far off. A stern goose was wandering about the yard, serenely preening its feathers. I caught up with it and bent it down to the ground; the goose's head cracked under my boot, cracked and overflowed. The white neck was spread out in the dung, and the wings began to move above the slaughtered bird.

'Mother of the Lord God and my soul,' I said, delving into the goose with the sword, 'roast it for me, ma'am.'

The old woman, glistening with blindness and glasses, picked the bird up, wrapped it in her apron and carried it off towards the kitchen.

'Comrade,' she said after a pause, 'it makes me want to hang myself,' and closed the door behind her.

But out in the yard the Cossacks were already sitting around their mess tin. They sat unmoving, straight as priests, and had paid no attention to the goose.

'The lad will do all right with us,' one of them said, referring to me, winking and scooping up some cabbage soup in his spoon.

The Cossacks had begun to eat their supper with the restrained elegance of muzhiks who respect one another, and I wiped the sword dry with sand, went out of the gate and returned again, in torment. The moon was already hanging above the yard like a cheap earring.

'Brother,' Surovkov, the most senior of the Cossacks, said to me all of a sudden, 'sit down and have some of our grub until your goose is ready . . .'

He produced a spare spoon from his boot and handed it to me. We gulped down the home-made cabbage soup and ate the pork.

'What do they write in the newspaper?' asked the lad with the flaxen hair, making a place for me.

'Lenin is writing in it,' I said, pulling out my copy of *Pravda*. 'He says that we have a shortage of everything . . .'

And loudly, like a deaf man triumphant, I read Lenin's speech to the Cossacks.

The evening tucked me up in the life-giving moisture of its crepuscular sheets, the evening placed its motherly palms on my burning forehead. I read and rejoiced and watched out, as I rejoiced, for anything crooked in the Lenin straightness.

'The truth* tickles every nostril,' said Surovkov, when I had finished, 'and how is a man to pull it from the pile, yet Lenin hits it at once, like a hen pecking a grain of corn . . .'

Surovkov, platoon commander of the staff squadron, said this about Lenin, and then we went up to sleep in the hayloft. Six of us slept there, warming one another with our bodies, our legs tangled together, under the roof in which there were holes that let in the stars. I had dreams and saw women in my dreams, and only my heart, stained crimson with murder, squeaked and overflowed.

The Rebbe

'. . . All things are mortal. Eternal life is destined only for the mother. And when the mother is no longer alive, she leaves the memory of herself, which no one has yet dared to profane. The memory of the mother feeds the compassion in us as the ocean, the boundless ocean, feeds the rivers that cleave the universe . . .'

These were Gedali's words. He pronounced them with gravity. The dying evening had surrounded him with the rosy mist of its sadness. The old man said:

'The windows and doors of the passionate edifice of

Hassidism have been knocked out, but it is immortal, like the soul of a mother ... Hassidism still stands, though with empty eye-sockets, at the crossroads of the furious winds of history.'

Thus spoke Gedali, and, having said his prayers in the synagogue, he led me to Rebbe Motale, the last rebbe of the Chernobyl dynasty.

Gedali and I ascended the main street. White Catholic churches gleamed in the distance like fields of buckwheat. The wheel of a gun was groaning around the corner. Two pregnant Ukrainian women came out of a gate, began to jingle their necklaces and sat down on a bench. The timid star began to shine in the orange battles of the sunset, and peace, a Sabbath peace, settled on the crooked rooftops of the Zhitomir ghetto.

'Here,' whispered Gedali, pointing out to me a long house with a broken upper façade.

We went into a room – empty and of stone, like a morgue. Rebbe Motale sat at a table, surrounded by those possessed of devils and the liars. He wore a sable cap and a white robe tied with a cord. The rebbe sat with his eyes closed, burrowing with his thin fingers in the yellow down of his beard.

'From where has the Jew come?' he asked, raising his eyelids.

'Odessa,' I replied.

'A pious city,'' the rebbe said suddenly, with extraordinary vigour. 'The star of our banishment, the involuntary well of our tribulations! ... With what does the Jew occupy himself?'

'I am putting into verse the adventures of Hershele Ostropoler.''

'A great labour,' the rebbe whispered, closing his eyelids again. 'The jackal moans when it is hungry, every fool is foolish enough to be unhappy, and only the wise man rends the veil of existence with laughter ... What has the Jew studied?'

'The Bible.'

'What does the Jew seek?'

'Merriment.'

'Reb Mordkhe,' said the *tsadik*, with a shake of his beard, 'let the young man take a place at the table, let him eat on this Sabbath evening together with the rest of the Jews, let him be happy that he is alive and not dead, let him clap his hands when his neighbours dance, let him drink wine, if he is served wine . . .'

And Reb Mordkhe leapt to my side, an inveterate buffoon with ectopic eyelids, a hunchbacked old codger no taller than a ten-year-old boy.

'Ah, my dear man, and so young,' said the ragged Reb Mordkhe, giving me a wink, 'ah, how many wealthy fools I have known in Odessa, how many destitute sages I have known in Odessa. But sit down at the table, young man, and drink the wine that you will not be served . . .'

We all seated ourselves next to one another – the possessed of devils, the liars and the moonstruck. In the corner broad-shouldered Jews who resembled fishermen or apostles suffered aloud over their prayer-books. Gedali in his green frock-coat drowsed by the wall like a multicoloured bird. And suddenly I caught sight of a youth behind Gedali's back, a youth with the face of Spinoza, with the mighty forehead of Spinoza, with the unhealthy-looking face of a nun. He was smoking, and quivering like an escaped prisoner brought back to prison after a chase. The ragged Mordkhe crept up to him from behind, tore the cigarette out of his mouth and darted back to me.

'This is the rebbe's son Ilya,' Mordkhe wheezed, as he moved close to me the bleeding flesh of his exposed eyelids, 'an accursed son, a bad son, a disobedient son . . .'

And Mordkhe threatened the youth with his small fist and spat in his face.

'Blessed is the Lord,' resounded the voice of Rebbe Motale Bratslavsky, and he broke the bread with his monastic fingers.

'Blessed is the God of Israel, who has chosen us from all the peoples on the earth . . .'

The rebbe blessed the food, and we sat down at table. Outside the window horses neighed and Cossacks yelled. The wilderness of war gaped outside the window. Amidst the silence and the prayer, the rebbe's son smoked one cigarette after another. When supper was over I got up first.

'My dear man, and so young,' Mordkhe began to mutter behind my back, and he tugged me by the waist, 'if there were no one in the world apart from wicked men of wealth and destitute vagrants, how would the holy men live?'

I gave the old man some money and went outside. Gedali and I said goodbye, and I went home to the station. There, at the station, in the agit-train of the First Cavalry Army, there awaited me the shining of a hundred lights, the magic brilliance of the radio station, the stubborn running of the machines in the printing-press and my unfinished article for the *Red Trooper* newspaper.*

The Way to Brody

I mourn for the bees. They have been tormented to death by the warring armies. In Volhynia there are no more bees.

We have defiled the indescribable hives. We have exterminated them with sulphur and blown them up with gunpowder. Smoke-blackened rags have given off an evil stink in the holy republics of the bees. As they died, they flew slowly, buzzing almost inaudibly. Deprived of bread, we got honey with our swords. In Volhynia there are no more bees.

The chronicle of our humdrum evil doings constricts me indefatigably, like a heart complaint. Yesterday was the day of carnage near Brody. Having lost our way in the blue land, we had had no suspicion of it – neither I, nor Afonka Bida, my friend. The horses had been getting grain since morning. The rye was tall, the sun was beautiful, and the soul, that did not deserve these radiant and fleeing skies, yearned for unhurried dolours. For this reason I compelled Afonka's steadfast mouth to bend forward to my sorrows.

'. . . The women of the Cossack settlement tell stories about the bee and its kind, friendly nature,' replied the platoon commander, my friend, 'all manner of stories. Whether men did Christ a wrong or whether there was no such wrong, others will come to know after the passage of time. "But here," the women of the Cossack settlement say, "is Christ on the cross. And all kinds of little midges are flying up to Christ, in order to torment him. And when he sees them his spirit fails him. But the countless midges cannot see him looking. At the same time a bee is flying around Christ . . . 'Kill him,' the midges shout to the bee. 'Kill him for us!' '. . . That I cannot do,' says the bee, raising his wings above Christ, "that I cannot do, for he is of the carpenter class . . ."''

'One must understand the bee,' Afonka, my platoon commander, says in conclusion. 'Well, let the bee overcome it. After all, we're drudging here for him too . . .'

And with a wave of his arms, Afonka launched into a song. It was the song about the light bay stallion. The eight Cossacks, Afonka's platoon, began to sing along, and even Grishchuk, who had been dozing on the box, moved his cap to the side.

The light bay stallion, Dzhigit by name, had belonged to a Cossack second-grade captain who got drunk on vodka on the day of his beheading. Thus did Afonka sing, drawing out his voice like a string, and falling asleep: Dzhigit was a faithful horse, and on holidays the second-grade captain knew no bounds to his desires. He was given five jugs of vodka on the day of the beheading. After the fourth the second-grade captain mounted his horse and began to ride towards heaven. The ascent was long, but Dzhigit was a faithful horse. They arrived in heaven, and the second-grade captain noticed that the fifth jug was missing. It had been left down on the earth, the last jug. Then the second-grade captain wept over the vanity of his exertions. He wept, and Dzhigit moved his ears as he looked at his master.

Thus did Afonka sing, clinking and falling asleep. The song floated over us like smoke. And we moved into the heroic sunset.

Its seething rivers trickled down the embroidered towels of the peasant fields. The silence was pink. The land lay like the spine of a cat, with a gleaming fur of grain. On a hillock huddled the mud-walled hamlet of Klekotov. Beyond the rise there awaited us a vision of the toothed and deathly Brody. But near Klekotov a shot burst resonantly in our faces. From behind a hut two Polish soldiers looked out. Their horses were tied up to posts. A light battery of the enemy was moving up the hillock in businesslike fashion. The bullets were stretching like threads along the road.

'Let's get out of here!' said Afonka.

And we fled.

Oh, Brody! The mummies of your trampled passions have breathed an overwhelming poison over me. I already sensed the mortal chill of eye sockets filled with tears that have grown cold. And now – a jolting gallop carries me away from the jagged stone of your synagogues . . .

Brody, August 1920

The Theory of the Tachanka

From headquarters I have been sent a driver, or, as we say, a 'vehicular'. His surname is Grishchuk. He is thirty-nine. His story is a dreadful one.

Grishchuk spent five years in captivity in Germany; a few months ago he escaped, got out through Lithuania and north-west Russia, reached Volhynia, was caught in Belyov by the most stupid mobilization commission in the world, and was returned to military service. He had had only fifty versts to go to the district of Kremenets, of which he was a native. In the district of Kremenets he has a wife and children. He has not been home for five years and two months. The mobilization commission made him my vehicular, and I have ceased to be a pariah among the Cossacks.

I am the owner of a *tachanka** and of a driver for it. *Tachanka!* That word has become the base of the triangle on which our ways are founded: sword – *tachanka* – horse . . .

The most ordinary priest's or assessor's* britzka* has, through a whim of our civil strife, become a formidable means of mobile battle, has created a new strategy and new tactics, has distorted the customary face of war, given birth to heroes and geniuses of the *tachanka*. Such is Makhno, whom we have suppressed, but who made the *tachanka* the axis of his mysterious and cunning strategy. Such is Makhno, who abolished infantry, artillery and even cavalry, and in the place of those primitive and clumsy implements screwed three hundred machine-guns on to britzkas. Such is Makhno, as many-faceted as nature. Haycarts, drawn up in battle formation, take possession of towns. A wedding procession, as it approaches a rural district's party headquarters, loses no time in opening concentrated fire, and the puny little priest, waving the black flag of anarchy above his head, demands that the authorities hand over the bourgeois, hand over the proletarians, the wine and the music.

An army of *tachanki* possesses an unprecedented manoeuvrability.

Budyonny has demonstrated this as well as Makhno. To fight such an army is difficult, to pin it down impossible. A machine-gun dug in under a hayrick, a *tachanka* stowed away in a peasant's threshing barn – they cease to be fighting units. These hidden emplacements, which are the hypothetical but intangible items of an addition sum, together make up the structure of the Ukrainian village of recent times – ferocious, insurgent and self-interested. Such an army, with its ammunition tucked away in various corners, Makhno will have ready for action within the space of a single hour; even less time is required to demobilize it.

Among us, in Budyonny's regular cavalry, the *tachanka* does not reign with such exclusive authority. Even so, all our machine-gun detachments travel solely in britzkas. Cossack ingenuity distinguishes between two kinds of *tachanka*: the colonial and the assessor's. And in fact, this is not ingenious – it is a distinction that actually exists.

It was on the assessor's britzka, that loose buggy made without love or inventiveness, that the wretched, red-nosed bureaucrats jolted their way across the wheaten steppes of Kuban, a sleep-starved bunch of men hurrying to post-mortems and criminal investigations, while the colonial *tachanka* came to us from the Volga territories of Samara and the Urals, the rich and fertile German colonies. The spacious oak seat back of the colonial *tachanka* is decorated with a thrifty art: puffy garlands of pink German flowers. The sturdy bottoms are bound with iron. One's journey is made upon unforgettable springs. The ardour of many generations do I sense in those springs, as now they bounce along the upturned Volhynia road.

I am experiencing the rapture of first possession. Each day after dinner we harness the horses. Grishchuk leads them out of the stable. They are recovering with each day that passes. With proud joy I already find a matt sheen on their groomed flanks. We massage the horses' swollen legs, clip their manes, throw on to their backs the Cossack harness – a tangled, shrivelled net of delicate thongs – and drive out of the yard at a trot. Grishchuk sits on the box, sideways; my seat is covered with flower-patterned bast canvas and hay that smells of scent and serenity. The tall wheels creak in the white, granular sand. Rectangles of flowering poppies paint the earth, ruined Catholic churches shine on hillocks. High above the roadway, in a niche that a shell has smashed, stands a brown statue of St Ursula* with bare, round arms. And ancient, narrow letters trace an uneven chain on the blackened gold of the pediment . . . 'To the greater glory of Jesus and His Holy Mother'.

Lifeless Jewish *shtetls* cluster round the Polish manor-houses. The prophetic peacock gleams on brick walls, an impassive spectre in the blue vastness. Concealed by a warren of hovels, a synagogue has squatted down on the destitute earth, eyeless, gap-toothed, round as a Hassidic hat. Narrow-shouldered Jews stand sadly at the crossroads. And in one's memory flares a picture of the southern Jews — jovial, pot-bellied, bubbling like cheap wine. There is no comparison between them and the bitter haughtiness of these long, bony backs, these tragic yellow beards. In their passionate features, painfully carved, there is no fat, or warm pulse of blood. The movements of the Volhynian and Galician Jew are unrestrained, abrupt, offensive to good taste, but the power of their grief is full of a gloomy grandeur and their secret contempt for the Polish *pan* is limitless. Looking at them, I have understood the fiery history of this outlying region, the stories that are told of Talmudists who were tenant landlords of taverns, rabbis who engaged in usury, girls who were raped by Polish troopers and on whose account Polish magnates shot themselves.

The Death of Dolgushov

The veils of battle were advancing towards the town. At midday Korochayev charged past us in a black felt cloak — a disgraced *nachdiv* 4, fighting alone and searching for death. As he rode by he shouted to me:

'Our communications are broken. Radziwiłłów and Brody are on fire! . . .'

And off he galloped – fluttering, entirely black, with pupils of coal.

On a plain as smooth as a board the brigades were regrouping. The sun was rolling through a crimson dust. In the ditches wounded men were eating. Nurses lay on the grass, singing in low voices. Afonka's reconnaissance troops were scouring the field, looking for corpses and uniforms. Afonka rode by two paces from me and said, without turning his head:

'They've given us a bloody nose. Two times two. There's talk about the *nachdiv*, he's being relieved of his command. The men are worried . . .'

The Poles had come up to the forest, about three versts away from where we were, and had set up machine-guns somewhere near by. The bullets were whining and shrieking. Their lament was growing unendurably loud. The bullets wounded the earth and swarmed in it, trembling with impatience. Vytyagaychenko, the regimental commander, who was snoring in the blazing sun, cried out in his sleep and woke up. He mounted his horse and rode over to the leading squadron. His face was crumpled, with red stripes left by his uncomfortable sleep, and his pockets were full of plums.

'The sons of bitches,' he said angrily and spat a plum stone from his mouth. 'What a filthy waste of time. Timoshka, hoist the flag!'

'What, are we off, then?' asked Timoshka, taking the pole from his stirrup and unfolding the banner, on which there was a star and some writing about the Third International.

'We're going to see what's going on over there,' said Vytyagaychenko, and suddenly he shouted wildly, 'All right, lassies, on your horsies! Call your people together, squadron leaders! . . .'

The buglers sounded the alarm. The squadrons formed up

into a column. Out of one of the ditches crawled a wounded man and, shading his eyes with his hand, said to Vytyagaychenko:

'Taras Grigoryevich, I've been asked to speak for us all. It seems as though we're going to stay here . . .'

'You'll be left behind . . .' muttered Vytyagaychenko, and he made his horse rear up on its hind legs.

'There's a kind of hope among us, Taras Grigoryevich, that we won't be left behind,' the wounded man said as he rode off.

'Stop your whining,' said Vytyagaychenko, turning round. 'Never fear, I won't leave you in the lurch.' And he gave the order to draw rein.

And immediately there rang out the wailing and womanish voice of Afonka Bida, my friend: 'Don't lead us there at the gallop, Taras Grigoryevich, it's five versts; how will we be able to fight if our horses are all worn out . . .? There's no point in rushing – you'll be there in plenty of time to pick pears with the Mother of God . . .'

'Quick march!' Vytyagaychenko ordered, without raising his eyes.

The regiment moved off.

'If the rumour about the *nachdiv* is right,' Afonka whispered, hanging back, 'and he is being relieved of his command, then all hell's going to break loose. Full stop.'

Tears trickled from his eyes. I stared at Afonka in utter amazement. He spun round like a top, clutched his cap, gave a hoarse cry and a whoop, and went charging off.

Grishchuk with his stupid *tachanka* and I – we were left alone and till evening rushed about between the fiery walls. The divisional staff had disappeared. No other unit would take us in. The Poles entered Brody and were repulsed by a counter-attack. We drove up to the town cemetery. A Polish mounted patrol sprang out from behind the gravestones and, shouldering their rifles, began to fire at us. Grishchuk turned around. His *tachanka* cried out with all its four wheels.

'Grishchuk!' I shouted through the whistling and the wind.

'Monkey tricks,' he replied sadly.

'It's all up with us!' I exclaimed, seized by the ecstasy of ruin. 'It's all up with us, father!'

'Why do women go to all that effort,' he replied, even more sadly, 'why the matchmakings and the marriages, why do the godfathers carouse at weddings . . .'

A pink tail shone in the sky and died. The Milky Way came out among the stars.

'It makes me want to laugh,' said Grishchuk, sorrowfully, and he pointed with his whip at a man who was sitting by the side of the road. 'It makes me want to laugh, why do women go to all that effort . . .'

The man who was sitting by the side of the road was Dolgushov, the telephonist. His legs spread apart, he was staring at us.

'Here, look,' said Dolgushov, when we drove up, 'I'm finished . . . Understand?'

'Yes,' Grishchuk replied, stopping the horses.

'You'll have to spend a cartridge on me,' Dolgushov said, sternly.

He sat leaning against a tree. His boots stuck out in opposite directions. Without lowering his eyes from me, he carefully loosened his shirt. His stomach had been torn out, his intestines had sagged down on to his knees, and the beating of his heart was visible.

'If the Poles come, they'll make a right ninny of me. Here's my passport, write to my mother and give her the particulars . . .'

'No,' I replied hollowly, and gave my horse a dig of the spurs.

Dolgushov spread out his blue palms on the earth and examined them with suspicion.

'You're running away,' he muttered, as he crawled down. 'Run, then, cur.'

The perspiration was crawling over my body. The machine-guns were chattering faster and faster, with hysterical obstinacy. Encircled by the halo of the sunset, Afonka Bida galloped up to us.

'We're giving them a fair old peppering,' he shouted, merrily. 'What's going on over here, then?'

I showed him Dolgushov and rode away.

They spoke briefly – I could not hear the words. Dolgushov handed the platoon commander his little book. Afonka stuck it in his boot and shot Dolgushov in the mouth.

'Afonya,' I said with a pathetic smile and rode over to the Cossack. 'You see, I couldn't do it.'

'Go away,' he replied, turning pale, 'or I'll kill you. You four-eyed lot have as much pity for us as a cat has for a mouse.'

And he cocked the trigger.

I rode off quickly, without turning round, my spine sensing coldness and death.

'Get out of here!' Grishchuk shouted from behind. 'Stop playing the fool!' And he grabbed Afonka by the arm.

'That damned lackey,' Afonka barked, 'he's not going to get away from me . . .'

Grishchuk caught up with me at the turning. There was no sign of Afonka. He had ridden away in the other direction.

'You see, Grishchuk?' I said. 'Today I have lost Afonka, my best friend . . .'

Grishchuk took out a wrinkled apple from under the seat.

'Eat it,' he told me. 'Eat it, please.'

And I accepted charity from Grishchuk and ate his apple with sadness and reverence.

Brody, August 1920

Kombrig 2

Budyonny was standing by a tree, in red trousers with a silver stripe. *Kombrig* 2 had just been killed. In his place the army commander* had appointed Kolesnikov.

An hour ago Kolesnikov had been colonel of a regiment. A week ago Kolesnikov had been the leader of a squadron.

The new *kombrig* was summoned to Budyonny. The commander was waiting for him, standing by the tree. Kolesnikov had come with Almazov, his commissar.

'The curs are giving us the squeeze,' the commander said with his dazzling grin. 'Either we win or we die. There is no other way. Got it?'

'Got it,' Kolesnikov replied, his eyes bulging.

'And if you run, I will shoot you,' the commander said, smiling, and turned to look at the section leader.

'Very well,' said the section leader.

'On you roll, Wheel,'* a Cossack shouted from the side.

Budyonny turned impetuously on his heel and saluted the new *kombrig*. The latter touched his peaked cap with five youthful red fingers, began to sweat and walked off along the ploughed-up path between the fields. His horses were waiting for him at a hundred sagenes'* distance. He walked with lowered head, his long and crooked legs moving with agonizing slowness. The blaze of the sunset washed over him, crimson and improbable as approaching death.

And suddenly, against the outstretched land, against the ploughed yellow nakedness of the fields we saw Kolesnikov's narrow back, his loosely hanging arms and his bowed head in its grey visored cap.

An orderly led up a horse for him.

He leapt into the saddle and galloped off to his brigade

136

without turning round. His squadrons were waiting for him by the main road, the well-worn road to Brody.

A groaning hurrah, torn by the wind, drifted over to us.

Training my binoculars, I could see the *kombrig* circling on his horse amidst columns of blue dust.

'Kolesnikov has led the brigade into battle,' said the observer in the tree above our heads.

'Very good,' replied Budyonny; he lit a cigarette and closed his eyes.

The hurrah ceased. The cannonade choked. Unnecessary shrapnel burst above the forest. And we heard the great silence of a sabre attack.

'He means business,' said the commander, getting up. 'Looking for honour. I should think he'll last the course.'

And, having requested horses, Budyonny rode off to the battlefield. The staff moved off after him.

I happened to catch sight of Kolesnikov again that same evening, an hour after the Poles had been annihilated. He was riding out in front of his brigade – alone – on a light bay stallion of unparalleled beauty, nodding in the saddle. His right arm was in a sling. Ten paces from him a mounted Cossack carried the unfurled banner. The front squadron was lazily leading the others in the singing of obscene couplets. The brigade stretched dusty and endless as a line of peasant carts going to a country fair. Puffing and panting in the rear came the weary brass bands.

In Kolesnikov's manner of sitting in the saddle that evening I saw the lordly indifference of a Tartar khan and recognized the training of the renowned Kniga, the self-willed Pavlichenko, the fascinating Savitsky.

Brody, August 1920

137

Sashka Christ

Sashka – that was his name, and he had been nicknamed 'Christ' because of his meekness. He was the public herdsman on a Cossack settlement, and had done no heavy work since the age of fourteen, when he had caught a foul disease. It had all happened like this:

Tarakanych, Sashka's stepfather, had gone off for the winter to the town of Grozny and had joined an *artel** there. It was an *artel* that had been knocked together successfully, and consisted of some Ryazan muzhiks. Tarakanych did carpentry work for them, and his income was increasing. He could not manage the business side of things and wrote back home asking the boy to come and work as his assistant: the settlement would get through the winter even without Sashka. Sashka worked with his father for a week. Then the Sabbath came, and they knocked off work and sat down to drink tea. It was October, but the air was mild. They opened a window and heated a second samovar. Under the windows a beggar woman was hanging around. She knocked on the window frame and said:

'Good day to you, peasants of another town. Please take notice of my position.'

'What position would that be?' said Tarakanych. 'Come in, cripple woman.'

The beggar woman began to fuss on the other side of the wall and then jumped up into the room. She came over to the table and bowed from the waist. Tarakanych seized her by her headscarf, threw the headscarf away and ran his fingers through her hair. The beggarwoman's hair was lustreless, grey, tufted and covered in dust.

'Fie upon you, what a muzhik, meddlesome and slim,' she said. 'It's nothing but a circus with you . . .'

138

'If you please, don't turn your nose up at me, an old woman,' she whispered with haste, clambering up on to the bench. Tarakanych lay down with her and got what fun he could. The beggar woman kept tilting her head to one side and laughing.

'Rain on an old woman,' she laughed. 'I'll give two hundred *poods* to the *desyatina** . . .'

And as she said this she caught sight of Sasha, who was drinking tea at the table, not raising his eyes to God's world.

'Your boy, is he?'

'Sort of mine,' Tarakanych replied. 'The wife's.'

'There's a good laddie, he's giving me the eye,' said the woman. 'Well, come here, then.'

Sashka went over to her – and caught a foul disease. At the time, however, no one was thinking of such things. Tarakanych gave the beggar woman the bones left over from dinner and a silver five-copeck piece, a very shiny one.

'Polish it with sand, prayerwoman,' said Tarakanych, 'and it will look even better. If you lend it to the Lord God on a dark night it will do instead of the moon . . .'

The cripple woman put her headscarf on again, pocketed the bones, and went. But two weeks later, all became plain to the muzhiks. They suffered greatly with the foul disease, spent all winter trying to get rid of it and dosing themselves with herbs. And when spring came they went back to the settlement and their work as peasants.

The settlement was nine versts' distance from the railway. Tarakanych and Sashka walked through the fields. The earth lay in an April dampness. In black pits emeralds gleamed. Green shoots embroidered the earth with a cunning stitch. And there was a sour smell from the earth, as from a soldier's wife at dawn. The first herds were flowing down the tumuli, the foals were frisking in the blue expanses of the horizon.

Tarakanych and Sashka walked along little paths that were barely detectable.

'Tarakanych, let me go back to the commune and be a herdsman again,' said Sashka.

'What's that?'

'I can't abide the herdsmen having such a fine life.'

'I don't consent to that,' said Tarakanych.

'Let me go, for God's sake, Tarakanych,' Sashka said again. 'All the hierarchs came from among the herdsmen.'

'Sashka the hierarch,' his stepfather laughed noisily. 'Got syphilis from the Mother of God . . .'

They passed the bend at Red Bridge, traversed the coppice and then the common pasture and caught sight of the cross on the settlement church. The women were still pottering about in the kitchen gardens, while the Cossacks, who had taken seats among the lilacs, were drinking vodka and singing. Tarakanych's *izba* was about half a verst's walk away.

'Please God let everything be all right,' he said, making the sign of the cross over himself.

They approached the hut and looked in its little window. There was no one in the hut. Sashka's mother was in the stable milking the cow. The muzhiks crept up inaudibly. Tarakanych laughed and shouted behind the woman's back:

'Motya, your highness, go and get your guests something for their supper.'

The woman turned round, began to flutter, ran out of the stable and went whirling about the yard. Then she returned to her place, flung herself on Tarakanych's chest and hid.

'My, how ugly and uninviting you are,' said Tarakanych, pushing her affectionately aside. 'Why don't you show us the children . . .'

'The children are gone,' said the woman, white all over, ran off about the yard again and fell to the ground. 'Oh,

Alyoshenka,' she cried wildly, 'our little children are gone, and they went feet first . . .'

Tarakanych made a hopeless gesture and went to the neighbours'. The neighbours said that the week before the Lord had taken away the little boy and the little girl with typhus. Motya had written to him, but he would not have had time to receive the letter. Tarakanych went back to the hut. His woman was lighting the stove.

'So you've finally got yourself free, Motya,' said Tarakanych. 'I'll need to teach you a lesson.'

He sat down at the table and began to pine – and pined until it was time to sleep, ate meat and drank vodka and did not go about his tasks. He snored at the table and kept waking up and then snoring again. Motya made up a bed for herself and her husband, and another for Sashka to one side. She blew out the lamp and lay down with her husband. Sashka tossed and turned on the hay in his corner, his eyes were open, he lay awake and saw, as in a dream, the interior of the hut, a star in the window and the edge of the table and the horse collars under his mother's bed. The compelling vision gained mastery over him, he yielded to dreams and rejoiced in his waking fantasy. He fancied that he saw two silver cords hanging down from the sky twisted into a thick rope, and a cradle fixed to them, a rosewood cradle with sinuous patterns on it. It swung high above the earth and far from the sky, the silver cords moving and gleaming. Sashka lay in the cradle, and the air fanned him with its currents. An air as loud as music, coming from the fields, and a rainbow flowering on the fields of unripe grain.

Sashka enjoyed his waking fantasy, closing his eyes now and then so as not to see the horse collars under his mother's bed. Then he heard a puffing sound from Motya's stovecouch, and thought about the fact that Tarakanych was tumbling his mother.

'Tarakanych,' he said loudly, 'I have some business with you.'

'What business can there be at night?' Tarakanych responded. 'Sleep, you bastard . . .'

'I swear by the cross, I've got business,' Sashka replied. 'Come out to the yard.'

And in the yard, under an unfading star, Sashka told his stepfather:

'Don't harm mother, Tarakanych, you're defiled.'

'What do you know about my character?' asked Tarakanych.

'I know your character, only you've seen mother, how sleek and fine she is? She has clean legs and breasts. Don't harm her, Tarakanych. We're defiled.'

'Dear fellow,' replied his stepfather, 'go away from blood and from my character. Look, here are twenty copecks for you, sleep the night, get sober . . .'

'Twenty copecks are no use to me,' Sashka muttered. 'Let me go and be a herdsman.'

'I don't agree to that,' said Tarakanych.

'Let me go and be a herdsman,' Sashka muttered, 'or else I'll tell mother all about us. Why should she suffer when she's so sleek and fine . . .'

Tarakanych turned away, went into the shed and brought out an axe.

'Hierarch Sashka,' he said in a whisper, 'it's a simple story, I'm going to cut you up, hierarch . . .'

'You won't cut me up for the sake of a woman,' said the boy, barely audibly, and he bent forward to his stepfather. 'Take pity on me, let me go and be a herdsman.'

'The deuce with you,' said Tarakanych, throwing away the axe. 'Go and be a herdsman.'

And he went back into the hut and spent the night with his wife.

That same morning Sashka went to the Cossacks to get himself hired for work, and from that time on he began to

live as a herdsman for the commune. He grew famed throughout the whole district for his open-heartedness, received from
the members of the settlement the nickname 'Sashka Christ',
and lived as a herdsman right up till the time when his call-up
came. Old muzhiks who were on the frail side would come
out to see him on the common pasture to have a chat, and
women would go to Sashka to recover from the crazy
habits of their muzhiks and were not angry with Sashka,
because of his love and because of his disease. Sashka's call-
up came in the first year of the war. He spent four years in
the war and returned to the settlement when the Whites
were having it their own way there. Sashka was egged on
to go to Platov settlement, where a detachment was being
formed to fight the Whites. A cavalry sergeant-major with a
long record of service, Semyon Mikhailovich Budyonny,
ran the show in this detachment, and with him there were
three brothers: Yemelyan, Lukyan and Denis. Sashka went
to the Platov settlement, and there his fate was settled. He
was in Budyonny's regiment, brigade, division and First
Cavalry Army. He went to rescue heroic Tsaritsyn, joined
forces with Voroshilov's Tenth Army, fought at Voronezh,
Kastornaya and at the General's Bridge on the Donets.
Sashka entered the Polish campaign as a transport driver,
because he had been wounded and was considered an
invalid.

That was how it all happened. Recently I have begun to
maintain an acquaintance with Sashka Christ and have transferred my little trunk to his wagon. Quite often we have
greeted the glow of morning and watched the sun go down
together. And when the capricious desire of battle has
brought us together, we have sat ourselves down in the
evenings by the shining earth mound outside a peasant's hut
or brèwed tea in the woods in a sooty kettle or slept side by
side in the mown fields, the hungry horses tethered to our
legs.

The Life Story of Pavlichenko,
Matvey Rodionych

Fellow villagers, comrades, my own brothers! Now harken in the name of mankind to the life-story of the Red general Matvey Pavlichenko. He was a pigkeeper, that general, a pigkeeper on the country estate of Lidino, in the employ of Nikitinsky, the landowner, where he tended the master's pigs until life sent him stripes on his shoulder straps, and then he began to tend cattle. And who can tell — had he been born in Australia, our Matvey Rodionych, light of our eyes, it is very possible, my friends, that he would have risen to elephants, he would have been tending elephants were it not that there is nowhere to get hold of elephants in our province of Stavropol. An animal bigger than a buffalo, I tell you frankly, does not exist in our wide realm of Stavropol. There is no comfort in buffaloes, a Russian finds it dull making fun of buffaloes; give us orphans a horse for the Eternal Judgement, a horse, so that our souls may come out on the boundary field with its flanks beneath them . . .

And so here I am tending my cattle, surrounded on all sides by cows, steeped all through with milk. I stink like a slit udder, bull calves walk around me for the sake of propriety, mousy bull calves, grey of hue. The freedom around me has lain down in the fields, the grass rustles all over the world, the heavens swing about above me like a concertina with many keyboards, and the heavens in the province of Stavropol, my lads, are very blue. And that is how I tend my cattle, playing my pipe to the winds for want of anything better to do, until a certain old man says to me:

'Matvey,' he says, 'off you go and see Nastya.'

'Why?' I say. 'Are you making mock of me, old man?'

'Off you go,' he says. 'She wishes it.'

And so off I go and see her.

'Nastya,' I say and blush deeply with all my blood.

'Nastya,' I say, 'are you making mock of me? . . .'

But she doesn't reply, and instead darts away from me at a run and runs as hard as she possibly can, and I run together with her, until we're on the common pasture, dead-beat, red and out of breath.

'Matvey,' Nastya says to me then, 'the Sunday before last, when it was the spring fishing and the fishermen were walking down to the shore, you walked with them like that, with your head lowered. Why did you have your head lowered, Matvey, was there some thought that oppressed your heart, answer me that? . . .'

And I answer her:

'Nastya,' I answer, 'I've no answer to give you, my head is not a rifle, and it has no front sight nor back sight neither, and you know my heart, Nastya, it's completely empty, it's most likely steeped in milk, it's a terrible thing how I stink of milk . . .'

And Nastya, I see, finds these words of mine amusing.

'I'll swear by the cross,' she says, and laughs fit to burst, laughs at the top of her voice, all over the steppe, as though she were playing a drum, 'I'll swear by the cross that you're exchanging winks with the young ladies . . .'

And after we'd spent a short while saying foolish things, she and I soon got married. And Nastya and I began to live as best we were able, and we were well able. We were hot all night, we were hot in winter, all the long night we went naked and tore the hide off each other. We lived as well as devils, and so it went on until the old man comes to see me for the second time.

'Matvey,' he says, 'the master was touching your wife in all the right places today, he's going to get her, the master . . .'

And I say:

'No,' I say, 'no. Take your leave of me, old man, or I'll cook your goose right here on the spot . . .'

And the old man, no doubt about it, left me at a fair old pace, and I covered twenty versts on foot that day, walked a long way that day, and in the evening I ended up in Lidino estate, at the home of my jolly Nikitinsky, the landowner. He was sitting in the living-room, that old old man, mending three saddles: an English one, a dragoon one and a Cossack one – and I stood outside his door like a burdock, stood for a whole hour, and all to no purpose. But then he cast eyes on me.

'What do you want?' he says.

'I want to settle my account.'

'Have you got designs on me?'

'I have no designs, but I honestly wish . . .'

At that point he looked away, turned away from the high road into a side-lane, spread out on the floor some crimson saddle-cloths, more crimson than the flags of the tsar they were, his saddle-cloths, he stood on them, the horrible old fellow, and began to puff himself up like a cockerel.

'Freedom for the free man,' he said, puffing himself up. 'I cockroached all your mothers, you Orthodox Christian peasants, you can have a settlement of your account, only do you not owe me, my dear friend Matyusha, some small trifle or other?'

'Hee, hee,' I reply, 'it's the joker you are, to be sure, so help me God, it's the joker you are, I think it's you who've got to pay me my wages . . .'

'Wages!' my master explodes, grinds out and throws me down on my knees and shuffles his feet and lands the Father, Son and Holy Ghost round about my earhole. 'Wages you want – have you forgotten that yoke of mine you broke last year, the one for the oxen, where is it, my yoke?'

'I'll give you your yoke back,' I answer my master and raise my simple eyes to him and sit there on my knees before him.

'I'll give you your yoke back, only don't you go pressing me with debts, old man, but wait a bit longer . . .'

And what do you suppose, you lads of Stavropol, my fellow villagers, comrades, my brothers, well, the master waited five years for me to pay his debts, five long years I lost, until the last one, the year '18, came visiting. On merry stallions it came, on its Kabardinian* horses. A long transport it brought behind it and all kinds of songs. And oh, my darling, year '18! Shall you and I really never step out again, little droplet of my blood, year '18? We have squandered your songs, drunk all your wine, decreed your laws, and only your writers are left to us. And oh, my darling! It was not writers who went flying about Kuban in those days, sending the souls of generals up into the air at one yard's distance. Matvey Rodionych lay in blood outside Prikumsk, and after the last march Matvey Rodionych was only five versts away from the estate of Lidino. And I went there, alone, without my detachment, and went into the living-room, entering it quietly. Some men from the district council were sitting in there. Nikitinsky was handing tea around to them and fawning upon one and all, but when he saw me he turned pale, and I took off my astrakhan hat to him.

'Good day,' I said to one and all, 'good day, well met. Will you receive a guest, master, or how shall it be with us?'

'It shall be quiet and decent with us,' a certain fellow replies to me then, and I can tell by the way he talks that he's a land surveyor. 'It shall be quiet and decent with us, but you, Comrade Pavlichenko, have evidently galloped from afar, for mud doth mar your appearance, and we, the district council, have a horror of such appearances – now why is it thus?'

'Because,' I reply, 'you cold-blooded district authorities, because in my appearance one of my cheeks has been burning for five years, burning in the trench, burning on the march, burning with a woman, and it will burn on Judgement Day. On Judgement Day,' I say, and look at Nikitinsky in a merry sort of way, but he hasn't got proper eyes now, just spheres in the middle of his face, as though spheres had been rolled into his forehead where his eyes used to be, and with these crystal spheres he winks at me, also in a merry sort of way, but very terrible to see.

'Matyusha,' he says to me, 'we used to be friendly in the old days, and now my spouse, Nadezhda Vasilyevna, who has lost her reason on account of these awful times, she was good to you, now, wasn't she, Nadezhda Vasilyevna? Matyusha, you used to respect her more than any other woman, do you really mean to tell me you won't see her now that she's bereft of light?'

'Very well,' I say, and he and I go into another room, and there he starts touching my hands, the right one, then the left.

'Matyusha,' he says, 'are you my destiny?'

'No,' I say, 'and stop using those words. God has given us, his lickspittles, the slip, our destiny is a turkey, our life is a copeck, stop using those words and hear, if you will, a letter from Lenin . . .'

'A letter to me, Nikitinsky?'

'That's right.' And I take out my book of decrees, open it at a blank page and read, though I am illiterate to the depths of my soul.

'In the name of the people,' I read, 'and for the foundation of a radiant future I order Pavlichenko, Matvey Rodionych, to take the lives of various people at his discretion . . . There,' I say, 'that's it, Lenin's letter to you . . .'

And he says to me, 'No!'

'No,' he says, 'Matyusha, our life has wasted away to the devil and blood has become cheap in the Russian Equiapostolic State, but whatever blood is due to you, you'll get it all the same and forget my dead eyes, and would it not be better if I showed you a certain floorboard?'

'All right,' I say, 'perhaps it would . . .'

And again he and I went through the rooms, went down

into the wine-cellar; there he pulled out a certain brick and behind that brick he found a casket. There were rings in it, that casket, necklaces, medals and a pearly icon. He threw it to me, sagging with fear.

'It's yours,' he says. 'Take possession of Nikitinsky's icon and off you go, Matvey, back to that den of yours at Prikumsk . . .'

And then I took him by the body, by the throat, by the hair.

'What about my cheeks?' I said. 'How am I going to live with my cheeks, brother of mine?'

And then he laughed of his own accord, too loud, and didn't try to tear himself free.

'Jackal's conscience,' he says, still not trying to tear himself free, 'I've been talking to you as though you were an officer of the Russian Empire, but you, you coarse villain, were suckled by a she-wolf. Shoot me, son of a bitch! . . .'

But I didn't shoot him, I didn't owe him any kind of shooting, I just dragged him upstairs into the drawing-room. There in the drawing-room was Nadezhda Vasilyevna, completely insane, pacing about the drawing-room with an unsheathed sabre and staring at herself in the mirror. But when I dragged Nikitinsky into the drawing-room, Nadezhda Vasilyevna ran to sit down in an armchair. She was decked out in a velvet crown with feathers, and sat down smartly in the armchair and presented arms to me with the sabre. And then I trampled on Nikitinsky, my master. I trampled on him for an hour or more than an hour, and during that time I got to know him and his life. Shooting – in my opinion – is just a way of getting rid of a fellow, to shoot him is to pardon him, and a vile compromise with yourself; with shooting you don't get to a man's soul, where it is in him and how it shows itself. But usually I don't spare myself, usually I trample my enemy for an hour or more than an hour, I want to find out about the life, what it's like with us . . .

The Cemetery in Kozin

The cemetery in a Jewish *shtetl*. Assyria and the mysterious decay of the East in the tall-weeded fields of Volhynia.

Grey stones, ground smooth, with three-hundred-year-old characters on them. Coarse high-relief patterns cut in granite. A carving of a fish and a sheep above a dead human head. Carvings of rabbis in fur caps. The narrow loins of the rabbis are girded with leather belts. And beneath their eyeless faces a waving line of curly stone beards. At the side, under an oak tree with its brains blown out by lightning, is the burial vault of Rabbi Azrael, who was murdered by the Cossacks of Bogdan Khmelnitsky.* Four generations lie in this tomb that is as beggarly as the habitation of a water-carrier, and the tablets, the tablets sing of them like an ornate Bedouin prayer:

'Azrael, son of Ananias, mouth of Jehovah.

'Elijah, son of Azrael, brain that joined in single combat with oblivion.

'Wolf, son of Elijah, prince abducted from the Torah in his nineteenth spring.

'Judah, son of Wolf, rabbi of Krakow and Prague.

'O death, O profit-seeker, O avaricious thief, why hast thou not just once taken pity on us?'

Prishchepa

I am making my way to Leszniów, where the divisional staff has taken up residence. My travelling companion is, as earlier, Prishchepa* – a young fellow from the Kuban, an unwearying boor, a kicked-out communist, a future rag-and-bone man, a happy-go-lucky syphilitic, an unhurried teller of fibs. He is wearing a crimson Circassian coat of fine cloth and a soft hood thrown over his back. On the way he told me about himself. I shall not forget his story.

A year ago Prishchepa ran away from the Whites. In revenge they took his parents as hostages and killed them at the counter-espionage HQ. Their belongings were looted by the neighbours. When the Whites were driven out of the Kuban, Prishchepa returned to his native Cossack settlement.

It was morning, dawn, the sleep of the muzhiks sighed in a stale fug. Prishchepa hired an official wagon and walked about the settlement collecting his gramophones, kvass jugs and towels that had been embroidered by his mother. He came out into the street in a black felt cloak with a curved dagger in his belt. The wagon trailed along behind. Prishchepa went from one neighbour to another, and the bloody imprint of his boot soles stretched after him. In those huts where the Cossack found things that had belonged to his mother, or a chibouk of his father's, he left old women nailed to the walls, dogs hung above wells and icons soiled with excrement. The men of the settlement smoked their pipes, morosely following his passage. The young Cossacks scattered out over the steppe, keeping a tally. The tally grew excessively large, and the settlement fell silent. When he had finished, Prishchepa returned to his father's devastated house. The furniture he had recovered he arranged in the order he recalled from his boyhood, and then he sent for vodka. Shutting himself up in the hut, he drank for two days and nights, sang, wept and slashed the tables with his sabre. On the third night the settlement saw smoke above Prishchepa's hut. Singed and lacerated, shuffling his feet, he led the cow out of her stall, put a revolver in her mouth and fired. The earth smoked under his feet, a blue ring of flame flew out of the chimney and melted away, in the stable an abandoned bull calf began to sob. The fire shone like a resurrection. Prishchepa untied the horse, leapt into the saddle, threw a lock of his hair into the blaze and vanished.

The Story of a Horse

Savitsky, our *nachdiv*, once took a white stallion from Khleb-nikov, the commander of the First Squadron. This was a horse which looked splendid, but its coarse lines always seemed a bit heavy to me. Khlebnikov had received in exchange a little black mare of not inferior breed, with a smooth trot. But he ill treated the little mare and thirsted for revenge and bided his time, and it came.

After the unsuccessful battles of July, when Savitsky was relieved of his command and sent back to the reserve of command personnel, Khlebnikov wrote an application to the cavalry staff for the horse to be returned to him. The chief of staff wrote on it the order, 'Said stallion to be restored to original status', and Khlebnikov, exultant, covered a hundred versts in order to find Savitsky, who at the time was living in Radziwillów, a wretched, mutilated little town that resembled a ragged boudoir gossip. He lived alone, the transferred *nachdiv*, and the lickspittles from the staffs did not want to know him any more. The lickspittles from the staffs fished for roast chicken in the army commander's smile and, acting in servile fashion, they turned away from the illustrious *nachdiv*.

Drenched in scent and looking like Peter the Great, he lived in disgrace, with the Cossack woman Pávla, whom he had taken away from a Jewish quartermaster, and twenty thoroughbred horses which we all looked upon as his property. In his yard, the sun was straining and languishing with the blindness of its own rays, the foals in his yard were impetuously suckling their dams, the stablemen with sweat-running backs were sifting oats on faded winnowing-machines, and only Khlebnikov, covered with the wounds of truth and driven on by vengeance, walked straight up to the barricaded yard.

'Is my identity familiar to you?' he asked Savitsky, who was lying on the hay.

'I might have seen you around,' Savitsky replied, and yawned.

'Then here is an order from the chief of staff,' Khlebnikov said firmly, 'and I would ask you, comrade from the reserve, to look on me with an official eye . . .'

'No problem,' Savitsky muttered in conciliatory fashion, took the document and began to read it for an uncommonly long time. Then he suddenly called the Cossack woman, who was combing her hair in the coolness under the awning.

'Pavla,' he said, 'we've been combing our hair ever since morning, now how about a nice little samovar . . .'

The Cossack woman put down her comb and, taking her hair in her hands, tossed it behind her back.

'All day we've been making a nuisance of ourselves, Konstantin Vasilyevich,' she said with a lazy, imperious smile. 'Now it's one thing you want, now it's another.'

And she walked over to the *nachdiv* in her high-heeled shoes, her breasts moving like an animal in a bag.

'All day we've been making a nuisance of ourselves,' the woman said again, beaming, and buttoned up the *nachdiv*'s shirt over his chest.

'Now I want one thing, and now another,' the *nachdiv* laughed, getting up; he embraced Pavla's surrendering shoulders and suddenly turned towards Khlebnikov a deathly pale face.

'I'm still alive, Khlebnikov,' he said from the Cossack woman's embrace, 'my legs can still walk, my horses can still gallop, my hands can still get you, and my gun is keeping warm next to my body . . .'

He took out the revolver resting against his bare belly and stepped up to the commander of the First Squadron.

The latter turned on his heel, his spurs began to moan, he walked out of the yard like an orderly who has received urgent mail, and again covered a hundred versts to find the chief of staff, but the latter told Khlebnikov to go away.

'Your business, commander, has been settled,' said the chief of staff. 'The stallion has been returned to you by me, and I have enough to worry about without you . . .'

He would not listen to Khlebnikov and at last the runaway commander returned to the First Squadron. Khlebnikov had absented himself for a week. During that time we were moved to a post in the Dubno forests. Khlebnikov returned, I remember, on the Sunday morning, the twelfth. He demanded from me more than a quire of paper, and some ink. The Cossacks planed a tree stump for him, he placed his revolver and the paper on the tree stump, and he wrote until evening, filling a large number of sheets with bad handwriting.

'A real Karl Marx,' the squadron's military commissar said to him in the evening. 'What are you writing, the devil take you . . .?'

'I am writing down various thoughts in accordance with my oath,' Khlebnikov replied, and handed the military commissar a declaration of withdrawal from the Communist Party of the Bolsheviks.

'The Communist Party,' it said in this declaration, 'was founded, I believe, for happiness and unwavering justice without limit, and also has a duty to look to the little man. Now I will touch upon the matter of a white stallion which I took away from some incredibly counter-revolutionary peasants, it having a wretched appearance, and many of my comrades laughed shameless mocking laughter at its appearance, but I had the strength to endure that cruel laughter and, gritting my teeth for the common cause, I groomed the stallion until the desired change, because, comrades, I am a lover of white horses and have put into them that small quantity of strength that has remained to me from the imperialist and civil wars, and stallions like that respond to my hand, and I was also able to feel his unspoken needs, but for an unjust black mare I have no use whatever, I cannot respond to her and cannot abide her, and all my comrades can confirm that if it goes on like this there will be trouble. And now the Party is unable to return my precious goods, according to the order, and I have no other way out but to write this declaration with tears that are not suited to a fighting man, but flow unceasingly and cut my heart, cut my heart to blood . . .'

This and much else was written in Khlebnikov's declaration, because he had been writing it all day, and it was very long. The military commissar and I struggled with it for about an hour and deciphered it to the end.

'What a fool,' said the military commissar, tearing up the document. 'Come and see me after supper, you're going to have a talk with me.'

'I don't want your talk,' Khlebnikov replied, quivering. 'You've lost me, military commissar.'

He stood with his hands placed at the seams of his trousers, trembling, not moving from the spot, and looking about him to each side as though he were deciding which way to flee. The military commissar walked right up to him, but did not see it through. Khlebnikov dashed away, running as fast as he could.

'Lost me!' he shouted wildly, getting up on to the tree stump and beginning to tear off his jacket and scratch his chest.

'Shoot, Savitsky,' he shouted, falling to the ground. 'Shoot me right now!'

Then we dragged him into his tent, and the Cossacks helped us. We brewed tea for him and rolled him cigarettes.* He smoked, still trembling. And only towards evening did our commander calm down. He said no more about his crazy declaration, but a week later travelled to Rovno, was examined at the medical commission and was demobilized, having six wounds.

That's how we lost Khlebnikov. I was terribly saddened by it, for Khlebnikov was a quiet man, like me in character. He was the only man in the squadron who had a samovar. On days when there was a lull he and I had drunk hot tea together. And he had told me about women in such detail that I had felt embarrassment and pleasure as I listened. This was, I think, because we were both affected by the same passions. We both looked upon the world as a meadow in May, a meadow across which women and horses moved.

Radziwillów, July 1920

Konkin

We were making mincemeat of the Poles near Belaya Tserkov. We were making mincemeat of them to our hearts' content, so that the trees sagged with bodies. I'd been hit that morning, but I'd mosquitoed my way out not too badly, just about OK. I remember that the day was inclining towards evening. I'd got separated from the *kombrig*, and only about five Cossacks of the proletariat were tagging along after me. Around me men were fighting with their arms round each other like priests with their wives, the blood was dripping out of me little by little, my horse was getting wet in front . . . In a word – two words . . .

Spirka Zabuty and I sped off as far as possible from the woods, we looked – and there was a nice bit of arithmetic . . . About three hundred sagenes away, no more, we could see the dust rising into the air from something that was either the staff or a transport. The staff would be OK, a transport even better. The lads' gear had got a bit ragged, and they had these little shirts that didn't even come down over their sexual maturity.

'Zabuty,' I said to Spirka, 'go f— your mother, I give you the floor, as a practised orator – I mean, that's their staff pulling out, isn't it . . .?'

'Of course it's their staff,' said Spirka. 'Only thing is – there's two of us and eight of them.'

'Blow wind, Spirka,' I said. 'All the same, I'm going to put some muck on their chasubles for them . . . Let's die for a pickled cucumber and the world revolution . . .'

And off we went. There were eight of them with swords. Two of them we unseated with our rifles. A third I saw Spirka take to Dukhonin's staff* to have his documents checked. And I went for the big shot. He was a crimson big shot, lads, with a chain and a gold watch. I squeezed him up against a farmhouse. The farm there was all apple trees and cherry trees. My big shot had a horse under him like a merchant's daughter, but it was tired. Then the *pan* general dropped his reins, aimed his Mauser at me and made a hole in my leg.

'Right,' I thought, 'you shall be mine, you're for it.'

I got a move on and put two rounds into the little horse. I felt sorry about that stallion. He was a little Bolshevik, that stallion, a real little Bolshevik. Red as a copper coin, a tail like a bullet, legs like strings. I'd planned to take him to Lenin alive, but it didn't work out. I liquidated that little horse. It tumbled down like a bride, and my big shot fell out of the saddle. He pulled himself to one side, then turned round one more time and made another hole in my body for the breeze to blow through. That meant that now I'd got three marks of distinction fighting the enemy.

'Jesus,' I thought, 'I bet he goes and kills me by accident . . .'

I galloped up to him, but he'd already whipped his sword out, and the tears were flowing down his cheeks. White tears, the milk of man.

'You'll get me the Order of the Red Banner,' I shouted. 'Surrender, Your Excellency, while I'm alive . . .'

'Can't do that, *pan*,' the old man answered. 'You'd better kill me . . .'

And there was Spiridon before me, like a leaf before the grass. He was in a lather, his eyes were popping out of his head.

'Vásya,' he shouted to me, 'you'd never believe the number of chaps I've put an end to! Here, that's a general you've got there, he's got the embroidery on him, I desire to put an end to him.'

'Go to the Turk,' I said to Zabuty, losing my temper. 'His embroidery has cost me blood.'

And with my mare I edged my general into a threshing barn; there was hay in there, or something. There was quiet in there, darkness, coolness.

'*Pan*,' I say, 'make life easy for yourself in your old age. Now for God's sake surrender to me, and you and I can relax, *pan* . . .'

But he was panting away against the wall, rubbing his forehead with a red finger.

'Can't do that,' he said. 'You'd better kill me. I will only give up my sword to Budyonny . . .'

He wants Budyonny. Ach, just my luck! Then the old fellow's number is up.

'Sir' I shout, wailing and gnashing my teeth, 'word of the proletariat, I myself am the commander-in-chief here. Don't go looking for the embroidery on me, 'cos I ain't got none, but I have got a title. My title is "musical eccentric and salon ventriloquist from the town of Nizhny . . . the town of Nizhny on the River Volga . . ."'

And the devil put me in a lather. The general's eyes winked like lamps in front of me. Before me a red sea opened. Resentment got into my wound like salt, for I could see that the old man didn't believe me. Then I shut my mouth, lads, tucked in my belly, breathed in and cursed in the old way, our way, the way of the fighting men, the way of Nizhny Novgorod, and I proved to the Pole that I was a ventriloquist.

At that the old man went white, grabbed at his heart and sat down on the ground.

'Now do you believe Vaska the eccentric, commissar of the Third Invincible Cavalry Brigade?'

'A commissar?' he shouted.

'That's right,' I said.

'A communist?' he shouted.

'That's right,' I said.

'At the hour of my death,' he shouted, 'as I take my last breath, tell me, my friend Cossack – are you really a communist?'

'That's right,' I said.

At that the old man sat up on the ground, kissed some incense-bag he had round his neck, broke his sword in two and lit two lampions in his eyes, two lamps above the dark steppe.

'Forgive me,' he said, 'I cannot surrender to a communist,' and he took my hand. 'Forgive me,' he said, 'and kill me in soldierly fashion . . .'

This story was told to us one day, with his usual buffoonery, during a halt, by Konkin the political commissar of the N— Cavalry Brigade, three times decorated with the Order of the Red Banner.

'And what did you agree with the *pan*, Vaska?'

'There was no agreeing anything with him . . . He turned out to be a stickler for honour. I greeted him again, but he was obstinate. Then we took his papers from him, what he had, we took his Mauser, his saddle, the funny old guy, and it's under me now. And then I looked – the blood was dripping out of me faster and faster, a terrible sleep was coming down over me, my boots were full of blood, I wasn't thinking about him . . .'

'So they lightened the old man's load?'

'It was a sin . . .'

Beresteczko

We were on the march from Khotin to Beresteczko. The men were drowsing in their high saddles. A song murmured like a stream running dry. Monstrous corpses lay about on burial mounds a thousand years old. Muzhiks in white shirts bowed to us ingratiatingly. The felt cloak of our *nachdiv*, Pavlichenko, fluttered above the staff officers like a dismal flag. His soft hood was thrown back over his cloak, and his curved sabre lay at his side as though it had been stuck on with glue.

We rode past the Cossack burial mounds and the tower of Bogdan Khmelnitsky.* From behind a gravestone an old man with a bandore* crept out and sang to us in a childlike voice of bygone Cossack glory. We listened to the song in silence, then unfurled our standards and burst into Beresteczko to the strains of a thundering march. The inhabitants had placed iron bars over their shutters, and silence, sovereign silence, had ascended her *shtetl* throne.

I ended up billeted in the house of a red-haired widow who smelled of widows' grief. I washed off the grime of the journey, and went out into the street. On the noticeboards were bills saying that the divisional military commissar Vino-gradov would that evening deliver a lecture on the Second Congress of the Comintern.* Directly under my window several Cossacks were shooting an old Jew with a silvery beard for espionage. The old man was screaming and trying to tear himself free. Then Kudrya from the machine-gun detachment took the old man's head and put it under his arm. The Jew calmed down and stood with his legs apart. With his right hand Kudrya pulled out his dagger and carefully cut the old man's throat, without splashing any blood on himself. Then he knocked on the closed window frame.

'If anyone's interested,' he said, 'they can come and get him. He's all yours . . .'

And the Cossacks turned the corner. I walked on after them and began to roam about Beresteczko. Most of the people here are Jews, but on the edges of the *shtetl* Russian artisan tanners have settled here and there. They live cleanly in white cottages behind white shutters. Instead of vodka the artisans drink beer or mead, cultivate tobacco in small front gardens and smoke it in long, curved chibouks, like the peasants of Galicia. The presence of three races, all of them active and businesslike, has made them dogged workers – sometimes a characteristic of the Russian when he has not yet acquired lice, taken to despair and drunk himself stupid.

The traditions of daily life had disappeared in Beresteczko, but they were solid here. Shoots that were over three centuries old still sprouted green in Volhynia from the warm mould of antiquity. Here with the threads of profit the Jews bound the Russian muzhik to the Polish *pan*, the Czech migrant settler to the Lodz factory. They were smugglers, the best on the frontier, and nearly always warriors of the faith. Hassidism held this bustling population of innkeepers, pedlars and brokers in stifling captivity. Boys in capotes still trod the the age-old road to the Hassidic *kheder*,* and old women drove their daughters-in-law to the *tsadik* with impassioned prayers for fertility.*

The Jews here live in spacious houses that have been daubed with white or watery-blue paint. The traditional poverty of the architecture goes back for centuries. Behind the house there invariably stretches a shed of two, sometimes three, storeys. These sheds never get any sun. Indescribably gloomy, they take the place of our yards. Secret passages lead to basements and stables. In time of war people take refuge in these catacombs from bullets and marauders. Here human waste and the dung of cattle pile up over many days. Dejection and horror fill the catacombs with a pungent stench and the rotten sourness of faeces.

Beresteczko stinks inviolably even to this day; from all and sundry a smell of rotten herring smites the nostrils. The *shtetl* stinks in expectation of a new era, and through it, instead of people, walk the faded plans of ill-conceived frontiers. By the end of the day I was sick of them. I walked out beyond the edge of the town and penetrated the ravaged castle of the Counts Raciborski, the recent owners of Beresteczko.

The tranquillity of the sunset had turned the grass near the castle blue. Above the pond had risen a moon green as a lizard. From the window I could see the estate of the Counts Raciborski – meadows and plantations of hops, concealed by the moiré ribbons of the dusk.

In the castle, earlier, there had lived a mad, ninety-year-old countess and her son. She had jeered at her son because he had given their dying stock no heirs, and – the muzhiks swore to me – the countess had beaten her son with her coachman's knout.

Below on the square a meeting was under way. Peasants, Jews and tanners from the outlying district had come there on foot. Above them had flared the ecstatic voice of Vinogradov and the clink of his spurs. He was speaking about the Second Congress of the Comintern, but I was roaming along walls where nymphs with hollow eyes were treading an ancient round dance. Then in a corner on the trampled floor I found the yellowed scrap of a letter. On it in faded ink was written: 'Berestetchko, 1820. Paul, mon bien aimé, on dit que l'empereur Napoléon est mort, est-ce vrai? Moi, je me sens bien, les couches ont été faciles, notre petit héros achève sept semaines . . .'

And below, the voice of the commissar talks on without

cease. He is passionately trying to convince the puzzled artisans and robbed Jews:

'You are the powers in charge. All that is here is yours. There are no gentry. I now pass on to the election to the Revolutionary Committee ...'

Salt

DEAR COMRADE EDITOR

I want to write to you about unconscious women who are harmful to us. The men hope and trust that, while you were travelling around the citizens' fronts, as you have made note, you did not miss the hardened station of Fastov, which is situated at the other end of the world, in a certain land, at an unknown distance; I have, of course, been there, and drunk home-brewed beer, wetting my whiskers but not my mouth. Concerning this above-mentioned station there are many things to write, but as we say in our simple way – you can't clear up the Lord's dirt for him. So I shall write to you only about what my eyes have seen with their own hands.

It was a quiet, glorious night seven days ago when our honoured cavalry train stopped there, loaded with fighting men. We were all burning to promote the common cause and had Berdichev as our destination. Only thing was, we noticed that our train wouldn't pull out, not for nobody's business, our Gavrilka wouldn't turn, and the men began to get worried, talking among themselves – what was the stop here for? And right enough, the stop turned out to be enormous for the common cause on occasion of the fact that the black-market traders, those vicious enemies, among whom there was also a countless number of the female sex, were acting in an insolent manner with the railway authorities. Fearlessly they grabbed hold of the handrails, those wicked enemies, they scooted over the iron roofs, romping around and stirring up trouble, and in each and every hand you could see the not-unfamiliar salt, sacks of up to five *poods*. But not for long did the capitalist triumph of the black-market traders last. The initiative of the soldiers, who clambered out of the wagon, gave the profaned authority of the railwaymen a chance to get some air in its belly. Only the females with their bags stayed around. Taking pity on them, the soldiers put some of the women in the goods vans, and some they didn't. In our wagon, belonging to the Second Platoon, there were two girls, as it turned out, and when the first bell went, an impressive-looking woman with a baby came over to us, saying:

'Let me on, kind Cossacks. All the war I've been suffering at stations with my babe-at-arms and now I want to see my husband, but because of the railway there's no way I can get to him. Haven't I deserved it of you?'

'Now, woman,' I said to her, 'whatever the platoon agrees, that's what we'll do.' And, turning to the platoon, I verified to them that the impressive-looking woman was requesting a ride to the place of destination of her husband and she really did have a bairn with her and what were they going to agree – to let her on or not?

'Let her on,' the lads shouted, 'after she's had us she won't want her husband . . .'

'Well,' I said to the lads, politely enough. 'I bow to you, platoon, only it surprises me to hear such stallion talk from you. Think of your own lives, platoon, and recall that you yourselves were babies in your mothers' arms once. It won't do to talk that way . . .'

And the Cossacks, saying to one another what a persuasive fellow he was, Balmashov, began to let the woman into the wagon, and she climbed in with gratitude. And each one of them, all a-boil with the truth of my words, found a seat for her, saying in eager rivalry:

'Sit down in the corner, woman, be nice to your little baby

in the way that mothers are, nobody's going to touch you in the corner, and you will reach your husband untouched, as you desire, and we're relying on your conscience to raise some new recruits for us, 'cos the old ones are getting older and as you can see there's not much young blood about. We have seen a lot of trouble, woman, both among the active and the re-enlisted, hunger has squeezed us, cold has burned us. But you sit here, woman, and have no fear . . .'

And when the third bell rang, the train moved off. And the glorious night spread itself over us like a marquee. And in that marquee there were stars like lanterns. And the men remembered the nights of Kuban and the green Kuban stars. And the thoughts flew by like birds. And the wheels went clackety-clack, clackety-clack . . .

After some time had passed, when the night was relieved at its post and the Red drummers had begun to beat the reveille on their Red drums, then the Cossacks came up to me, seeing that I was sitting there not sleeping and lonely as hell.

'Balmashov,' the Cossacks said to me, 'what are you doing sitting there all alone and not asleep?'

'Low do I bow to you, fighting men, and I ask your pardon, but allow me to have a couple of words with that citizeness . . .'

And trembling all over, I rose from my reclining bower, from which the sleep had fled like a wolf from a pack of evil hounds, I walked over to her and took the bairn from her arms and tore the swaddling off it and the rags and saw underneath the swaddling a good little *pood* of salt.

'Here's an interesting bairn, comrades, one that doesn't ask for a tit, doesn't pee on your skirt and doesn't wake up in the night . . .'

'Forgive me, kind Cossacks,' the woman says, butting into our conversation very cool-headed like. 'It was not I that deceived you – it was my trouble that deceived you.'

'Balmashov will forgive your trouble,' I reply to the

woman. 'It's not much cost to Balmashov. For what Balmashov buys he sells again. But turn around, woman, and take a look at the Cossacks who have raised you up on high as a toiling mother of the Republic. Turn around and look at those two girls who are crying because we have made them suffer this night. Turn around and look at our wives in the wheatfields of the Kuban who are exhausting their womanly strength without husbands, and those others, who are also on their own, who from evil necessity are raping the girls that pass into their lives ... But nobody has laid a finger on you, wretched woman, though they should have done. Turn around and look at Russia, overwhelmed by suffering ...'

And she to me:

'I have been deprived of my salt. I'm not frightened of the truth. You don't care about Russia, you're just saving the Yids Lenin and Trotsky ...'

'We're not talking about the Yids just now, you harmful citizeness. The Yids don't come into it. By the way, I will not speak for Lenin, but Trotsky is the desperate son of a Tambov governor and he joined the toiling class though he came from another class. Like men sentenced to hard labour they — Lenin and Trotsky — are leading us out on to the free road of life, while you, you vile woman, are more of a counter-revolutionary than the White general who threatens us with a sharp sabre, riding a horse that cost thousands ... He can be seen, that general, from every road, and the toiler cherishes his dream of cutting his throat, while you, countless citizenry with your interesting little children that don't ask for bread and don't go running in the wind — you cannot be seen, you're like a flea, and you bite, bite, bite ...'

And truly, I confess, I threw that woman off, down beside the rails, but she, being very coarse, just sat and waved her skirts, and then went her own little low-down way. And, when I saw that woman unharmed, with untold Russia all around her, and the peasants' fields without an ear of corn, and the violated girls, and the comrades many of whom go to the front but few come back, I wanted to jump down from the wagon and kill myself or kill her. But the Cossacks had pity on me and said:

'Give her one from your rifle.'

And taking my trusty rifle from the wall, I wiped that infamy from the face of the working land and the Republic.

And we, the fighting men of the Second Platoon, swear before you, dear comrade editor, and before you, dear comrades of the editorial office, that we will deal mercilessly with all traitors who haul us into a pit and want to turn back the tide and strew Russia with corpses and dead grass.

For all the fighting men of the Second Platoon –
NIKITA BALMASHOV, SOLDIER OF THE REVOLUTION.

Evening

Oh, Rules of the Russian Communist Party. Through the sour dough of Russian narratives you have laid impetuous rails. Three bachelor hearts with the passions of Ryazan Christs, you have converted into writers for the *Red Trooper* newspaper, have done this so that each day they may write a rollicking newspaper full of courage and coarse good spirits.

Galin with his wall-eye, the consumptive Slinkin, Sychov with his rotten intestines – they are plodding along in the barren dust of the rear, spreading the mutiny and fire of their broadsheets through the ranks of pensioned-off Cossacks, the reserve pilferers who are listed as Polish interpreters and the young girls who are sent to our Politotdel train from Moscow to be put back on the straight and narrow.

Only towards nightfall is the newspaper ready – a dynamite fuse placed under the army. In the sky the squint-eyed lamp of the provincial sun is extinguished, the lights of the printing coach, scattering, blaze uncontrollably, like the passion of a machine. And then, towards midnight, Galin comes out of the coach in order to explore the wound of his unrequited love for the train laundress, Irina.

'Last time,' says Galin, narrow in the shoulders, pale, unseeing, 'last time, Irina, we examined the shooting of Nicholas the Bloody, who was executed by the proletariat of Yekaterinburg. Now we shall go on to other tyrants who died the deaths of dogs. Peter III was strangled by Orlov, his wife's lover, Paul was torn to pieces by courtiers, and his son, Nicholas Palkin, poisoned himself, his son fell on the first of March, and his grandson died of drink* ... You need to know those things, Irina ...'

And, raising to the laundress an eye full of naked adoration, Galin indefatigably stirs up the burial vaults of emperors gone to their doom. Round-shouldered, he is bathed in the light of the moon that sticks out up there like a cheeky splinter: the printing presses hammer away somewhere close to him and the radio station shines with a pure radiance. Rubbing against the shoulder of the cook, Vasily, Irina listens to the obscure and preposterous muttering of love; above her in the black seaweed of the sky trail the stars, the laundress drowses, makes the sign of the cross over her pouting mouth and looks at Galin wide-eyed. Thus does a girl who thirsts for the inconveniences of conception look at a professor who is devoted to learning.

And next to Irina yawns the heavy-jowled Vasily, who views mankind with disdain, as do all cooks. Cooks – they have much to do with the flesh of dead animals and with the appetites of live ones, and so in politics cooks seek things that do not concern them. Thus, too, Vasily, the heavy-jowled conqueror. Pulling his trousers up to his nipples, he asks Galin about the civil lists of various kinds, the dowry for the daughters of the tsars, and then says, yawning, 'It's night-time, Arisha, and tomorrow will be a long day. Come and crush the fleas ...'

And they closed the kitchen door, leaving Galin alone with the moon that stuck out up there like a cheeky splinter . . . And, facing the moon, on the slope by the pond that had fallen asleep, I sat wearing my spectacles, with boils on my neck and my feet in bandages. With confused, poet's brains I was digesting the class struggle, when Galin came up to me with his gleaming wall-eyes.

'Galin,' I said, overcome by self-pity and loneliness, 'I'm ill, it's clear that my end has come, Galin, and I'm tired of living in the Cavalry Army . . .'

'You're a driveller,' Galin replied, and the watch on his thin wrist showed one o'clock in the morning. 'You're a driveller and it's our bad luck to have to put up with you drivellers . . . The whole Party is wearing aprons that are smeared with blood and shit, we peel the shell from the kernel for you; after a little time has passed you will see that shelled kernel, and then you will take your finger out of your nose and will sing the glories of the new life in remarkable prose; but for the moment sit quiet, driveller, and don't whine in our way . . .'

He moved closer to me, adjusted the bandages that were coming apart on my scabby wounds, and lowered his head on to his pigeon chest. The night consoled us in our sorrows, a light wind fanned us like a mother's skirt, and the grasses below gleamed with dewy freshness.

The thundering of the train printing press shrank to a squeak and then fell silent, the dawn drew a line near the edge of the earth, the door to the kitchen squeaked and opened a little way. Four feet with fat heels were thrust out into the coolness, and we saw Irina's loving calves and Vasily's big toe with its black and crooked toenail.

'Vasilyok,' the woman whispered in the intimate, sinking accents of a Russian, 'get out of my bed, trouble-maker . . .'

But Vasily merely jerked his heels and moved closer.

'The Cavalry Army,' Galin said to me then, 'the Cavalry

Army is a social focus produced by the Central Committee of our party. The curve of the revolution has thrown to the fore Cossack freebooters who are steeped in many prejudices, but the Central Committee will, by manoeuvring, tear through them like an iron brush . . .'

And Galin began to talk about the political education of the First Cavalry Army. He talked for a long time, in a muffled voice, with perfect clarity. His eyelid twitched above his wall-eye, and the blood trickled from my lacerated palms.

Kovel, 1920

Afonka Bida

We were fighting near Leszniów. The wall of the enemy cavalry was appearing everywhere. The spring of the Polish strategy now being established was uncoiling with an ominous whistle. We were being squeezed. For the first time in the whole campaign we could feel at our backs the devilish sharpness of breaches in the rear and of flank attacks – the merciless bites of the weapon which had served us so long and so happily.

The front at Leszniów was held by the infantry. Along crookedly dug trenches loafed Whitish, unshod Volhynian muzhiks. These men had been taken from the plough the day before in order to form foot reserves for the Cavalry Army. The peasants had come with a will. They fought with the greatest assiduity. Their puffing Cossack ferocity amazed even the Budyonny men. Their hatred for the Polish landowner was made of unassuming but durable material.

In the second period of the war, when whooping had ceased to have any effect on the imagination of the enemy and cavalry attacks on an entrenched adversary had become impossible, this homespun infantry would have brought the Cavalry Army great advantage. But our destitution got the upper hand. The muzhiks were given one rifle between three and cartridges of the wrong size. The undertaking had to be called off, and this authentic people's volunteer corps was disbanded and sent home.

Now let us turn to the fighting at Leszniów. The foot soldiers had dug themselves in three versts from the town. In front of their front line a stoop-shouldered youth in spectacles was walking up and down. At his side dangled a sword. He was moving along in starts, with a discontented air, as though his boots were pinching him. This muzhik commander, who had been chosen by them and was loved by them, was a Jew, a weak-sighted Jewish youth, with the unhealthy-looking and studious face of a Talmudist. In battle he manifested the circumspect courage and cool-headedness of a distracted dreamer.

It was the third hour of a long July afternoon. In the air shone an iridescent gossamer of heat. Beyond the hills flashed a festive band of full-dress coats and horses' manes braided with ribbons. The youth gave the signal to get ready. The muzhiks, slapping along in their bast sandals, ran to their posts and held their guns at the ready. But it proved to be a false alarm. Maslak's flowery squadrons were coming out on to the Leszniów road. Their emaciated but cheerful horses were going at a round pace. On gilded poles weighed down by velvet tassels, in fiery pillars of dust, sumptuous standards swayed. The horsemen rode with a majestic and insolent coldness. Dishevelled foot soldiers crawled out of their trenches and, mouths agape, followed the resilient elegance of this unswift flood.

At the head of the regiment, on a bow-legged little horse, rode *kombrig* Maslak, full of drunken blood and the rottenness of his own fatty juices. His stomach, like a large tomcat, lay on the silver pommel. At the sight of the foot soldiers he turned a merry purple and beckoned the platoon commander, Afonka Bida, to him. We called the platoon commander 'Makhno'* on account of the likeness he bore to the renowned leader. They whispered for a minute, the commander and Afonka. Then the platoon commander turned to the First Squadron, bent forward and gave the quiet command, 'Give rein!' Platoon by platoon, the Cossacks moved into a trot. They drove their horses into a passion and tore over to the trenches, out of which the foot soldiers were staring, over-joyed by the spectacle.

'Prepare for battle!' sang the mournful and almost remote voice of Afonka.

Maslak, wheezing, coughing and enjoying himself, rode off to the side; the Cossacks hurled themselves into the attack. The poor foot soldiers ran for it, but too late. Cossack lashes were already flailing up and down their ragged coats. The horsemen circled about the field, twirling their whips in their hands with uncommon skill.

'What are you playing around for?' I shouted to Afonka.

'For fun,' he replied to me, fidgeting about in his saddle, as he retrieved from a bush a young lad who had hidden himself there.

'For fun!' he shouted, as he jabbed at the frenzied lad.

The fun came to an end when Maslak, mollified and majestic, waved his podgy hand.

'That'll teach you to keep a better look-out, foot soldiers,' Afonka shouted, superciliously straightening his puny body. 'Go and catch fleas, foot soldiers . . .'

The Cossacks, exchanging smiles, assembled in ranks. As for the foot soldiers, the bird had flown. The trenches were empty. And only the stoop-shouldered Jew stood in his previous place, peering at the Cossacks attentively and haught-ily.

The firing from the direction of Leszniów did not let up. The Poles were surrounding us. Through binoculars the separate figures of the mounted scouts were visible. They were galloping out of the town and disappearing like weighted, wobbling toys. Maslak formed up the squadrons and scattered them on both sides of the highway. Above Leszniów a glittering sky had arisen, inexpressibly empty, as always at hours of danger. The Jew, throwing his head back, mournfully and violently whistled on his metal pipe. And the foot soldiers, those unique and well-whipped foot soldiers, returned to their posts.

Bullets were flying thickly in our direction. The brigade headquarters had come within range of the machine-guns. We rushed into the wood and began to tear our way through the bushes along the right-hand side of the road. The machine-gunned branches groaned fretfully above us. By the time we managed to get out of the bushes, the Cossacks were no longer in their former places. On the *nachdiv's* orders they had withdrawn towards Brody. Only the muzhiks snarled sparse shots from their trenches, and the lagging Afonka was catching up with his platoon.

He was riding on the very edge of the road, looking around him and and sniffing the air. For a moment, the firing died away. The Cossack decided to take advantage of the breathing-space and moved off at full gallop. At that moment a bullet punctured the neck of his horse. Afonka rode on for some hundred yards, and then, in our ranks, the horse meekly bent its forelegs and fell to the ground.

Unhurriedly, Afonka extricated his crushed leg from the stirrup. He squatted down and dug about in the wound with a copper-coloured finger. Then Bida straightened up and took in the gleaming horizon with a wearied gaze.

'Farewell, Stepan,' he said in a wooden voice, stepped back from the expiring beast and bowed to it from the waist. 'How will I return to the quiet settlement without you? What will I do with your embroidered saddle? Farewell, Stepan,' he repeated more loudly, choked, squeaked like a caught mouse, and began to howl. The bubbling howl reached our ears, and we saw Afonka bowing like a hysterical peasant woman in church. 'Well, I won't submit to selfish fate!' he shouted, taking his hands away from his deathly pale face. 'I shall cut down the unspeakable Poles without mercy! To the last gasp, to the last of their blood and the blood of the Mother of God . . . In front of the men of the settlement, dear brothers, I promise you, Stepan . . .'

Afonka lay down with his face to the wound and fell silent. Turning a deep, shining, violet eye on its master, the horse listened to Afonka's painful wheeze. In tender oblivion it drew its fallen muzzle over the ground, and the streams of blood, like two ruby-red ribbons, trickled down the white muscles of its breast.

Afonka lay without stirring. Delicately picking his way on his fat legs, Maslak walked up to the horse, put his revolver in its ear and fired. Afonka leapt up and turned to Maslak a terrible, pock-marked face.

'Gather up the harness, Afanasy,' Maslak said gently, 'and go to your unit . . .'

And from the slope we saw Afonka, bent under the weight of the saddle, with a face moist and red as cut meat, stroll off to his squadron, boundlessly alone in the dusty, blazing desert of the fields.

Late in the evening I encountered him at the transport unit. He was sleeping on a cart that contained his property — swords, field jackets and gold coins with holes in them. The platoon commander's blood-caked head with its twisted, dead mouth flopped as though crucified on the bend of the saddle. Beside him was placed the harness of the dead horse, and the intricate and fanciful garb of a Cossack steed — breastplates with black tassels, supple harness studded with coloured stones and a bridle embossed with silver.

The darkness was growing thicker and thicker. The transport crawled viscously along the road to Brody; modest stars rolled along the milky ways of heaven, and far-off villages burned in the cool depth of the night. Assistant squadron commander Orlov and the long-moustached Bitsenko were sitting right there in Afonka's cart and discussing Afonka's plight.

'He brought that horse from home,' said Bitsenko of the moustaches. 'Where will he find another horse like that?'

'A horse – it is a friend,' replied Orlov.

'A horse – it is a father,' sighed Bitsenko. 'It saves your life countless times. A fat lot Bida will be able to do without a horse.'

But by morning Afonka had vanished. The fighting at Brody began and ended. Defeat was replaced by temporary victory, we experienced a change of *nachdiv*, but still there was no sign of Afonka. And only the ominous grumbling in the villages indicated the vicious, predatory trail of Afonka's brigandage.

'He's procuring a horse,' was what was said in the squadron, and during the immense evenings of our wanderings I heard not a few stories about this fierce, lonely quest.

Men from other units stumbled on Afonka a few dozen versts from our position. He had been lying in ambush waiting for Polish cavalrymen who had got left behind, or scouring the woods, tracking down hidden herds of peasant horses. He had been setting fire to villages and shooting Polish headmen for receiving stolen goods. To our admiring ears came echoes of this furious single-handed combat, echoes of the desperate and thievish attack of a solitary wolf upon a leviathan.

Another week passed. The bitter concerns of the day replaced the stories of Afonka's gloomy daring in our conversation, and 'Makhno' began to be forgotten. After that a rumour went round that he had been slaughtered by Galician peasants somewhere in the woods. And on the day of our entry into Beresteczko, Yemelyan Budyak of the First Squadron, making no bones about it, went to the *nachdiv* to ask him for Afonka's saddle with its yellow saddlecloth. Yemelyan intended to go on parade with a new saddle, but he did not get the chance.

We entered Beresteczko on 6 August. At the head of our division moved a quilted Asiatic coat and the knee-length coat of the new *nachdiv*. Levka, the crazy lickspittle, led a stud mare along behind the *nachdiv*. A battle march, full of long-drawn-out menace, flew along the pretentious, destitute streets. Ramshackle cul-de-sacs, a painted forest of decrepit and twisted cross-beams, lay all over the little town. Its heartwood, eaten away by time, breathed a melancholy decay over us. Smugglers and pious hypocrites hid away in their roomy, twilit *izbas*. Only Pan Ludomirski, the bell ringer, in a green frock-coat, greeted us outside the church.

We crossed the river and passed deep into the artisans' quarter. We were approaching the house of the priest when round a corner, on a burly grey stallion, rode Afonka.

'My compliments,' he said in a baying voice and, shoving the men apart, took his place in the ranks.

Maslak fixed his eyes on the colourless distance and wheezed, without turning round, 'Where did you get the horse?'

'It's my own,' Afonka replied, rolling a cigarette and wetting it with a brief movement of his tongue.

The Cossacks rode up to him one after the other and said hello to him. In the place where his left eye had been a monstrous pink swelling shone repulsively on his charred face.

And next morning Bida went on the spree. In the church he smashed the shrine of St Valentine and attempted to play the organ. He had on a jacket cut from blue carpet with a lily embroidered on its back, and his sweaty forelock was combed over his missing eye.

After dinner he saddled up his horse and fired his rifle at

the shattered windows of the castle of the Counts Raciborski. The Cossacks stood around him in a semicircle. They tugged at the stallion's tail, felt its legs and counted its teeth.

'A fine mount,' said Orlov, the squadron commander's assistant.

'A horse in good nick,' the long-moustached Bitsenko confirmed.

At St Valentine's

Our division occupied Beresteczko last night. The staff has put up in the house of the Roman Catholic priest Tuzinkiewicz. Dressed up as a woman, Tuzinkiewicz fled from Beresteczko before the entry of our troops. Of him I know that he busied himself with God in Beresteczko for about forty-five years, and was a good priest. When the inhabitants want us to grasp this, they say that the Jews loved him. During Tuzinkiewicz's time the old Roman Catholic church was restored. The repair work was finished on the day of the church's three-hundredth anniversary. On that day the Bishop came from Zhitomir. Prelates in silk cassocks held a service in front of the church. Large of belly, soft and pleasing, they stood like bells in the dewy grass. From neighbouring villages flowed the obedient rivers. The muzhik knee was bent, there was kissing of hands and in the heavens that day there flamed unprecedented clouds. Heavenly flags flew in honour of the old church. The Bishop himself kissed Tuzinkiewicz on the forehead and named him Father of Beresteczko, *pater Beresteckae.*

I learned this story in the morning at staff headquarters, where I was looking through a report from our flank column, which had been out on reconnaissance in Lwow, in the Radzichow district. I read the documents, and the snoring of the orderlies behind my back spoke of our never-ending homelessness. The scribes, damp with insomnia, were writing orders for the division, eating cucumbers and sneezing. Only when I became free, at noon, did I walk over to the window and see the church of Beresteczko – mighty and white. It shone in the tepid sunshine like a porcelain tower. The lightnings of noon gleamed in its lustrous sides. Their convex line began among the ancient green of the cupolas and ran lightly downwards. Pink veins smouldered in the white stone of the pediment, and at the summit there were columns as slender as candles.

Then the singing of the organ struck my ears, and at once in the doorway of staff headquarters an old woman with flowing yellow hair appeared. She moved like a dog with a broken paw, wheeling round and limping over the ground. Her eyes were filled with the white moisture of blindness and were streaming with tears. The sounds of the organ, now dragging, now hurried, floated over to us. Their flight was difficult, their resonance plaintive and long-drawn-out. The old woman wiped away her tears with her yellow hair, sat down on the floor and began to kiss the knees of my boots. The organ fell silent and then burst into a bass guffaw. I seized the old woman by the arm and looked round. Clerks were hammering their typewriters, orderlies were snoring ever more exuberantly, their spurs cutting the thick felt under the velvet upholstery of the sofas. The old woman kissed my boots tenderly, embracing them as though they were an infant. I dragged her towards the way out and shut the door behind us. The church rose before us as dazzling as the scenery in a theatre. The side gate was open, and strewn on the graves of Polish officers were the skulls of horses.

We ran into the yard, went down a gloomy corridor and ended up in a rectangular room which had been built on to the chancel. There Sashka, a nurse of the 31st regiment, ran the show. She was rummaging about in some silks which had been thrown on the floor. A deathly aroma of brocade, of scattered flowers, of fragrant putrefaction streamed into her quivering nostrils, tickling and poisoning. Then some Cossacks came into the room. They began to hoot with laughter, grabbed Sashka by the arms and hurled her with all their might on to a heap of cloth and books. Sashka's body, blooming and stinking like the flesh of a cow that has just been slaughtered, was bared, her raised skirts revealed her squadron lady's legs, cast-iron, shapely legs, and Kurdyukov, the silly fellow, having sat down astride Sashka bouncing as if he were in the saddle, then pretended to be seized by passion. She threw him off and rushed to the door. And only then, crossing the chancel, did we get into the church.

It was full of light, this church, it was full of dancing beams, airy columns, a kind of cool rejoicing. How can I forget the picture that hung on the right side-chapel painted by Apolek? In this picture twelve rosy *paters* are rocking a chubby infant Jesus in a cradle entwined with ribbons. The toes of his feet are spread wide, his body is shining with a hot, matutinal sweat. The child lies on his plump, creased back and twelve apostles in cardinals' tiaras are bent over the cradle. Their faces have been shaven to the point of blueness, burning cloaks bulge out over their bellies. The apostles' eyes sparkle with wisdom, determination, gaiety; at the corners of their mouths hover thin, ironic smiles; on their double chins fiery warts have been planted, crimson warts like radishes in May.

In this Beresteczko church there was a peculiar, seductive view of the mortal sufferings of the sons of men. In this church saints went to their doom with the theatricality of Italian opera singers, and the executioners' black hair gleamed like the beard of Holofernes. Here, too, above the altar, I spotted a blasphemous painting of John that was also the work of Apolek's heretical and entrancing brush. In this painting the Baptist was beautiful, with that ambiguous and only half-expressed beauty for the sake of which the concubines of kings lose their half-lost honour and their blossoming lives.

Distracted by the memory of my daydreaming about Apolek, I did not notice the traces of destruction in the church, or else they did not seem great to me. The only thing that had been broken was the shrine of St Valentine. Pieces of mouldering cotton wool lay about beneath it and the ridiculous bones of the saint, which resembled more than anything else the bones of a chicken. And Afonka Bida was still playing the organ. He was drunk, Afonka, wild and badly cut about the body. Only yesterday had he returned to us with the horse he had taken from the muzhiks. Afonka was stubbornly attempting to pick out a march on the organ, and someone was remonstrating with him in a sleepy voice: 'Give it up, Afonka, let's go and get some grub.' But the Cossack would not give it up, and there were a lot of them, Afonka's songs. Each sound was a song, and all the sounds were separated one from the other. The song – its thick melody – would last for a moment and then pass into another ... I listened, looked around, and the traces of destruction did not seem very great to me. But that was not the view of Pan Ludomirski, the bell-ringer of St Valentine's and the husband of the old blind woman.

Ludomirski had crept out from somewhere. He had entered the church at an even pace, his head lowered. The old man could not bring himself to throw a sheet over the ejected relics, because a man of low rank is not permitted to touch holy things. The bell-ringer fell on the blue flagstones of the floor; he raised his head and his dark blue nose stood above him like a flag above a corpse. The dark blue nose quivered above him, and at that moment the velvet curtain by the altar began to undulate and, quivering, crept back to one side. In the depths of the niche that had been revealed, against the backdrop of a sky entirely furrowed with dark clouds, was a little bearded figure in an orange caftan, running – barefoot, with a lacerated and bleeding mouth. Then a hoarse wail rent my ears. We retreated with misgiving in the face of horror, horror overtook us and with dead fingers probed our hearts. I looked again: the man in the orange caftan was being pursued by hatred and was being overtaken by his pursuer. He raised his hand in order to ward off the blow that was being aimed at him, and the blood was flowing from his hand in a purple flood. The little Cossack who was standing beside me began to shout and, lowering his head, started to run off, even though there was nothing to flee from, because the figure in the niche was only Jesus Christ – the most unusual depiction of God of any I have seen in my life.

Pan Ludomirski's Saviour was a curly-headed little Yid with a small, tufted beard and a low, wrinkled forehead. His sunken cheeks were touched with carmine, and above his eyes, closed in pain, curved thin, ginger eyebrows.

His mouth was lacerated, like the lip of a horse, his Polish caftan was gathered in by a precious belt, and below the caftan writhed porcelain feet, painted, naked, cut to pieces by silver nails.

Pan Ludomirski stood beneath the statue in a green frock-coat. He raised a withered hand and cursed us. The Cossacks popped their eyes and spread out their straw-like forelocks. In a thunderous voice the bell-ringer of the church of St Valentine anathematized us in the purest Latin. Then he turned away, fell to his knees and embraced the legs of the Saviour.

Returning to my quarters at the staff HQ, I wrote a report to the divisional commander about an affront to the religious feelings of the local population. The order was given for the church to be closed, and the guilty persons, having been subjected to a disciplinary inquiry, were consigned to the jurisdiction of a military tribunal.

Beresteczko, August 1921

Squadron Commander Trunov

At noon we brought the bullet-riddled body of Trunov, our squadron leader, to Sokal. He was killed this morning in a battle with enemy planes. All the hits on Trunov were to his face, his cheeks were peppered with wounds, his tongue torn out. We washed the dead man's face as best we could, in order to make it look less fearsome. We put a Caucasian saddle at the head of the coffin and dug a grave in a ceremonial spot, in the public gardens, in the middle of town, right by the cathedral. At that spot our squadron assembled on horseback, together with the regimental staff and the division's military commissar. And at two o'clock by the cathedral clock our decrepit little cannon gave the first shot. It saluted the dead commander, our old three-inch cannon, it performed a complete salute, and we bore the coffin to the open pit. The lid of the coffin was open, the clean, midday sun lit the long corpse and its mouth, with its broken teeth, and the brushed boots, their heels placed together, as if on drill.

'Men,' said Pugachov, colonel of the regiment, looking at the dead man and stationing himself by the edge of the hole, 'men,' he said, trembling and standing erect with his hands on the seams of his trousers, 'let us bury Pasha Trunov, world hero, let us render Pasha the final honour . . .'

And, raising to heaven eyes that were red-hot with lack of sleep, Pugachov shouted out a speech about the dead fighters of the First Cavalry, about that proud phalanx that was beating the hammer of history on the anvil of the ages to come. Pugachov shouted his speech loudly, he clenched the handle of a curved Chechen cavalry sword and dug up the earth with his torn feet in silver spurs. After his speech the band played the Internationale and the Cossacks took their leave of Pashka Trunov. The entire squadron leapt onto their horses and fired a volley into the air, our three-incher mumbled a second time, and we sent three Cossacks for a wreath. They whirled away as fast as they were able, firing at full gallop, falling out of their saddles and giving a display of trick riding, and brought back whole handfuls of red flowers. Pugachov scattered the flowers beside the grave, and we began to go up to Trunov for the final kiss. I stood at the back, I touched with my lips the now serene forehead, surrounded by the saddle, and went off into the town, into Gothic Sokal, which lay in blue dust and invincible Galician dejection.

A large square stretched to the left of the gardens, a square built round with ancient synagogues. Jews in ragged frockcoats hurled abuse at one another in that square and in obscure blindness pulled each other about. Some of them, the Orthodox ones, were extolling the teaching of Adasia, rabbi of Belz, and for this they were being attacked by Hassidim of moderate persuasion, pupils of the Gusyatin rabbi, Judah. The Jews were arguing about the Kabbala, mentioning in their disputations the name of Elijah, the Vilna Gaon, the opponent of the Hassidim . . .*

'Elijah!' they shouted, twisting and writhing, and opening wide their beard-tangled mouths.

Having forgotten the war and the shooting, the Hassidim were reviling the very name of Elijah, the high priest of Vilna, and I, pining with sorrow for Trunov, I too jostled among them and for my own relief shouted along with them, until I beheld in front of me a Galician as tall and deathly pale as Don Quixote.

This Galician was dressed in a white shirt of coarse linen that reached down to his toes. He was dressed as though for a burial or for communion, leading on a rope a dishevelled little cow he had. On his gigantic torso he had the mobile, tiny, wholly shaven head of a snake; it was covered by a countryman's broad-brimmed straw hat which kept coming loose. The pathetic little cow followed the Galician on its rope: he led it self-importantly, intersecting with the gallows of his long bones the hot brilliance of the heavens.

At a solemn pace, avoiding the square, he went down a crooked side-lane steeped in thick, nauseous vapours. In wretched, charred little houses, in destitute kitchens Jewesses were fussing about, Jewesses who resembled old Negro women, Jewesses with outrageous breasts. The Galician went past them and stopped at the end of the lane by the pediment of a shattered building. There, by the pediment, by a white, warped pillar a gypsy blacksmith sat shoeing horses. The gypsy beat the hooves with a hammer, and kept shaking his greasy hair, whistling and smiling. A few Cossacks with horses stood around him. My Galician went up to the blacksmith; saying nothing, he gave him a dozen baked potatoes and, without looking at anyone, turned back. I was about to set off after him, for I could not understand what sort of a man he was and what kind of life he could lead here, in Sokal, but I was stopped by a Cossack who was holding an unshod horse at the ready. The name of this Cossack was Seliverstov. He had at some point left Makhno and was now serving in the 33rd Cavalry Regiment.

'Lyutov,' he said, greeting me by shaking my hand, 'you bully everybody, the devil is in you. Lyutov, why did you maim Trunov this morning? . . .'

And Seliverstov shouted at me a piece of stupid hearsay, pure preposterous nonsense about how I had allegedly beaten Trunov, my squadron leader. Seliverstov reproached me for this in every possible way, he reproached me in front of all the Cossacks, but there was no truth in his story. Trunov and I had quarrelled that morning, to be sure, because Trunov was forever wasting time with the prisoners; he and I had had a quarrel, but he is dead, Pashka, he will have no more judges in this world – I was the last of them all. This was why our quarrel had arisen:

We took today's prisoners at dawn, at Zawada station. There were ten of them. They were in their underwear when we took them. There was a pile of clothes beside the Poles – this was a ruse of theirs so that we should not be able to tell, by their uniforms, the officers from the men. They themselves had thrown off their clothes, but on this occasion Trunov decided to obtain the truth.

'Officers, step forward,' he commanded, going up to the prisoners and drawing his revolver.

Trunov had already been wounded in the head this morning; his head was bound with a cloth, the blood trickling from it like rain from a hayrick.

'Officers, confess,' he repeated and began to nudge the Poles with the butt of the revolver.

Then from the group there stepped forward a thin, old man with large bare bones on his back, yellow cheek-bones and a drooping moustache.

'This war finish,' said the old man with unintelligible rapture, 'all officers run away, this war finish . . .'

And the Pole stretched out his blue hands to the squadron leader.

'Five fingers,' he said, sobbing and twisting an enormous, flabby hand, 'with these five fingers I reared my family . . .'

The old man choked, began to sway, dissolved in rapturous tears and fell on his knees before Trunov, but Trunov warded him off with his sword.

'Your officers are reptiles,' said the squadron leader, 'your officers have thrown their clothes here . . . Whoever deserves punishment will get what's coming to him. I'm going to make a check . . .'

And there and then the squadron leader selected from the pile of clothes a cap with piping and pulled it over the old man's eyes.

'It fits,' muttered Trunov, moving closer and lisping slightly, 'it fits.' And he stuck his sword into the prisoner's gullet. The old man fell, his legs moved, and from his throat gushed a foaming coral stream. Then up to him stole, with a gleam of earring and round rustic neck, Andryushka Vosmiletov. Andryushka undid the Pole's buttons, shook him lightly and began to pull the trousers off the dying man. He threw them on to his saddle, took another two uniforms from the pile, and rode away from us, flicking his whip. At that moment the sun came out from behind the clouds. It swiftly surrounded Andryushka's horse, its spirited trot, the carefree swayings of its docked tail. Andryushka was riding along the path towards the forest; in the forest stood our transport, the drivers of the transport raging, whistling and making signs to Vosmiletov as though he were deaf and dumb.

The Cossack had already got halfway there, but then Trunov, suddenly falling to his knees, croaked after him:

'Andrey,' said the squadron leader, looking at the ground, 'Andrey,' he said again, still not raising his eyes from the ground, 'our Soviet Republic is still alive, it's too soon to divide it up. Drop the rags and bones, Andrey . . .'

But Vosmiletov did not even turn round. He went on riding at his astonishing Cossack trot, his little horse pertly throwing its tail out from under itself, as though brushing us aside.

'Treason,' Trunov muttered then, surprised. 'Treason,' he said. He hastily brought his carbine to his shoulder and fired, and in his hurry missed. But this time Andrey stopped. He turned the horse round towards us and began to bounce in the saddle like a woman; his face turned red and angry, and his legs started to jerk.

'Listen, fellow-countryman,' he shouted, riding up to the man, and he at once calmed down at the sound of his own deep and powerful voice. 'I ought really to send you to kingdom come, fellow-countryman . . . All you're supposed to do is clean up a dozen Poles and look at the panic you get into. We've each cleaned up a hundred – and we didn't ask for your assistance ... If you're a worker, then do your work ...'

And, throwing the trousers and the two uniforms off the saddle, Andryushka gave a snort and, turning away from the squadron leader, began to help me compile a list of the remaining prisoners. He hung about beside me, grunting extraordinarily loudly, and his fussing annoyed me. The prisoners howled and ran from Andryushka, and he ran after them and took them by the armful as a hunter takes an armful of reeds in order to get a proper view of a flock of birds that is flying towards a river at dawn.

In attending to the prisoners I exhausted all the curses and somehow managed to write down the names of eight men, the numbers of their units and the type of gun they had, and then passed on to the ninth. This ninth man was a young man who resembled a German gymnast from a good circus, a young man with a proud German chest and sideburns, wearing an open sleeveless jacket and a pair of Jäger drawers. He turned to me the two nipples on his high chest, tossed back his fair, sweaty hair and named his unit. Then Andryushka seized him by the drawers and sternly inquired:

'Where did you get the underwear?'

'My mother knitted it,' the prisoner replied, swaying.

'Your mother must be a manufacturer,' said Andryushka, still studying the drawers, and with the pads of his fingers he touched the Pole's well-manicured fingernails. 'Your mother must be a manufacturer; the likes of us didn't make stuff like that ...'

Again he felt the drawers and took the ninth man by the arm in order to lead him over to the other prisoners who had already had their names written down. At that moment, however, I saw Trunov crawling out from behind a hillock. Blood was trickling from the head of the squadron leader, like rain from a hayrick, his dirty bandage had come undone and was hanging down, he was crawling on his belly and held a carbine in his arms. It was a Japanese carbine, varnished and with a powerful charge. From twenty paces Pashka blew the youth's skull open, and his brains spattered my hands. Then Trunov ejected the cartridges from the gun and came over to me.

'Cross out one of them,' he said, pointing at the list.

'No, I won't,' I replied, shuddering. 'It's obvious that Trotsky doesn't write orders for you, Pavel . . .'

'Cross out one of them,' Trunov said again, poking a black finger at the sheet of paper.

'No, I won't!' I shouted with all my might. 'There were ten and now there are eight, and they won't want to know you at headquarters, Pashka . . .'

'At headquarters they'll see it in terms of the wretched life we lead,' Trunov replied, and he began to advance on me, torn all over, hoarse and covered in smoke, but then stopped, raised his bloodied head to the heavens and said, with bitter reproach, 'Buzz, buzz,' he said, 'and there's another one buzzing . . .'

And the squadron leader showed us four dots in the sky, four bombers sailing through the radiant, swan-like clouds. These were planes from the air squadron of Major Faunt Le Roy, large armoured planes.

'To horse!' the platoon commanders shouted, at the sight of them. They led the squadron over towards the forest at a trot, but Trunov did not go with his squadron. He remained near the station building, leaned against the wall and fell silent. Andryushka Vosmiletov and two machine-gunners, two barefoot lads in crimson riding-breeches, stood beside him, fussing anxiously.

'Cut a thread in your bores, lads,' Trunov said to them, and the blood began to drain from his face, 'here's a dispatch from me to the Pugach . . .'*

And in gigantic muzhik letters Trunov wrote on an obliquely torn-out sheet of paper:

'It being my duty to perish this day,' he wrote, 'I find it my duty to add two dead to the possible defeat of the enemy and at the same time give command to Semyon Golov, the platoon commander . . .'

He sealed the letter, sat down on the ground and, putting his back into the job, pulled off his boots.

'Make good use of them,' he said, giving the machine-gunners the dispatch and the boots. 'Make good use of them, those boots are new . . .'

'Good luck to you, commander,' the machine-gunners muttered back to him, shifting from leg to leg and delaying their departure.

'And good luck to you,' said Trunov, 'one way or the other, lads,' and he walked towards the machine-gun that stood on a hillock near the station hut. There waiting for him was Andryushka Vosmiletov, the rag-and-bone man.

'One way or the other,' Trunov said to him, proceeding to aim the machine-gun, 'are you going to stay with me for a bit, eh, Andrey? . . .'

'Oh Lord Jesus,' Andryushka replied fearfully, uttered a sob, turned white and began to laugh, 'by the banner of the mother of Lord Jesus! . . .'

And he began to aim the second machine-gun at the planes.

But the planes had begun to climb ever more steeply above the station, they crackled fussily in the heights, descended, described arcs, and the sun lay, a pink ray, on the yellow lustre of their wings.

By now we, the fourth squadron, were in the forest. There in the forest we waited for the end of the unequal battle between Pashka Trunov and the American airforce major, Reginald Faunt Le Roy.* The major and his three bomb-throwers displayed great ability in this battle. They descended to three hundred metres and blasted first Andryushka and then Trunov with their machine-guns. None of the many cartridges discharged by our men caused the Americans any harm; they flew off to the side without noticing the squadron that was hidden in the forest. And so, after half an hour's wait, we were able to go and collect the corpses. The body of Andryushka Vosmiletov was picked up by two relatives of his who served in our squadron, while Trunov, our dead commander, we took to Gothic Sokal and buried him in a ceremonial spot there, in the public gardens, in a flower-bed, in the middle of the town.

The Ivans

Deacon Ageyev had fled from the front twice. For this he was transferred to the Moscow 'branded'* regiment. The commander-in-chief Kamenev*, Sergey Sergeich, inspected this regiment in Mozhaysk before it was dispatched to its position.

'I don't need them,' said the commander-in-chief, 'Send them back to Moscow, to clean latrines.'

In Moscow the 'branded' men had somehow been licked into a draft company. The deacon had ended up among their number. He arrived at the Polish front and there claimed to have gone deaf. The medical assistant Barsutsky, from the first-aid division, having spent a week fussing over him, was surprised at the deacon's stubbornness.

'The deuce take him, the deaf fellow,' said Barsutsky to Soychenko, the medical orderly. 'Rustle up a wagon from the transports, we'll send the deacon to Rovno for tests . . .'

Soychenko went off to the transport and obtained three wagons: on the first of them sat the driver Akinfiev.

'Ivan,' Soychenko said to him, 'you'll take the deaf fellow to Rovno.'

'I can take him,' Akinfiev replied.

'And you'll bring me back a receipt . . .'

'Naturally,' said Akinfiev. 'And what's the cause of it, his deafness?'

'One's own bast mat is dearer than another's mug,'* said Soychenko, the medical orderly. 'That's the only cause of it. He's a freemason,* not deaf.'

'I can take him,' Akinfiev said again, and rode off after the other carts.

Outside the first-aid station were assembled three wagons in all. In the first of them had been put a nurse who was being posted to the rear, the second had been set aside for a Cossack who was suffering from an inflammation of the kidneys, and into the third climbed Ivan Ageyev, the deacon.

Having seen to everything, Soychenko summoned the medical assistant.

'Our freemason's on his way,' he said. 'I've loaded him into the Revtribunal* wagon against a receipt. They'll be off in a moment.'

Barsutsky glanced out of the little window, saw the wagons and rushed out of the building, red all over and without his hat.

'Oh, but you'll kill him!' he shouted to Akinfiev. 'You'll have to put the deacon in another wagon.'

'Why bother?' the Cossacks who were standing near by replied, and they laughed. 'Our Vanya will get him anywhere . . .'

Akinfiev, knout in hand, was standing right there, beside his horses. He took off his hat and said politely, 'Good day, comrade.'

'Good day, friend,' replied Barsutsky, 'you're a wild beast, you know – the deacon must be put in another wagon . . .'

'I want to know,' said the Cossack, shrilly, and his upper lip shuddered, crept along and began to tremble over his dazzling teeth, 'I want to know whether it's all right or not all right, that when the enemy is tyrannizing us unspeakably, when the enemy is beating us to the last breath, when he's hanging on to our legs like a ton weight and tying our arms like snakes, whether it's all right for us to caulk up our ears in this hour of death and danger?'

'Vanya's standing up for the little commissars,' Korotkov, the driver of the first wagon, shouted. 'Oh, how he's standing up for them . . .'

'What do you mean, standing up for them?' muttered Barsutsky, turning away. 'We're all standing up for them. Only the business has to be done according to the rule book.'

'Well, he can hear all right, anyway, our deaf fellow can,' Akinfiev suddenly interrupted, twirled his knout in his pudgy fingers, laughed and winked at the deacon. The latter was sitting on the cart, his enormous shoulders lowered, and moving his head all the while.

'Well, off you go, and God be with you,' the doctor shouted in despair. 'You'll answer to me for it all, Ivan . . .'

'I agree to that,' Akinfiev pronounced reflectively, and he inclined his head. 'Make yourself comfortable,' he said to the deacon, without turning round. 'Make yourself even more comfortable,' he repeated, gathering the reins in his hand.

The wagons formed up in a row and one after the other rolled off along the high road. Korotkov led the way. Akinfiev was third. He whistled a tune and shook the reins. In this fashion they rode some fifteen versts and towards evening were overrun by a sudden enemy attack.

On this day, 23 July, the Poles, by means of a swift manoeuvre, mangled the rear of our army, swooped down into the town of Kozin and took prisoner many men of the eleventh division. The squadrons of the sixth division were rushed to the region around Kozin in order to make a counter-movement on the foe. The units' lightning-fast manoeuvring scattered the transports; the Revtribunal wagons wandered about for two whole days along the seething fringes of the battle and only on the third night did they manage to get out on to the road along which the rearguard staff were moving. It was on this road, at midnight, that I encountered them.

Numb with despair, I encountered them after the battle of Khotin. In the battle of Khotin my horse, Lavrik, my comfort upon earth, had been killed. Having lost him, I transferred to an ambulance cart and picked up the wounded until evening. Then those who were not wounded were thrown off the cart, and I remained alone beside a ruined peasant house. Night flew towards me on swift horses. The wail of the transports filled the universe. On the earth, girded round with screams, the roads were dying. The stars crept out of the night's cool belly, and abandoned villages flared up above the horizon. Carrying my saddle on my back, I walked across a havoc-torn boundary field and at the turning stopped to attend to a call of nature. Having relieved myself, I did up my flies and felt splashes on my hand. I switched on my flashlight, turned round and saw on the earth the corpse of a Pole, drenched in my urine. It was pouring out of his mouth, spluttering between his teeth and collecting in his empty eye sockets. A notebook and fragments of the proclamations of Pilsudski lay beside the corpse. In the Pole's notebook there were notes of minor expenses, the order of the shows at the Krakow Theatre and the birthday of a woman named Maria-Luiza. With one of the proclamations of Pilsudski, marshal and commander-in-chief, I wiped the stinking liquid from the skull of my unknown brother and walked away, bent under the weight of the saddle.

Now wheels were groaning somewhere near at hand.

'Stop,' I shouted, straightening up, 'who goes there?'

Night flew towards me on swift horses, fires meandered on the horizon.

'Revtribunal folk,' replied a voice, crushed by darkness.

I ran forward and knocked into a wagon.

'My horse was killed,' I said, unusually loudly. 'My horse was called Lavrik . . .'

No one made me any reply. I got up on to the wagon, put the saddle under my head, fell asleep and slept until dawn, kept warm by musty hay and the body of Ivan Akinfiev, my chance companion.

In the morning the Cossack woke up later than I did.

'It's getting light, thank God,' he said, hauling his revolver out from under his box and firing over the deacon's ear. The latter was sitting right in front of us, driving the horses. Above the dome of his balding pate flew feathery grey hair. Akinfiev fired another shot over his ear and then put the revolver away in its holster.

'Good morning, Vanya,' he said to the deacon, grunting and putting his boots on, 'let's have some grub, eh?'

'Look here, lad,' I cried, coming to my senses, 'what are you doing?'

'Whatever it is, it isn't enough,' Akinfiev replied as he got out the food. 'He's been trying it on with me for three days now.'

And then from the first wagon, Korotkov, whom I knew from the 31st Regiment, answered, and told the whole story of the deacon from the beginning. Akinfiev listened to him attentively, pinning back his ears, and then hauled out a roast leg of ox from under his saddle. It was covered in thick canvas and stuck all over with straw. The deacon climbed across to us from the driver's seat, sliced the green meat with a little knife and gave us each a piece. Breakfast over, Akinfiev tied the ox leg up again in its bag and shoved it away in the hay.

'Vanya,' he said to Ageyev, 'let's go and drive out the devil. It doesn't matter if we stop, the horses have to get a drink . . .'

From his pocket he took a bottle of medicine and a Tarnovsky syringe,* and gave them to the deacon. They climbed down from the wagon and walked off some twenty yards into the fields.

'Nurse,' Korotkov shouted in the first wagon, 'look the other way, you'll be blinded by Akinfiev's riches . . .'

'I don't give a shit for you or your tool,' the woman muttered, and she turned away.

Then Akinfiev lifted up his shirt. The deacon knelt in front of him and performed the syringing. Then he wiped the syringe with a rag and held it up to the light. Akinfiev pulled up his trousers; seizing the moment, he went behind the deacon's back and again fired a shot right above his ear.

'All the best to you, Ivan,' he said, as he buttoned himself up.

The deacon put the bottle down on the grass and got up off his knees. His feathery hair flew up.

'The Supreme Judge will judge me,' he said, dully, 'you are not placed above me, Ivan . . .'

'Now everybody's judging everybody else,' interrupted the driver of the second wagon; he resembled a pushy hunchback. 'And they're dealing out death, very simply . . .'

'Even better,' Ageyev pronounced, straightening up. 'Kill me, Ivan . . .'

'Don't play games, deacon,' said Korotkov, whom I knew from earlier times, coming over to him. 'You have to realize what kind of man you're riding with. Another man would have sewn you up like a duck, without a quack, but he's fishing the truth out of you and teaching you, you unfrocked priest . . .'

'Or even better,' the deacon said again, stubbornly, and he stepped forward. 'Kill me, Ivan.'

'You'll kill yourself, you bastard,' Akinfiev replied, turning pale and lisping, 'you'll dig a hole for yourself, and fill it in on top of yourself, too . . .'

He waved his arms in the air, tore at his collar and fell on the ground in a fit.

'Oh, little droplet of my blood,' he shouted wildly and began to sprinkle his face with sand, 'oh, bitter little droplet of my blood, Soviet power of mine . . .'

'Vanya,' Korotkov said, coming up to him and tenderly placing a hand on his shoulder, 'don't lash about, dear friend, don't get upset. We must be on our way, Vanya . . .'

Korotkov took some water in his mouth and sprayed it on Akinfiev, then he carried him over to the cart. The deacon got up on his seat again, and we rolled off.

We had only two versts to go to the town of Verby. That morning countless transports had met in the town. Here were the eleventh division, and the fourteenth and the fourth. Jews wearing waistcoats stood in their doorways with hunched shoulders like ragged birds. Cossacks walked about the yards collecting towels and eating unripe plums. No sooner had they arrived than Akinfiev climbed into the hay and fell asleep, while I took a blanket from his wagon and went to look for a place in the shade. On both sides of the road, however, the fields were strewn with excrement. A bearded muzhik in copper-rimmed spectacles and a Tyrolean hat who was reading a newspaper on the side intercepted my gaze and said:

'We call ourselves human beings, yet we make a worse mess than jackals. Makes you feel ashamed for the village . . .'

And turning away, he again began to read his newspaper through his large spectacles.

Then I made for the coppice on the left and caught sight of the deacon, who was getting closer and closer to me.

'Where are you kittening off to, countryman?' Korotkov shouted to him from the first wagon.

'To put myself in order,' the deacon muttered, seizing my hand and kissing it.

'You're a wonderful gent,' he whispered, grimacing, shivering and catching his breath; 'if you have a free moment I'd like to ask you to write a letter for me to the town of Kasimov, and let my lady wife weep for me . . .'

'Are you deaf, father deacon,' I shouted at him, point-blank, 'or aren't you?'

'Guilty,' he said, 'guilty,' – and strained his ear.

'Are you deaf, Ageyev, or aren't you?'

'That's right, I'm deaf,' he said hurriedly. 'The day before yesterday my hearing was perfect, but comrade Akinfiev has ruined my hearing with his firing. His duty was to deliver me to Rovno, comrade Akinfiev, but I hardly think he'll do it . . .'

And falling to his knees, the deacon crawled head first between the wagons, completely entangled in his priestly, tousled hair. Then he got up from his knees, slipped out between the carts and walked up to Korotkov. The latter gave him some tobacco, they rolled cigarettes and lit each other's.

'That's the right way to do it,' said Korotkov, and he made room beside him. The deacon sat down beside him, and they fell silent.

Then Akinfiev woke up. He threw the ox leg out of his bag, sliced the green meat with his little knife and gave us all a piece. At the sight of that rotten leg I felt weakness and despair, and gave my share back.

'Goodbye, lads,' I said. 'Good luck to you . . .'

'Goodbye,' replied Korotkov.

I took my saddle from the wagon and as I left I could hear the interminable muttering of Ivan Akinfiev.

'Vanya,' he was saying to the deacon, 'that was a big mistake you made, Vanya. You ought to have been terrified at the sound of my name, but you went and got in my wagon. Well, you could still jump about until you ran into me, but I'm going to treat you something horrible, Vanya, I swear it, I'm going to treat you something horrible . . .'

A Sequel to the Story of a Horse

Four months ago Savitsky, our former *nachdiv*, took a white stallion from Khlebnikov, the commander of the First Squadron. Then Khlebnikov left the army, and today Savitsky had a letter from him.

Khlebnikov had written to Savitsky:

... And I can have no more spite against Budyonny's army. I understand my sufferings in that army and hold them in my heart with more reverence than a sacred relic. But the working masses of the wretched Vitebsk region, where I am president of the district revolutionary committee, cry to you, Comrade Savitsky, as to a universal hero, 'Give us world revolution!' and desire that your white stallion will tread beneath you for long years along easy paths to the benefit of the freedom beloved of all and of the brotherly republics – in which we must keep a particular eye on the authorities in the provincial organizations and on the district units in an administrative respect ...

And Savitsky to Khlebnikov:

True and devoted Comrade Khlebnikov!

In respect of the letter you have written me, it is very praiseworthy for the common cause, all the more so, I may say, after your folly, when you covered your eyes with your own skin and left our Bolshevik Communist Party. Our Communist Party is, Comrade Khlebnikov, an iron rank of fighting men who give up their blood on the front line, and when from iron blood doth flow, then that is not a joke, comrade, it's victory or death. The same as regards the common cause, which I do not expect to see the dawn of, because the fighting is fierce and I change the command personnel once every two weeks. For thirty days I have been fighting a rearguard action, protecting the invincible First Cavalry and finding myself under effective rifle, artillery and air fire from the enemy. Tardy has been killed, as have Lukhmanikov, Lykoshenko, Gulevoy and Trunov, and there is no white stallion underneath me, so on account of the alteration in our military fortunes, you should not expect to see your beloved *nachdiv* Savitsky again, Comrade Khleb-nikov; but we shall see each other, to put it bluntly, in the Kingdom of Heaven, though rumour has it that the old man in the heavens doesn't have a kingdom, but a bordello with all the trimmings, and there's enough gonorrhoea on the earth already, so perhaps we won't see each other again after all. And with that, farewell, Comrade Khlebnikov.

Galicia, September 1920

The Widow

Shevelyov, the colonel, is dying in the ambulance cart. A woman is sitting at his feet. The night, pierced by the reflections of the cannonade, has bent in an arch over the dying man. Lyovka, the *nachdiv*'s driver, is warming up food in a saucepan. Lyovka's forelock is hanging over the fire, the hobbled horses are munching in the bushes. Lyovka stirs the saucepan with a twig and says to Shevelyov, who is stretched out in the ambulance cart:

'I used to work, dear comrade, in Temryuk town, I worked at display riding, and I was also a lightweight athlete. Of course, a small town is boring for a woman, the little ladies would catch sight of me, pull down the walls ... "Lev

Gavrilych, don't say no to a cold snack *à la carte*, you won't regret the time lost . . ." I took one of them off to an eating-house. We ordered two portions of veal, we ordered a half-jug of vodka, we sat completely quiet, drinking . . . I looked – some sort of gentleman was shoving his way over to me, dressed OK, neatly, but in his personality I noticed a large imagination, and he was somewhat the worse for wear.

'"Excuse me," he says, "but what, incidentally, is your nationality?"

'"Why," I ask, "do you, a gentleman, trouble me for my nationality, especially when I am in the company of a lady?"

'"What sort of an athlete," he says, "are you . . .? In French wrestling they make mincemeat out of your kind. Tell me your nationality . . ."

'But, I don't lash out yet.

'"Why do you –" I say, "I don't know your name and patronymic – provoke such a misunderstanding, that one of us must certainly perish here at the present time, or, in other words, lie down unto the final expiration?" Lie down to the last,' Lyovka repeats with ecstasy and stretches his arms to the sky, surrounding himself with night as with a nimbus.

The unwearying wind, the pure wind of the night, is singing, suffused with the sound of bells, rocking souls. The stars are glowing here and there in the dark like wedding rings, they are falling on Lyovka, getting tangled in his hair and fading in his shaggy head.

'Lev,' Shevelyov whispers to him suddenly with blue lips, 'come here. What gold there is – is for Sashka,' says the wounded man, 'the rings, the harness – all are for her. We lived as best we could, I shall make amends to her. My clothes, my underwear, my medal for bravery, are for my mother on the Terek. Send them with a letter and write in the letter – the commander sends his greetings, and do not weep. The hut is yours, old woman, live. If anyone lays a finger on you, go straight to Budyonny and say, "I'm Shevelyov's mother." My horse Abramka I endow to the regiment, I endow my horse for the remembrance of my soul . . .'

'I've understood about the horse,' Lyovka mutters and he waves his arms. 'Sash,' he shouts to the woman, 'did you hear what he said? . . . Own up to him – will you give the old woman what's hers or won't you?'

'To the devil with your mother,' replies Sashka and walks off into the bushes, straight as a blind woman.

'Will you give her the orphan's share?' says Lyovka, catching up with her and seizing her by the throat. 'Say it to his face . . .'

'Yes. Let go.'

And then, having extracted this declaration, Lyovka took the saucepan from the fire and began to pour the soup into the dying man's stiffened mouth. Cabbage soup trickled out of Shevelyov, the spoon clanked on his flashing dead teeth and the bullets sang ever more mournfully, ever more powerfully in the dense expanses of the night.

'He's firing his rifles, the reptile,' said Lyovka.

'The aristo lackey,' replied Shevelyov, 'he's cutting us open with machine-guns on our right flank . . .'

And, having closed his eyes, as majestic as a corpse on a table, Shevelyov began to listen to the fighting with his large, waxen ears. At his side Lyovka chewed meat, crunching and panting. The meat finished, Lyovka licked his lips and pulled Sashka into a narrow gully.

'Sash,' he said trembling, belching and wringing his hands, 'Sash, to God our sins are just like so many weeds . . . We live once, and we die once. If you'll yield to me, Sash, I'll serve you even if it's with my blood . . . His day is past, Sash, but God has plenty more . . .'

They sat down in the high grass. The lingering moon crept out from behind the clouds and paused on Sashka's bare knee.

'Keeping yourselves warm,' Shevelyov muttered, 'but it looks as if the enemy's routed the fourteenth division.'

Lyovka crunched and panted in the bushes. The hazy moon loafed about the sky like a beggarwoman. Distant gunfire floated on the air. The feather-grass rustled on the troubled earth, and into the grass fell the August stars.

Then Sashka returned to her former place. She began to change the wounded man's bandages, and raised a flashlight over the suppurating wound.

'By tomorrow you'll be gone,' said Sashka, as she sponged Shevelyov, who was sweating a cold sweat. 'By tomorrow you'll be gone, it's in your intestines, death . . .'

And at that moment a many-voiced, solid blow fell on the earth. Four fresh brigades, which had been brought into the fighting by the enemy's high command, had fired their first shell over Busk and, tearing our communications to pieces, lit up the watershed of the Bug. Obedient fires rose up on the horizon, the heavy birds of a cannonade flew out of the flames. Busk burned, and Lyovka, the frantic lackey, flew through the forest in *nachdiv* 6's swaying carriage. He pulled on the crimson reins and rammed the varnished wheels against tree stumps. Shevelyov's ambulance cart careered after him, the attentive Sashka guiding the horses that were straining on their harness.

Thus did they arrive at the forest's edge, where the first-aid post was. Lyovka unharnessed the horses and went to see the chief medic to ask for a horse-cloth. He walked through the forest, which was cluttered with wagons. The bodies of ambulance men stuck out from under the wagons, a timid dawn struggled above soldiers' sheepskins. The boots of the sleepers were thrown apart, their pupils turned up to the sky, the black pits of their mouths distorted.

It turned out that the chief medic had a horse-cloth; Lyovka went back to Shevelyov, kissed him on the forehead and covered him from the head downwards. Then Sashka approached the cart. She had tied her kerchief under her chin and shaken the straw from her dress.

'Pavlik,' she said, 'my Jesus Christ,' and lay down sideways beside the dead man, covering him with her immoderate body.

'She's grieving,' Lyovka said then. 'You can't deny it, they had a good life. Now she'll have to go running around the whole squadron again. It's no joke . . .'

And he rode on into Busk, where the staff of the 6th cavalry division was.

There, ten versts from the town, a battle against the Savinkov Cossacks was taking place. The traitors were fighting under the command of Cossack captain Yakovlev, who had gone over to the Poles. They were fighting courageously. The *nachdiv* had been with the troops for nearly two whole days, and Lyovka, not finding him at staff headquarters, had returned to his hut, cleaned his horses, poured water over the wheels of the carriage and lain down to sleep in the shed. The shed was full of fresh hay, as inflammable as scent. Lyovka had a good sleep and then sat down to have dinner. The landlady had cooked him potatoes which she had covered with sour clotted milk. Lyovka was already sitting at the table, when outside in the street there resounded a funereal wail of bugles and the thud of many hooves. The squadron with its buglers and standards was coming along the winding Galician street. The body of Shevelyov, placed on a gun-carriage, had been covered with banners. Sasha rode behind the coffin on Shevelyov's stallion; a Cossack song oozed from the ranks at the back.

The squadron passed along the main street and turned towards the river. Then Lyovka, barefoot and without his hat, set off at a run after the retreating detachment and caught the horse of the squadron commander by the reins.

Neither the *nachdiv*, who had stopped at the crossroads and saluted the dead commander, nor his staff could hear what Lyovka said to the squadron commander.

'The underwear . . .' came the fragments of words on the

wind, '. . . mother on the Terek . . .' – we heard Lyovka's incoherent shouts. The squadron commander, without hearing him to the end, freed his reins and pointed to Sashka. The woman shook her head and rode on. Then Lyovka jumped up into her saddle, seized her by the hair, bent her head back and smashed her face with his fist. Sashka wiped the blood away with the hem of her skirt and rode on. Lyovka got down from the saddle, tossed back his forelock and bound a red scarf round his hips. And the calls of the bugles led the squadron onward, towards the shining line of the Bug.

He soon returned to us, Lyovka, the *nachdiv*'s lackey, and shouted, his eyes ablaze:

'I gave it to her hot . . . "I'll send the things to his mother," she says, "when the time comes. I have a good memory," she says, "I'll remember myself." Well make sure you remember and don't forget, you bone of a viper . . . And if you forget – we'll remind you one more little time. The second time you forget – we'll remind you a second time . . .'

Galicia, August 1920

Zamość

The *nachdiv* and his headquarters staff were lying in a mown field three versts from Zamość. The troops had before them the prospect of a night attack on the town. The order of the day required that we stay the night in Zamość, and the *nachdiv* was awaiting reports of a victory.

It was raining. Over the saturated earth flew wind and darkness. All the stars had been suppressed by clouds swollen with ink. The exhausted horses were sighing and shifting from one foot to another in the murk. There was nothing to give them. I tied my horse's reins to my foot, wrapped myself up in my cloak and lay down in a hole that was full of water. The sodden earth revealed to me the soothing embrace of the grave. The horse gave its reins a pull and hauled me off by my leg. It found a tuft of grass and began to nibble it. Then I fell asleep and dreamed of a shed spread with hay. Above the shed droned the dusty gold of harvest time. The sheaves of wheat lay about the sky, the July day was moving towards evening, and the chalices of the sunset were being thrown back over the village.

I was stretched out on a silent couch, and the hay's caress under the nape of my neck was driving me out of my mind. Then the doors of the shed parted with a whistle. A woman, dressed for a ball, drew close to me. She took a breast from the black lace of her bodice and brought it to me cautiously, like a wet-nurse bringing a feed. She put her breast against my own. An agonizing warmth shook the foundations of my soul, and drops of sweat, living, moving sweat, began to seethe between our nipples.

'Margot,' I wanted to shout, 'the earth is pulling me along on the cord of its disasters like a stubborn cur, yet all the same I have seen you, Margot . . .'

I wanted to shout this, but my jaws, which were clenched together by a sudden chill, would not unclench. Then the woman moved away from me and fell to her knees.

'Jesus,' she said, 'receive the soul of thy departed servant . . .'

She placed two worn five-copeck pieces on my eyelids and stuffed the opening of my mouth with fragrant hay. A howl vainly thrashed about the circle of my fettered jaws, my dimming pupils slowly turned up under the copper coins, I was unable to open my hands and . . . I woke up.

A muzhik with a tumbledown beard lay in front of me. He was holding a rifle. The spine of my horse cut the sky like a black crossbar. The bridle-rein was gripping my leg in a tight loop, making it stick up in the air.

'You fell asleep, countryman,' said the muzhik, smiling with nocturnal, sleepless eyes, 'your horse has hauled you half a verst . . .'

I disentangled the strap and got up. Over my face, which had been lacerated by the tall weeds, blood was flowing.

Right there, two steps from us, lay the front line. I could see the chimneys of Zamość, thievish lights in the ravines of its ghetto and the watch-tower with its broken lamp. The damp dawn was flowing down on us like waves of chloroform. Green rockets flew up above the Polish camp. They trembled in the air, shed their petals like roses under the moon and died.

And in the silence I sensed the remote breath of a groan. The smoke of hidden murder wandered around us.

'Someone is being killed,' I said. 'Who is it? . . .'

'The Pole is agitated,' the muzhik replied to me, 'the Pole is killing Jews.'

The muzhik transferred his rifle from his right hand to his left. His beard had curled completely to one side. He looked at me affectionately and said:

'They're long, these nights on the line, there's no end to these nights. And then a man gets an itch to talk to another man, but where will you find him, that other man? . . .'

The muzhik made me light my cigarette from his.

'The Jew is guilty before all men,' he said, 'both ours and yours. There will be very few of them left when the war is over. How many Jews are there in the world?'

'Ten million,' I replied and began to bridle my horse.

'There'll be two hundred thousand of them left,' the muzhik exclaimed and touched me on the forearm, fearing that I would leave. But I got up into my saddle and galloped off to the place where the staff were.

The *nachdiv* was already preparing to move out. The orderlies stood at attention before him, asleep on their feet. Dismounted squadrons crawled over the wet hillocks.

'They've settled our hash,' the *nachdiv* whispered, and rode off.

We followed him along the road to Sitanets.

It rained again. Dead mice floated along the roads. The autumn ambushed our hearts, and trees, bare corpses placed on both legs, began to sway at the crossroads.

We arrived at Sitanets in the morning. I was with Volkov, the billeting officer. He found us a vacant hut on the edge of the village.

'Vodka,' I said to the landlady, 'vodka, meat and bread!'

The old woman was sitting on the floor, feeding from her hand a calf hidden under the bed.

'*Nic nema*,'* she replied indifferently. 'And I don't remember a time when there was . . .'

I sat down at the table, took off my revolver and fell asleep. A quarter of an hour later I opened my eyes and saw Volkov stooped over the windowsill. He was writing a letter to his fiancée.

'Dear Valya,' he had written, 'do you remember me?'

I read the first line, then took the matches out of my pocket and set fire to a heap of straw on the floor. The released flame began to flare up and swept towards me. The old woman lay bosom-down on the fire and extinguished it.

'What are you doing, *pan*?' said the old woman, and she stepped back in horror.

Volkov turned round, fixed the landlady with empty eyes and resumed his letter.

'I'll burn you, old woman,' I muttered as I fell asleep. 'I'll burn you and your stolen calf.'

'*Czekaj*,'* the landlady shouted in a high voice. She ran into the passage and came back with a pitcher of milk and a loaf.

We had not even had time to eat half of it when shots began to ring out in the yard. There were a lot of them. They rang out for a long time and got on our nerves. We finished the milk, and Volkov walked off into the yard in order to find out what was up.

'I've saddled your horse,' he said to me through the little window. 'They've done for mine, good and proper. The Poles are setting up machine-guns a hundred yards away.'

And there we were, only one horse between the two of us. It barely managed to carry us out of Sitanets. I got into the saddle. Volkov squeezed himself in behind.

Transports were moving forward, roaring and sinking into the mire. The morning was seeping over us like chloroform seeping over a hospital table.

'You married, Lyutov?' Volkov said suddenly, sitting behind me.

'My wife left me,' I replied; I dozed off for a few moments and thought I was sleeping in my bed.

Silence.

Our horse stumbles.

'The mare will be done for in another two versts,' says Volkov, sitting behind me.

Silence.

'We've lost the campaign,' mutters Volkov and gives a snore.

'Yes,' I say.

Sokal, September 1920

Treason

Comrade Investigator Burdenko. To your question I reply that my Party number is 2400, issued to Nikita Balmashov by the Krasnodar Party Committee. My life before 1914 I explain as domestic: I did arable farming with my parents and transferred from arable farming into the ranks of the Imperialists to defend Citizen Poincaré* and the butcher of the German Revolution, Ebert-Noske* – they, one must suppose, were asleep and as they slept dreamed of a way to lend assistance to my native settlement of St Ivan in the Kuban district. And so the rope uncoiled until the time when Comrade Lenin together with Comrade Trotsky redirected my brutal bayonet and pointed it towards a given set of intestines and a new piece of belly fat that suited it better. Ever since that day, I bear the number 2400 on the butt of my sharp-eyed bayonet, and it is rather embarrassing and all too ridiculous for me to hear now from you, Comrade Investigator Burdenko, this unseemly cock and bull story about the unknown N— Hospital. I don't give a shit about that hospital, and almost never fired at it or attacked it – it could not have happened. Being wounded, we all three of us, namely the soldier Golovitsyn, the soldier Kustov and I, had a fever in our bones, and did not attack, but only wept, standing in hospital dressing-gowns in the square amidst the free population, Jews by nationality.* And regarding the three panes of glass which we damaged with an officer's revolver, I tell you on my honour that the panes were not serving their appointed purpose, being in the storeroom where they were not needed. Even Dr Yaveyn, seeing this bitter shooting of ours, merely made mockery with various smiles, standing at the window of his hospital, which can also be confirmed by the above-mentioned free Jews of the town of Kozin. Concerning Dr Yaveyn I can also, Comrade Investigator, submit the material evidence that he made fun of us when the three of us wounded men, namely the soldier Golovitsyn, the soldier Kustov and I, originally presented ourselves for treatment, and with his very first words he announced to us, all too coarsely: 'You fighting men will each of you go and take a bath in the bathroom and drop your weapons and your clothes this minute; I'm afraid there'll be an infection from them, they're going straight into my storeroom . . .' Whereupon, beholding in front of him a beast, and not a man, soldier Kustov stuck out his broken leg and questioned how there could be any infection in a sharp Kuban sabre, except for the enemies of our revolution, and was also interested to find out more about the storeroom, whether there was really a Party soldier there in charge of the stuff or, on the contrary, one of the non-Party masses. Then Dr Yaveyn evidently realized that we were perfectly able to understand treason. He turned his back and, without another word, sent us off to the ward, and again with various smiles, where we went hobbling on various legs, waving our crippled arms and holding on to one another, as the three of us are countrymen from the St Ivan settlement, namely Comrade Golovitsyn, Comrade Kustov and I, we are countrymen with the same fate and whoever's got a broken leg holds his comrade by the arm, and whoever doesn't have an arm leans on his comrade's shoulder. In accordance with the order that had been issued, we went into the ward, where we expected to see cultural-education work and devotion to the cause, but what did we see as we entered the ward? We saw Red Army men, all of them infantry, sitting on the made beds playing draughts, and with them tall nurses, completely smooth, standing by the windows and doling out sympathy. At the sight of this, we stopped as though we had been struck by thunder.

'Your war's over, lads,' I exclaim to the wounded men.

'That's right, it is,' the wounded men reply, moving their draughts that are made of bread.

'It's a bit soon,' I says to the wounded men, 'it's a bit soon for you soldiers to have finished with the war when the enemy is moving about softly-softly fifteen versts from the town and when one reads in the *Red Trooper* newspaper that our international position is just horrible and the horizon is filled with clouds.' But my words bounced off the heroic soldiers like sheep droppings off a regimental drum, and instead of a proper conversation what happened was that the sisters of mercy led us over to our beds and again began to go on and on about giving up our arms, as though we'd already been beaten! They caused Kustov no end of agitation on that account, and he began picking at his wound, which was situated on his left shoulder, above the valiant heart of a fighting man and proletarian. Seeing this, the nurses quietened down a bit, but they quietened down only for a very short time, and then started once more to engage in the jeering that is common to the non-Party masses and began to send those who were willing to haul the clothes off us as we slept or made us play theatrical roles for cultural-educational work dressed in women's clothes, which is not seemly.

Unmerciful sisters. Several times they tried using sleeping powder to get our clothes, so we began to take turns at sleeping, keeping one eye open, and even went to the toilet on lesser business in full uniform with revolvers. And when we had suffered like this for a week and a day we began to ramble in our speech, had visions and, finally, waking up on the accursed morning of 4 August, saw that we were lying in numbered overalls like penal convicts, without our weapons and without the clothes that had been woven by our mothers, those weak old women in the Kuban ... And the sun, we saw, was shining gloriously, and the trench soldiers, among whom we three Red cavalrymen had suffered so much, were making fools of us, and with them the unmerciful sisters, having slipped us sleeping powder the night before, were now shaking their young breasts at us and bringing us cocoa in dishes, and milk in the cocoa enough to drown in! At the sight of this merry carousal the soldiers thumped their crutches horribly loud and pinched our sides as though we were prostitutes, saying that Budyonny's First Cavalry Army had finished its war, too. But no, curly-headed comrades who feed your very marvellous bellies so that at night you sound like machine-guns, it has not finished its war, and all it was was that, having asked to leave the room like it was for necessary business, the three of us went outside into the yard and from the yard we rushed all in a fever and with black gaping wounds to Citizen Boyderman, the chairman of the district revolutionary committee, without whom, Comrade Investigator Burdenko, this misunderstanding about the shooting most possibly would never have existed, i.e. without that chairman who made us completely lose our wits. And although we can give no firm material evidence against Citizen Boyderman, the thing is that when we looked in ˙on the chairman we directed our attention upon a citizen of elderly years in a sheepskin coat, a Jew by nationality, who was sitting at a table, a table so piled with papers that it is not a pretty sight to see . . . He casts his eyes now this way, now that, and it's plain to see that he can't make head nor tail of those papers, those papers are a misery to him, all the more so when I tell you that unknown but honoured soldiers go in threateningly to see Citizen Boyderman and ask him for rations, and if it's not them it's local Party workers reporting on counter-revolution in the surrounding villages, and then immediately rank and file workers from the Centre appear, wanting to get married in the district revolutionary committee in the very shortest time and without delay . . . So we too with raised voices explained the incident of treason at the hospital, but Citizen Boyderman only stared at us, and cast his eyes now this way, now that, and stroked our shoulders, which is not authority and is unworthy of authority, issued no resolution of any kind, but merely announced: 'Comrade soldiers, if you love Soviet authority, then leave these premises, to which we were unable to agree, i.e. to leave the premises, but demanded to see his identity card, on the non-production of which we lost consciousness. And, being without consciousness, we came out on to the square in front of the hospital, where we disarmed the militia in the person of one cavalryman and with tears in our eyes violated three poor-quality panes of glass in the above-mentioned storeroom. In the face of this inadmissible fact, Dr Yaveyn made faces and mocking grimaces, and this at the moment when Comrade Kustov was about to die of his illness within four days!

In his short Red life Comrade Kustov was agitated about treason beyond all bounds, that treason that is winking at us from the window, there it goes, mocking at the coarse proletariat, but the proletariat, comrades, knows itself that it's coarse, this causes us pain, it burns our souls and tears with fire the prisons of our bodies and the gaols of our hateful ribs . . .

Treason, I tell you, Comrade Investigator Burdenko, is laughing at us from the window, treason is up and about in our house with its boots off, treason has thrown its boots over its shoulder so as not to make the floorboards creak in the house it is burgling . . .

Czesniki

The Sixth Division had mustered in the forest that lies outside the village of Czesniki, and was waiting for the signal for the attack. But Pavlichenko, *nachdiv* 6, was waiting for the Second Brigade and had not given the signal. Then up to the *nachdiv*'s side rode Voroshilov. He shoved him in the chest with his horse's muzzle and said:

'We're procrastinating, *nachdiv* 6, we're procrastinating.'

'The Second Brigade,' Pavlichenko replied hollowly, 'according to your orders, is proceeding at a trot towards the place of engagement.'

'We're procrastinating, *nachdiv* 6, we're procrastinating,' said Voroshilov, and gave his reins a jerk. Pavlichenko stepped back a pace.

'In the name of conscience,' he shouted, beginning to wring his raw fingers, 'in the name of conscience, don't hurry me, Comrade Voroshilov . . .'

'Don't hurry him,' whispered Klim Voroshilov, member of the revolutionary war council, and closed his eyes. He sat on his horse, his eyes were hooded, he said nothing though his lips were moving. A Cossack in bast sandals and a bowler hat looked at him in bewilderment. The army staff, stalwart general staffers in trousers redder than human blood, performed gymnastics behind his back and exchanged smiles with one another. The galloping squadrons blew through the forest as the wind blows, breaking branches. Voroshilov combed the mane of his horse with his Mauser.

'Commander,' he shouted. Then he turned round to face Budyonny, and fired in the air. 'Say a word of parting to the troops. There he is on the hillock, the Pole, he's there like a picture, laughing at you . . .'

The Poles were indeed visible through binoculars. The army staff leapt to its horses, and the Cossacks began to flow towards it from all sides.

Ivan Akinfiev, ex-Revtribunal transport, rode past and shoved me with his stirrup.

'Are you in action, Ivan?' I said to him, 'I mean to say, you haven't any ribs, have you? . . .'

'I don't give a shit about those ribs,' replied Akinfiev, who was sitting sideways on his horse, 'let me hear what the man's got to say.'

He rode forward and squeezed hard up against Budyonny.

The latter started, and said softly:

'Lads,' said Budyonny, 'our position is bad, we need more life in it, lads . . .'

'Give us Warsaw!' shouted the Cossack in bast sandals and bowler hat, He opened his eyes wide and slashed the air with his sword.

'Give us Warsaw!' shouted Voroshilov, making his horse rear in the air and riding into the midst of the squadrons.

'Men and commanders,' he said with passion, 'in Moscow, the ancient capital, an unprecedented power is struggling. A workers' and peasants' government, the first in the world, orders you, fighters and commanders, to attack the enemy and bring victory.'

'Swords at the ready,' Pavlichenko began to sing in the distance behind the commander's back, and his twisted crimson lips began to gleam with foam in the ranks. The *nachdiv*'s red coat was torn, his meaty, loathsome face distorted. With the blade of his precious sword he saluted Voroshilov.

'In accordance with the duty of the revolutionary oath,' said *nachdiv* 6, hoarsely, looking around him, 'I report to the war council of the First Cavalry: the Second Invincible Cavalry Brigade is approaching the place of engagement.'

'Carry on,' replied Voroshilov and gave a wave of his arm. He touched the bridle-rein. Budyonny rode off beside him. They rode side by side on long chestnut mares, in matching military jackets and shining trousers embroidered with silver. The fighting men, with a whoop, moved off after them, and pale steel glimmered in the ichor of the autumn sun. But I heard no unanimity in the Cossack whoop and, as I waited for the attack, I walked off into the forest, into its depths, towards the first-aid station.

Two plump nurses in aprons had lain down there on the grass. They were prodding each other with their young breasts and pushing each other off again. They were laughing in dying female giggles and winking to me from below, not blinking. Thus do village wenches with bare legs wink at a lad whose tongue is hanging out, village wenches who squeal like fondled puppies, spending the night in the yard in the languorous pillows of the hayrick. Somewhat further away from the nurses lay a wounded Red Army man in a delirium, and Styopka Duplishchev, a quarrelsome little Cossack, was curry-combing Hurricane, a thoroughbred stallion that belonged to the *nachdiv* and was descended from Lyulyusha, the Rostov champion. The wounded man was reminiscing in a quick patter about Shuya, about a certain heifer and about some flax tow or other, but Duplishchev, drowning his pitiful muttering, was singing a song about a batman and a fat general's wife, singing louder and louder, waving the curry-comb and stroking the horse. He was, however, interrupted by Sashka, plump Sashka, the lady of all the squadrons. She rode up to the boy and jumped to the ground.

'Are we going to settle it, then?' said Sashka.

'Push off,' replied Duplishchev, turning his back on her and beginning to plait ribbons into Hurricane's mane.

'Do you keep your word, Styopka,' said Sashka then, 'or are you bootwax?'

'Push off,' replied Styopka, 'I keep my word.'

He plaited all the ribbons into the mane and suddenly shouted to me in despair:

'You see, Kirill Vasilyich,* just look how outrageously she treats me. For a whole month I've been putting up with I can't tell you what. Wherever I turn – there she is, wherever I go – she gets in my way; let her have the stallion, she says, and again, let her have the stallion. Well, when the *nachdiv*'s ordering me every day: "With a stallion like that, Styopa," he says, "there'll be a lot of people asking you to let them have the stallion, but you mustn't let anyone else have him until he's into his fourth year . . ."'

'I bet you'll be into your fifteenth year before you let anyone have you . . .' muttered Sashka and turned away. 'Into your fifteenth year, I bet, and you'll be no trouble, you won't say anything, just let out bubbles . . .'

She went back to her mare, fixed the saddle-girth and got ready to ride. The spurs on her shoes jingled, her open-work stockings were spattered with mud and adorned with straw, her monstrous breasts swung behind her back.

'I brought a rouble,' said Sashka, aside, and placed her shoe with its spur into the stirrup. 'Brought it, and now I'll have to take it away again.'

The woman fished out two brand-new fifty-copeck pieces,

played with them a little on her palm and put them back in her bosom again.

'Are we going to settle it, then?' Duplishchev said, never taking his eyes off the silver, and walked the stallion over. Sashka selected a sloping place in the clearing and stood her mare there.

'It seems you're the only person on earth with a stallion,' she said to Styopka and began to guide Hurricane. 'It's just that my little mare's a trench horse, hasn't been covered for two years, so I thought perhaps I'd get hold of some good pedigree . . .'

Sashka managed the stallion and then led her horse to one side.

'There we are with our stuffing, girl,' she whispered, kissed her mare on its wet, horsy, piebald lips with their pendant lines of spittle, rubbed herself against the horsy muzzle and began to listen closely to the sound that was stamping through the forest.

'The Second Brigade's on the move,' said Sashka sternly, and turned to me. 'We must ride, Lyutych . . .'

'Maybe it is, and maybe it isn't,' shouted Duplishchev, and something caught in his throat. 'Come on, deacon, place your bet . . .'

'I've got the money right here,' muttered Sashka, and leapt on to her mare,

I rushed after her, and we moved off at a gallop. A whoop from Duplishchev resounded behind us and the gentle tap of a shot.

'Will you look at that!' shouted the young Cossack, and he began to race about the woods with all his might.

The wind leapt among the branches like a maddened hare, the Second Brigade flew through the Galician oak trees, the serene dust of a bombardment ascended above the earth as above a peaceful peasant hut. And at a sign from the *nachdiv* we moved into the attack, the unforgettable attack at Czesniki.

After the Battle

The story of my quarrel with Akinfiev goes like this:

On the thirty-first the attack at Czesniki took place. The squadrons had gathered in the forest close by the village and after five o'clock in the evening they hurled themselves upon the enemy. He was waiting for us on an elevation at a distance of three versts. We galloped the three versts on horses that were infinitely exhausted, and, having leapt up the hill, we saw a deathly wall of black uniforms and pale faces. These were Cossacks who had betrayed us at the beginning of the Polish fighting and had been thrown together into a brigade by Cossack Captain Yakovlev. Having formed his horsemen into a square, the captain waited for us with his sabre unsheathed. In his mouth gleamed a gold tooth, a black beard lay on his chest like an icon on a corpse. The enemy machine-guns were firing from twenty paces away, and men fell wounded in our ranks. We trampled them and attacked the enemy, but his square did not falter; then we ran for it.

Thus was the short-lived victory gained by Savinkov's men over the Sixth Division. It was gained because the object of the attack did not turn away his face before the lava of our onward-flying squadrons. The captain stood his ground on this occasion, and we fled without having crimsoned our swords in the pitiful blood of traitors.

Five thousand men, the whole of our division, rushed down the slopes pursued by no one. The enemy remained on the hill. He did not believe in his improbable victory and could not bring himself to ride in pursuit. Therefore we remained alive and slipped down unharmed into the valley, where we were greeted by Vinogradov, *nachdiv* 6. Vinogradov was racing about on a furious fast horse, returning the escaping Cossacks to the battle.

'Lyutov,' he shouted, catching sight of me, 'turn the men back for me, or I'll dispatch your soul . . .'

Vinogradov thrashed his swaying stallion with the handle of his Mauser, he screeched, summoning the men together. I freed myself from him and rode across to the Kirghiz Gulimov, who was galloping along not far away:

'Uphill, Gulimov,' I said, 'turn your horse back . . .'

'Turn that mare of yours first,' replied Gulimov, and looked round. He looked round thievishly, fired and singed the hair above my ear.

'Turn your own horse,' Gulimov whispered; he took me by the shoulders and tried to draw his sword with his other hand. The sword sat tight in its sheath. The Kirghiz shivered and looked around him, he embraced my shoulder and inclined his head ever closer.

'Yours first,' he said again, barely audibly; 'mine will follow after you . . .' and he lightly tapped me on the chest with the blade of his averted sword. I felt nauseous from death's proximity and its narrowness; with my palm I pushed away the Kirghiz's face, which was hot as a stone in the sun, and scratched it as deeply as I possibly could. Warm blood stirred beneath my fingernails, began to tickle them; I rode away from Gulimov, out of breath as after a long journey. My tormented friend, the horse, moved slowly. I rode without seeing the way, I rode without turning round, until I encountered Vorobyov, the commander of the First Squadron. Vorobyov was looking for his billeting officers and could not find them. He and I got as far as the village of Czesniki together and sat down there on a bench with Akinfiev, the former Revtribunal vehicular. Past us walked Sashka, the nurse from 31st Cavalry Regiment, and two commanders sat down near us on the bench. These commanders began to doze and said nothing; one of them, shell-shocked, kept shaking his head uncontrollably and winking from a wide-open, staring eye. Sashka went to make a report to the hospital about him and then came back to us, pulling her horse by the reins. Her mare was being stubborn, making its feet slide in the wet clay.

'Where are you sailing off to?' Vorobyov said to the nurse. 'Sit with us for a bit, Sash . . .'

'I'm not sitting with you,' replied Sashka and gave her mare a slap on the belly. 'I'm not . . .'

'Why not?' shouted Vorobyov, laughing, 'or have you thought the better of drinking tea with the menfolk, Sashka? . . .'

'I've thought the better of it with you,' the woman said, turning to the commander, throwing the reins far away from her, 'I've thought better of drinking tea with you, Vorobyov, because I saw you today, you heroes, and I saw your ugly work, commander . . .'

'Well, when you saw it,' muttered Vorobyov, 'that was when you should have fired . . .'

'Fired,' Sashka said with despair and tore the hospital armband from her sleeve. 'Was I supposed to fire with this, then?'

And just then Akinfiev, the former Revtribunal vehicular, with whom I had some old unfinished business to settle, drew near to us.

'You've got nothing to fire with, Sashok,' he said, calmingly. 'Nobody's blaming you for that, the people I blame are the ones that get mixed up in a fight but don't put any cartridges in their revolvers . . . You took part in the attack,' Akinfiev shouted to me suddenly, and a spasm spread over his face, 'you took part and you didn't put any cartridges in, what was the reason for that? . . .'

'Leave me alone, Ivan,' I said to Akinfiev, but he would not leave me in peace and came closer, all crooked, epileptic and without ribs.

'The Pole shot at you, and you didn't shoot back,' muttered the Cossack, fidgeting and turning his shattered hip. 'What was the reason for it? . . .'

'The Pole shot at me,' I replied insolently, 'and I didn't shoot back . . .'

'So you're a Milk-drinker,' Akinfiev whispered, stepping back.

'So what if I am,' I said, louder than before. 'What do you want, Ivan? . . .'

'I want to know that you're in your right mind,' Ivan shouted in wild triumph, 'that you're in your right mind. I have an order written about the Milk-drinkers, they're to be shot, they worship God . . .'

Gathering a crowd, the Cossack went on shouting about the Milk-drinkers without cease. I began to move away from him, but he came after me and, having caught me up, punched me in the back with his fist.

'You didn't put any cartridges in,' Akinfiev whispered with a dying thrill right into my ear and began to get busy, trying with his large fingers to tear my mouth apart, 'you worship God, traitor . . .'

He tugged and tore my mouth. I shoved the hysterical fellow away and socked him in the face. Akinfiev fell sideways to the ground and, falling, hurt himself so badly that he bled.

Then Sashka approached him, her breasts dangling. The woman sluiced him with water and removed a long tooth from his mouth – it had been swaying in that black mouth like a birch tree on a bare high road.

'All that cockerels care about,' said Sashka, 'is knocking their beaks together, but what has happened today makes me want to close my eyes so as not to see . . .'

She said this with sorrow and took back with her the shattered Akinfiev, while I dragged myself off to the village of Czesniki, which had slipped in the unwearying Galician rain.

The village was floating and swelling, purple clay flowed from its dismal wounds. A first star gleamed above me and fell into clouds. Rain whipped the white willows and spent its force. The evening flew up towards the sky, like a flock of birds, and the darkness laid its wet wreath upon me. I was exhausted and, bent under the sepulchral crown, moved forward, begging fate for the simplest of abilities – the ability to kill a man.

Galicia, September 1920

The Song

While we were billeted in the small village of Budyatichi I had the misfortune to get a bad landlady. She was a widow, she was poor; I shot up a lot of locks in her storerooms, but I never found any poultry.

All I could do was to play the crafty game for all I was worth, and one day, having returned home early, before twilight, I saw my landlady closing the door of the oven on a stove that was still warm. In the hut there was a smell of cabbage soup – there could have been meat in that soup. I smelt meat in that soup and put my revolver on the table, but the old woman obstinately denied it. Spasms showed in her face and in her black fingers, she went dark and looked at me with fright and astonishing hatred. But nothing would have saved her, I'd have harassed her to death with my revolver, had I not been hindered in this by Sashka Konyayev, otherwise known as Sashka Christ.

He came into the shack with a concertina under his arm, his handsome legs dangling in boots that were shapeless from wear.

'We'll play some songs,' he said and raised to me his eyes that were crammed to overflowing with blue, sleepy chunks of ice. 'We'll play some songs,' said Sashka, sitting down on the bench, and he played his way through an introduction.

This pensive introduction came as if from far off; the Cossack broke off and had a fit of melancholy with his blue eyes. He turned away from everyone and, knowing what would please me, began a song from the Kuban.

'. . . Star of the fields,' he began to sing, 'star of the fields above my father's house, and the sad hand of my mother . . .'

I loved that song, in love for it I attained an exalted ecstasy of the heart. Sashka knew about that, because we both of us – he and I – had heard it for the first time in '19 in the Don estuary, at the Kagalnitskaya Cossack settlement.

A certain hunter who worked the protected waters there had taught us that song. There, in the protected waters, fish spawn and there are countless flocks of birds. The fish propagate in the estuary in inexpressible abundance, they can be caught in ladles or even simply with the hands, and if one puts an oar in the water it will stand upright – the fish will hold the oar and carry it along with them. We had seen this ourselves, we would never forget the protected waters at Kagalnitskaya. All the authorities banned hunting there – a proper and justified ban – but in the year '19 a fierce battle was being fought in the estuary, and the hunter Yakov, who had been plying his improper trade before our very eyes, made a present of his concertina as a decoy to our squadron singer Sashka Christ. He taught Sashka his songs; many of them were of the old, heartfelt kind. We forgave the crafty hunter everything, for his songs were necessary to us: no one then could see any end to the war, and only Sashka covered our wearisome roads with tintinnabulation and with tears. A trail of blood moved along that road. The song flew above our trail. So it was in the Kuban and on the Green campaigns,* so it was in Uralsk and in the foothills of the Caucasus and is still, even to this day. The songs are necessary to us, no one sees an end to the war, and Sashka Christ, the squadron singer, is not yet ripe for death . . .

And on that evening too, when I had been cheated of my

landlady's cabbage soup, Sashka pacified me with his half-strangled and swaying voice.

'Star of the fields,' he sang, 'star of the fields above my father's house, and my mother's sad hand . . .'

And sprawled in a corner on the rotten bedding, I listened to him. The dream was breaking my bones, the dream was shaking the decomposing hay beneath me, through its hot downpour I could barely discern the old woman supporting her faded cheek in her hand. Having let fall her badly stung head, she stood by the wall without stirring and did not move from the spot when Sashka finished playing. Sashka finished playing and put the concertina on one side; he yawned and laughed as after a long sleep, and then, seeing the desolation of our widow's shack, flicked the sweepings off the bench and hauled a pail of water into the hut.

'Look, my heart,' the landlady said to him, scratched her back against the door and pointed at me, 'your chief came here today, shouted at me, stamped his feet, got rid of the locks and laid out weapons in front of me . . . It's a sin from God – to lay out weapons in front of me, I mean, I'm a woman . . .'

Again she scratched herself against the door and began to throw sheepskins over her son. Her son was snoring under the icon on a large bed that was strewn with rags. He was a mute boy with a swollen, bloated white head and gigantic feet like those of a grown muzhik. His mother wiped his dirty nose and returned to the table.

'Dear landlady,' Sashka said to her then and touched her shoulder, 'if you wish, I will do you a courtesy . . .'

But it was as if the woman did not hear his words.

'I haven't seen any cabbage soup,' she said, supporting her cheek. 'It's gone, my cabbage soup. Men show me weapons, and when a good man does turn up and a woman might as well enjoy herself with him, I feel so sick that even sin doesn't cheer me up . . .'

She drawled her mournful complaints and, as she muttered, moved the mute boy away towards the wall; Sashka lay down with her on the rag bed, and I tried to fall asleep and began to think up dreams for myself, in order to fall asleep with pleasant thoughts.

The Rebbe's Son

... Do you remember Zhitomir, Vasily? Do you remember the Teterev, Vasily, and that night when the Sabbath, the young Sabbath stole along the sunset, crushing the stars with her little red heel?

The thin horn of the moon was bathing its arrows in the dark water of the Teterev. Absurd Gedali, the founder of the Fourth International,* had taken us to the home of Rebbe Motale Bratslavsky for evening prayers. Absurd Gedali was waving the cockerel feathers of his top hat in the red smoke of the evening. The predatory eyes of candles blinked in the Rebbe's room. Inclined over prayer-books, broad-shouldered Jews were groaning hollowly, and the old buffoon of the Chernobyl *tsadikkim** was jingling the copper coins in his tattered pocket ...

... Do you remember that night, Vasily? ... Outside the window horses neighed and Cossacks shouted. The desert of war yawned outside the window, and Rebbe Motale Bratslavsky, clutching his prayer-shawl in his worn fingers, prayed by the east wall. Then the veil of the Ark was drawn back, and in the funereal light of the candles we saw the scrolls of the Torah, wrapped in coverings of purple velvet and blue silk,* and, hanging above the Torah, the lifeless, submissive, handsome face of Ilya, the Rebbe's son, the last prince of the dynasty ...*

And then, Vasily, the day before yesterday, the regiments

of the Twelfth Army opened the front at Kovel. In the town the scornful cannonade of the vanquishers thundered. Our troops wavered and got mixed up together. The Politotdel train began to creep away along the dead spine of the fields. And monstrous Russia, improbable as a swarm of clothes lice, began to tramp in its bast sandals on both sides of the carriages. The typhus-ridden muzhik horde rolled in front of itself its customary hump of a soldier's death. It jumped on to the footboards of our train and fell off, knocked down by blows from rifle-butts. It puffed, scrabbled, flew forward and said nothing. And at the twelfth verst, when I had run out of potatoes, I chucked a pile of Trotsky's leaflets at them. But only one of them stretched out a dirty, dead hand for a leaflet. And I recognized Ilya, the son of the Zhitomir Rebbe. I recognized him immediately, Vasily. And so painful was it to see a prince who had lost his trousers, broken in two by a soldier's knapsack, that, breaking the regulations, I hauled him into our carriage. His bare knees, as clumsy as an old woman's, bumped against the rusty iron of the steps; two plump-breasted girl typists in sailor's jackets dragged the long, shy body of the dying man along the floor. We put him down in a corner of the editorial office, on the floor. Cossacks in wide red oriental trousers adjusted his fallen clothes. The girls, having placed on the floor the bandy legs of simple cows, coldly observed his sexual parts, the wilted, curly virility of a Semite worn to a shadow. While I, who had seen him on one of my nights of stray wandering, began to pack the scattered belongings of the Red Army soldier Bratslavsky into a trunk.

Here everything was dumped together – the warrants of the agitator and the commemorative booklets of the Jewish poet. Portraits of Lenin and Maimonides lay side by side. Lenin's nodulous skull and the tarnished silk of the portraits of Maimonides. A strand of female hair had been placed in a book of the resolutions of the Sixth Party Congress, and in the margins of communist leaflets swarmed crooked lines of Ancient Hebrew verse. In a sad and meagre rain they fell on me – pages of the Song of Songs and revolver cartridges. The sad rain of sunset bathed my hair, and I said to the youth, who was dying in the corner on a torn mattress:

'Four months ago, on a Friday evening, Gedali, the junk dealer, brought me to your father, Rebbe Motale, but you were not in the Party then, Bratslavsky . . .'

'I was in the Party then,' the boy replied, scratching his chest and writhing in fever, 'but I couldn't leave my mother . . .'

'And now, Ilya?'

'In a revolution a mother is a minor episode,' he whispered. 'My letter came up, the letter B, and the organization sent me away to the front . . .'

'And you ended up in Kovel, Ilya?'

'I ended up in Kovel,' he shouted in despair. 'The kulak rabble opened the front. I took over a scratch regiment, but it was too late. I didn't have enough artillery . . .'

He died before we got to Rovno. He died, the last prince, among poems, phylacteries* and foot-bindings. We buried him at a forgotten station. And I – who am barely able to accommodate the storms of my imagination within my ancient body – I received my brother's last breath.

Argamak*

I decided to move to the front. When he heard of this, the *nachdiv* made a wry face.

'Why poke your nose in there? . . . As soon as you open your mouth they'll shoot you as a counter-revolutionary . . .'

I got my own way. Not only that. My choice fell on the

most bellicose division – the sixth. I was appointed to the fourth squadron of the 23rd Cavalry Regiment. The squadron was commanded by a locksmith from the Bryansk factory named Baulin, only a boy. As a warning to others he had grown a beard. Ashy tufts twisted on his chin. At the age of twenty-two, Baulin let nothing bother him. This quality, proper to thousands of Baulins, was an important element in the triumph of the revolution. Baulin was firm, laconic, obstinate. The path of his life had been decided. He had no doubts about the rightness of that path. Hardship came easy to him. He was able to sleep standing up. He slept pressing one hand with the other, and when he woke up the passage from oblivion to wakefulness was not noticeable.

To expect mercy under Baulin's command was out of the question. My service began with a rare foretokening of success – I was given a horse. There were no horses, either in the army stables or among the peasants. Chance had a hand in it. The Cossack Tikhomolov had killed two captive officers without permission. He had been entrusted with escorting them to brigade headquarters, for officers might be able to give important information. Tikhomolov did not take them that far. The Cossacks decided to try him before the Revtribunal, but then decided not to. Squadron Commander Baulin imposed a retribution more terrible than the tribunal – he took Tikhomolov's stallion, nicknamed Argamak, away from him and sent Tikhomolov himself to the transport wagons.

The torment I endured with Argamak very nearly surpassed the measure of human strength. Tikhomolov had brought the horse from the Terek, his home. It had been taught the Cossack trot, the special Cossack full gallop – dry, frenzied, sudden. Argamak's stride was long, stretched, stubborn. With that devilish stride he carried me out of the ranks, I would become separated from the squadron and, deprived of my sense of direction, I would wander around in search of my unit for whole days and nights thereafter, end up in the enemy lines, spend the night in a ravine, try to attach myself to other units and be told to go away. My war experience was limited to service in the German war, in the artillery division of the 15th Infantry Regiment. Usually this entailed sitting in solemn state on top of an ammunition wagon; from time to time we rode in a gun team. There was nowhere where I could have got used to the hard, swinging trot of Argamak. Tikhomolov had bequeathed to his mount all the devils of his fall. I jolted, like a sack, on the stallion's long, dry back. I wore out his back. It became covered in sores. Metallic flies fed on these sores. Hoops of coagulated black blood girdled the horse's belly. Because of clumsy shoeing Argamak began to overreach, his hind legs swelled up at the fetlock and became elephantine. His eyes were suffused with the peculiar fire of a tormented horse, the fire of hysteria and obstinacy. He would not let himself be saddled.

'You've annulled that mount, four-eyes,' said the platoon commander.

In my presence the Cossacks said nothing; behind my back they got ready in the way that plunderers get ready, in somnolent and perfidious immobility. They did not even ask me to write letters . . .

The cavalry had taken Novograd-Volynsk. In a twenty-four-hour period we were having to cover sixty, eighty versts. We were getting close to Rovno. One-day rests were practically non-existent. Night after night I had the same dream. I was tearing along at a trot on Argamak. There were fires at the side of the road. Cossacks were cooking their food. I rode past them, they did not raise their eyes to me. Some greeted me, others did not look up – they were not interested in me. What did it mean? Their indifference signified that there was nothing special about my manner of sitting in the saddle, I rode the way everyone else did, there was no reason to look at me. I galloped on my way and was happy. My thirst for peace and happiness was not quenched when I was awake – that was why I had these dreams.

There was no sign of Tikhomolov. He was keeping an eye on me somewhere on the edges of the march, in the sluggish tail-ends of wagons stuffed with rags.

One day the platoon commander said to me:

'Pashka keeps asking after you . . .'

'Why does he want me?'

'Apparently he does . . .'

'I suppose he thinks I have offended him? . . .'

'Well, haven't you? . . .'

Pashka's hatred came to me over forests and rivers. I felt it with my skin and shivered. Eyes suffused with blood were fixed upon my path.

'Why did you give me an enemy?' I asked Baulin.

The squadron commander rode past and yawned.

'It's no concern of mine,' he replied, without turning round, 'it's your concern . . .'

Argamak's back would heal a little, then open up again. I put three cloths under the saddle, but the ride was not right, the weals did not heal over. The knowledge that I was sitting on an open wound nagged at me.

One Cossack from our platoon, Bizyukov by name, was a countryman of Tikhomolov's, and knew Pashka's father, down there on the Terek.

'His father, Pashka's,' Bizyukov said to me one day, 'breeds horses for the hunt . . . He's a perky rider, a plump chap . . . He arrives at the herd – has to choose a horse straight away . . . They lead them in. He stands in front of the horse, puts his legs apart, looks . . . What do you want? . . . Well, what he wants is, he waves his massive great fist, gives the horse a belt between the eyes – and the horse is out of the game. "What did you nobble the horse for, Kalistrat? . . ." "When I go out on my terrible hunts," he says, "that sort of horse wouldn't be any good to me . . . That horse didn't come up to my hunting standards . . . My kind of hunt," he says, "is a hunt to the death . . ." A perky rider, and no mistake.'

And so it was that Argamak, left by Pashka's father in the land of the living, chosen by him, came into my hands. What should I do next? In my mind I turned over a large number of plans. The war saved me from my worries.

The cavalry attacked Rovno. The town was taken. We spent two days and nights in it. The following night the Poles pushed us back out. They gave battle in order to bring out their retreating units. The manoeuvre was successful. For cover the Poles had the assistance of a hurricane, lashing rain, a heavy summer thunderstorm that capsized on the world in floods of black water. We evacuated the town for twenty-four hours. In this nocturnal battle the Serb Dundich fell, one of the bravest of men. In this battle Tikhomolov also fought. The Poles swooped down on his transport. The spot was flat, without cover. Pashka lined up his wagons in a battle order that was known only to him. The Romans probably used to line their chariots up in a formation like that. Pashka, as it turned out, had a machine-gun. He must have stolen it and kept it hidden away for such an eventuality. With this machine-gun Tikhomolov beat off the assault, saved his property and withdrew the entire transport, except for two carts whose horses had been shot.

'Why are you keeping the men hanging about?' people at brigade headquarters said to Baulin a few days after this battle.

'If I'm keeping them hanging about, it must be necessary . . .'

'Watch out, you'll get trouble . . .'

Pashka had not been pardoned, but we knew he would come. He arrived in galoshes and no socks. His toes had been chopped off; ribbons of black gauze hung from them. They trailed after him like a mantle. Pashka arrived in the village of Budyatichi on the square in front of the church where our horses were standing by the tethering post. Baulin sat on the steps of the church, steaming his feet in a tub. His toes had begun to rot slightly. They were pinkish, the pink of iron at the beginning of tempering. Tufts of youthful, straw-like hair stuck to Baulin's forehead. The sun burned on the bricks and tiles of the church. Bizyukov, who stood beside the squadron commander, stuffed a cigarette into the other man's mouth and lit it. Tikhomolov, trailing his torn mantle, walked towards the tethering post. His galoshes slapped. Argamak stretched out his long neck amd neighed a welcome to his master, neighed softly and shrilly, like a horse in the wilderness. On his back the ichor snaked like lace between the bands of lacerated flesh. Pasha stood beside the horse. The dirty ribbons lay motionless on the ground.

'So that's the way it is,' the Cossack articulated, barely audibly.

I stepped forward.

'Let's make it up, Pasha. I'm glad that the horse is going to you. I can't cope with him . . . Let's make it up, shall we?'

'It's not Easter yet, to be making it up.' The platoon commander was rolling a cigarette behind my back. His oriental trousers were spread out, his shirt unbuttoned on his copper chest, as he rested on the church steps.

'Give him a triple kiss,* Pashka,' muttered Bizyukov, Tikhomolov's countryman, who knew Kalistrat, Pashka's father. 'He wants to give you one . . .'

I was alone among these men, whose friendship I had not succeeded in obtaining.

Pashka, as though rooted to the spot, was standing in front of the horse. Argamak, breathing powerfully and freely, stretched out his muzzle to him.

'So that's the way it is,' the Cossack said again; he turned sharply towards me and said steadily, 'I'm not going to make it up with you.'

Shuffling in his galoshes, he began to walk away along the limy, heat-scorched road, his bandages sweeping the dust of the village square. Argamak went after him, like a dog. The reins swung under his muzzle, his long neck lay low. Baulin was still rubbing the reddish iron rottenness of his feet in the tub.

'You've given me an enemy,' I said to him, 'but how am I to blame?'

The squadron commander raised his head.

'Go on.'

'All right, I will . . .'

'I understand you,' the commander interrupted, 'I understand you completely . . . Your aim is to live without making enemies . . . Everything you do is aimed that way – so you won't have any enemies.'

'Give him a triple kiss,' muttered Bizyukov, turning away.

On Baulin's forehead a fiery spot was imprinted. His cheek twitched.

'Do you know what the end of this is?' he said, unable to control his breathing properly. 'The end of it is boredom . . . go away to the ragged mother . . .'

I had to leave. I got a transfer to the the sixth squadron. There things went better. Somehow or the other, Argamak had taught me how to sit in the saddle the Tikhomolov way. My dream was fulfilled. The Cossacks stopped following me and my horse with their eyes.

ODESSA STORIES

The King

The wedding ceremony was at an end. The rabbi wearily lowered himself into an armchair. Then he went out of the room and saw tables placed the whole length of the courtyard. There were so many of them that they thrust their tail out of the front gate, into Hospital Street. The velvet-covered tables coiled about the yard like snakes that had had patches of every colour applied to their bellies, and they sang in thick voices, these patches of orange and red velvet.

The apartments had been turned into kitchens. Through soot-grimed doorways beat a corpulent flame, a drunken and pudgy flame. In its smoky rays baked old women's faces, bumpy female chins, well-thumbed breasts. Sweat as pink as blood, as pink as the foam of a rabid dog, flowed round these heaps of burgeoning, sweetly stinking human flesh. Three cooks, not counting the dish-washers, were preparing the wedding supper. Over them reigned the eighty-year-old Reyzl, as traditional as a scroll of the Torah, tiny and hunch-backed.

Before the supper, a young man unfamiliar to the guests wormed his way into the courtyard. He asked for Benya Krik.* He took Benya Krik to one side.

'Listen, King,' said the young man, 'I must have a word with you. Auntie Khana from Kostetskaya Street sent me.'

'Oh, very well,' replied Benya Krik, whose nickname was 'the King', 'what is this word?'

'A new superintendent came to the police station yesterday, Auntie Khana told me to tell you.'

'I knew about this the day before yesterday,' replied Benya Krik. 'Go on.'

'He gathered the constables together and gave a speech.'

'A new broom sweeps clean,' replied Benya Krik. 'He wants to make a raid. Go on.'

'But when will the raid be, King?'

'It will be tomorrow.'

'King, it will be today.'

'Who told you this, boy?'

'Auntie Khana told me. Do you know Auntie Khana?'

'I know Auntie Khana. Go on.'

'He gathered the constables together and gave them a speech. "We must get rid of Benya Krik," said the superintendent, "because where there is an emperor, there there is no king. Today – when Krik gives his sister in marriage and everyone will be there. We must make the raid today."'

'Go on.'

'So the cops began to get scared. They said if we make a raid today, when he is having a celebration, Benya will be angry, and much blood will flow. But the superintendent said self-respect is more important . . .'

'Well, go on,' replied the King.

'What shall I say to Auntie Khana about the raid?'

'Tell her Benya knows about the raid.'

And he went away, this young man. He was followed by about three of Benya's friends. They said they would return in half an hour. And they returned in half an hour. That is all.

They did not sit down at table in order of seniority: stupid old age is just as pitiful as cowardly youth. Or in order of wealth, either: the lining of a heavy purse is sewn with tears.

In the place of honour sat the bride and groom. This was their day. In the next place sat Sender Eykhbaum, the King's father-in-law. This was his right. You should know Sender Eykhbaum's story, because it is not a common story.

How did Benya Krik, gangster and king of gangsters, become Eykhbaum's son-in-law? How did he subsequently become a man who had sixty milch cows except for one? It all had to do with a robbery. A year earlier Benya had written Eykhbaum a letter:

Monsieur Eykhbaum, I ask you to put twenty thousand roubles in the gateway of No. 17 Sofiyevskaya tomorrow morning. If you do not do this, there will await you such a thing that it is not heard of, and all Odessa will talk about you.

Yours faithfully
BENYA THE KING.

Three letters, each one clearer than the last, had remained unanswered. Then Benya took measures. They arrived by night, nine men with long sticks in their hands. The sticks were bound around with tar-coated oakum. Nine blazing stars flared up in Eykhbaum's cattleyard. Benya smashed the locks on the shed door and began to lead out the cows one by one. A lad with a knife was waiting for them. He felled each cow with a single blow and sank the knife into the cow's heart. On the blood-soaked earth the torches bloomed like fiery roses. The dairymaids were driven off with shots. The gangsters fired into the air – if you don't fire into the air, someone may get killed. When the sixth cow fell with a mortal bellow at the King's feet, Eykhbaum, who had come running out into the yard in his underpants, asked:

'What will be from this, Benya?'

'If I am not to have my money, you will have no cows, Monsieur Eykhbaum. That is adding two and two together.'

'Come in, Benya.'

They came to an agreement. The slaughtered cows were shared between them. Eykhbaum received a guarantee of personal immunity and was given a certificate with a seal to that effect. But the miracle came later.

At the time of the robbery, on that terrible night when skewered cows bellowed and calves slipped on their mothers' blood, when torches danced like black maidens, and the dairymaids dashed aside, squealing, under the muzzles of friendly Brownings – out into the yard in a low-cut chemise ran old man Eykhbaum's daughter, Tsilya. And the King's triumph became his defeat.

Two days later, without warning, Benya returned to Eykhbaum all the money he had taken from him. In the evening he presented himself on a visit. Under his orange cuff shone a diamond bracelet. He asked Eykhbaum for the hand of his daughter Tsilya. The old man suffered a slight stroke, but he got better. There was life in the old man yet, enough for another twenty years.

'Eykhbaum,' the King said to him, 'when you die I shall bury you in the First Jewish Cemetery, right by the gate. I shall place to you a monument of pink marble. I shall make you an Elder of the Brody Synagogue.* I shall give up my trade, Eykhbaum, and enter your business as a partner. We shall have two hundred cows, Eykhbaum. I shall kill all the milk traders, except for you. No thief shall walk the street where you live. I shall build you a dacha at the sixteenth stop* . . . you were no rabbi in your young days either, after all. Who forged that will, or should we not speak about that? . . . And the King will be your son-in-law, not a milksop, but the King, Eykhbaum . . .'

And he got his way, Benya Krik, because he was passionate, and passion holds sway over the world. The newly-weds spent three months in fertile Bessarabia among grapes, abundant food and the sweat of love. Then Benya returned to Odessa in order to give in marriage his forty-year-old sister Dvoyra, who suffered from goitre. Now let us return to the wedding of Dvoyra Krik, the King's sister.

For supper they served turkeys, roast chickens, geese, *gefilte* fish and fish soup in which lemon lakes shone like mother-of-pearl. Above the heads of the dead geese flowers swayed like splendid plumes. But do the foamy breakers of Odessa's sea cast up roast chickens on the shore?

On that blue, starry night, all that is noblest in our contraband, all for which the land is famed from end to end, performed its destructive, seductive task. The foreign wine warmed stomachs, sweetly fractured legs, stupefied brains and called forth eructations sonorous as the summons of a battle horn. The black cook from the *Plutarch*, which had arrived a couple of days earlier from Port Said, had wafted through the customs pot-bellied bottles of Jamaican rum, oily Madeira, cigars from the plantations of Pierpont Morgan and oranges from the environs of Jerusalem. That is what the foamy breakers of Odessa's sea cast up upon the shore.

The Jewish beggars, having imbibed their fill like *tref* swine, thundered deafeningly with their crutches. Eykhbaum, who had loosened his waistcoat, surveyed the raging assembly with a screwed-up eye and hiccupped lovingly. The band played a flourish. It was like a divisional parade. A flourish – nothing but a flourish. The gangsters, who sat in serried ranks, were at first embarrassed by the excessive accumulation of outsiders. Then they let themselves go. Lyova Katsap smashed a bottle of vodka on the head of his beloved. Monya Artillerist fired in the air. But the limits of their ecstasies were reached only when, in accordance with ancient custom, the guests began to bestow gifts upon the newly-weds. The synagogue beadles, leaping up on to the tables, sang out to the tones of each seething flourish the number of roubles and silver spoons that had been bestowed. And then the King's friends showed the true worth of blue blood and the not-yet defunct chivalry of the Moldavanka. With an inexpressible, casual movement of their hands they threw coins, rings and strings of coral on to the golden trays. Tightening their belts and thrusting forth their bellies, they got up from their seats.

Moldavanka aristocrats, they were squeezed into crimson waistcoats, their steel shoulders enveloped in red-brown jackets, and on their fleshy legs swelled buttoned leather the colour of an azure sky. Drawing themselves up to their full stature, the bandits clapped in time to the music, shouted 'Bitter!'* and threw the bride flowers, while she, the forty-year-old Dvoyra Krik, the sister of Benya Krik, the sister of the King, disfigured by illness, with her swollen goitre and eyes that were bulging out of their sockets, sat on a mountain of cushions beside the puny boy who had been bought with Eykhbaum's money and was speechless with melancholy.

The ritual of bestowal was drawing to a close, the beadles had grown hoarse and the bass was out of tune with the violin. Over the little courtyard spread a gentle smell of burning.

'Benya,' said Papasha Krik, the old drayman,* who had a reputation among the draymen as a crude fellow, 'Benya, you know what I think? I think the soot by us is burning.'

'Papasha,' the King replied to his drunken father, 'please, eat and drink, let not these foolish things excite you.'

Papasha Krik followed his son's advice. He ate and drank. But the small cloud of smoke was growing ever more poisonous. And here and there the edges of the sky were already turning pink. And then a tongue of flame, narrow as a sword, shot up high in the air. The guests, half getting up, began to sniff the air like hounds. Women squealed. The gangsters exchanged glances with one another. Benya was inconsolable.

'They are mining my party!' he cried, full of despair. 'Friends, I beg you, eat and drink . . .'

At this moment the young man who had arrived at the beginning of the evening appeared in the courtyard.

'King,' he said, 'I must have a word with you . . .'

'Go on then,' the King assented, 'you always have a word or two in stock . . .'

'King,' said the unknown young man, giggling, 'this is plain ridiculous, the police station is burning like a candle . . .'

The delicatessen owners were struck dumb. The gangsters smirked. The sixty-year-old Manka, progenitrix of the out-of-town bandits, putting two fingers in her mouth, whistled so piercingly that those next to her gave a start.

'Manya, you are not at work,' Benya Krik observed to her. 'More gently, Manya.'

The young man who had brought the startling piece of news shook with suppressed laughter. He was giggling like a bashful schoolgirl.

'About forty of them came out of the police station,' he related, moving his jaws, 'they were coming on a raid, but when they had gone about fifteen paces, the place caught fire . . .'

Benya forbade his guests to go and watch the fire. He set off with two companions. The police station was meticulously ablaze on all four sides. Policemen, their backsides a-jog, were running up and down the smoke-filled stairways throwing boxes out of the windows. On the quiet the prisoners were making themselves scarce. The firemen were full of zeal, but it turned out that there was no water in the nearby hydrant. The superintendent, the new broom, stood on the opposite pavement, biting his moustache. Without movement, the new broom continued to stand. Benya, as he walked past the superintendent, gave him a military salute.

'Good health, your excellency,' he said sympathetically. 'What can one say of this misfortune? Why, it's a nightmare.'

He fixed his eyes dully on the burning building, shook his head and smacked his lips:

'Ai-ai-ai.'

When Benya returned home again the little lamps were already going out in the courtyard and the dawn was breaking in the sky. The guests had dispersed. The musicians were drowsing, their heads lowered on to the fingerboards of their basses. Dvoyra was nudging her husband towards the door of their nuptial chamber, looking at him carnivorously, like a cat which, holding a mouse in her jaws, gently tests it with her teeth.

How It was Done in Odessa

I began.

'Reb Arye-Leyb,'* said I to the old man, 'let us talk of Benya Krik. Let us talk of his lightning-swift beginning and terrible end. Three black shadows obstruct the paths of my imagination. Here is Froim Grach.* The red steel of his deeds – will it not stand comparison with the strength of the King? Here is Kolka Pakovsky. The simple-hearted fury of that man contained within it all that was necessary in order for him to exert power. And did Chaim Drong really not possess the ability to tell the light of a star that is new from one that is unfading? But then why was Benya Krik the only one to climb to the top of the rope ladder, while all the rest hung below, on unsteady rungs?'

Reb Arye-Leyb remained silent as he sat on the cemetery wall. Before us stretched the green tranquillity of the graves. A man who thirsts for an answer must stock up with patience. A man who acquires knowledge is best suited by solemnity. So Arye-Leyb remained silent as he sat on the cemetery wall. At last, he said:

'Why him? Why not them, you want to know? Well then – forget for a while that you have glasses on your nose, and autumn in your soul. Stop brawling at your writing-desk and stuttering in the presence of others. Imagine for a moment that you do your brawling on the squares and your stuttering on paper. You are a tiger, you are a lion, you are a cat. You can spend the night with a Russian woman, and the Russian woman will be satisfied with you. You are twenty-five years old. If heaven and earth had rings attached to them, you would seize hold of those rings and pull heaven down to earth. But your Papasha is the drayman Mendel Krik. What does such a Papasha think about? He thinks about drinking a good cup of vodka, about giving someone a sock in the mug, about his horses – and that is all. You want to live, but he compels you to die twenty times a day. What would you do in Benya Krik's place? You would do nothing. But he did something. And that is why he is the King, while you're nothing.

'He went to Froim Grach, who even then looked at the world with only one eye and was what he is. He said to Froim, "Take me. I want to get across to your shore. The shore I get across to will gain from it."

'Grach asked him: "Who are you, where do you come from and what do you breathe with?"'

'"Try me, Froim," replied Benya, "and let us stop spreading buckwheat porridge on a clean table."

'"Let us stop spreading porridge," replied Grach, "I will try you."

'And they called together a council, so that they could think about Benya Krik. I was not at that council. But it is said that they called together a council. The head of it then was Lyovka Byk,* now deceased.

'"What goes on under his hat, this Benchik boy?" asked the deceased Byk.

'And the one-eyed Grach said what he thought, "Benya talks little, but he talks with relish. He says little, but you want him to say more."

'"If that's so," the deceased Lyovka exclaimed, "then let us try him on Tartakovsky."

'"Yes, let us try him on Tartakovsky," the council decided, and all in whom conscience still resided blushed when they heard this decision. Why did they blush? You will learn of this if you come where I will take you."

'We called Tartakovsky "Yid-and-a-Half" or "Nine Raids". He got the name "Yid-and-a-Half" because no one Jew could ever have held in himself as much insolence and money as there was in Tartakovsky. He was taller than the tallest policeman in Odessa, and weighed more than the fattest market woman. And Tartakovsky was nicknamed "Nine Raids" because the firm of Lyovka Byk & Co. had made upon his office not eight raids and not ten, but precisely nine. To the lot of Benya Krik, who at that time was not yet King, fell the honour of accomplishing the tenth raid on Yid-and-a-Half. When Froim informed him of this, he said yes and went out, slamming the door. Why did he slam the door? You will learn of this if you come where I will take you.

'Tartakovsky has the soul of a murderer, but he is one of us. He has come from us. He is our blood. He is our flesh, as though born of the same mother. Half Odessa works in his shops. And he suffered from his own Moldavanka boys. Twice they kidnapped him for a ransom, and once during a pogrom they buried him, with choirboys. The Sloboda hoods were beating Jews on Bolshaya Arnautskaya. Tartakovsky got away from them and met a funeral procession, complete with choirboys, on Sofievskaya.

'"Who is having a funeral with choirboys?" he asked.

'The passers-by replied that it was him, Tartakovsky. The procession reached the Sloboda Cemetery. Then our Molda-vanka boys took a machine-gun out of the coffin and began to spray the Sloboda hoods with bullets. But Yid-and-a-Half had not foreseen this. Yid-and-a-Half was scared to death. And what boss would not have been scared in his place?

'A tenth raid on a man who had already been buried once, this was a crude act. Benya, who was not yet King, understood that better than anyone. But he said yes to Grach, and that same day he wrote Tartakovsky the usual sort of letter:

DEAR RUVIM OSIPOVICH

Please be so kind as to put under the water-butt by Saturday . . . et cetera. In the case of your refusal, as you have recently begun to permit yourself this, a great disappointment in your family life awaits you.

With respect, your acquaintance

BENTSION KRIK

'Tartakovsky was not too lazy to reply without delay:

BENYA

If you were an idiot, I would write to you as to an idiot. But I do not think you are, and may God save you from being thought one. It is plain that you are young. Do you really not know that this year the harvest in Argentina is so big it would bury you, and we sit here unable to sell our wheat. And I will tell you, with my hand on my heart, I am sick of eating such a bitter crust of bread and experiencing such misery in my declining years, after having worked all my life like the lowest drayman. And what do I have to show for this endless travail? Ulcers, sores, trouble and insomnia. Give up these foolish ideas, Benya.

Your friend, far more than you suppose,

RUVIM TARTAKOVSKY

'Yid-and-a-Half had done his thing. He had written a letter. But the mail delivered the letter to the wrong address. Receiving no answer, Benya got annoyed. The following day he presented himself at Tartakovsky's office with four friends. Four young guys with masks and revolvers fell into the room.

'"Hands up!" they said and began to wave their pistols.

'"Calm down, Solomon," Benya observed to one of them who was shouting louder than the others, "it's no use the way you get keyed up on the job," – and, turning round to face the shop assistant, who was as white as death and yellow as clay, he asked him:

'"Is Yid-and-a-Half on the premises?"

'"He's not on the premises," replied the assistant, whose last name was Muginshteyn,* and whose first name was Iosif and who was the unmarried son of Auntie Pesya, the poultry seller from Seredinskaya Square.

'"Then who's acting for the boss here?" they began to ask the unhappy Muginshteyn.

'"I am acting for him," said the assistant, as green as green grass.

'"Then with God's help, open the safe for us!" Benya commanded him, and an opera in three acts began.

'The nervous Solomon packed a suitcase full of money, securities, watches and monograms, the now-deceased Iosif stood in front of him with his hands raised, and Benya meanwhile related stories from the life of the Jewish people.

'"Since he is making of himself a Rothschild," said Benya, about Tartakovsky, "let him be burned by fire. Explain to me, Muginshteyn, as to a friend, when he received from me a business letter, why could he not sit for five copecks on the tramcar and come to me in my apartment and drink a glass of vodka with my family and take a bite of what God has sent? What stopped him from speaking out his soul before me? 'Benya,' he could have said to me, 'either way, here for you is my balance-sheet, just give me a couple of days, let me take a breath, give me to lift my hands.' What would I have replied to him? Pig does not meet with pig, but man meets with man. Do you understand, Muginshteyn?"'

'"I understand," said Muginshteyn, lying, because it was quite beyond his understanding why Yid-and-a-Half, a venerable and wealthy man, and a man of the first importance, had to ride the tramcar for zakuski* with the family of drayman Mendel Krik.

'And all the while misfortune loafed under the windows like a beggar at dawn. Misfortune burst into the office with a din. And though it came in the form of the Jew Savka Butsis, it was as drunk as a water-carrier.

'"Ho-hoo-ho," shouted Savka the Jew, "forgive me, Benchik, I am late," and he began to stamp his feet and wave his arms. Then he fired, and the bullet hit Muginshteyn in the stomach.

'Are words needed here? A man was and a man is no more. A blameless bachelor was living like a bird on a branch – and now he is dead through a foolishness. A Jew arrived, who looked like a sailor, and fired not at a target in a shooting gallery, but at a living man. Are words needed here?

'"Get the hell out of the office," cried Benya, and ran off last. As he left, however, he managed to say to Butsis, "I swear by my mother's coffin, Savka, you will lie beside him . . ."

'Now tell me, young gentleman who cuts the coupons on other people's shares, what would you have done in Benya Krik's place? You do not know what to do. But he knew. That is why he is the King, while you and I sit on the wall of the Second Jewish Cemetery, screening ourselves from the sun with our hands.

'Auntie Pesya's unfortunate son did not die at once. An hour after he had been taken to the hospital, Benya turned up there. He had the head doctor and a sick-nurse brought out to him and told them, keeping his hands in the pockets of his cream trousers, "I have an interest the patient Iosif Muginshteyn should get well. In any case, allow me to introduce myself – Bentsion Krik. Camphor, air-cushions, a private room – give them with an open heart. And if you don't, every doctor, be he even a doctor of philosophy, will get just six feet of earth."

'But Muginshteyn died that same night. And only then did Yid-and-a-Half raise the alarm through all Odessa.

'"Where do the police begin," he cried, "and where does Benya end?"

'"The police end where Benya begins," sensible people replied, but Tartakovsky would not calm down. In the end, he heard, on Serdinskaya Square, a red motor car with a musical box play the first march from the opera *I Pagliacci*. In broad daylight the motor car swept up to the little house where Auntie Pesya lived.

'With a thunder of wheels, a spitting of smoke, a shining of brass and a stink of petrol the motor car played arias on its horn. Someone leapt out of the motor car and went round to the kitchen, where little Auntie Pesya was writhing on the earthen floor. Yid-and-a-Half was sitting on a chair waving his arms.

'"Hooligan mug!" he shouted, catching sight of his guest. "Bandit, may the earth cast you out, a fine fashion you have picked yourself – killing live men!"

'"Monsieur Tartakovsky," Benya Krik replied, in a quiet voice, "for two whole days and nights now I have wept for the dear deceased as for my own brother. But I know that you wished to spit on my young tears. Shame, Monsieur Tartakovsky – in what flameproof safe have you hidden your shame? You had the insolence to send the mother of our departed Iosif a hundred wretched roubles. My brain, together with my hair, stood on end when I heard that piece of news . . ."

'Here Benya paused. He wore a chocolate jacket, cream trousers and raspberry-coloured lacing boots.

'"Ten thousand in a lump sum," he roared, "ten thousand in a lump sum and a pension until her death, though she live to be a hundred and twenty. And if not, then we shall leave these premises, Monsieur Tartakovsky, and get into my motor car . . ."

'Then they quarrelled with each other. Yid-and-a-Half quarrelled with Benya. I was not present at that quarrel. But those who were, they remember. They agreed on five thousand in ready cash and fifty roubles a month.

'"Auntie Pesya," Benya said then to the dishevelled old woman who lay on the floor, "if you need my life you can have it, but everyone makes mistakes, even God. There has been a huge mistake, Auntie Pesya. But was it not a mistake on God's part to settle the Jews in Russia, where they have been tormented as if in hell? And what would be the harm if the Jews were to live in Switzerland, where they would be surrounded by first-class lakes, mountain air and nothing but Frenchmen? Everyone makes mistakes, even God. Listen to me with your ears, Auntie Pesya. You have five thousand in hand and fifty roubles a month until you die – live a hundred and twenty years. Iosif's funeral will be first class: six horses like six lions, two hearses with wreaths, the choir from the Brody Synagogue. Minkovksy himself will come to sing the burial service for your departed son . . ."

'And the funeral took place the following morning. About that funeral ask the beggars of the cemetery. Ask the beadles from the Synagogue of Kosher Poultry Vendors or the old women from the Second Almshouse about it. Such a funeral as Odessa had never seen before, and the world will never see again. That day the policemen put on cotton gloves. In the synagogues, twined with greenery and with doors open wide, electricity burned. Black plumes swayed on the white horses that were harnessed to the hearse. Sixty choristers walked at the head of the procession. The choristers were boys, but they sang with the voices of women. The elders of the Synagogue of Kosher Poultry Vendors helped Auntie Pesya along by the arm. Behind the elders walked the members of the Society of Jewish Shop Assistants, and behind the Jewish Shop Assistants, barristers, doctors of medicine and doctors' assistant-midwives. On one side of Auntie Pesya were the female poultry sellers from Stary Bazaar, and on her other side were the honourable dairymaids from Bugayevka, tucked up in orange shawls. They were stamping their feet like gendarmes on parade on their holiday. From their broad hips came a smell of sea and milk. And behind them all trudged the employees of Ruvim Tartakovsky. There were a hundred of them, or two hundred, or two thousand. They were dressed in black frock-coats with silk lapels and new boots that squeaked like piglets in a sack.

'And now I shall speak as the Lord spake in the burning bush on Mount Sinai. Take my words into your ears. All that I saw, I saw with my own eyes, sitting here, on the wall of the Second Cemetery, beside lisping Moyseyka and Shimshon from the funeral parlour. It was I who saw it – Arye-Leyb, a proud Jew who lives in the presence of the dead.

'The hearse rolled up to the Cemetery Synagogue. They placed the coffin on the step. Auntie Pesya trembled like a little bird. The cantor got out of the phaeton and began the funeral service. The sixty choirboys accompanied him. And at that moment a red motor car swept round the bend. It played "On with the Motley" and came to a halt. People were as silent as the slain. The trees, the choirboys, the beggars were all silent. Four men got out from under the red roof and slowly carried to the hearse a peerless wreath of roses. And when the funeral service was at an end, the four men raised the coffin on their steel shoulders, and with blazing eyes and protruding chests they strode along with the members of the Society of Jewish Shop Assistants.

'In front walked Benya Krik, whom no one yet called the King. He was the first to approach the grave, ascend the mound and stretch out his hand.

'"What do you want, young man?" asked Kofman from the funeral brotherhood, running up to him.

'"I want to give a speech," answered Benya Krik.

'And he gave a speech. It was heard by all who wished to hear it. It was heard by me, Arye-Leyb, and lisping Moyseyka, who sat on the wall beside me.

'"Ladies and gentlemen," said Benya Krik, "ladies and gentlemen," he said, and the sun rose above his head like a sentry with a rifle. "You have come to pay your last respects to an honest toiler who died for a copper half copeck. In my own name and in the name of all who are not present here, I thank you, ladies and gentlemen. What did our dear Iosif see in his life? He saw a couple of trifles. What did he do? He counted other people's money. Why did he die? He died for the whole toiling class. There are some who are already condemned to death. And there are some who have not yet begun to live. And then a bullet, flying into the condemned breast, makes a hole in Iosif, who has seen nothing in his life but a couple of trifles. There are those who can drink vodka, and there are those who can't but who drink it all the same. And the former get their enjoyment out of misery and joy, while the latter suffer for all those who drink vodka and are not able to drink it. Therefore, ladies and gentlemen, after we have said a prayer for our poor Iosif, I ask you to accompany to his grave the deceased – although you do not know it – Savely Butsis."

'And when he had made this speech, Benya Krik came down from the grave mound. The people, the trees and the cemetery beggars were silent. Two gravediggers carried an unpainted coffin to the adjacent grave. The cantor, stuttering, ended the prayer. Benya threw in the first spadeful of earth and went over to Savka. After him, like sheep, went all the barristers and ladies with brooches. He made the cantor sing the full funeral service, and the sixty choirboys accompanied him. Savka had never dreamt of such a funeral – believe the words of Arye-Leyb, an old, old man.

'It is said that on that day Yid-and-a-Half decided to go out of business. I was not there at the time. But the fact that neither the cantor, nor the choir, nor the funeral brotherhood asked any money for the funeral – this I saw, with the eyes of Arye-Leyb (such is my name). And more than that I could not see, because people, after slowly walking away from Savka's grave, threw themselves into flight, as from a fire. They flew in phaetons, in wagons and on foot. And only the four who had arrived in the red motor car left in it again. The musical box played its march, the car gave a start and whirled away.

' "The King," said the lisping Moyseyka, looking after it as it went, the same Moyseyka who always takes from me the best seat on the wall.

'Now you know it all. You know who first uttered the name "King". It was Moyseyka. You know why he didn't give the name to the one-eyed Grach or to the crazy Kolka. You know it all. But what is the use, if you still have glasses on your nose, as you had before, and autumn in your soul?'

Justice in Brackets

The first deal I had was with Benya Krik, the second with Lyubka Shneyveys.* Can you understand the meaning of such words? Can you begin to relish them? On this road of death Seryozhka Utochkin* was missing. I did not meet him on this occasion, and so I am still alive. Like a monument of bronze he stands above the town, he – Utochkin, red of hair and grey of eye. All people will have to run between his legs of bronze.

One day he'll sit on them and they'll die. Or else – everyone will sit on Utochkin and he'll die. Who can tell? I should not lead the story off down side-streets. I should not do it even when in the side-streets the acacias are in bloom and the chestnuts are ripening. First about Benya, then about Lyubka Shneyveys. On that let us end. And everyone will say the full stop comes where it should come.

Since I was blessed with being born a Jew, I became a broker. Having become an Odessa broker, I covered myself in leaves and put forth shoots. Burdened with shoots, I felt unhappy. For what reason? The reason is competition. Otherwise I would not even have blown my nose at this justice. In my hands the work is not hidden. Before me stands the air. It glistens like the sea beneath the sun, the beautiful and empty air. The shoots want to eat. I have seven of them, and my wife is the eighth shoot. I did not blow my nose at justice. No. Justice blew its nose at me. For what reason? The reason is competition.

The cooperative was called 'Justice'. Nothing bad can be said about it. Anyone who says anything bad about it takes upon himself an injustice. It was run by six partners, *primo di primo*, who were moreover specialists in their branch. Their shop was full of merchandise, and the point–duty militiaman there was Motya from Golokovskaya. What more do you want? Nothing more, it seems. This deal was offered me by the bookkeeper from Justice. An honest deal, a safe deal, an easy deal. I cleaned my body with a clothes brush and sent it to Benya. The King pretended he had not seen my body. Then I coughed and said:

'Whenever you like, Benya.'

The King was having *zakuski*. A small decanter of vodka, a fat cigar, a wife with a little belly, the seventh or the eighth month, I cannot say for sure. Around the terrace, nature and wild vines.

'Whenever you like,' I say.

'When?' he asks me.

'Now that you have asked me,' I reply to the King, 'I am bound to express my opinion. In my opinion, the night of Saturday to Sunday would be best of all. The man on point duty, by the way, is none other than Motya from Golokov-skaya. A weekday would also be OK, but why make a quiet deal into a noisy one?'

Such was my opinion. And the King's wife agreed with it.

'Child,' Benya said to her then, 'I want you should go and rest on the couch.'

Then with slow fingers he tore the gold fillet from his cigar and turned round to Froim Shtern:

'Tell me, Grach, are we busy on Saturday, or are we not busy on Saturday?'

But Froim Shtern is a man with all his wits about him. He is a red-haired man with only one eye in his head. To reply with an open soul Froim Shtern cannot do.

'On Saturday,' he replied, 'you promised to go to the Mutual Credit Society . . .'

Grach pretends that he has nothing further to say, and he unconcernedly rams his only eye into the farthest corner of the terrace.

'Excellent,' Benya Krik follows on, 'remind me to go there on Saturday for Tsudechkis, write that down for yourself, Grach. Go back to your family, Tsudechkis,' the King says to me. 'On Saturday evening, in all probability, I shall pay a visit to Justice. Take my words with you, Tsudechkis, and go.'

The King speaks little, and he speaks politely. This frightens people so badly that they never ask him to repeat. I made my departure, and set off along Gospitalnaya, turned into Stepovaya, then stopped in order to examine Benya's words. I tried them by feel and by weight, I held them between my front teeth and saw that these were in no way words I needed.

'In all probability,' said the King, with slow fingers removing the gold fillet from his cigar. The King speaks little, and he speaks politely. Who can understand the meaning of the King's few words? In all probability I shall go, or in all probability I shall not go. Between yes and no lie five thousand brokerages. Not counting the two cows which I keep for my needs, I have ten hungry mouths to feed. Who gave me the right to take risks? After the bookkeeper from Justice came to see me, did he not go to see Buntselman? And Buntselman, in his turn, did he not run off to Kolya Shtift, that fellow Kolya who is hot-tempered to the point of impossibility? The King's words had descended like a boulder on that path where hunger roams, multiplied by nine heads. More simply speaking, I precipitated Buntselman by half a breath. He was going in to Kolya at the same moment as I was coming out from Kolya. It was hot, and he had begun to sweat. 'Hold your ground, Buntselman,' I said to him, 'your hurry is in vain, and so is your sweat. Here I eat. *Und damit Punktum,** as the Germans say.'

And then there was the fifth day. And then there was the sixth day. The Sabbath walked up and down the streets of the Moldavanka. Motya was on duty already, I was asleep in my bed already. Kolya was toiling at Justice. He had loaded half a draycart, and his aim was to load another half a draycart. Just then in the lane a noise was heard, iron-bound wheels began to rumble; Motya from Golokovskaya took hold of a telegraph pole and asked, 'Shall I let it fall?' Kolya replied, 'It's not time yet.' (The fact was that in case of need this pole could fall.)

A wagon drove slowly into the lane and approached the shop. Kolya realized that the police were coming, and his heart began to tear itself to pieces, because he was loth to give up his work.

'Motya,' he said, 'when I fire, the pole will fall.'

'Absolutely,' Motya replied.

Shtift returned to the shop, and all his helpers went with him. They stood along the wall and drew their revolvers. Ten eyes and five revolvers were aimed at the door, as well as the sawn pole. The young fellows were full of impatience.

'Clear off, militia,' whispered an impatient one, 'clear off, 'cos we're going to kill him . . .'

'Be quiet,' said Benya Krik, jumping down from the mezzanine. 'Where do you see militia, ugly mug? The King is here.'

Much longer, and there would have been trouble. Benya knocked Shtift to the ground and grabbed his revolver from him. People began to fall from the mezzanine like rain. In the darkness one could make out nothing.

'Well, well,' Kolka shouted then, 'Benya is trying to kill me, that is rather interesting . . .'

For the first time in his life, the King had been taken for a police officer. That was worthy of laughter. The gangsters roared with full-throated laughter. They switched on their flashlights, they split their sides, they rolled about the floor, choking with laughter.

Only the King did not laugh.

'In Odessa they will say,' he began in a businesslike voice, 'in Odessa they will say the King was tempted by his comrade's earnings.'

'They will say that once,' Shtift replied to him. 'No one will say that twice.'

'Kolya,' the King went on solemnly and in a quiet voice, 'do you believe me, Kolya?'

And here the gangsters stopped laughing. In each of their hands a flashlight burned, but laughter went creeping out of the Justice cooperative.

'What do you want me to believe, King?'

'Do you believe me, Kolya, when I tell you I have nothing to do with this?'

And he sat down on a chair, that subdued King, he covered his eyes with a dusty sleeve and began to weep. Such was the pride of this man that it made him burn like a fire. And all the gangsters, all of them to a man, saw their King weeping from wounded pride.

Then they stood facing each other. Benya stood, and Shtift stood. They began to shake hands, they apologized, they kissed each other on the lips, and each of them shook the hand of his comrade with such force as though he wanted to tear it off. Dawn was already beginning to gaze blankly with its weak eyes, Motya had already returned to the police station to go off duty, already two full draycarts had carted away that which had once been called the Justice cooperative, but the King and Kolya were still exchanging greetings and, their arms thrown round each other's necks, kissing as tenderly as drunks.

Who was fate looking for that morning? It was looking for me, Tsudechkis, and it found me.

'Kolya,' the King asked at last, 'who directed you to Justice?'

'Tsudechkis. And what about you, Benya, who directed you to it?'

'Tsudechkis.'

'Benya,' Kolya cried, 'are we really going to let him live?'

'Certainly not,' says Benya, turning to one-eyed Shtern, who is standing on one side, giggling, because he has fallen out with me. 'You order the brocade coffin, Froim, and I will go and get Tsudechkis. After all, Kolya, once you have begun something, you have to go through with it, and I earnestly invite you on my own behalf and that of my spouse to come to me in the morning and take *zakuski* in the circle of my family.'

At about five o'clock in the morning, or rather at about four o'clock in the morning, and it may not even have been four, the King came into my bedroom, took me, if you will excuse me, by the back, took me off the bed, placed me on the floor and put his foot on my nose. Hearing various sounds and the like, my spouse leapt down and asked Benya:

'Monsieur Krik, why do you attack my Tsudechkis?' 'What do you mean, why?' replied Benya, not taking his foot off the bridge of my nose, and the tears began to trickle from his eyes. 'He has cast a shadow on my name, he has shamed me in front of comrades, you can say goodbye to him, Madame Tsudechkis, for my honour is dearer to me than my happiness and he cannot remain alive . . .'

Continuing to weep, he stamped on me with his feet. My spouse, seeing that I was distraught, began to scream. This happened at half-past four, and she finished at eight. But she taught him a lesson, oh, how she taught him a lesson! This was splendid!

'Why are you angry with my Tsudechkis,' she cried, standing on the bed, and I, writhing on the floor, looked at her in admiration. 'Why are you beating my Tsudechkis? Because he wanted to feed his nine hungry little chicks? You so-and-so, you are the King, you are the son-in-law of a rich man and a rich man yourself, and your father is a rich man. You are a man who has the world at his feet, what is one unsuccessful deal to you, Benchik, when next week will bring you seven successful ones? Do not dare to beat my Tsudechkis! Do not dare!'

She saved my life.

When the children woke up, they began to scream too. Even so, Benya had spoilt as much of my health as he knew he had to spoil. He left two hundred roubles for medical treatment and went away. I was taken to the Jewish Hospital. On Sunday I was dying, on Monday I was getting better, and on Tuesday I had my crisis.

That is my first story. Who is to blame, and what is the reason? Is Benya really to blame? There is no point in hiding our eyes from one another. Another man such as Benya the King does not exist. Exterminating falsehood, he seeks justice, both that justice which is in brackets and that which is not in brackets. But you see, all the rest of them are as cold as jellied fish, they do not like to seek, they will not seek, and that is worse.

I recovered. And this in order to escape from Benya's hands and fall into Lyubka's. First about Benya, then about Lyubka Shneyveys. On that let us end. And then everyone will say the full stop comes where it should come.

Lyubka Kózak*

In the Moldavanka, on the corner of Dalnitskaya and Balkovskaya Streets, stands the house of Lyubka Shneyveys. In this house there is a wine cellar, a coaching inn, an oat shop, many other shops and a dovecot for a hundred pairs of Kryukov and Nikolayev doves. These shops, and also Odessa stone quarry number forty-six, all belong to Lyubka Shneyveys, nicknamed Lyubka Kózak – all except the dovecot, which is the property of the watchman Yevzel, a retired soldier with a medal. On Sundays Yevzel goes out to the hunters' market with his doves and sells them to civil servants from the town and to the boys of the neighbourhood. In addition to the watchman, also living on Lyubka's courtyard are Pesya-Mindl, a cook and procuress, and the manager Tsudechkis, a little Jew similar in stature and little beard to our renowned Moldavanka Rebbe Ben-Zkharya. I know many interesting stories about this Tsudechkis. The first is the story of how Tsudechkis became the manager of Lyubka's coaching inn, Lyubka who is nicknamed Kózak.

About ten years ago Tsudechkis brokered the sale of a horse-driven threshing machine to a certain landowner, and in the evening brought the landowner to see Lyubka in order to celebrate the purchase of the threshing machine. His purchaser not only had a moustache but side-moustaches as well and wore patent-leather boots. For supper Pesya-Mindl gave him *gefilte* fish, and then a very pretty young lady, Nastya by name. The landowner stayed overnight, and in the morning Yevzel woke Tsudechkis, who had curled up like a bun outside the door of Lyubka's room.

'Here,' said Yevzel, 'last night you boasted that a landowner had bought a threshing machine through you – well let me tell you, having stayed the night here, he ran off at dawn like the lowest of the low. It is plain that you are a crook. Now fork out two roubles for the eats and four roubles for the young lady. It is plain that you are an old hand . . .'

But Tsudechkis would not pay the money. Then Yevzel shoved him into Lyubka's room and locked the door.

'Now,' said the watchman, 'you will stay here, and then Lyubka will come back from the quarry and, with God's help, will take your soul out of you. Amen.'

'Convict,' Tsudechkis replied to the soldier, beginning to look around his new room, 'you know nothing, convict, except your doves, but I still believe in God, and he will lead me out of here as he has led all the Jews – first out of Egypt and then out of the wilderness . . .'

The little broker wanted to say much more to Yevzel, but the soldier took the key with him and went away with a rumble of boots. Then Tsudechkis turned round and saw the procuress Pesya-Mindl by the window; she was reading a book entitled *The Miracles and the Heart of the Baal-Shem.** She was reading the Hassidic book with its gilt edges and rocking an oak cradle with her foot. In this cradle Lyubka's son, Davidka, lay crying.

'Fine customs I see on this Sakhalin,* said Tsudechkis to Pesya-Mindl. 'A child is crying fit to burst, pitiful to watch, and you, you fat woman, sit like a stone in the forest and don't give him his bottle . . .'

'You give him the bottle,' replied Pesya-Mindl, without taking her eyes off her book, 'that is if he will take it from you, you old deceiver – look, he's as big as a Cossack now, and all he wants is his mama's milk, but his mama is galloping round her stone quarries, drinking tea with Jews at the Bear Inn, buying contraband at the harbour and thinking no more of her son than of last year's snow . . .'

'Yes,' the little broker said to himself then, 'you are in the hands of Pharaoh, Tsudechkis' – and he withdrew to the eastern wall,* muttered the whole of the morning prayer, with supplements, and then took the crying infant in his arms. Davidka looked at him in bewilderment and waved his little crimson legs with their infant sweat, and the old man began to walk about the room and, rocking to and fro like a *tsadik* at prayer, began to sing a never-ending song.

'Ah-ah-ah,' he sang, 'now all the other children shall have hard pears, but our Davidochka shall have buns, so that he will sleep both day and night . . . Ah-ah-ah, now all the children shall have fists . . .'

And Tsudechkis showed Lyubka's son his small fist with its grey hair, and repeated his song about hard pears and fists until the boy had fallen asleep and the sun had reached the middle of the radiant sky. It reached the middle and began to quiver like a fly enfeebled by the heat. Wild muzhiks from Nerubaysk and Tatarka who were staying at Lyubka's coaching inn got down under their wagons and fell into a restless, noisy sleep, a drunken apprentice went out to the gate and, having thrown his plane and saw to the winds, fell to the ground in a heap, fell in a heap and began to snore in the midst of the world, covered in golden flies and the blue lightnings of July, and not far from him, in the cool, wrinkled German settlers who had brought Lyubka wine from the Bessarabian border sat down and made themselves comfortable. They lit pipes, and the smoke from their curved chibouks began to mingle with the silver stubble of their unshaven, old men's cheeks. The sun hung from the sky like the pink tongue of a thirsty dog, the gigantic sea rolled on to Peresyp,* and the masts of far-off ships rocked on the emerald water of Odessa Bay. The day sat in a decorated barque, the day sailed on towards evening, and only halfway towards evening, some time after four o'clock, did Lyubka return from the town. She arrived on a little roan horse with a large belly and a mane that was too long. A fat-legged lad in a printed cotton shirt opened the gate for her. Yevzel supported her horse's bridle, and then Tsudechkis cried out to Lyubka from his cell:

'Regards to you, Madame Shneyveys, and good day. You rode away for three years on business and threw your hungry child into my arms . . .'

'Shut up, ugly mug,' replied Lyubka to the old man, and got down from the saddle. 'Who's that gaping over there in my window?'

'It's Tsudechkis, the old hand,' the soldier with the medal replied and he began to tell his mistress about the whole of the episode with the landowner, but he did not reach the end, because the broker, interrupting him, began to shout with all his might:

'What impudence,' he began to shout, flinging his skullcap down, 'what impudence, to throw a child that is not my own into my arms and to vanish for three years yourself. Come here and feed him . . .'

'I'll come and sort you out, you crook,' muttered Lyubka, and she ran towards the stairs. She came into the room and took a breast from her dusty blouse.

The boy stretched towards her, bit hard on her monstrous nipple, but obtained no milk. A vein distended on the mother's brow, and Tsudechkis said to her, shaking his skull-cap:

'You want to have everything for yourself, greedy Lyubka, you pull the whole world towards you as children pull at the tablecloth to get the breadcrumbs; you want the best wheat and the best grapes; you want to bake white loaves in the blaze of the sun, while your little child, a child like a little star, must waste away without milk . . .'

'How can I have any milk,' cried the woman, turning away and squeezing her breast, 'when the *Plutarch* arrived at the harbour today and I've done fifteen versts in the heat? . . . But that's a long story you've started, old Jew – you'd do better to give me the six roubles . . .'

But again Tsudechkis would not pay the money. He rolled up his sleeve, exposed his arm and stuck his thin, dirty elbow into Lyubka's mouth.

'Choke, prisoner,' he said, and spat into the corner.

Lyubka kept the elbow that was not her own in her mouth for a bit, then took it out, locked the door and went into the courtyard. There already waiting for her was Mr Trottyburn,* who resembled a column of reddish meat. Mr Trottyburn was the *Plutarch's* chief engineer. He had brought two sailors with him to Lyubka's. One of the sailors was an Englishman, the other was a Malayan. All three together, they lugged the contraband that had been brought from Port Said into the courtyard. The box was too heavy, they dropped it on the ground, and out of it fell cigars entangled with

Japanese silk. A large number of women came running up to the box, and two newly arrived gypsies, undulating and jangling, came in from the side.

'Away, jackdaws!' Lyubka shouted at them and led the seamen into the shade of the acacias.

They sat down at the table, Yevzel served them with vodka, and Mr Trottyburn unfurled his wares. From the bale he produced cigars and fine silks, cocaine and filing tools, loose tobacco from the state of Virginia and red wine that had been purchased on the island of Chios. Each article of merchandise had its own special price, each figure was washed down with Bessarabian wine that smelt of sun and bedbugs. Twilight was already flowing over the courtyard, like an evening wave on a broad river, and the drunken Malayan, full of surprise, touched Lyubka's breast with his finger. He touched it with one finger, then with each finger in turn. His soft, yellow eyes hung above the table like paper lanterns on a street in China; barely audibly, he began to sing, and he fell to the ground when Lyubka gave him a push with her fist.

'Look what a well-mannered one he is,' Lyubka said to Mr Trottyburn, 'the last of my milk will vanish because of this Malayan, and yet that Jew has already been nagging me for that milk . . .'

And she pointed at Tsudechkis who, standing at the window, was washing his socks. A small lamp smoked in Tsudechkis's room, his washtub foamed and hissed, he leaned out of the window, sensing that he was being talked about, and shouted in despair:

'Stand up for me, people!' he shouted, and waved his arms.

'Shut up, ugly mug!' Lyubka burst out laughing. Then, 'Shut up!' she shouted, and she threw a stone at the old man but did not hit him first time, and then she grabbed an empty wine-bottle. But Mr Trottyburn, the chief engineer, took the bottle from her, aimed and hurled it through the open window.

'Miss Lyubka,' the chief engineer said then, getting up and gathering towards him his drunken legs, 'many worthy people come to me, Miss Lyubka, for merchandise but I don't give it to anyone, neither to Mr Kuninzon nor to Mr Bat, nor to Mr Kupchik, to no one but you, because your conversation is agreeable to me, Miss Lyubka . . .'

And, steadying himself on legs that faltered, he took his sailors by the shoulder, one an Englishman, the other a Malayan, and went dancing with them about the courtyard, which had begun to grow cold. The men from the *Plutarch* danced in thoughtful silence, and an orange star that had rolled right down to the horizon gazed at them for all it was worth. After that, they took their money, joined arms and went out into the street, swaying as a pendent lamp sways on board a ship. From the street they could see the sea, the black water of Odessa Bay, toy flags on sunken masts and piercing lights kindled in spacious depths. Lyubka accompanied her dancing guests to the crossroads; when she was alone in the empty street, she began to laugh at her thoughts and then returned home. The sleepy lad in the printed cotton shirt bolted the gate behind her. Yevzel brought his mistress the takings for the day, and she went upstairs to go to bed. There Pesya-Mindl, the procuress, was already dozing, and Tsudechkis rocked the oak cradle with his naked feet.

'Oh, you have worn us out, shameless Lyubka,' he said, taking the child out of the cradle, 'but now learn from me, foul mother . . .'

He placed a small comb on Lyubka's breast and put her son into her bed. The child stretched out towards his mother, pricked himself on the comb and began to cry. Then the old man shoved the bottle at him, but Davidka turned away from the bottle.

'Are you practising sorcery on me, old swindler?' muttered Lyubka, falling asleep.

'Be quiet, foul mother,' Tsudechkis answered her. 'Be quiet and learn from me, the devil take you . . .'

The child again pricked himself on the comb, hesitantly took the bottle and began to suck it greedily.

'There,' said Tsudechkis, and he laughed, 'I have weaned your child for you; learn from me, the devil take you . . .'

Davidka lay in the cradle, sucked the bottle and dribbled blissfully. Lyubka woke up, opened her eyes and closed them again. She saw her son, and the moon, forcing its way in at her window. The moon was bounding in black clouds like a calf that was lost.

'Very well,' Lyubka said then, 'show Tsudechkis the door, Pesya-Mindl, and let him come tomorrow for a pound of American tobacco.'

And the following day Tsudechkis came for a pound of loose tobacco from the state of Virginia. He received it and a quarter of tea as well. And at the end of the week, when I came to Yevzel's to buy doves from him, I saw the new manager in Lyubka's courtyard. He was as tiny as our Rebbe Ben-Zkharya. Tsudechkis was the new manager. He has remained at his post for fifteen years,* and during that time I have heard a large number of stories about him. And, if I can, I shall tell them all, one after the other, because they are very interesting stories.

The Father

Froim Grach was married once. That was a long time ago; twenty years have passed since that time. Froim's wife bore him a daughter and died in childbirth. The little girl was given the name Basya. Her grandmother on her mother's side lived in Tulchin, that self-seeking, weak-sighted little town. The old woman did not like her son-in-law. She said of him: Froim is a drayman by occupation, he has black horses, but Froim's soul is blacker than the black coats of his horses . . .

The old woman did not like her son-in-law and took the newborn girl to her own home. There she spent twenty years, with the girl, and then died. Then Baska returned to her father. It all happened like this:

On Wednesday the fifth, Froim Grach took wheat from the warehouses of the Dreyfus Company to the port, to the steamship *Caledonia*. By evening he had finished the job and drove home. At the turning off Prohorovskaya Street he encountered the blacksmith Ivan Pyatirubel.

'Respect to you, Grach,' said Ivan Pyatirubel, 'some woman is hammering on the door of your abode.'

Grach drove on and saw a woman of gigantic stature in his courtyard. She had enormous thighs, and cheeks that were brick-red in colour.

'Papasha,' said the woman in a deafening bass, 'the devils are snatching me with boredom. I have been waiting for you all day . . . I have come to tell you that Grandmother has died in Tulchin.'

Grach stood in his draycart and stared at his daughter for all he was worth.

'Do not dance about in front of the horses,' he shouted in despair, 'take the shaft horse's bridle. Do you want to break my horses' legs . . .'

Grach stood in the cart and brandished his knout. Baska took the shaft horse by the bridle and led the horses to the stable. She unharnessed them and went off to work in the kitchen. The girl hung her father's foot-bindings on the line, she cleaned the grimy teapot with sand and started to warm up a meatball in a cast-iron pot.

'The filth here is unbearable, Papasha,' she said, and threw his sour sheepskins, that lay strewn about the floor, out of the window. 'But I will get rid of this dirt,' Baska yelled, giving her father his supper.

The old man drank vodka out of the enamelled teapot and ate the meatball, which smelled like a happy childhood. Then he picked up his knout and went out through the gate. Baska came out after him. She put on a pair of men's lacing boots, she put on an orange dress, she put on a hat covered with birds, and settled down on a small bench. The evening slouched along past the small bench, the radiant eye of the sunset fell into the sea beyond Peresyp, and the sky was as red as a red-letter day in the calendar. All commerce had ceased on Dalnitskaya, and the gangsters were already driving over to Glukhaya Street and Ioska Samuelson's brothel. They drove in varnished carriages, dressed up like hummingbirds in coloured jackets. Their eyes were bulging, each had one leg stuck out towards the footboard, and in an outstretched steel hand each held a bouquet wrapped in rice paper. Their varnished droshkys moved slowly; in each carriage sat one man with a monstrous bouquet, and the coachmen, jutting aloft on high seats, were adorned with bows like best men at weddings. Old Jewish women wearing head-dresses idly watched the flow of this customary procession; they were indifferent to everything, the old Jewish women, and only the sons of shopkeepers and shipwrights envied the kings of the Moldavanka. Solomonchik Kaplun, * the grocer's son, and Monya Artillerist, the smuggler's son, were among those who endeavoured to avert their eyes from the splendour of other men's success. They both walked past Baska Grach and gave her a wink. They walked past her, swaying like girls who have discovered love, they whispered to each other and began to move their arms, demonstrating how they would embrace Baska if she felt like it. And now Baska immediately felt like it, because she was an ordinary girl from Tulchin, that self-seeking, weak-sighted little town. She weighed five poods and a few pounds more; all her life she had lived with the poisonous offshoots of Podolian brokers, wandering book pedlars, lumber contractors, and had never seen men like Solomonchik Kaplun. And so, having set eyes on him, she began to shuffle her fat feet, shod in men's lacing boots, on the ground, and said to her father:

'Papasha,' she said in a thunderous voice, 'look at that little gentleman – he has feet like dollies'. I would smother feet like that . . .'

'Eheh, *panie* Grach,' an old Jew, who was sitting alongside, said, an old Jew, Golubchik * by name. 'I see your child is asking for the grass.'

'Then there will be trouble on my head,' Froim replied to Golubchik, toying with his knout a little, and went off to bed and fell peacefully asleep, because he did not believe the old man. He did not believe the old man and he turned out to be dead wrong. Golubchik was the one who was right. Golubchik engaged in matchmaking on our street, at nights he recited prayers over the well-to-do when they died and he knew everything about life that there is to be known. Froim Grach was wrong. Golubchik was the one who was right.

And indeed, from that day forth Baska spent all her evenings outside the gate. She sat on the little bench and sewed herself a trousseau. Pregnant women sat beside her, piles of cloth crept over her mighty, bandy-legged knees, the pregnant women swelled with all kinds of things as cows' udders swell at pasture with the rosy milk of spring, and one by one their husbands came home from work. The husbands of the quarrelsome wives wrung out their tousled beards under the watertap and then ceded place to hunchbacked old women. The old women bathed fat infants in troughs, they smacked their grandsons on their shining buttocks and rolled them up in their threadbare skirts. And thus Baska from Tulchin first saw the life of the Moldavanka, our generous mother – a life stuffed with sucking infants, drying rags and conjugal nights full of suburban chic and military tirelessness. The girl wanted the same kind of life for herself, but then she discovered that the daughter of the one-eyed Grach could not count on a worthy match. So she stopped calling her father her father.

'Red-headed thief,' she would shout to him in the evenings, 'red-headed thief, come and get your supper.'

And this continued until Baska had sewed herself six night-gowns and six pairs of drawers with lace frills. When she had finished the hemming of the frills, she began to weep in a thin voice that was unlike her usual voice, and said through her tears to the steadfast Grach:

'Every other girl,' she said to him, 'has her interest in life, but I am living like a nightwatchman in someone else's warehouse. Either do something for me, Papasha, or I will make an end to my life . . .'

Grach heard his daughter to the end, and next day he put on a sailcloth cloak and set off to visit Kaplun, the grocer on Privoznaya Square.

Above Kaplun's shop glittered a golden sign. This was the best shop on Privoznaya Square. Its interior smelt of many seas and wonderful lives unknown to us. A boy was watering the cool depths of the shop with a watering-can and singing a song which it is decent only for grown-ups to sing. Solomon-chik, the owner's son, stood behind the counter – on this counter were displayed olives that had come from Greece, oil from Marseilles, coffee beans, Lisbon Malaga, sardines from the firm of Philippe & Canot and cayenne pepper. Kaplun himself sat in his waistcoat in the full blaze of the sun, in a small glass annexe, eating watermelon – red watermelon with black seeds, slanting seeds like the eyes of sly Chinese girls. Kaplun's belly lay on the table under the sun, and the sun could do nothing about it. But then the grocer caught sight of Grach in his sailcloth cloak, and turned pale.

'Good day, Monsieur Grach,' he said, and moved aside. 'Golubchik warned me that you would be coming here, and I have made you up such a nice little pound of tea, a positive rarity . . .'

And he began to talk about a new variety of tea that had been brought to Odessa on the Dutch ships. Grach listened to him patiently; then, however, he interrupted, because he was a simple man without guile.

'I am a simple man without guile,' said Froim. 'I stay with my horses and occupy myself with my work. I am giving for Baska new underwear and a few old quarter-copeck bits, and I myself stand for Baska; and if that isn't enough for anyone, let him burn in fire . . .'

'Why should we burn?' Kaplun replied in a quick patter, giving the drayman's arm a stroke, 'such words are not called for, Monsieur Grach, after all, you are known among us as a man who can help others, and, by the way, you may offend others. You're not a Krakow rabbi,* and I did not stand at the altar with the niece of Moses Montefiore* . . . but Madame Kaplun . . . we have Madame Kaplun, a grand lady and God himself does not know what she wants . . .'

'Well, I know,' Grach said, interrupting the shopkeeper with terrible calm, 'I know that Solomonchik wants Baska, but Madame Kaplun does not want me.'

'That's right, I don't want you,' cried Madame Kaplun, who had been listening at the door, and she came into the small glass annexe, glowing all over, with heaving bosom. 'I don't want you, Grach, just as people do not want death; I don't want you just as a bride does not want pimples on her face. Do not forget that our deceased grandfather was a grocer, that our deceased Papasha was a grocer, and we have a duty to stick to our branch of business.'

'Stick to your branch of business, then,' Grach replied to the blazing Madame Kaplun, and he went off home.

There, waiting for him, was Baska, dressed up in her orange dress, but the old man, without a glance at her, spread out his sheepskin coat under the carts, lay down to sleep and slept until Baska's mighty hand drew him out from under the cart.

'Red-headed thief,' the girl said in a whisper that was not like her usual whisper, 'why must I endure your drayman's habits, and why are you as silent as a tree-stump, red-headed thief?'

'Baska,' Grach enunciated then with terrible calm, 'Solomonchik wants you, but Madame Kaplun does not want me . . . They are looking for a grocer there . . .'

And, having straightened out his sheepskin coat, the old man again got under the cart, and Baska disappeared from the premises . . .

All this happened on a Saturday, a non-working day. The sunset's purple eye, as it rummaged over the earth, stumbled in the evening upon Grach, snoring under his drayman's cart. An impetuous ray fixed the sleeping man with fiery reprimand and led him out to a Dalnitskaya Street that was as dusty and as glittering as the green rye in the wind. Tartars were walking up Dalnitskaya, Tartars and Turks with their mullahs. They were returning from a pilgrimage to Mecca back to their homes in the Orenburg steppes and Transcaucasia. A steamship had brought them to Odessa, and they were going from the port to the coaching inn of Lyubka Shneyveys, nicknamed Lyubka Kózak. Stiff striped robes covered the Tartars and flooded the roadway with the bronze sweat of the desert. White towels were wound around their fezzes, and this signified a man who had worshipped at the shrine of the Prophet. The pilgrims reached the corner and turned towards Lyubka's courtyard, but they were unable to get through there because a large number of people had gathered at the gate. Lyubka Shneyveys, her purse at her side, was beating a drunken muzhik and shoving him into the roadway. She was beating him in the face with her clenched fist, like a tambourine, and with her other hand she was supporting the muzhik so that he did not fall. Small streams of blood were creeping between the muzhik's teeth and behind his ear; he was reflective and looking at Lyubka as though he did not know her, and then he collapsed on the stones and fell asleep. Then Lyubka gave him a shove with her foot and went back inside her shop. Her watchman Yevzel closed the gates behind her and waved an arm at Froim Grach, who was walking by.

'Respect to you, Grach,' he said. 'If you want to observe something of life, then pay a visit to our courtyard, there is something there that will make you laugh . . .'

And the watchman led Grach over to a wall where the pilgrims who had arrived the night before were sitting. An old Turk in a green turban, an old Turk as green and light as a leaf was lying on the ground. He was covered in a pearly sweat, he breathed with difficulty and rolled his eyes.

'There,' said Yevzel and adjusted the medal on his threadbare jacket, 'there is a scene of life from the opera *The Turkish Disease*. He is dying, the little old man, but there can be no question of calling the doctor for him, because whoever dies on the road home from the God Mahomet is considered by them to be a most fortunate and wealthy man . . . Halvash,' Yevzel shouted to the dying man, roaring with laughter, 'here's the doctor come to see to you . . .'

The Turk gave the watchman a look of childish fear and hatred, and turned away. Then Yevzel, pleased with himself, led Grach to the wine cellar on the opposite side of the courtyard. In the cellar lamps were already lit and an orchestra was playing. Old Jews with dirty beards were playing Romanian and Jewish songs. At a table, Mendel Krik was drinking wine from a green glass and describing how his own sons – Benya the elder and Lyovka the younger – had maimed him. He bawled his story in a hoarse and terrible voice, showed his ground teeth and let people feel the wounds on his belly. Volhynian *tsadiks* with porcelain faces stood behind his chair and listened in frozen amazement to Mendel Krik's outrageous boasting. They were astonished at everything they heard, and Grach despised them for this.

'The old boaster,' he muttered, of Mendel, and ordered wine for himself.

Then Froim called to his side the mistress of the house, Lyubka Kózak. She was spouting foul language by the door and drinking vodka, standing up.

'Go on then, speak,' she shouted to Froim, her eyes squinting in mad fury.

'Madame Lyubka,' Froim replied to her, and made her sit down beside him, 'you are a clever woman, and I have come to you as I would to my own mother. I trust in you, Madame Lyubka, first in God, then in you . . .'

'Speak,' cried Lyubka, ran round the whole cellar and then returned to her seat.

And Grach said:

'In the colonies,' he said, 'the Germans have a rich wheat harvest, but in Constantinople groceries go for half of nothing. You can buy a pood of olives in Constantinople for three roubles, while here they sell for thirty copecks a pound . . . Grocers have begun to live well, Madame Lyubka, grocers live off the fat of the land, and if he approaches them with delicate hands a person could become happy . . . But I am now alone in my work, the deceased Lyova Byk is dead, for me from nowhere is there help and here I am alone, as God is alone in heaven . . .'

'Benya Krik,' said Lyubka then, 'you tried him on Tartakovsky, what is wrong with Benya Krik?'

'Benya Krik,' Grach repeated, surprised, 'he is a bachelor too, it occurs to me?'

'He is a bachelor,' said Lyubka. 'Splice him with Baska, give him money, take him out to people . . .'

'Benya Krik,' the old man repeated, like an echo, like a distant echo. 'Of him I did not think.'

He stood up, muttering and stuttering. Lyubka ran ahead and Froim trudged along after her. They crossed the courtyard and went up to the second floor. There, on the second floor, lived the women who Lyubka kept for visitors.

'Our bridegroom is with Katyusha,' said Lyubka to Grach, 'wait for me in the passage,' and she went along to the room at the far end where Benya Krik was in bed with the woman called Katyusha.

'That's enough dribbling,' said the mistress of the house to the young man. 'You must get fixed up with some sort of a job first, Benchik, and then you can dribble . . . Froim Grach is looking for you. He is looking for a man to help him with his work, and cannot find one . . .'

And she told all that she knew about Baska and the business affairs of the one-eyed Grach.

'I will think about it,' Benya answered her, covering Katyusha's bare legs with the sheet, 'I will think about it, let the old man wait for me a bit.'

'You'll have to wait for him a bit,' said Lyubka to Froim, who had stayed out in the passage, 'you'll have wait for him a bit, he's going to think about it.'

The mistress of the house pulled up a chair for Froim, and he sank into boundless expectation. He waited patiently, like a muzhik in a government office. On the other side of the wall Katyusha moaned and roared with laughter. The old man dozed for two hours outside her locked door, two hours, perhaps longer. Evening had long ago become night, the sky had turned black, and its milky ways had filled with gold, brilliance and coolness. Lyubka's cellar was closed now, the drunks lay about the courtyard like broken furniture, and by midnight the old mullah in the green turban was dead. After that came the music from the sea, French horns and trumpets from the English ships: the music came from the sea and died away, but Katyusha, reliable Katyusha, was still incandescing for Benya Krik her painted, Russian and rosy paradise. She moaned on the other side of the wall and roared with laughter: old Froim sat unmoving outside the door, he waited until one o'clock in the morning and then knocked.

'Man,' he said, 'are you laughing at me?'

Then Benya opened, at last, the door of Katyusha's room.

'Monsieur Grach,' he said in embarrassment, beaming and covering himself with the sheet, 'when we are young, we think of women as merchandise, but all they are is straw that burns from nothing . . .'

And, having put his clothes on, he set Katyusha's bed straight, plumped up her pillows and went out with the old man into the street. As they walked along they reached the Russian cemetery, and there, outside the cemetery, the interests of Benya Krik and the bent Grach, the renowned gangster, coincided. They coincided in an agreement that Baska would bring her future husband* a dowry of three thousand roubles, two blood horses and a pearl necklace. They coincided in an agreement that Kaplun should be obliged to pay two thousand roubles to Benya, Baska's bridegroom. He was guilty of family pride – Kaplun of Privoznaya Square, he had got rich on Constantinople olives, he had not spared Baska's first love, and therefore Benya Krik decided to take upon himself the task of getting two thousand roubles out of Kaplun.

'I shall take this upon myself, Papasha,' he said to his future father-in-law. 'God will help us, and we shall punish all grocers . . .'

This was said at break of day, when the night had already passed, and it is here that a new story begins, the story of the fall of the house of Kaplun, the tale of its slow ruin, of acts of arson and shots in the night. And all this – the fate of the arrogant Kaplun and the fate of the daughter Baska – was decided that night when her father and her unexpected fiancé walked along by the Russian cemetery. Lads were then pulling girls behind fences, and kisses resounded on the gravestones.

Sunset

One day Lyovka, the youngest of the Kriks, saw Lyubka's daughter Tabl. Tabl means 'dove' in Russian. He saw her and left home for three days and nights. The dust of other people's roadways and the geraniums in other people's windows brought him consolation. After three days and nights Lyovka returned home and found his father in the front garden. His father was having his supper. Madame Gorobchik sat beside her husband looking round her like a murderess.

'Go away, coarse son,' said Papasha Krik, when he saw Lyovka.

'Papasha,' replied Lyovka, 'take a tuning-fork and tune your ears.'

'What is the matter?'

'There is a girl,' said his son. 'She has blond hair. Her name is Tabl. Tabl means "dove" in Russian. I have got my eye on this girl.'

'You have got your eye on a slut,' said Papasha Krik, 'and her mother runs a brothel.'

Hearing these fatherly words, Lyovka rolled up his sleeves and raised a sacrilegious hand against his father. But Madame Gorobchik jumped up from her chair and stood between them.

'Mendel,' she screeched, 'put up a sign for Lyovka!* Eleven of my meatballs has he eaten . . .'

'Eleven of your mother's meatballs have you eaten!' shouted Mendel and went up to his son, but the latter slipped away and ran out of the house, and Benchik, his elder brother, tagged along after him. Until night-time they whirled about the streets, they panted like yeast fermenting revenge, and at last Lyovka said to his brother Benya, who in a few months' time was destined to become Benya the King:

'Benchik,' he said, 'let us take this job on ourselves, and people will come and kiss our feet. Let us kill Papasha, whom the Moldavanka no longer calls Mendel Krik. The Moldavanka calls him Mendel the Pogrom. Let us kill Papasha – can we wait any longer?'

'It is not yet time,' replied Benchik, 'but time is passing. Listen to its footsteps and make way for it. Step aside, Lyovka.'

And Lyovka stepped aside, in order to make way for time. It started on its path – time, the old cashier – and on its path it met Dvoyra, the King's sister, Manasse, the driver, and the Russian girl Marusya Yevtushenko.

Even ten years ago I knew men who wanted Dvoyra, the daughter of Mendel the Pogrom, but now Dvoyra's goitre dangles under her chin and her eyes are starting out of their sockets. Nobody wants Dvoyra. But not long ago there appeared an elderly widower with grown-up daughters. He needed a one-and-a-half-ton cart and a pair of horses. Hearing of this, Dvoyra washed her green dress and hung it out in the courtyard. She was going to go to the widower in order to find out how advanced in years he was, what kind of horses he needed and whether she could have him. But Papasha Krik did not want any widowers. He took the green dress, hid it in his dray and went off to work. Dvoyra heated the iron to iron her dress, but she could not find the dress. Then Dvoyra fell to the ground and had a fit. Her brothers hauled her over to the tap and sluiced her with water. Do you recognize, people, the hand of their father, nicknamed Pogrom?

Now about Manasse, the old driver, who was driving Fräulein and Solomon the Wise. To his perdition he discovered that the horses of old Butsis, and Froim Grach, and Chaim Drong were shod with rubber. Looking at them, Manasse went to Pyatirubel and had Solomon the Wise shod with rubber. Manasse loved Solomon the Wise, but Papasha Krik said to him:

'I am not Chaim Drong and I am not Nicholas the Second that my horses should work on rubber.'

And he took Manasse by the collar, lifted him up into his dray and drove out of the yard. Manasse dangled from his outstretched hand as from a gallows. The sunset was stewing in the sky, a sunset as thick as jam, the bells were groaning in the church of St Alexis, the sun was setting behind Blizhnie Melnitsy,* and Lyovka, the boss's son, walked behind the dray like a dog behind its master.

An immense crowd ran after the Kriks, as though they were an ambulance, and Manasse was dangled tirelessly in Mendel Krik's iron hand.

'Papasha,' Lyovka said to his father, 'you are crushing my heart in your outstretched hand. Drop it, and let it roll in the dust.'

But Mendel Krik did not even turn round. The horses went at a gallop, the wheels thundered, a ready-made circus. The dray came out on to Dalnitskaya and Ivan Pyatirubel's smithy. Mendel wiped the driver Manasse against the wall and threw him into the smithy on to a heap of iron. Lyovka ran to fetch a pail of water and poured it over the old driver Manasse. Do you recognize now, people, the hand of Mendel, father of the Kriks, nicknamed Pogrom?

'Time is passing,' Benchik said one day, and his brother Lyovka stepped aside in order to make way for it. And Lyovka stood to one side like that until Marusya got a bun in the oven.

'Marusya is pregnant,' people began to whisper and Papasha Krik laughed when he heard them.

'Marusya is pregnant,' he would say, and laugh like a child, '*vay Israel*, who is this Marusya?'

Just at that moment Benchik came out of the stable and put his hand on his Papasha's shoulder.

'I care about women,' said Benchik sternly, and handed his Papasha twenty-five roubles, because he wanted the abortion to be done by the doctor at the clinic and not at Marusya's home.

'I will give her the money,' his Papasha replied; 'let her get herself an abortion, otherwise I will not live to see happiness.'

And next morning, at the usual time, he drove out with Gangster and Gentle Spouse, and at dinnertime Marusya Yevtushenko appeared in the courtyard of the Kriks.

'Benchik,' she said, 'I loved you, may you be accursed.'

And she flung ten roubles in his face. Two five-rouble notes – this was never more than ten.

'Let's get rid of Papasha,' said Benchik to his brother Lev, and they sat down on the small bench outside the gate, and beside them sat Semyon, the son of Anisim the yardkeeper, a *mensh* of seven years. And there, who can say that such a seven-year-old nothing is unable to love and that he is able to hate? Who would have thought that he loved Mendel the Pogrom, yet love him he did.

The brothers sat on the bench and worked out how old their Papasha might be, and how long was the tail of debt behind his sixty years, and Semyon, the son of Anisim the yardkeeper, sat beside them.

At that time the sun had not yet reached Blizhnie Melnitsy. It was pouring into dark clouds, like the blood from a ripped boar, and in the streets rumbled the carts of old Butsis, returning from work. The dairy women were already milking the cows for the third time, and Madame Parabellum's housemaids were hauling the pails of evening milk on to her front steps. And Madame Parabellum stood on the steps, clapping her hands.

'Women!' she shouted. 'My women and other women, Berta Ivanovna, ice-cream sellers and *kefir** sellers! Come and get your evening milk.'

Berta Ivanovna, the German teacher, who charged two quarts of milk per lesson, received her portion first. After her came Dvoyra Krik in order to see how much water Madame Parabellum mixed with her milk and how much soda she put in it.

But Benchik took his sister aside.

'This evening,' he said, 'when you see that the old man has done for us, go up to him and bash in his head with the milk-strainer. And let there be an end to the firm of Mendel Krik & Sons.'

'Amen – not before time,' replied Dvoyra, and she went out of the gate. And she saw that Semyon, Anisim's son, was no longer in the courtyard and that the whole of the Molda-vanka was coming to visit the Kriks.

The Moldavanka came in droves, as though going to a roll-call in the courtyard of the Kriks. The people came as they come to the fairground on the second day of Passover. Ivan Pyatirubel the blacksmith brought along his pregnant daughter-in-law and his grandchildren. Old Butsis brought his niece who had come from Kamenets-Podolsk for a visit to the coast. Tabl appeared with a Russian man. She leaned on his arm and played with the ribbon of her plait. Last of all came Lyubka galloping on a roan stallion. And only Froim Grach came quite alone, his hair as red as rust, one-eyed and in a sailcloth cloak.

People settled down in the front garden and took out the picnics they had brought with them. The artisans took their shoes off, sent their children to fetch beer, and put their heads on the bellies of their wives. And then Lyovka said to Benchik, his brother:

'Mendel the Pogrom is our father,' he said, 'and Madame Gorobchik is our mother, but people are curs, Benchik. We work for curs.'

'Let's think,' replied Benchik, but no sooner had he uttered these words than thunder burst on Golokovskaya. The sun flew upwards and began to spin like a red bowl on the point of a spear. The old man's dray was rushing towards the gate. Gentle Spouse was in a lather, Gangster tore at the harness. The old man raised his knout above the frenzied horses. His straddled legs were enormous, a crimson sweat boiled on his face, and he sang songs in a drunken voice. And at that point Semyon, Anisim's son, slid like a snake past someone's legs, jumped out into the street and began to shout with all his might, 'Turn your cart round, Uncle Krik, for your sons want to kill you.'

But it was too late. Papasha Krik, his horses a-lather, flew into the courtyard. He raised his knout, he opened his mouth and – was silent. The people who had seated themselves in the front garden goggled at him. Benchik stood on the left by the dovecot. Lyovka stood on the right by the yardkeeper's lodge.

'Servants and masters!' said Mendel Krik barely audibly, lowering his knout. 'See how my blood raises its hand against me.'

And, having jumped down from the dray, the old man rushed at Benya and smashed the bridge of his nose with his fist. Then Lyovka arrived in the nick of time and did what he could. He shuffled his father's face as though it were a new pack of cards. But the old man was sewn from the devil's skin, and the holes in that skin were sewn up with cast iron. The old man wrenched Lyovka's arm and threw him to the ground beside his brother. He sat on Lyovka's chest, and the women shut their eyes so as not to see the old man's broken teeth and his face, which was running with blood. And at that moment the inhabitants of the indescribable Moldavanka heard the swift steps of Dvoyra, and her voice.

'For Lyovka,' she said, 'for Benchik, for me, Dvoyra, and for everyone,' and she bashed her Papasha's head with the milk-strainer. Everyone leapt to their feet and ran towards him, waving their arms. They dragged the old man over to the tap, as they had once dragged Dvoyra, and turned it on. Blood flowed along the gutter like water, and the water flowed like blood. Madame Gorobchik elbowed her way to them through the crowd, hopping like a sparrow.

'Don't be silent, Mendel,' she said in a whisper. 'Say something, Mendel . . .'

But, hearing the silence in the courtyard and seeing that the old man had come back from work and the horses were unharnessed and no one was pouring water on the heated wheels, she rushed away and ran about the courtyard like a dog with three legs. And then the honourable masters came closer. Papasha Krik lay with his beard in the air.

'That's the end of him,' said Froim Grach, and turned away.

'Curtains,' said Chaim Drong, but Ivan Pyatirubel the blacksmith waved his index finger right in front of his nose.

'Three against one,' said Pyatirubel. 'Shame on the whole Moldavanka, but it is not evening yet. I've never seen the boy who could finish off old man Krik . . .'

'It is evening,' interrupted Arye-Leyb, who had appeared no one knew from where, 'it is evening, Ivan Pyatirubel. Do not say "no", Russian, when life is saying "yes" to you.'

And, settling down beside Papasha Krik, Arye-Leyb wiped his lips with a handkerchief, kissed him on the forehead and told him about King David, the King of the Jews, who possessed many wives, many estates and treasures, and yet knew how to weep at the proper time.

'Stop that whimpering, Arye-Leyb,' Chaim Drong shouted to him, and began to shove Arye-Leyb in the back, 'stop reciting that funeral service to us, you're not at home in the cemetery now.'

And, turning to face Papasha Krik, Chaim Drong said, 'Get up, old drayman, rinse out your gullet and say something coarse to us like you usually do, you old rascal, and get me a couple of carts ready for the morning, for I have some rubbish to be carted away . . .'

And the whole crowd began to wait to see what Mendel would say about the carts. But for a long time he said nothing; then his eyes opened and his mouth, stuck with filth and hair, gaped and blood came out between his lips.

'I have no carts,' said Papasha Krik, 'my sons have killed me. Let my sons be the bosses.'

Well, the boss who inherited the bitter legacy of Mendel Krik was not to be envied. He was not to be envied because all the troughs in the stable had long ago decayed and half of the wheels needed new tyres. The sign above the gate had collapsed, one could not read a single word on it, and the last of the drivers' white shirts had rotted away to dust. Half the town owed money to Mendel Krik, but the horses, as they took the oats from the trough, licked off, together with the oats, the figures that had been written on the wall in chalk. All that day muzhiks of some kind or other came to the dumbfounded heirs demanding money for chaff and barley. All that day women came and got their gold rings and nickel-plated samovars out of pawn. Peace departed from the house of the Kriks, but Benya, who in a few months' time was fated to become Benya the King, did not give in, and he ordered a new sign that read: 'Mendel Krik & Sons, Carriage and Carting'. This was to be written in gold letters on a blue background and interwoven with horseshoes picked out in bronze. He also bought a piece of striped ticking for the drivers' linen and an unprecedented amount of timber for the repair of the carts. He hired Pyatirubel for a whole week and wrote receipts for each customer. And by the evening of the following day, hear this, people, he was more exhausted than if he had made fifteen round trips from Arbuznaya Harbour to Odessa-Tovarnaya.* That evening, I would have you know, he found at home neither a crumb of bread nor a single clean plate. Now you will embrace with your mind the inveterate barbarism of Madame Gorobchik. The unswept sweepings lay in the rooms, a splendid jellied veal was thrown out to the dogs. And Madame Gorobchik stood erect by her husband's stove-bench like a slop-drenched crow on an autumn bough.

'Keep them under observation,' Benchik said to his younger brother, 'keep them under the microscope, the newly-weds, because I think, Lyovka, they are hatching a plot against us.'

That was what Benchik said to his brother Lyovka, who saw through everyone with the eyes of Benya the King, but Lyovka, the herdsman, did not believe him and went off to bed. His Papasha was already snoring on his boards, and Madame Gorobchik was tossing and turning from side to side. She spat on the walls and expectorated on the floor. Her bad character prevented her from sleeping, but at last she too fell asleep. The stars were scattered like soldiers drawn up in their ranks, green stars on a dark blue background. A gramophone obliquely, at Petka Ovsyanitsy's, began to play Jewish songs, and then even the gramophone fell silent. The night got on with its business, and the air, the rich air, poured in through the window to Lyovka, the youngest of the Kriks. He loved the air, Lyovka. He lay and breathed, and drowsed, and toyed with the air. He was experiencing a rich mood, and this lasted until he heard a rustle and a creak from his father's stove-bench. Then the lad covered his eyes and pricked up his ears. Papasha Krik raised his head like a mouse sniffing the air, and crawled down from the stove-bench. The old man pulled a little bag of cash out from under his pillow and threw his boots over his shoulder. Lyovka let him go, for where could he go to, the old cur? Then the lad went out after his father and saw Benchik creeping along at the other side of the courtyard, keeping to the wall. The old man stole inaudibly up to the drays, stuck his head into the stable, and whistled to the horses, and the horses came running and rubbed their muzzles against Mendel's head. It was night in the courtyard, night sprinkled with stars, dark blue air and silence.

'Sh–sh,' said Lyovka, putting a finger to his lips, and Benchik, who had come over from the other side of the courtyard, also put a finger to his lips. Their Papasha whistled to the horses, as to small children, and then he ran between the carts and spurted through the gateway.

'Anisim,' he said in a quiet voice, knocking at the window of the yardkeeper's lodge. 'Anisim, my heart, open the gate for me.'

Anisim came out of the lodge, as tousled as hay.

'Old master,' he said, 'I beg you, do not bring shame upon yourself before me, a simple man. Go back and rest, master . . .'

'Open the gate for me,' the Papasha whispered, even more quietly. 'Anisim, my heart . . .'

'Go back to your room, Anisim,' said Benchik then, and he came out to the yardkeeper's lodge and put his hand on his Papasha's shoulder. And Anisim saw before him the face of Mendel the Pogrom, white as paper, and turned away, in order not to see his master with such a face.

'Do not beat me, Benchik,' said old Krik, retreating. 'Where is the end to your father's torments . . .'

'Oh, wretched father,' Benchik replied, 'how could you say what you have just said?'

'I could!' cried Mendel, striking himself about the head with his fist, 'I could, Benchik!' he cried with all his might and began to sway like a man in a seizure. 'Look, in this courtyard I have served half a lifetime. It has seen me, this courtyard, as the father of my children, the husband of my wife and the master of my horses. It has seen my glory and my twenty stallions and my twelve carts bound with iron. It has seen my legs, as firm as pillars, and my arms, my wicked arms. But now, dear sons, open the gate for me, and let me have my way; let me leave this courtyard which has seen too much . . .'

'Papasha,' replied Benya, without raising his eyes, 'go back to your wife.'

But there was no need to return to her, to Madame Gorobchik. She herself came rushing through the gateway, sweeping along the ground, her old yellow legs dangling in the air.

'Oh,' she cried as she swept along the ground, 'Mendel the Pogrom and my sons, my lazy good-for-nothings . . . What have you done to me, my lazy good-for-nothings, what have you done with my hair, my body, my teeth, where are they, where is my youth . . .?'

The old woman screeched, tore her nightgown from her shoulders and, getting to her feet, began to go round and round on the spot like a dog trying to bite its tail. She scratched her sons' faces badly; she kissed her sons' faces and tore their cheeks.

'Old thief,' Madame Gorobchik howled, galloping round her husband, twisting his moustache and tugging it, 'old thief, my old Mendel . . .'

All the neighbours were woken by her howling, and the whole courtyard came running to the gateway, and bare-bellied children began to blow their fifes. The Moldavanka was gathering to see the scandal. And Benya Krik, who had turned grey with shame before people's eyes, barely managed to chase his newly-weds into the apartment. He drove the people away with a stick, he pushed them back towards the gate, but Lyovka, his younger brother, took him by the collar and began to shake him as if he were a pear tree.

'Benchik,' he said, 'we're tormenting the old man. The tears are choking me, Benchik . . .'

'So tears are choking you,' Benchik replied, and, gathering the spittle in his mouth, he spat in Lyovka's face. 'Oh, base brother,' he whispered, 'vile brother, untie my hands and do not get under my feet.'

And Lyovka untied his hands. The lad slept in the stable until daybreak and then he disappeared from the house. The dust of other people's roadways and the geraniums of other people's windows brought him consolation. The youth measured the roads of sorrow, went missing for two days and nights and, returning on the third, saw the blue sign glowing above the house of the Kriks. The blue sign nudged his heart, the velvet tablecloths knocked Lyovka's eyes off their feet, velvet tablecloths were spread on the tables and large numbers of guests were roaring with laughter in the front garden. Dvoyra was moving among the guests in a white head-dress, stiff-starched women gleamed in the grass like enamelled teapots, and swaying artisans, who had already thrown off their jackets, seized hold of Lyovka and pushed him into the apartment. Mendel Krik, the eldest of the Kriks, was already sitting there, his face badly bruised. Usher Boyarsky, proprietor of the firm Chef D'Oeuvre, the hunchbacked tailor's cutter Yefim and Benya Krik were all hovering around the disfigured Papasha Krik.

'Yefim,' Usher Boyarsky was saying to the tailor's cutter, 'please come a little closer and measure Monsieur Krik for a striped suit of *prima* quality, as if it were for yourself, and make so bold as to inquire as to the exact cut required – English naval double-breasted, English military single-breasted, Lodz *demi-saison* or Moscow thick.'

'What kind of overalls do you wish to have made for you?' Benchik asked Papasha Krik. 'Come on, tell Monsieur Boyarsky.'

'It depends how angry you are with your father,' Papasha Krik replied, brushing a tear from his eye; 'that kind of overalls.'

'Since Papasha is not a sailor,' Benya interrupted his father, 'the military cut will be the most suitable. Choose, to start with, a suit for every day.'

Monsieur Boyarsky leaned forward and listened.

'Say what you are thinking,' he said.

'This is what I think,' replied Benya. 'He's a Jew, [who has spent all his life ill-clothed, barefoot and begrimed as a penal settler from Sakhalin Island ... And now that, God be thanked, he has reached his old age, it is necessary to make an end of this permanent penal servitude, it is necessary to keep the Sabbath as the Sabbath ...']*

The End of the Almshouse

At the time of the famine there was no one in Odessa who could have lived better than the almsfolk at the Second Jewish Cemetery. The cloth merchant Kofman had once erected an almshouse beside the cemetery wall to the memory of his wife Izabella. Much fun was made of this location at the Café

Franconi.* But Kofman turned out to have done the right thing. After the revolution the old men and women who found refuge at the cemetery got jobs as gravediggers, cantors and washers of corpses. They got hold of an oak coffin and a pall with silver tassels, and hired it out to people who were poor.

Timber at that time had vanished from Odessa. The rented coffin did not lie idle. At home and during the funeral service the deceased person remained inside the oak box; but he was put into the grave wrapped only in a shroud. This is a forgotten Jewish law.

The wise men taught that one should not prevent the worms from uniting with the carrion, for it is unclean. 'For dust thou art, and unto dust shalt thou return.'*

Because the old law had been revived, the old people received in their rations food that no one in those years ever dreamed of. In the evenings they drank long and deep in the cellar of Zalman Krivoruchka and gave their neighbours the leavings.

Their prosperity was not disturbed until the uprising in the German colonies took place. In the fighting the Germans killed the garrison commander, Gersh Lugovoy.

He was buried with full honours. The troops came to the cemetery with bands, field kitchens and machine-guns on carts. By the open grave orations were made and vows were taken.

'In 1911,' cried Lenka Broytman, the commander of the division, exerting himself, 'Comrade Gersh joined the Bolshevik Workers' Party* and worked as a propagandist and liaison agent. In 1913 Comrade Gersh began to undergo repression together with Sonya Yanovskaya, Ivan Sokolov and Monoszon in the town of Nikolayev . . .'

Arye-Leyb, the administrative head of the almshouse, stood with his comrades at the ready. Scarcely had Lenka finished his valedictory address than the old folk began to turn the coffin on its side in order to empty out the dead man, who was covered with a banner. Lenka nudged Arye-Leyb imperceptibly with his spur.

'Leave it,' he said, 'leave it as it is . . . Gersh did service to the Republic . . .'

Before the eyes of the horrified old folk Lugovoy was buried, and with him the oak coffin, the tassels and the black pall on which stars of David and a verse from an ancient Hebrew prayer for the dead had been woven in silver.

'We are dead people,' said Arye-Leyb to his comrades after the funeral, 'we are in the hands of Pharaoh . . .'

And he rushed off to see Broydin, the cemetery's manager, with a request for the issue of boards for a new coffin and cloth for a pall. Broydin promised to look into it, but did nothing. The enrichment of old folk was no part of his plans. In the office, he said:

'My heart aches more for the unemployed municipal workers than it does for these speculators . . .'

Broydin promised to look into it, but did nothing. In Zalman Krivoruchka's cellar Talmudic curses rained down on his head and on the heads of the members of the Union of Municipal Workers. The old folk cursed the marrow of Broydin's bones and the bones of the members of the union and the fresh seed in the wombs of their wives, and wished upon each one of them a particular kind of palsy and sores.

Their income shrank. Now their rations consisted of a dark blue soup with fishbones. The second course was barley porridge without butter.

An old person from Odessa can eat any kind of a soup, no matter what it is made of, as long as it contains bay leaf, garlic and pepper. Here there were none of these.

The Izabella Kofman Almshouse shared the common lot. The fury of the starving old folk grew. It broke upon the head of the person who was least expecting it. This person was the woman doctor Judith Shmayser,* who had come to the almshouse to inoculate them against smallpox.

The provincial executive committee had issued a decree that made inoculation against smallpox compulsory. Judith Shmayser laid out her instruments on the table and lit a spirit lamp. Outside the window stood the emerald walls of the cemetery shrubs. The small blue tongue of flame mingled with the June lightning.

Closest to Judith stood Meyer Beskonechny,* an emaciated old man. Morosely he followed her preparations.

'Now let me give you a jab,' Judith said to him, brandishing her tweezers. She began to pull from his rags the blue whiplash of his arm.

The old man jerked his arm away: 'I've got nothing for you to jab . . .'

'It won't hurt,' Judith exclaimed, 'a jab in the flesh doesn't hurt.'

'I have no flesh,' said Meyer Beskonechny, 'I have nothing for you to jab . . .'

From a corner of the room came muted sobbing. It was Doba-Leya, who had formerly been a cook at circumcisions. Meyer contorted his decayed cheeks.

'Life is sweepings,' he muttered, 'the world is a brothel, people are crooks . . .'

The pince-nez on Judith's little nose gave a lurch, her breasts protruded under her starched white coat. She opened her mouth to explain the benefits of smallpox inoculation, but was stopped by Arye-Leyb, the head of the almshouse.

'Young lady,' he said, 'a mama bore us just as a mother bore you. This woman, our mother, bore us in order that we might live, not live in torment. She wanted us to live well, and she was right as only a mother can be. Anyone who is satisfied with what Broydin serves up to him is not worthy of the material that went into making him. Your purpose, young lady, is to inoculate against smallpox, and, with God's help you will do so. Our purpose is to live our life to its end,

THE END OF THE ALMSHOUSE

and not to torment it to its end, and we are not fulfilling that purpose.'

Doba-Leya, a whiskery old woman with a leonine face, began to sob even louder, having heard these words. She began to sob in a bass voice.

'Life is sweepings,' repeated Meyer Beskonechny, 'people are crooks . . .'

The paralysed Simon-Wolf seized the steering bar of his invalid carriage and, screeching and twisting his hands, advanced towards the door. The skullcap slipped from his swollen, crimson head.

Down the main avenue, snarling and grimacing, all thirty old men and women poured after Simon-Wolf. They brandished their crutches, braying like hungry asses.

Catching sight of them, the watchman banged the gates of the cemetery shut. The gravediggers raised their spades in the air, the earth and roots of grass still sticking to them, and paused in amazement.

At the sound the bearded Broydin came out, wearing leggings, a cycling cap and a tight, short jacket.

'Crook!' Simon-Wolf shouted at him. 'We have nothing for her to jab . . . there is no flesh on our arms . . .'

Doba-Leya bared her teeth and began to snarl. She started to run the paralysed man's invalid carriage into Broydin. Arye-Leyb began, as always, with allegories, with parables that crept up from a distance towards a goal that was not immediately obvious.

He began with the parable of Rabbi Hosea,* who gave his property to his children, his heart to his wife, his fear to God, his taxes to Caesar and who kept for himself only a place under an olive tree, where the sun, as it set, shone longest of all. From Rabbi Hosea, Arye-Leyb passed on to the boards for the new coffin and the rations.

Broydin spread his legginged legs and listened, without raising his eyes. The brown barrier of his beard lay motionless on the new service jacket; he seemed to have given himself up to sad and peaceful thoughts.

'You will forgive me, Arye-Leyb,' Broydin sighed, turning to the cemetery sage, 'you will forgive me if I say that I cannot help perceiving in you a secret motive and a political element. Behind your back, Arye-Leyb, I cannot help perceiving others who know what they are doing, just as you yourself know what you are doing . . .'

At this point Broydin raised his eyes. They were suffused with the white water of rabid fury. The trembling hills of his pupils fixed themselves on the old people.

'Arye-Leyb,' said Broydin in a loud voice, 'read these cables from the Tartar Republic, where large numbers of Tartars are starving like madmen . . . Read the appeal of the St Petersburg proletariat, who are working and waiting, starving, by their lathes.'

'I have no time to wait,' Arye-Leyb said, interrupting the manager, 'I have no time . . .'

'There are people,' Broydin thundered, hearing nothing, 'who are worse off than you, and there are thousands upon thousands of people who are worse off than the ones who are worse off than you . . . You're sowing trouble for yourself, Arye-Leyb, you'll reap the whirlwind. You will be dead men if I turn away from you. You will die if I go my way and you go yours. You will die, Arye-Leyb. You will die, Simon-Wolf. You will die, Meyer Beskonechny. But before you die, tell me − I am curious to know this − do we have Soviet power or do we perhaps not? If we do not and I am wrong − then take me to Mr Berzon's, on the corner of Deribasovskaya and Yekaterininskaya, where I worked as a waistcoat maker all the years of my life . . . Tell me I am wrong, Arye-Leyb . . .'

And the manager of the cemetery went right up to the cripples. His quivering eyes were let loose on them. They swept over the petrified, moaning herd like the beams of searchlights, like tongues of flame. Broydin's leggings creaked, the sweat boiled on his pock-marked face, he came closer and closer to Arye-Leyb, demanding a reply to whether he was wrong to believe that Soviet power had already begun . . .

Arye-Leyb was silent. This silence might have been his downfall, had not Fedka Stepun, in a sailor's shirt, appeared at the end of the avenue.

Fedka had been shell-shocked at Rostov* and was receiving medical treatment; he lived in a shanty next to the cemetery, wore a whistle on an orange police cord and a revolver with no holster.

Fedka was drunk. His curls were spread out on his forehead like volutes carved in stone. Under them, high cheek-bones. He was grimacing convulsively. He approached Lugovoy's grave, which was surrounded by faded wreaths.

'Where were you, Lugovoy,' said Fedka to the deceased, 'when I was taking Rostov? . . .'

Gritting his teeth, the sailor blew his police whistle and drew the revolver from his belt. The revolver's blue steel muzzle glinted.

'They've killed the tsars,' Fedka shouted, 'there aren't any tsars . . . Let them all lie without coffins . . .'

The sailor was clutching his revolver. His chest was exposed. On it were tattooed the word 'Riva' and a dragon, the head of which curved towards one nipple.

The gravediggers with their lifted spades crowded around Fedka. The women who were washing corpses came out of their storerooms and prepared to bawl together with Doba-Leya. Wailing waves beat against the closed gates of the cemetery.

Relatives who had brought their dead on wheelbarrows demanded to be admitted. Beggars banged their crutches against the railings.

'They've killed the tsars.' The sailor fired in the air.

People went dashing off in leaps and bounds along the avenue. Broydin slowly went pale. He raised his arm, agreed to all the almshouse demands and, doing an about-turn in military style, went back to the office. At that same instant, the gates opened. The relatives of the dead, pushing their wheelbarrows in front of them, wheeled them smartly along the walkways. In piercing falsettos self-styled cantors began to sing *El moley rahamim** over the freshly dug graves. In the evening everyone celebrated the victory at Krivoruchka's. They brought Fedka three quarts of Bessarabian wine.

'*Hevel havolim*,' said Arye-Leyb, clinking glasses with the sailor, 'you're a good soul, one can get along with you . . . *Vehakol hevel . . .*'*

The mistress of the house, Krivoruchka's wife, was washing used glasses behind the wall.

'If a Russian happens to have a good character,' said Madame Krivoruchka, 'then that's really something special . . .'

Fedka was helped outside at one o'clock in the morning.

'*Hevel havolim*,' – he muttered the dire, incomprehensible words as he picked his way along Stepovaya Street – '*kuloy hevel . . .*'

On the following day the old folk at the almshouse were each given four pieces of lump sugar, and meat for their bortsch. In the evening they were taken to the municipal theatre for an event arranged by the Department of Social Security. It was a performance of *Carmen*. For the first time in their lives the disabled and deformed people saw the gilt tiers of the Odessa theatre, the velvet of its partitions, the oily brilliance of its chandeliers. At the intervals they were all served with liver-sausage sandwiches.

The old folk were driven back to the cemetery in an army truck. Rumbling and exploding, it trundled its way through the deserted streets. The old folk fell asleep with full bellies. They belched in their sleep and quivered with satiety like dogs that have run themselves out.

In the morning Arye-Leyb got up before the others. He turned to the east in order to pray, and saw a notice on the door. On this sheet of paper Broydin announced that the almshouse was being closed for repairs and that all those in receipt of its charity must that day report to the Provincial Department of Social Security for re-registration for work.

The sun surfaced above the leafy treetops of the cemetery. Arye-Leyb put his fingers to his eyes. Out of their dimmed hollows crept a tear.

An avenue of chestnuts, shining, stretched towards the mortuary. The chestnuts were in flower, the trees carried tall, white flowers on their outspread boughs. An unknown woman in a shawl fastened tightly over her breasts was managing things in the mortuary. There everything had been redone – the walls adorned with fir branches, the tables scraped clean. The woman was washing a dead infant. She turned it deftly from side to side; the water flowed in a diamond stream along its hollow, blotchy spine.

Broydin sat in his leggings on the mortuary steps. He had the air of a man who was resting. He removed his cycling cap and wiped his brow with a yellow handkerchief.

'It's what I told Comrade Andreychik at the Union.' The unknown woman's voice was melodious. 'We're not work-shy . . . let them ask about us in Yekaterinoslav . . . Yekaterinoslav knows our work . . .'.

'Calm down, Comrade Blyuma, calm down,' Broydin said peaceably, putting the yellow handkerchief away in his pocket. 'I'm easy to get along with . . . Easy to get along with . . .' he repeated and turned his flashing eyes towards Arye-Leyb, who had dragged himself right up to the front steps. 'Just don't spit in my porridge, that's all . . .'

Broydin did not finish his speech: outside the gates a droshky harnessed to a tall black horse had stopped. Out of the droshky got the municipal services manager in a shirt with a turn-down collar. Broydin joined him and led him to the cemetery.

The old tailor's apprentice showed his superior the centennial history of Odessa resting under the granite slabs. He showed him the memorials and burial vaults of the wheat exporters, of ships' brokers and merchants who had built a Russian Marseilles on the site of the settlement of Hadjibey.* Here they lay – their heads towards gates – the Ashkenazys, the Hessens and the Efrussis, the polished misers, the philosophical *flâneurs*, the creators of fortunes and of Odessa anecdotes. They lay under memorials of labradorite and pink marble, screened off by rows of acacia and chestnut trees from the plebs, who were huddled against the walls.

'They didn't let us live while they were alive,' Broydin kicked a memorial with his boot, 'they didn't let us die after they were dead . . .'

Warming to his subject, he told the municipal services manager about his programme for the reorganization of the cemetery and his plan for a campaign against the Funeral Brotherhood.

'And they've got to go,' the manager pointed to the beggars who were lined up outside the gates.

'It's being seen to,' replied Broydin, 'little by little it's all being seen to . . .'

'Well, carry on,' said manager Mayorov, 'you've got things in order here, old chap . . . Carry on . . .'

He put his foot on the running-board of the droshky and remembered about Fedka.

'What was that Punch-and-Judy show all about? . . .'

'A lad who was shell-shocked,' Broydin said, his eyes lowered, 'and he loses his self-control now and then . . . But it's been explained to him now, and he apologizes . . .'

'The pot's on the boil,' said Mayorov to his travelling companion as he rode away, 'everything is turning over nicely . . .'

The tall horse drew him and the manager of the Department of Public Services off towards the town. Along the way they encountered the old men and old women who had been thrown out of the almshouse. They were hobbling along, stooped under bundles, trudging their way in silence. Sprightly Red Army men were driving them together into a line. The invalid carriages of paralysed folk creaked. The whistle of asthma, an obedient wheezing, escaped from the chests of retired cantors, wedding jesters, circumcision cooks and superannuated shop assistants.

The sun was high in the sky. The heat tormented the heap of rags that was dragging itself across the earth. Their road lay along a joyless, scorched and stony highway, past wattle-and-daub shanties, past fields choked by stones, past gaping houses that had been destroyed by shells, and past Plague Hill. Once upon a time in Odessa this inexpressibly melancholy road had led from the town to the cemetery.

Karl-Yankel

In the time of my childhood Jonah Brutman had a smithy in Peresyp. In it gathered horse dealers, draymen – in Odessa they are called *bindyuzhniki* – and butchers from the municipal slaughterhouses. The smithy was located near the Balta Road. Having selected it as an observation post, one could intercept muzhiks bringing oats and Bessarabian wine to the town. Ioyna was a timid, small man, but he was schooled in wine and he had the soul of an Odessa Jew.

In my time he had three sons growing up at home. They had the best dovecot in town. The blacksmith's sons used to come to the Aleksandrovsky Market with a hundred pairs of doves. Just before the war they started to rear carrier doves. It was a bird factory; it took up as much room as the smithy itself did. You would not even think of fighting Jonah's sons. There were three of them. Their father came up to their waists. It was on the beach at Peresyp that I reflected for the first time on the power of the forces that dwell secretly in nature. Three fattened bulls with purple shoulders and feet like spades, they carried the dried-up little Jonah down to the water as one carries an infant. And yet he, no one else, had begotten them. There were no doubts about that. The blacksmith's wife was devout, with a fanatical devotion. In Volhynia, her native land, in the *shtetl* of Medzhibozh,* the doctrine of Hassidism was born. The old woman went to the synagogue twice a week – on Friday evening and Saturday morning; the synagogue was a Hassidic one, and there at Passover people would dance themselves into a frenzy, like dervishes. Jonah's wife paid tribute to the emissaries whom the Galician *tsadiks* sent into the southern provinces. The blacksmith did not interfere in his wife's relations with God – after work he went off to a wine-cellar near the slaughter-houses and there, as he sipped the cheap pink wine, he meekly listened to what people were talking about – the price of cattle, and politics.

The sons resembled their mother in stature and strength; two of them, having grown up, went off and joined the partisans. The eldest was killed at Voznesensk; the second Brutman, Semyon, went over to Primakov and joined a division of Red Cossacks. He was made commander of a Cossack regiment, and later, when the division was expanded into a corps, he became corps commander. He and a few other lads from the *shtetl* were the beginning of the breed – conspicuous by its unexpectedness and picturesque quality – of Jewish fighters, raiders and partisans.

The third son inherited the blacksmith's trade. He works at the Gen plough factory in the reorganized old part of town. He has not married and has begotten no one.

Semyon's children roamed from place to place with his division. The old woman needed a grandson to whom she could tell stories about the Baal-Shem. She expected a grandson from her youngest daughter Polya. Alone of all the family the young girl resembled little Jonah. She was timid, short-sighted, with delicate skin. Many men sought her hand. Polya chose Ovsey Belotserkovsky. We did not understand this choice. Even more astonishing was the news that the young couple were happy together. Women have their own way of keeping house: an outsider cannot see the pots being broken. But in this case the person who broke the pots was Ovsey Belotserkovsky. A year after his marriage he brought a legal action against his mother-in-law, Brana Brutman. Taking advantage of the fact that Ovsey was away on an official journey and Polya had gone into hospital to be treated for mastitis, the old woman kidnapped her newly born grandson, took him to the little operator Naftula Gerchik, and there in the presence of ten ruins,* ten ancient and destitute old men, habitués of the Hassidic synagogue, the rite of circumcision was performed upon the babe.

Ovsey Belotserkovsky learned this after he returned. Ovsey was registered as a candidate for the Party. He decided to take counsel with the secretary of the Department of State Trade cell, Bygach.

'You have been morally defiled,' Bygach told him, 'you must take this matter further . . .'

The Odessa Public Procurator's Office decided to hold a show trial at the Petrovsky factory. The little operator Naftula Gerchik and Brana Brutman – who was sixty-two years of age – found themselves in the dock.

Naftula was just as much a part of Odessa's municipal property as the Duc de Richelieu* monument was. I remember how he used to walk past our windows on Dalnitskaya holding his trepan and grease-stained midwife's bag. This bag contained his unpretentious instruments. From it he would extract now a knife, now a bottle of vodka and a piece of gingerbread. He would sniff the gingerbread before drinking, and, having drunk, begin to intone some prayers. He was red-haired,

Naftula, as red-haired as the first red-haired man upon earth.
When cutting off what was his due, he did not filter off the
blood through a glass tube, but sucked it out with his inverted
lips. The blood smeared his dishevelled beard. He came out to
the guests tipsy. His bear-like eyes shone with a rabid merriment. As red-haired as the first red-haired man upon earth, he
intoned through his nose a blessing over the wine. With one
hand Naftula knocked the vodka back into the overgrown,
crooked, fire-breathing pit of his mouth, in his other hand
there was a plate. On it lay the knife, crimsoned with the
baby's blood, and a piece of gauze. As he collected his money,
Naftula would go round the guests with this plate: he would
jostle among the women, fall down on them, grab their
breasts and bawl to the whole street.

'Fat mamas,' the old man would bawl, his coral eyes
flashing, 'print boys for Naftula, thresh wheat on your bellies,
make an effort for Red Naftula ... Print boys, fat
mamas ...'

The husbands flung money in his plate. The wives wiped
the blood from his beard with table-napkins. The courtyards
of Glukhaya and Gospitalnaya Streets were not depleted.
They seethed with children as the mouths of rivers seethe
with roe. Naftula trudged about with his bag like a tax-
collector. Public Procurator Orlov stopped Naftula in his
interminable rounds.

The public procurator thundered from the rostrum, striving
to prove that the little operator was the servant of a priest.
The shaggy nut of Naftula's head drooped low, somewhere
near the legs of the guards. The genius of the race spoke in
the old man – he shrank in the court, shrivelled up, decreased
improbably in size.

'Do you believe in God?' the public procurator asked him.

'Let the man who has won two hundred thousand believe
in God,' Naftula replied.

'Were you not surprised by the arrival of Citizen Brutman

302

at such a late hour, at night, in the rain, with a newborn
infant in her arms?'

'I am surprised,' said Naftula, 'when human beings do
something human, but when they perform mad tricks I am
not surprised . . .'

These replies did not satisfy the public procurator. He
pressed Naftula more and more violently. The matter at issue
was the glass tube. The public procurator contended that, by
sucking out the blood with his lips, the defendant was exposing tens of thousands of children to the danger of infection.
Naftula's head drooped nearly to the floor. He sighed, covered
his eyes and wiped his collapsed mouth with a small fist.

'What are you muttering, Citizen Gerchik?' the court
chairman asked him.

Naftula fixed his lacklustre gaze on Public Procurator Orlov.

'The late Monsieur Zusman,' he said, sighing, 'your deceased papa, had a head you could not match in all the world
. . . And, thanks be to God, he had no apoplexy when thirty
years ago he summoned me to your circumcision. And now
we see that you have grown into a big man under Soviet
power and that Naftula did not take along with that little
piece of nonsense anything that would have been of any good
to you later on . . .'

He began to blink his bear-like eyes, shook his red nut
sorrowfully and fell silent. He was answered by a burst of
laughter, thunderous salvoes of guffawing. Orlov, né Zusman,
swinging his arms, was shouting something but it was impossible to make it out in the cannonade. He was demanding that
it be entered in the protocol that . . . Sasha Svetlov, the
topical satirist of the *Odessa News*, sent him a note from the
press box: 'You're a dolt, Syoma,' the note said, 'destroy him
with irony; only the ludicrous destroys . . . Yours, Sasha.'

The chamber quietened down when the witness Belotserkovsky was led in. The witness repeated his written statement.
He was lanky, in riding-breeches and cavalry jackboots. Ac-

cording to Ovsey, the Tiraspol and Balta district Party committees had cooperated fully in the procuring of oilcake. When the work was in full swing he had received a telegram with the news of the birth of a son. After having a word with the organization manager of the Balta district committee, he decided not to interrupt the procurement and to confine himself to the dispatch of a congratulatory telegram ... He himself returned only two weeks later. In all, sixty-four thousand poods of oilcake had been collected. At his lodgings, apart from the witness Kharchenko, a neighbour, a laundress by profession, and his son, he had found no one. His spouse was away in a clinic, and the witness Kharchenko, as she rocked the cradle, an obsolete custom, was singing a lullaby over him. Knowing the witness Kharchenko to be an alcoholic, he did not consider it necessary to try to understand the words of her singing, but was merely surprised that she called the boy Yasha, when he had directed that his son was to be called Karl, in honour of the teacher Karl Marx. Having unswaddled the child, he was convinced of his misfortune.

A few questions were asked by the public procurator. The defence announced that it had no questions. The bailiff led in the witness Polina Belotserkovsky. Staggering, she approached the bar. A bluish spasm of recent motherhood distorted her face, on her tender forehead stood drops of sweat. She took in with her gaze the little blacksmith who was arrayed as though for a holiday, in a bow and new lacing boots – and the coppery, grey-whiskered face of her mother. The witness Belotserkovskaya did not reply to the question as to what she knew about the present case. She said that her father was a poor man, and had worked in the smithy on the Balta Road for forty years. Her mother had given birth to six children: three of them had died, one was a Red commander, another worked at the Gen factory ...

'Mother is very devout, anyone can see that, she has always

suffered because her children are not believers, and could not endure the thought that her grandchildren would not be Jews. You have to take into account the kind of family Mother grew up in . . . Everyone knows the *shtetl* of Medzhibozh, to this day the women there wear wigs . . .'"

'Tell us, witness . . .' a sharp voice interrupted her. Polina fell silent, the drops of sweat coloured on her forehead. It seemed as though the blood were seeping through her thin skin. 'Tell us, witness . . .' mumbled a voice that belonged to the former barrister Samuil Lining . . .

If the Sanhedrin existed in our day, Lining would be its head. But there is no Sanhedrin, and Lining, who learned to read and write Russian at the age of twenty-five, began in his fourth decade to write appeals to the Senate that in no way differed from the treatises of the Talmud . . .

The old man had slept through the whole trial. His jacket was covered in ash. He had woken up at the sight of Polya Belotserkovskaya . . .

'Tell us, witness,' – the fish-like row of his dark-blue, falling-out teeth began to crackle – 'did you know of your husband's decision to call his son Karl?'

'Yes.'

'What did your mother call him?'

'Yankel.'

'And you, witness, what did you call your son?'

'I called him darling.'

'Why darling, precisely?'

'I call all children darling.'

'Let us proceed further,' said Lining – his teeth fell out, he caught them with his lower lip and stuffed them back into his jaw. 'Let us proceed further. In the evening, when the child was taken to the home of the defendant Gerchik, you were not there, you were in a clinic . . . Do I state the matter correctly?'

'I was in a clinic.'

'At which clinic were you being treated?'

'The one on Nezhinskaya Street, run by Doctor Drizo.'

'You were being treated by Doctor Drizo?'

'Yes.'

'You are sure of that?'

'How could I not be? . . .'

'I shall present a document to the court.' Lining's big-eared face raised itself above the table. 'From this document the court will see that at the time in question Doctor Drizo was absent, at a congress of paediatricians in Kharkov . . .'

The public procurator made no objection to the filing of the document.

'Let us proceed further,' said Lining, his teeth crackling.

The witness leaned on the bar with the whole of her body. Her whisper was barely audible.

'Perhaps it wasn't Doctor Drizo,' she said, lying on the bar. 'I can't remember everything, I'm exhausted . . .'

Lining combed his yellow beard with his pencil, rubbed his round-shouldered back against the bench and adjusted his false teeth.

On being requested to produce her health insurance certificate, Belotserkovskaya replied that she had lost it . . .

'Let us proceed further,' the old man said.

Polina ran her hand across her brow. Her husband was sitting at the end of the bench, separated from the other witnesses. He was sitting up straight, his long legs in their cavalry jackboots tucked under him . . . The sun fell on his face, which was stuffed with the cross-pieces of small, malicious bones.

'I'll find the certificate,' Polina whispered, her hands sliding from the bar. At that instant a child's crying rang out. Behind the door a baby was weeping and moaning.

'What are you thinking of, Polina?' the old woman said in a thick voice. 'The child hasn't been fed since this morning, the child is weak with crying . . .'

The Red Army men, with a start, picked up their rifles. Polina slid ever lower, her head flew back and landed on the floor. Her arms flew up, began to move in the air and then collapsed.

'The court is adjourned!' the chairman cried.

A roar exploded in the chamber. His green eye sockets a-glitter, Belotserkovsky approached his wife with crane-like steps.

'Feed the child!' their hands cupped like megaphones, people shouted from the back rows.

'They'll feed it,' a woman's voice replied from afar, 'now that you're here . . .'

'The daughter's mixed up in it,' said a broad-faced worker who was sitting beside me, 'the daughter's in it . . .'

'It's a family, brother,' his neighbour pronounced. 'Things happen at night, things you can't see in the dark . . . At night they get it tangled up, by day you can't untangle it . . .'

With slanting rays the sun sliced through the chamber. The crowd slowly tossed and turned, breathing fire and sweat. With some difficulty, I elbowed my way out into the corridor. The door of the red corner* was slightly open. From inside came the moaning and champing of Karl-Yankel. In the red corner hung a portrait of Lenin, the one where he is speaking from the armoured car on the square of the Finland Station; the portrait was surrounded by coloured diagrams made in the Petrovsky factory. Along the walls there were banners and rifles in wooden mounts. A woman worker with the face of a Kirghiz, her head inclined, was feeding Karl-Yankel. He was a plump little man five months old, in knitted socks and with a white topknot on his head. Clinging to the Kirghiz woman by suction, he was rumbling and hammering on the breast of his nurse with his small, clenched fist.

'What a racket he made,' said the Kirghiz woman. 'He'll never be at a loss to find someone to feed him . . .'

Hanging about in the room there was also a girl of about

seventeen in a red kerchief, with cheeks that stuck out like pine-cones. She was wiping Karl-Yankel's oilskin dry.

'He's going to be a soldier,' the girl said, 'look at the way he's hitting you . . .'

The Kirghiz woman, gently pulling, took her nipple out of Karl-Yankel's mouth. He began to growl, and in desperation threw back his head with its little white topknot . . . The woman freed her other breast and gave it to the boy. He looked at the nipple with small, turbid eyes; something flashed in them. The Kirghiz woman looked down at Karl-Yankel, squinting with her dark eye.

'Why a soldier,' she said, adjusting her bonnet, 'he's going to be one of our airmen, he's going to fly about under the sky . . .'

In the chamber the hearing had been resumed.

A battle was in progress between the public procurator and the experts, who had reached a conclusion that was full of Jesuitical evasiveness. The public prosecutor, having risen, was banging the desk with his fist. I could see the foremost rows of the public – Galician *tsadiks* with their beaver-fur hats on their knees. They had come for a hearing at which, according to the Warsaw newspapers, the Jewish religion was to be put on trial. The faces of the rebbes, as they sat in the front row, floated in the stormy, dusty radiance of the sun.

'Down with them!' yelled a young communist who had managed to get right up to the stage itself.

The battle flared up.

Karl-Yankel, his eyes fixed unseeingly on me, sucked the Kirghiz woman's breast. The woman was slightly pock-marked.

From the window flew the straight streets that I had walked all over in my childhood and youth – Pushkinskaya stretched towards the station, Malo-Arnautskaya extended into the park beside the sea.

I had grown up in these streets, now it was Karl-Yankel's

turn, but no one had fought for me as they were fighting for him ... Not many people had been much concerned with me ...

'It's impossible,' I whispered to myself, 'that you will not be happy, Karl-Yankel ... It's impossible that you will not be happier than I ...'

NOTES

Notes

EARLY STORIES

ILYA ISAAKOVICH AND MARGARITA PROKOFYEVNA

five *poods*: one *pood* was equivalent to 36 lb avoirdupois (16.38 kg).

SHABBOS NAKHAMU

***Shabbos Nakhamu*:** the name of the first Sabbath after the ninth day of the month of Av (*tisha be'av*) – the day of mourning and fast in memory of the destruction of Jerusalem. On this Sabbath the words of the Prophet Isaiah are read in the synagogues: *Nakhamu, nakhamu ami* . . . ('Comfort ye, comfort ye, my people . . .')

the 'Hershele' cycle: Babel intended to write a whole cycle of stories about Hershele Ostropoler, the eighteenth-century Jew from Ostropol who was famed for his wit and his mockery of ignoramuses and moneybags. The present story is based on the Yiddish folk-tale *Di mayse mit Shabbos Nakhamu*.

. . . sixth day: a modified quotation from the Book of Genesis.

all Ostropol, all Berdichev, all Vilyuysk: Russian towns within the Jewish Pale which had predominantly Jewish populations.

***Pan*:** a Polish gentleman.

For every wife . . . feet: here, as elsewhere, Babel consciously uses the syntax and grammar of Yiddish speech. These phrases are based on the Yiddish idiomatic expressions *a man vi a mensh* ('a man like a human being') and *er kormit mikh mit tsuzogen* ('he feeds me with promises') (Efraim Sicher, *Style and Structure in the Prose of Isaak Babel*, p. 73).

Rebe Borochl: Baruch ben Iehiel Tulniczer, the grandson of the Baal Shem Tov, the founder of the mystical movement known as Hassidism, which was widespread in Galicia, Volhynia, Lithuania, Poland and Belorussia. Rebbe Boruchl was the Medzhibozh *rebbe* whom Hershele served as a court jester. A *rebbe* (the Yiddish word), or *tsadik*, was a spiritual leader among the Hassidim. His followers ascribed supernatural powers to him, and he was considered capable of prophecy and of direct communication with God.

tsadik: literally 'righteous man' (Hebrew). Another name for a *rebbe* among the Hassidim.

Count Potocki: probably Count Andrzej Potocki (1861–1908), the governor-general of Galicia who was assassinated in 1908 by the student Siczynski.

'AUTOBIOGRAPHICAL' STORIES

CHILDHOOD. AT GRANDMOTHER'S

the uprising: the Polish uprising of 1861.

and: Babel's manuscript breaks off at this point, and the end of the story is found, with some text illegible, on a separate sheet.

THE STORY OF MY DOVECOT

the Volozhin Yeshivah: a yeshivah is a Jewish religious higher institute of learning. The Lithuanian town of Volozhin was famous for its yeshivah, which attracted students from many lands until its closure in 1892.

Hassidic songs . . . : in fact, these songs usually have no words at all.

tsitsit: tassels that are fastened to the four corners of the *tales-kotn* (lesser *talith*, or ritual undergarment).

shtetl: a Jewish town or settlement.

FIRST LOVE

the Japanese war: the Russo-Japanese war of 1903–4, in which the Japanese were the victors.

the Milk-drinkers: the Molokanye, an extreme Russian religious sect whose members consumed milk products during Lent, and refused to serve in the military or to shed blood.

the Old Believers: an Old Believer was a Russian Orthodox believer who did not accept the liturgical reforms introduced by Patriarch Nikon in the mid seventeenth century.

NOTES

IN THE BASEMENT

Langeron: Langeron Beach. The name comes from that of Count Aleksandr Fyodorovich Langeron (1763–1831), an infantry general who served in the French army before the French revolution, but later emigrated to Russia and joined the Russian army, serving mostly in the south of the country. A street in Odessa, Lanzheronovskaya, is named after him.

the Sanhedrin: in ancient Jerusalem, the council of the elders; in seventeenth-century Amsterdam, the leaders of the Jewish community, who sentenced Spinoza to *herem*, or excommunication, for his freethinking.

Bolshoy Fontan: part of Odessa's seaside health resort.

Count Branitsky (1732–1819): a Polish state functionary who helped to draw up the plans for the first partition of Poland.

Yom Kippur and Rosh Hashana: Yom Kippur is the name of the fast that begins ten days after the New Year. Rosh Hashana is the feast of the Jewish New Year.

castor oil: i.e. a laxative.

AWAKENING

Mischa Elman (1891–1967), **Ephraim Zimbalist** (1889–1985), **Jascha Heifetz** (1901–1987): famous violinists. **O. Gabrilowich** (1878–1931): famous pianist and conductor.

Zagursky: in real life, P.S. Stolyarsky (1871–1944), the famous Odessa violin teacher who taught Babel, but also David Oistrakh and many others who later became violin virtuosi.

Auer: Leopold Auer, the great violinist and music teacher who was for a long time a professor of the St Petersburg Conservatoire.

Benvenuto Cellini (1500–1571): the Italian sculptor.

the Gemara: the Babylonian and Jerusalem Talmud.

the Cadet Corps: a closed and privileged educational establishment which prepared the sons of noblemen for service in the tsar's army. It is obvious that the hero of the present story could not possibly have studied in the Cadet Corps.

DI GRASSO

Anselmi and Titto-Ruffo: C. Titta Ruffo (1877–1953) was an internationally famous Italian baritone who sang in Russia from 1905 onwards. Giuseppe Anselmi (1876–1929), likewise renowned, was an Italian tenor who sang in Russia for the first time in 1904.

Di Grasso: a tragic actor from Sicily who worked in Russia.

Kremenchug: a provincial town in the Kharkov district.

Utochkin: S.I. Utochkin (1876–1916), a Russian airman from Odessa who was renowned for his bravery.

GUY DE MAUPASSANT

Russian philology: here, in an ironically pompous use of the old-fashioned term *russkaya slovesnost* – Russian literature.

Peski: a suburb of St Petersburg.

Blasco Ibáñez: Vicente Blasco Ibáñez (1867–1928), a Spanish novelist who was popular in Russia.

Roerich: Nikolay Roerich (1874–1947), the Russian painter.

Judith: an opera by the Russian composer A.N. Serov.

Édouard de Maynial – *La Vie et l'oeuvre de Guy de Maupassant*: the book was published in Paris in 1907.

THE JOURNEY

Muravyov: M.A. Muravyov, a Bolshevik military commander who was notorious for his cruelty.

Lunacharsky: A.V. Lunacharsky (1875–1933), commissar of education at the time of the story.

tref: 'unkosher' (Hebrew).

Antloyf, Khaim . . . : 'Get lost, Khaim' (Yiddish).

Cheka: abbreviation of *chrezvychaynaya komissiya* – 'Special Commission', the name of the organization set up by the Bolsheviks to root out counter-revolutionary activity.

Yehuda Halevi (1075–1141): the greatest poet of the Jewish Middle Ages, who lived in Toledo, Spain, but voyaged to Palestine at the very end of his life.

Klodt: Pyotr Karlovich Klodt (1805–67), a sculptor who among other works created a group of horses on Anichkov Bridge in St Petersburg.

Aleksandr Aleksandrovich: Tsar Alexander III (1845–94).

Queen Louise: the wife of the Danish King Christian IX. Her daughter Dagmar married the Russian Tsar Alexander III and became Maria Fyodorovna. Her second daughter was the wife of the English King Edward VII and her son George became king of Greece. Maria Fyodorovna's son was Nicholas II, the last Russian tsar, shot in 1918.

Uritsky: Moysey Solomonovich Uritsky (1873–1918): the president of the Petrograd Cheka. He was murdered by Social Revolutionaries.

RED CAVALRY

CROSSING THE ZBRUCZ

nachdiv 6: abbreviation of *nachal'nik divizii* – 'divisional commander'. The '6' refers to the number of the division; i.e. 'the commander of the sixth division'.

kombrig: abbreviation of *komandir brigady* – 'brigade commander'.

Panie: 'Sir' (Polish).

Papasha: 'papa', 'Daddy'.

THE CATHOLIC CHURCH IN NOVOGRAD

Pani: 'Mrs', 'Madam' (Polish).

Radziwill ... Prince Sapieha: the Radziwills and the Sapiehas were the ancient and most aristocratic families of the *Rzeczpospolita*. Here the reference is to Prince Janusz Radziwill and Prince Justach Sapieha, Polish political leaders of the twentieth century who continued the fight against Russia.

A LETTER

Comrade Budyonny: S.M. Budyonny (1883–1973), a Don Cossack who served in the tsarist army and after the revolution formed a cavalry detachment of Cossacks, which subsequently progressed to being a regiment, then a brigade, then a division and ultimately a corps. From 1919 onwards he was the commander of the First Cavalry Army, and later became a marshal and a Hero of the Soviet Union.

samogon: moonshine, illicit home-distilled vodka.

Denikin: A.I. Denikin (1872–1947), the White general who led the anti-Bolshevik army in the south of Russia.

Senka: familiar form of Semyon.

THE *KONZAPAS* COMMANDER

konzapas: abbreviation of *konniy zapas* (literally 'horse reserve', or remount stable).

PAN APOLEK

Leo XIII (1810–1903): he became Pope in 1878.
Luca della Robbia (1399–1482): the Italian sculptor.
O, ten czlowiek: 'Oh, that man' (Polish).

THE SUN OF ITALY

the soundless Zbrucz rolled its dark and glassy wave: the town of Novograd-Volynsk is in fact on the river Slucz, not the river Zbrucz.

Makhno: Nestor Ivanovich Makhno (1889–1934), the Ukrainian anarchist leader who during the Russian Civil War fought both the White and the Red Army, though he occasionally formed temporary alliances with the latter.

Tsekists: members of the Central Committee (TsK, or 'Tseka') of the Bolshevik Party.

GEDALI

Ibn-Ezra: Avraham ibn-Ezra (1089–1167), the famous Jewish poet in Muslim Spain, and Bible commentator.

the shy star: sunset ushers in the Jewish Sabbath and at nightfall the Sabbath eve prayers commence in the synagogue.

Rashi: abbreviation of the name of Rabbi Shlomo Yitshaki (1040–1105), a famous commentator on the Bible and the Talmud. The commentary itself is also given this name.

Maimonides: Moshe ben Maimon (1135–1204), the famous Jewish philosopher and scholar.

And now out of the blue darkness . . . Sabbath: here Babel alludes to the ancient poetic prayer-image of the Sabbath as a queen and bride.

MY FIRST GOOSE

izba: cottage; also a room in a cottage.

Comintern: the Third International, an international organization created in 1919 in order to unite the forces of communism. The Second Congress of the Comintern was held on 19 July 1920.

the truth: in Russian, *pravda*.

THE REBBE

a pious city: the Rebbe is being ironic, for Odessa was famed as the centre of the Jewish enlightenment.

Hershele Ostropoler: see notes to the story 'Shabbos Nakhamu', above.

the *Red Trooper* newspaper: Babel wrote for this newspaper, the official organ of the political section of the First Cavalry Army, under the pseudonym 'K. Lyutov'.

THE THEORY OF THE *TACHANKA*

tachanka: a machine-gun cart.

assessor: tsarist government official of the rank of 'assessor'.

britzka: a light carriage, sometimes covered.

a brown statue of St Ursula: according to legend, St Ursula perished together with eleven thousand maidens in Cologne in the fourth century AD.

KOMBRIG 2

army commander: i.e. Budyonny.

'Wheel': the name 'Kolesnikov' means 'wheelwright', and is derived from the Russian word *koleso*, 'wheel'.

sagenes: a sagene, or *sazhen*, was equivalent to 2.134 metres.

SASHKA CHRIST

artel: cooperative association.
desyatina: measure of land – 2.7 acres.

THE LIFE STORY OF PAVLICHENKO, MATVEY RODIONYCH

Kabardinian: from Kabardin, a region of the northern Caucasus.

THE CEMETERY IN KOZIN

Bogdan Khmelnitsky (1595–1657): hetman of the Ukraine who led the rising of the Cossacks against Poland, a process that ended with the union of the Ukraine with Russia. During the rising many Jews were massacred.

PRISHCHEPA

Prishchepa: Prishchepa is not mentioned in the earlier stories, but is given a detailed and unsympathetic description in Babel's diary as a cruel and stupid anti-Semite who forces Jews to cook potatoes on the Sabbath, eve of the Fast of Av, and who harasses a young Jewish woman.

THE STORY OF A HORSE

cigarettes: *papirosy*, Russian cigarettes, consisting of a cardboard tube tipped with a small amount of coarse, strong tobacco.

KONKIN

take to Dukhonin's staff: in army slang, a euphemism for 'shoot', 'execute'. General Dukhonin was supreme commander-in-chief after the flight of Kerensky, and was murdered by his soldiers at the end of 1917. His name contains the word *dukh*, or 'spirit'.

BERESTECZKO

the tower of Bogdan Khmelnitsky: Beresteczko was the site of a battle Khmelnitsky lost to the Poles (see note to *The Cemetery in Kozin*, above).

bandore: Ukrainian stringed instrument.

Comintern: see note to 'My First Goose', p. 319.

kheder: the elementary religious school.

with impassioned prayers for fertility: the Hassidim ascribed supernatural powers to the *tsadik*.

EVENING

Last time . . . drink: Tsar Nicholas II, the last Russian tsar, was murdered in the town of Yekaterinburg in 1918. Tsar Peter III was assassinated by the brothers Orlov in a plot with Catherine the Great. Tsar Paul I, Catherine's son, was strangled in 1801, probably with the consent of his son Alexander, who became tsar; his brother Nicholas I, nicknamed Nicholas Palkin ('The Rod') because of the cruelty he fostered in the Russian army, is officially supposed to have died of illness in 1855, but there were rumours that he committed suicide in consequence of the defeat of the Russian army in the Crimean War; his son Alexander II was assassinated on 1 March 1881 by terrorists belonging to the 'People's Will' group. His son Alexander III is thought to have been an alcoholic.

AFONKA BIDA

Makhno: see 'The Sun of Italy', note 2, p. 318.

SQUADRON COMMANDER TRUNOV

Elijah, the Vilna Gaon, the opponent of the Hassidim: Rabbi Eliyahu ben Shlomo (1720–97), the great scholar and Talmudist who led Lithuanian Jewry.

the Pugach: literally, 'the toy pistol', but also a reference to Pugachov.

Faunt Le Roy: the name of the American airforce captain was actually Cedric E., not Reginald, Faunt Le Roy.

THE IVANS

'branded': i.e. in disgrace.

Kamenev: S.S. Kamenev (1881–1936): Soviet military leader. Before the revolution he was an officer in the tsarist army, but from 1919 until 1924 was commander-in-chief of the Soviet armed forces.

one's own bast mat is dearer than another's mug: a Russian proverb that means, roughly, 'one cares more for one's own interests than those of others.'

Revtribunal: abbreviation of 'revolutionary tribunal'.

Tarnovsky syringe: a syringe used in the treatment of syphilis. Named after the Russian venereologist.

ZAMOŚĆ

nic nema: 'there isn't anything' (Polish).
czekaj: 'wait' (Polish).

TREASON

Poincaré: President of the French Republic.

Ebert-Noske: Ebert was the President of the German Weimar Republic, and Noske his Minister of Defence. Balmashov conflates them into one person.

Jews by nationality: in the USSR, the Jews were recognized as a nationality.

CZESNIKI

Kirill Vasilyich: the Christian name and patronymic of 'Lyutov', the narrator, who is subsequently referred to as 'Lyutych'.

THE SONG

Green campaigns: the campaigns against the 'Greens' – armed bands of peasants who were deserters from the tsarist army and hid in the woods and forests (hence their name).

THE REBBE'S SON

the Fourth International: the Third International was the Comintern. Gedali dreams of an ideal 'International' (see the story 'Gedali').

the old buffoon of the Chernobyl *tsadikkim*: Reb Mordkhe, from the story 'The Rebbe'. Religious Jews are forbidden to handle money on the Sabbath.

coverings of purple velvet and blue silk: the sewn and ornamented veil in which the scrolls of the Torah are wrapped. In fact, we ought not to be able to see the coverings, as on the Sabbath eve the scrolls are kept inside the ark of the Torah.

the last prince of the dynasty: see the story 'The Rebbe'.

phylacteries: in Hebrew *tfillin*, small, specially shaped boxes containing excerpts from the Torah written on parchment. The boxes are fixed to the forehead and to one arm by means of thongs during morning prayer.

ARGAMAK

Argamak: the word is used in Russian to refer to a central Asian breed of saddle-horse.

Give him a triple kiss: as an Easter salutation. – the verb used in the Russian text, *pokhristosovat'sya*, literally means to 'Christ'.

ODESSA STORIES

THE KING

Krik: the name means 'Yell', or 'Shout', 'Benya the Yell'.

the Brody Synagogue: a famous Odessa synagogue. In a sketch for his unfinished Red Cavalry story 'Demidovka' Babel depicts his father praying in this synagogue.

at the sixteenth stop: at the sixteenth station of Bolshoy Fontan, the most fashionable part of Odessa's seaside health resort.

'bitter': *gor'ko* – a Russian wedding toast.

drayman: Babel uses the Ukrainian–Odessan word *bindyuzhnik*, rather than the standard Russian *izvozchik*.

HOW IT WAS DONE IN ODESSA

Arye-Leyb: the name is compounded from the Hebrew and Yiddish words for 'lion'.

Froim Grach: 'Ephraim the Rook'.

Who are you . . . ?: a version of the Yiddish greeting *fun vanen kumt a yid?* ('where does the Jew come from?').

Byk: 'the Bull'.

Muginshteyn: in Yiddish the name means 'stomach-stone'.

zakuski: snacks.

JUSTICE IN BRACKETS

Shneyveys: in Yiddish the name means 'snow-white'.

Seryozhka Utochkin: Sergey Utochkin, a famous Russian aviator who was one of the first people in Odessa to own an automobile. The implication is the danger of being run over by a car.

Und damit Punktum: 'and with that, a full stop' (German).

LYUBKA KÓZAK

Kózak: the Yiddish word for 'Cossack'. In Yiddish, the word is also associated with 'trouble'. Thus, 'Lyubka the Cossack', but also 'Lyubka the Trouble'.

The Miracles and the Heart of the Baal-Shem: Rabbi Israel ben Eliezer of Medzhibozh, known as the Baal Shem Tov, or by the acronym 'Besht', was the founder of Hassidism. There are several collections of his legends and teachings compiled by his followers, such as *The Miracles of the Baal Shem Tov*. The name 'Baal Shem Tov' in Hebrew means 'possessing the name of God', and it was adopted by wise men and sages who were then considered to have the power to work miracles.

Sakhalin: the Russian penal colony island in the Pacific.

the eastern wall: at prayer, Jews usually stand facing east, towards Jerusalem.

Peresyp: a district of Odessa's port.

Mr Trottyburn: see the story 'Awakening'.

fifteen years: there seems to be an inconsistency here, as at the beginning of the story the narrator says that the action took place 'about ten years ago'.

THE FATHER

Kaplun: the name means 'capon'.

Golubchik: the name means 'dear fellow', and is derived from *golub*, meaning 'dove'.

a Krakow rabbi: Krakow was a centre of Rabbinical learning and culture.

Moses Montefiore (1784–1885): the Anglo-Jewish philanthropist who championed the cause of oppressed Russian Jewry and who helped to found the Jewish resettlement in Palestine.

her future husband: there is an inconsistency here – in the story 'The King' Benya Krik marries Eykhbaum's daughter, Tsilya.

SUNSET

put up a sign for Lyovka!: i.e. lay down the law.

Blizhnie Melnitsy: a district of Odessa lying beyond the Moldavanka.

kefir: a kind of yoghurt.

Odessa-Tovarnaya: the railway station for goods trains.

who has spent ... Sabbath: the manuscript breaks off after the word 'Jew' – the conclusion of the story has been borrowed from Babel's play *Sunset*, which contains the words supplied.

THE END OF THE ALMSHOUSE

Café Franconi: a high-class café in Odessa.

For dust thou art ... : cf. Genesis 3:19.

Workers' Party: Revolutionary Social Democratic Workers' Party.

Shmayser: the name means 'subduer', 'bossy-boots' (German Yiddish).

Beskonechny: the name means 'endless'.

Rabbi Hosea: Rabbi Hosea of Palestine, a religious teacher of the second century AD.

Rostov: the site of military operations against General Denikin's White forces in January 1920.

El moley rahamim: a Hebrew prayer for the dead.

Hevel havolim ... Vehakol hevel: 'vanity of vanities ... all is vanity' (Ecclesiastes 12:8).

Hadjibey: the Turkish settlement that was ceded to Russia at the Treaty of Yassy in 1791.

KARL-YANKEL

Medzhibozh: the home town of Israel ben Eliezer the Baal Shem Tov and a centre of Hassidism. The Hassidic *tsadiks* sent their emissaries around the Jewish *shtetls* in search of new adherents to the movement.

ten ruins: according to Judaic ritual any gathering for prayer must consist of at least ten men.

Duc de Richelieu: a French aristocrat who was governor of Odessa – a monument was erected to him in 1826.

wigs: devout married Jewish women cover their hair with a kerchief or wig, in order not to attract the attention of men.

the red corner: *krasniy ugolok,* a special room for reading and study, containing a small library, the works of Lenin and Marx, and official Communist Party literature.

Textual Notes

The following textual annotations provide the reader with a selection of the most important changes in the text of the stories in previous versions or subsequent editions. Some of these changes were stylistic and indicate Babel's stylistic development and meticulous craftsmanship; many, however, were dictated by the censor or editors for political reasons. The situation is complicated by numerous misprints and alterations whose authorship is unclear. As space is limited, we have referred to 'late editions' meaning collections of Babel's works published in the mid thirties which were the basis for the posthumous Soviet and post-Soviet Russian collections, which have only partially restored expurgated passages.

The text of *Red Cavalry* is taken from the first 1926 edition with the restoration by the translator of a few phrases from earlier versions and with the addition of 'Argamak'. 'Argamak' and the rest of the stories are taken from their first publication or from Babel's archives, except for 'The King', 'How It was Done in Odessa', and 'Lyubka Kózak' which follow the versions in Moscow journals.

THE STORY OF MY DOVECOT

p. 28, *Now, after two decades, it is very hard to say how horribly I was afraid of them.* Missing in late editions.

p. 29, *Our little town whispered for a long time about my extraordinary success, and Father was so pitifully proud of it that I could not bear to think about his restless instability and about how he submitted so helplessly to any change and was either gladdened or depressed by it.*

The teacher Karavayev was better than a father to me. Missing in late editions.

p. 29, *as it does on the cheeks of peasant children who do not engage in heavy work, a not repulsive mole sat on one of those cheeks.* In late editions, this becomes 'as on the cheeks of peasant children, a mole sat'.

p. 29, *squealing, choking.* In late editions these words are omitted.

p. 30, *my exhausted dreams.* In late editions the word 'exhausted' is omitted.

p. 30, *the little schoolboys.* In late editions this becomes simply 'the schoolboys'.

p. 32, *our ancient family would one day become stronger and more sublime than the other people on the earth.* In late editions, this becomes: 'our family would one day become stronger and more wealthy than the other people on the earth'.

p. 32, *not afraid of anyone, not afraid of the fact that he was loved by no one in the world.* Missing in late editions.

p. 33, *our stalwart people.* In late editions this becomes 'our people'.

p. 33, *even mother got drunk.* In late editions this becomes 'even mother took a sip of wine'.

p. 33, *when she began to enjoy the happiness of making sandwiches for me before I left for the gymnasium and when she went.* In late editions this becomes 'when in the mornings before I left for the gymnasium she began to make sandwiches for me, when we went'.

p. 34, *over things that smell of a tender dampness and the coolness of new things.* In late editions, this is simply 'over new things'.

p. 34, *the unforgettable morning twilight.* In late editions the word 'unforgettable' is omitted.

p. 34, *but sudden disasters blocked my path.* In late editions, this is changed to 'But in my path stood unexpected obstacles'.

p. 36, *I watched them go, the old man, his cobbler's chair and the beloved cages wrapped up in coloured rags.* In late editions this passage is missing.

p. 36, *across a square that had suddenly capsized.* In late editions: 'across a square that had suddenly capsized in my eyes'.

p. 37, *But the lad, hearing about Sobornaya, did not waste any time hanging about.* Missing in late editions.

p. 38, *like an inevitable echo.* Missing in late editions.

p. 38, *He struck me a swinging blow, his hand now clenched; the dove cracked on my temple.* In late editions: 'He struck me a swinging blow with his palm clutching the bird'.

p. 38, *on a lame and lively horse.* In late editions: 'on a big horse'.

p. 39, *on Shoyl's corpse laying out the dead man.* In late editions: 'and laid out the dead Shoyl'.

FIRST LOVE

p. 41, *In her exultant eyes I saw.* In late editions: 'I saw in them'.

p. 42, *They caused me suffering. Unbridled fantasies tormented me, but this is not worth talking about, for the love and jealousy of ten-year-old boys are in every respect similar to the love and jealousy of grown men, except that in boys these feelings are more secret, more exalted, more ardent.* In late editions the words 'Unbridled fantasies tormented me' and 'except that in boys these feelings are more secretive, more exalted, more ardent' have been cut.

p. 43, *Babel.* The name Babel is omitted here and elsewhere in this story in late editions.

p. 44, *and its thick, patient, hairy muzzle.* Missing in late editions.

p. 45, *and began to tremble with love for me.* Missing in late editions.

p. 46, *flushed with a merciless winter gaiety, like a rich girl at a skating rink.* Missing in late editions.

p. 47, *Father's face, which had tightened into a spasm, was rent by exultation, and he was preparing to bawl as Jewish widows bawl at funerals or like old women in Morocco, old women who have landed in misfortune.* Missing in late editions.

p. 47, *His dying eyes were surrounded by tears.* Missing in late editions.

p. 48, *rolling in my own green vomit.* Missing in late editions.

p. 48, *be brave, my poor Babel.* Missing in late editions.

p. 49, *So the doctor was surprised to find I had such a strange illness.* Omitted in late editions.

p. 49, *And now, when I remember those sad years, I find in them the beginning of the ailments that torment me, and the causes of my premature and dreadful decline.* Removed in the last Stalinist editions, possibly out of political prudence.

IN THE BASEMENT

p. 57, *He was shouting what he always shouted.* Missing in late editions.

p. 57, *'You are pulling out of me the glue,' my uncle complained in a thunderous voice, 'you are pulling out of me the glue in order that you should stuff your dog-mouths. A stone you have put on my neck, a stone* *hangs on my neck . . .'.* In late editions, two sentences are inserted after 'your dog-mouths': 'Work has taken away my soul. I have nothing to work with, I have no arms, I have no legs . . .'

p. 58, *Resolve and calm took hold of me.* Missing in late editions.

p. 59, *I gave them up to it.* Missing in late editions.

AWAKENING

p. 64, *among the last dregs of a tribe that did not know how to die.* Missing in late editions.

p. 66, *There was no salvation.* Missing in late editions.

GUY DE MAUPASSANT

p. 80, *and ate his own excrement.* Excised from editions that appeared after Babel's death.

THE JOURNEY

p. 81, *At the telegraphist's back stood a big, round-shouldered muzhik in a fur cap with unfastened ear flaps and back flap. The superior winked to the muzhik, the latter put his lamp on the floor, undid the dead man's flies, cut off his sexual organs with a small knife and began to stuff them into his wife's mouth.*
'You wouldn't touch tref,' said the telegraphist, 'so eat something kosher.' In the collections of Babel's stories that appeared in 1957 and 1966 this passage is omitted.

CROSSING THE ZBRUCZ

p. 91, *along the unfading high road.* These words are omitted in late editions.

PAN APOLEK

p. 107, *– a war as merciless as the passion of a Jesuit.* Missing from editions published from the early 1930s.

p. 108, *the blooms of a tropical garden.* Missing in late editions.

p. 111, *slyly turning away her gaze.* Missing in late editions.

THE SUN OF ITALY

p. 112, *My soul, filled with the tormenting intoxication of a dream, smiled at persons unknown, and my imagination, a blind and happy old hag, swirled before me like a July mist.* Missing in late editions.

p. 113, *The vague intoxication fell from me.* Missing in late editions. The version of the story pubished in the journal *Krasnaya nov'* has: 'The vague intoxication fell from me, like the scales from a sloughing snake.'

p. 113, *the long snake of his muzhik's grin.* Editions published from the early 1930s have: 'his muzhik's grin'.

GEDALI

p. 116, *Oh, Talmuds of my childhood, turned to dust! Oh, dense sadness of memories!* Missing in late editions.

MY FIRST GOOSE

p. 120, *'I say!' he cried, and cut the air with his switch. Then he read the document concerning my attachment to divisional staff.* In late editions this paragraph is replaced by: 'I handed him the document concerning my attachment to divisional staff.'

p. 120, *The billeting officer carried my trunk on his shoulder.* Editions from 1924 to 1931 have: 'The billeting officer carried my mess-tin on his shoulder' – probably a misprint in the Russian text (*kotelok* for *sunduchok*).

THE REBBE

p. 124, *the furious winds of history.* In late editions the word 'furious' is omitted.

p. 124, *'From where has the Jew come?'.* In Russian, *Otkuda priyekhal yevrey?* – a translation of the normal greeting in Yiddish (*fun vanen kumt a yid?*) among Jews. The Russian edition of 1926 has, erroneously: *Otkuda priyekhal, yevrey?* ('Where have you come from, Jew?').

THE WAY TO BRODY

p. 126, *the indescribable hives.* In late editions 'indescribable' is missing.

p. 127, *and even Grishchuk, who had been dozing on the box, moved his cap to the side.* This phrase has been taken by the translator from early editions of *Red Cavalry*; it is not in the first edition.

p. 127, *For this reason I compelled Afonka's steadfast mouth to bend forward to my sorrows.* Missing in late editions.

p. 128, *into the heroic sunset.* 'Heroic' is missing in late editions.

THE THEORY OF THE *TACHANKA*

p. 128, *His story is a dreadful one.* Missing in late editions.

p. 129, sword – *tachanka* – horse . . . In editions from 1936: 'sword – *tachanka* – blood . . .'.

p. 129, *Such is Makhno, whom we have suppressed.* In later editions 'whom we have suppressed' is omitted.

THE DEATH OF DOLGUSHOV

p. 135, *And I accepted charity from Grishchuk and ate his apple with sadness and reverence.* In the volume of Babel's stories entitled *Rasskazy* (Moscow-Leningrad 1925), the words 'from Grishchuk' are followed by the insertion of 'a simple man'. In the edition of 1931 the words 'with sadness and reverence' are omitted, and in late editions the entire sentence is missing.

KOMBRIG 2

p. 137, *amidst columns of blue dust.* In editions published from 1931 onwards: 'amidst columns of thick dust'.

p. 137, *'Very good,' replied Budyonny; he lit a cigarette and closed his eyes.* The text of the story as it was published in the journal *Lef*, 1923, no. 4, had read:

'Very good,' replied Budyonny.
And at that moment the first Polish shell began to trace above us its howling flight.
'They're going at a trot,' said the observer.

'Very good,' replied Budyonny, lit a cigarette and closed his eyes. A hurrah, barely audible, moved away from us like a tender song.

'They're going at a gallop,' said the observer, stirring the branches a little. Budyonny smoked without opening his eyes.

The cannonade filled the air with dust, spread out, shone with lightnings, clouded the vaults, hammered them with blows and thunder.

'The brigade is attacking the enemy,' sang the observer up there overhead.

SASHKA CHRIST

p. 139, *and got what fun he could.* Missing in late editions.

THE STORY OF A HORSE

p. 156, *And he had told me about women in such detail that I had felt embarrassment and pleasure as I listened.* Missing in late editions.

BERESTECZKO

p. 160, *as though it had been stuck on with glue.* In early editions this was followed by the sentence: 'Its handle of black bone was inlaid with a sumptuous pattern, and the sheath was kept by the orderlies who led the lively horses behind the *nachdiv*.' In late editions the words 'as though it had been stuck on with glue' are missing.

p. 161, *The presence of three races, all of them active and business-like, has made them dogged workers − sometimes a characteristic of the Russian when he has not yet acquired lice, taken to despair and drunk himself stupid.* Omitted from editions published after Babel's rehabilitation, obviously for reasons of censorship.

SALT

p. 166, *because we have made them suffer this night.* In late editions 'as ones that have suffered'.

p. 166, *'you're just saving the Yids Lenin and Trotsky . . .'*
'We're not talking about the Yids just now, you harmful citizeness. The Yids don't come into it. By the way, I will not speak for Lenin, but Trotsky is the desperate son of a Tambov governor and he joined the toiling class though he came from another class. Like men sentenced to hard labour they – Lenin and Trotsky – are leading us out on to the free road of life . . .'
In all late editions the words 'Lenin and Trotsky' and also the entire passage from 'By the way' to 'road of life' are missing. It seems to have been a fact that many Cossacks thought Lenin was of Jewish descent.

EVENING

p. 168, *Thus does a girl who thirsts for the inconveniences of conception look at a professor who is devoted to learning.* Missing in early and late editions.
p. 168, *the heavy-jowled conqueror.* Missing in late editions.
p. 169, *The whole Party is wearing aprons that are smeared with blood and shit.* Missing in late editions.
p. 169, *in the intimate, sinking accents of a Russian,* 'of a Russian' was removed from the beginning of the thirties.

AFONKA BIDA

p. 175, *Another week passed.* In an early publication of the story, this was followed by: 'The replacement of the *nachdiv* overshadowed in everyone's minds the small consumptive figure of Afonka, his flat, seminarist's Makhno curls.'

AT ST VALENTINE'S

p. 178, *There Sashka, a nurse of the 31st regiment, ran the show.* In an early publication of the story this was followed by: 'She had torn up the chasubles and had ripped the silk from someone's garments.'
p. 179, *They began to hoot with laughter, grabbed Sashka by the arms and hurled her with all their might on to a heap of cloth and books. Sashka's body, blooming.* Instead of this, an early publication of the story had: 'They began to hoot with laughter and seized her by the bosom and stuck gilded sticks from the canopy under her skirts.

Kurdyukov, a half-baked fellow, struck her on the nose with a thurible, while Bitsenko threw her with all his might on to a heap of cloth and sacred books. The Cossacks began to bare Sashka's body, which was blooming . . .'

p. 179, *She threw him off and rushed to the door. And only then, crossing the chancel, did we get into the church.* An early publication of the story had: 'She threw him off, smashed his head and rushed towards her bag. The Cossacks and I – we only just managed to drive her away from the silks. Aiming her revolver at us, she went away, swaying, growling like an angry hound, and dragging her bag behind her. She took the bag away with her, and only then, crossing the chancel, did we get into the church.'

p. 180, *Distracted by the memory of my daydreaming about Apolek.* In editions published from the early 1930s onwards, these words are missing.

p. 181, *We retreated with misgiving in the face of horror, horror overtook us and with dead fingers probed our hearts.* Missing in late editions.

p. 181, *was a curly-headed little Yid.* In late editions: 'was a curly-head Jew'.

SQUADRON COMMANDER TRUNOV

p. 183, *'Elijah!' they shouted, twisting and writhing, and opening wide their beard-tangled mouths.* Missing in late editions.

p. 184, *for I could not understand what sort of a man he was and what kind of life he could lead here, in Sokal.* Missing in late editions.

p. 187, *a young man with a proud German chest.* In late editions, 'proud' becomes 'white'.

p. 188, *'It's obvious that Trotsky doesn't write orders for you, Pavel . . .'.* In editions from 1933 onwards, Trotsky's name is omitted. The sentence becomes: 'Somehow I don't think that orders are written for you, Pavel . . .' This refers to Trotsky's decree that prisoners of war should not be executed.

THE IVANS

p. 193, *Lavrik, my comfort upon earth.* Missing in late editions.

p. 193, *It was pouring out of his mouth, spluttering between his teeth and* *collecting in his empty eye sockets.* Missing from editions published after Babel's rehabilitation.

THE WIDOW

p. 201, *The aristo lackey.* In editions published after Babel's rehabilitation, this phrase was changed from *Vot kholuyskoye znat'ye* ('The aristo lackey') to *Vot kholuyskoye zanyat'ye* ('There's a lackey's occupation').

p. 201, . . . *crunching and panting. The meat finished, Lyovka licked his lips and pulled Sashka into a narrow gully.*

'Sash,' he said trembling, belching and wringing his hands, 'Sash, to God our sins are just like so many weeds . . . We live once, and we die once. If you'll yield to me, Sash, I'll serve you even if it's with my blood . . . His day is past, Sash, but God has plenty more . . .'

· They sat down in the high grass.

The whole of this episode as well as the words 'on Sashka's bare knee' and the sentence 'Lyovka crunched and panted in the bushes', are omitted from editions published during the 1930s, but restored in editions published after Babel's posthumous rehabilitation.

p. 204, *Lyovka, the* nachdiv's *lackey.* Missing in late editions.

ZAMOŚĆ

p. 204, *All the stars had been suppressed.* In late editions this is altered to 'All the stars had been put out' (*zadusheny* is altered to *potusheny*).

p. 205, *living, moving sweat.* These words are not found in earlier published versions of the story.

TREASON

p. 209, *I don't give a shit about that hospital.* These words are excluded from editions published from the beginning of the 1930s as being indecent.

p. 213, *and the gaols of our hateful ribs* . . . Missing in late editions.

p. 213, *in the house it is burgling* . . . In the text of the story as it was published in the almanach *Proletariy* in 1926, this was followed by a concluding sentence: 'But we shall tear off the floorboard that has risen up against our innocent coarseness, and shall fill with black blood the boots that have been trained not to creak.'

CZESNIKI

p. 214, *The army staff, stalwart general staffers in trousers redder than human blood, performed gymnastics behind his back and exchanged smiles with one another.* This sentence is omitted from all editions published from the beginning of the 1930s onwards. The reason for the exclusion was obviously one of censorship.

p. 214, *Then he turned round to face Budyonny, and fired in the air.* This is actually an early version. Later versions of the story simply have: '. . . turning round to face Budyonny,' etc.

p. 215, *Two plump nurses in aprons had lain down there on the grass. They were prodding each other with their young breasts and pushing each other off again. They were laughing in dying female giggles and winking to me from below, not blinking. Thus do village wenches with bare legs wink at a lad whose tongue is hanging out, village wenches who squeal like fondled puppies, spending the night in the yard in the languorous pillows of the hayrick. Somewhat further away from the nurses . . .* Missing in late editions.

THE SONG

p. 223, *I loved that song, in love for it I attained an exalted ecstasy of the heart.* This sentence is missing from later editions.

p. 224, *if you wish, I will do you a courtesy . . .'* These words were missing from early versions of the story.

THE REBBE'S SON

p. 226, *And monstrous Russia, improbable as a swarm of clothes lice, began to tramp in its bast sandals on both sides of the carriages.* The whole of this sentence is omitted from editions published after Babel's rehabilitation, obviously for reasons of censorship.

p. 226, *I chucked a pile of Trotsky's leaflets at them.* Trotsky's name is missing from all editions published from 1933 onwards.

ARGAMAK

p. 233, *'Go on.'*
'All right, I will . . .'
Missing from separate editions of *Red Cavalry*.

THE KING

p. 241, *That is what the foamy breakers of Odessa's sea cast up upon the shore.* In late editions, the sentence continues, after a comma: 'that is what the Odessa beggars sometimes get at Jewish weddings. They got Jamaican rum at Dvoyra Krik's wedding, and so, having imbibed their fill like *tref* swine, the Jewish beggars' and so on as in the text.

p. 241, *raging.* In Russian, *bushuyushchee.* Babel's original text had *budushchee* – 'future'.

p. 241, *Tightening their belts and thrusting forth their bellies, they got up from their seats.* Missing in late editions.

p. 243, *He was giggling like a bashful schoolgirl.* Missing in late editions.

HOW IT WAS DONE IN ODESSA

p. 251, *the beadles from the Synagogue of Kosher Poultry Vendors.* In Babel's original Russian text this is *Sprosite ob nikh u shamesov iz sinagogi torgovtsev koshernoy ptitsey.* In editions from 1925 this was misprinted: *Sprosite ob nikh u shamesov iz sinagogi, torgovtsev koshernoy ptitsey,* which gives the meaning: 'Ask the beadles from the synagogue about them, the vendors of kosher poultry.'

THE FATHER

p. 267, *that self-seeking, weak-sighted little town.* Missing in late editions.

p. 269, *Baska Grach and gave her a wink. They walked past her.* Missing in late editions.

p. 272, *with terrible calm.* Missing in late editions.

p. 273, *then with terrible calm.* Missing in late editions.

p. 276, *outside her locked door, two hours.* Missing in late editions.

KARL-YANKEL

p. 299, *They had the best dovecot in town. The blacksmith's sons used to come to the Aleksandrovsky Market with a hundred pairs of doves. Just before the war they started to rear carrier doves. It was a bird factory; it took up as much room as the smithy itself did. You would not even think of fighting Jonah's sons. There were three of them.* Missing in editions from 1932.

p. 300, *The blacksmith's wife was devout, with a fanatical devotion. In Volhynia, her native land, in the shtetl of Medzhibozh, the doctrine of Hassidism was born.* Missing in editions from 1932.

p. 300, *and later, when the division was expanded into a corps, he became commander of it.* Missing in late editions.

p. 300, *the breed – conspicuous by its unexpectedness and picturesque quality –.* In late editions: 'this unexpected breed'.

p. 302, *the servant of a priest.* In editions from 1932: 'the servant of a cult'.

p. 302, *The shaggy nut of Naftula's head drooped low, somewhere near the legs of the guards. The genius of the race spoke in the old man – he shrank in the court, shrivelled up, decreased improbably in size.* Missing in late editions.

p. 303, *He pressed Naftula more and more violently.* In editions from 1932 this sentence is missing.

p. 308, *a conclusion that was full of Jesuitical evasiveness.* In editions from 1932: 'an evasive conclusion'.

p. 308, *The woman was slightly pock-marked.* Missing in late editions.

Appendix

A good many years ago, in 1929, I chanced to read a book which disturbed me in a way I can still remember. The book was called *Red Cavalry*; it was a collection of stories about Soviet regiments of horse operating in Poland. I had never heard of the author, Isaac Babel – or I. Babel as he signed himself – and nobody had anything to tell me about him, and part of my disturbance was the natural shock we feel when, suddenly and without warning, we confront a new talent of great energy and boldness. But the book was disturbing for other reasons as well.

In those days one still spoke of the 'Russian experiment' and might still believe that the light of dawn glowed on the test-tubes and crucibles of human destiny. And it was still possible to have very strange expectations of the new culture that would arise from the Revolution. I do not remember what my own particular expectations were, except that they involved a desire for an art that would have as little ambiguity as a proposition in logic. Why I wanted this I don't wholly understand. It was as if I had hoped that the literature of the Revolution would realize some simple, inadequate notion of the 'classical' which I had picked up at college; and perhaps I was drawn to this notion of the classical because I was afraid of the literature of modern Europe, because I was scared of its terrible intensities, ironies, and ambiguities. If this is what I really felt, I can't say that I am now wholly ashamed of my

340

cowardice. If we stop to think of the museum knowingness about art which we are likely to acquire with maturity, of our consumer's pride in buying only the very best spiritual commodities, the ones which are sure to give satisfaction, there may possibly be a grace in those moments when we lack the courage to confront, or the strength to endure, some particular work of art or kind of art. At any rate, here was Babel's book and I found it disturbing. It was obviously the most remarkable work of fiction that had yet come out of revolutionary Russia, the only work, indeed, that I knew of as having upon it the mark of exceptional talent, even of genius. Yet for me it was all too heavily charged with the intensity, irony, and ambiguousness from which I wished to escape.

There was anomaly at the very heart of the book, for the Red cavalry of the title were Cossack regiments, and why were Cossacks fighting for the Revolution, they who were the instrument and symbol of Tsarist repression? The author, who represented himself in the stories, was a Jew; and a Jew in a Cossack regiment was more than an anomaly, it was a joke, for between Cossack and Jew there existed not merely hatred but a polar opposition. Yet here was a Jew riding as a Cossack and trying to come to terms with the Cossack ethos. At that first reading it seemed to me — although it does not now — that the stories were touched with cruelty. They were about violence of the most extreme kind, yet they were composed with a striking elegance and precision of objectivity, and also with a kind of lyric *joy*, so that one could not at once know just how the author was responding to the brutality he recorded, whether he thought it good or bad, justified or not justified. Nor was this the only thing to be in doubt about. It was not really clear how the author felt about, say, Jews; or about religion; or about the goodness of man. He had — or perhaps, for the sake of some artistic effect, he pretended to have — a secret. This alienated and disturbed me. It was impossible not to be overcome by admiration for *Red Cavalry*, but it was not at all the sort of book that I had wanted the culture of the Revolution to give me.

And, as it soon turned out, it was not at all the sort of book that the Revolution wanted to give anyone. No event in the history of Soviet culture is more significant than the career, or, rather, the end of the career, of Isaac Babel. He had been a protégé of Gorky, and he had begun his career under the aegis of Trotsky's superb contempt .for the pieties of the conventional 'proletarian' aesthetics. In the last years of the decade of the twenties and in the early thirties he was regarded as one of the most notable talents of Soviet literature. This judgement was, however, by no means an official one. From the beginning of his career, Babel had been under the attack of the literary bureaucracy. But in 1932 the Party abolished RAPP – the Russian Association of Proletarian Writers – and it seemed that a new period of freedom had been inaugurated. In point of fact, the reactionary elements of Soviet culture were established in full ascendancy, and the purge trials of 1937 were to demonstrate how absolute their power was. But in the five intervening years the Party chose to exercise its authority in a lenient manner. It was in this atmosphere of seeming liberality that the first Writer's Congress was held in 1934. Babel was one of the speakers at the Congress. He spoke with considerable jauntiness, yet he spoke as a penitent – the stories he had written since *Red Cavalry* had been published in a volume at the end of 1932 and since that time he had written nothing, he had disappointed expectation.

His speech was a strange performance.* It undertook to be

---

* I am indebted to Professor Rufus Mathewson for the oral translation of Babel's speech which he made for me. Professor Mathewson was kindness itself in helping me to information about Babel; he is, of course, not accountable for any inaccuracy or awkwardness that may appear in my use of the facts.

humorous; the published report is punctuated by the indica-
tion of laughter. It made the avowals of loyalty that were by
then routine, yet we cannot take it for granted that Babel was
insincere when he spoke of his devotion to the Revolution, to
the Government, and to the State, or when he said that in a
bourgeois country it would inevitably have been his fate to
go without recognition and livelihood. He may have been
sincere even when he praised Stalin's literary style, speaking
of the sentences 'forged' as if of steel, of the necessity of
learning to work in language as Stalin did. Yet beneath the
orthodoxy of this speech there lies some hidden intention.
One feels this in the sad vestiges of the humanistic mode that
wryly manifest themselves. It is as if the humour, which is
often of a whimsical kind, as if the irony and the studied
self-depreciation, were forlorn affirmations of freedom and
selfhood; it is as if Babel were addressing his fellow-writers in
a dead language, or in some slang of their student days, which
a few of them might perhaps remember.

Everything, he said at one point in his speech, is given to us
by the Party and the Government; we are deprived of only
one right, the right to write badly. 'Comrades,' he said, 'let us
not fool ourselves: this is a very important right, and to take
it away from us is no small thing.' And he said, 'Let us give
up this right, and may God help us. And if there is no God,
let us help ourselves . . .'

The right to write badly – how precious it seems when
once there has been the need to conceive of it! Upon the right
to write badly depends the right to write at all. There must
have been many in the audience who understood how serious
and how terrible Babel's joke was. And there must have been
some who had felt a chill at their hearts at another joke that
Babel had made earlier in his address, when he spoke of
himself as practising a new literary genre. This was the genre
of silence – he was, he said, 'the master of the genre of
silence'.

Thus he incriminated himself for his inability to work. He made reference to the doctrine that the writer must have respect for the reader, and he said that it was a correct doctrine. He himself, he said, had a very highly developed respect for the reader; so much so, indeed, that it might be said of him that he suffered from a hypertrophy of the faculty of respect – 'I have so much respect for the reader that I am dumb.' But now he takes a step beyond irony; he ventures to interpret, and by his interpretation to challenge, the official doctrines of 'respect for the reader'. The reader, he says, asks for bread, and he must indeed be given what he asks for – but not in the way he expects it; he ought to be surprised by what he gets; he ought not be given what he can easily recognize as 'a certified true copy' of life – the essence of art is unexpectedness.

The silence for which Babel apologized was not broken. In 1937 he was arrested. He died in a concentration camp in 1939 or 1940. It is not known for certain whether he was shot or died of typhus. Both accounts of the manner of his death have been given by people who were inmates of the camp at the time. Nor is it known for what specific reason he was arrested. Raymond Rosenthal, in an admirable essay on Babel published in *Commentary* in 1947, says, on good authority, that Babel did not undergo a purge but was arrested for having made a politically indiscreet remark. It has been said that he was arrested when Yagoda was purged, because he was having a love-affair with Yagoda's sister. It has also been said that he was accused of Trotskyism, which does indeed seem possible, especially if we think of Trotsky as not only a political but a cultural figure.

But no reason for the last stage of the extinction of Isaac Babel is needed beyond that which is provided by his stories, by their method and style. If ever we want to remind ourselves of the nature and power of art, we have only to think of how accurate reactionary governments are in their awareness of that nature and that power. It is not merely the content of art that they fear, not merely explicit doctrine, but whatever of energy and autonomy is implied by the aesthetic qualities a work may have. Intensity, irony, and ambiguousness, for example, constitute a clear threat to the impassivity of the State. They constitute a *secret*.

Babel was not a political man except as every man of intelligence was political at the time of the Revolution. Except, too, as every man of talent or genius is political who makes his heart a battleground for conflicting tendencies of culture. In Babel's heart there was a kind of fighting – he was captivated by the vision of two ways of being, the way of violence and the way of peace, and he was torn between them. The conflict between the two ways of being was an essential element of his mode of thought. And when Soviet culture was brought under full discipline, the fighting in Babel's heart could not be permitted to endure. It was a subversion of discipline. It implied that there was more than one way of being. It hinted that one might live in doubt, that one might live by means of a question.

It is with some surprise that we become aware of the centrality of the cultural, the moral, the *personal* issue in Babel's work, for what strikes us first is the intensity of his specifically aesthetic preoccupation. In his schooldays Babel was passionate in his study of French literature; for several years he wrote his youthful stories in French, his chief masters being Flaubert and Maupassant. When, in an autobiographical sketch, he means to tell us that he began his mature work in 1923, he puts it that in that year he began to express his thoughts 'clearly, and not at great length'. This delight in brevity became his peculiar mark. When Eisenstein spoke of what it was that literature might teach the cinema, he said that 'Isaac Babel will speak of the extreme laconicism of literature's expressive means – Babel, who, perhaps, knows in practice better than anyone else that great secret, "that there is no iron that can enter the human heart with such stupefying effect, as a period placed at just the right moment." ⃰ Babel's love of the laconic implies certain other elements of his aesthetic, his commitment (it is sometimes excessive) to *le mot juste*, to the search for the word or phrase that will do its work with a ruthless speed, and his remarkable powers of significant distortion, the rapid foreshortening, the striking displacement of interest and shift of emphasis – in general his pulling all awry the arrangement of things as they appear in the 'certified true copy'.

Babel's preoccupation with form, with the aesthetic surface, is, we soon see, entirely at the service of his moral concern. James Joyce has taught us the word *epiphany*, a showing forth – Joyce had the 'theory' that suddenly, almost miraculously, by a phrase or a gesture, a life would thrust itself through the veil of things and for an instant show itself forth, startling us by its existence. In itself the conception of the epiphany makes a large statement about the nature of human life; it suggests that the human fact does not dominate the scene of our existence – for something to 'show forth' it must first be hidden, and the human fact is submerged in and subordinated to a world of circumstance, the world of things; it is known only in glimpses, emerging from the danger or the sordidness in which it is implicated. Those writers who by their practice subscribe to the theory of the epiphany are drawn to a particular aesthetic. In the stories of Maupassant, as in those of Stephen Crane, and Hemingway, and the Joyce of *Dubliners*, as in those of Babel himself, we perceive the writer's intention to create a form which shall in itself be shapely and autonomous and at the same time unusually responsible to the truth

---

⃰ Eisenstein quotes from Babel's story, 'Guy de Maupassant'. The reference to Babel occurs in the essay of 1932, 'A Course in Treatment', in the volume *Film Form: Essays in Film Theory*, edited and translated by Jay Leyda, New York, 1949.

of external reality, the truth of things and events. To this end he concerns himself with the given moment, and, seeming almost hostile to the continuity of time, he presents the past only as it can be figured in the present. In his commitment to events he affects to be indifferent to 'meanings' and 'values'; he seems to be saying that although he can tell us with unusual accuracy what is going on, he does not presume to interpret it, scarcely to understand it, certainly not to judge it. He arranges that the story shall tell itself, as it were; or he tells it by means of a narrator who somehow makes it clear that he has no personal concern with the outcome of events – what I have called Babel's lyric joy in the midst of violence is in effect one of his devices for achieving the tone of detachment. We are not, of course, for very long deceived by the elaborate apparatus contrived to suggest the almost affectless detachment of the writer. We soon enough see what he is up to. His intense concern with the hard aesthetic surface of the story, his preoccupation with things and events, are, we begin to perceive, cognate with the universe, representative of its nature, of the unyielding circumstance in which the human fact exists; they make the condition for the epiphany, the showing forth; and the apparent denial of immediate pathos is a condition of the ultimate pathos the writer conceives.

All this, as I say, is soon enough apparent in Babel's stories. And yet, even when we have become aware of his pathos, we are, I think, surprised by the kind of moral issue that lies beneath the brilliant surface of the stories, beneath the lyric and ironic elegance – we are surprised by its elemental simplicity. We are surprised, too, by its passionate subjectivity, the intensity of the author's personal involvement, his defenceless commitment of himself to the issue.

The stories of *Red Cavalry* have as their principle of coherence what I have called the anomaly, or the joke of a Jew who is a member of a Cossack regiment – Babel was a supply officer under General Budyonny in the campaign of 1920.

Traditionally the Cossack was the feared and hated enemy of the Jew. But he was more than that. The principle of his existence stood in total antithesis to the principle of the Jew's existence. The Jew conceived his own ideal character to consist in his being intellectual, pacific, humane. The Cossack was physical, violent, without mind or manners. When a Jew of Eastern Europe wanted to say what we mean by 'a bull in a china shop', he said 'a Cossack in a *succah*' – in, that is, one of the fragile decorated booths or tabernacles in which the meals of the harvest festival of *Succoth* are eaten: he intended an image of animal violence, of aimless destructiveness. And if the Jew was political, if he thought beyond his own ethnic and religious group, he knew that the Cossack was the enemy not only of the Jew – although that in special – but the enemy also of all men who thought of liberty; he was the natural and appropriate instrument of ruthless oppression.

There was, of course, another possible view of the Cossack, one that had its appeal for many Russian intellectuals, although it was not likely to win the assent of the Jew. Tolstoy had represented the Cossack as having a primitive energy, passion, and virtue. He was the man as yet untrammelled by civilization, direct, immediate, fierce. He was the man of enviable simplicity, the man of the body – and of the horse, the man who moved with speed and grace. We have devised an image of our lost freedom which we mock in the very phrase by which we name it: the noble savage. No doubt the mockery is justified, yet our fantasy of the noble savage represents a reality of our existence, it stands for our sense of something unhappily surrendered, the truth of the body, the truth of full sexuality, the truth of open aggressiveness. Something, we know, must inevitably be surrendered for the sake of civilization; but the 'discontent' of civilization which Freud describes is our self-recrimination at having surrendered too much. Babel's view of the Cossack was more consonant with that of Tolstoy than with the traditional view of his own people. For him the Cossack was indeed the noble savage, all too savage, not often noble, yet having in his savagery some quality that might raise strange questions in a Jewish mind.

I have seen three pictures of Babel, and it is a puzzle to know how he was supposed to look. The most convincing of the pictures is a photograph, to which the two official portrait sketches bear but little resemblance. The sketch which serves as the frontispiece to Babel's volume of stories of 1932 makes the author look like a Chinese merchant – his face is round, impassive, and priggish; his nose is low and flat; he stares through rimless glasses with immovable gaze. The sketch in the *Literary Encyclopedia* lengthens his face and gives him horn-rimmed spectacles and an air of amused and knowing assurance: a well-educated and successful Hollywood writer who has made the intelligent decision not to apologize for his profession except by his smile. But in the photograph the face is very long and thin, charged with emotion and internality; bitter, intense, very sensitive, touched with humour, full of consciousness and contradiction. It is 'typically' an intellectual's face, a scholar's face, and it has great charm. I should not want to speak of it as a Jewish face, but it is a kind of face which many Jews used to aspire to have, or hoped their sons would have. It was surely this face, or one much like it, that Babel took with him when he went among the Cossacks.

We can only marvel over the vagary of the military mind by which Isaac Babel came to be assigned as a supply officer to a Cossack regiment. He was a Jew of the ghetto. As a boy – so he tells us in his autobiographical stories – he had been of stunted growth, physically inept, subject to nervous disorders. He was an intellectual, a writer – a man, as he puts it in striking phrase, with spectacles on his nose and autumn in his heart. The orders that sent him to General Budyonny's command were drawn either by a conscious and ironical Destiny with a literary bent – or at his own personal request. For the reasons that made it bizarre that he should have been attached to a Cossack regiment are the reasons why he was there. He was there to be submitted to a test, he was there to be initiated. He was there because of the dreams of his boyhood. Babel's talent, like that of many modern writers, is rooted in the memory of boyhood, and Babel's boyhood was more than usually dominated by the idea of the test and the initiation. We might put it that Babel rode with a Cossack regiment because, when he was nine years old, he had seen his father kneeling before a Cossack captain who wore lemon-coloured chamois gloves and looked ahead with the gaze of one who rides through a mountain pass.

Isaac Babel was born in Odessa, in 1894. The years following the accession of Nicholas II were dark years indeed for the Jews of Russia. It was the time of the bitterest official anti-Semitism, of the Pale, of the Beilis trial, of the Black Hundreds and the planned pogroms. And yet in Odessa the Jewish community may be said to have flourished. Odessa was the great port of the Black Sea, an eastern Marseille or Naples, and in such cities the transient, heterogeneous population dilutes the force of law and tradition, for good as well as for bad. The Jews of Odessa were in some degree free to take part in the general life of the city. They were, to be sure, debarred from the schools, with but few exceptions. And they were sufficiently isolated when the passions of a pogrom swept the city. Yet all classes of the Jewish community seem to have been marked by a singular robustness and vitality, by a sense of the world, and of themselves in the world. The upper classes lived in affluence, sometimes in luxury, and it was possible for them to make their way into a Gentile society in which prejudice had been attenuated by cosmopolitanism. The intellectual life was of a particular energy, producing writers, scholars, and journalists of very notable gifts; it is in Odessa that modern Hebrew poetry takes its rise with Bialyk and Tchernokovsky. As for the lower classes, Babel himself represents them as living freely and heartily. In their ghetto, the Moldavanka, they were far more conditioned by their economic circumstances than by their religious ties; they were not at all like the poor Jews of the *shtetln*, the little towns of Poland, whom Babel was later to see. He represents them as characters of a Breughel-like bulk and brawn; they have large, coarse, elaborate nicknames; they are draymen and dairy-farmers; they are gangsters – the Jewish gangs of the Moldavanka were famous; they made upon the young Babel an ineradicable impression and to them he devoted a remarkable group of comic stories.

It was not Odessa, then, it was not even Odessa's ghetto, that forced upon Babel the image of the Jew as a man not in the actual world, a man of no body, a man of intellect, or wits, passive before his secular fate. Not even his image of the Jewish intellectual was substantiated by the Odessa actuality – Bialyk and Tchernokovsky were anything but men with spectacles on their noses and autumn in their hearts, and no one who ever encountered in America the striking figure of Dr Chaim Tchernowitz, the great scholar of the Talmud and formerly the Chief Rabbi of Odessa, a man of Jovian port and large, free mind, would be inclined to conclude that there was but a single season of the heart available to a Jew of Odessa.

But Babel had seen his father on his knees before a Cossack captain on a horse, who said, 'At your service,' and touched his fur cap with his yellow-gloved hand and politely paid no heed to the mob looting the Babel store. Such an experience, or even a far milder analogue of it, is determinative in the life of a boy. Freud speaks of the effect upon him when, at twelve, his father told of having accepted in a pacific way the insult of having his new fur cap knocked into the mud by a Gentile who shouted at him, 'Jew, get off the pavement.' It is clear that Babel's relation with his father defined his relation to his Jewishness. Benya Krik, the greatest of the gangsters, he who was called King, was a Jew of Odessa, but he did not wear glasses and he did not have autumn in his heart – it is in writing about Benya that Babel uses the phrase that sets so far apart the intellectual and the man of action. The exploration of Benya's pre-eminence among gangsters does indeed take account of his personal endowment – Benya was a 'lion', a 'tiger', a 'cat'; he 'could spend the night with a Russian woman and satisfy her'. But what really made his fate was his having had Mendel Krik, the drayman, for his father. 'What does such a father think about? He thinks about drinking a good glass of vodka, of smashing somebody in the face, of his horses – and nothing more. You want to live and he makes you die twenty times a day. What would you have done in Benya Krik's place? You would have done nothing. But *he* did something ...' But Babel's father did not think about vodka, and smashing somebody in the face, and horses; he thought about large and serious things, among them respectability and fame. He was a shopkeeper, not well to do, a serious man, a failure. The sons of such men have much to prove, much to test themselves for, and, if they are Jewish, their Jewishness is ineluctably involved in the test.

Babel, in the brief autobiographical sketch to which I have referred, speaks with bitterness of the terrible discipline of his Jewish education. He thought of the Talmud Torah as a prison shutting him off from all desirable life, from reality itself. One of the stories he tells – conceivably the incident was invented to stand for his feelings about his Jewish schooling – is about his father's having fallen prey to the Messianic delusion which beset the Jewish families of Odessa, the belief that any one of them might produce a prodigy of the violin, a little genius who could be sent to be processed by Professor Auer in Petersburg, who would play before crowned heads in a velvet suit, and support his family in honour and comfort. Such miracles had occurred in Odessa, whence had come Elman, Zimbalist, Gabrilowitsch, and Heifetz. Babel's father hoped for wealth, but he would have foregone wealth if he could have been sure, at a minimum, of fame. Being small, the young Babel at fourteen might pass for eight and a prodigy. In point of fact, Babel had not even talent, and certainly no vocation. He was repelled by the idea of becoming a musical 'dwarf', one of the 'big-headed freckled children with necks as thin as flower stalks and an epilectic flush on their cheeks'. This was a Jewish fate and he fled from it, escaping to the port and the beaches of Odessa. Here he tried to learn to swim and could not: 'the hydrophobia of my ancestors – Spanish rabbis and Frankfurt money-changers – dragged me to the bottom.' But a kindly proof-reader, an elderly man who loved nature and children, took pity on him. 'How d'you mean, the water won't hold you? Why shouldn't it hold you?' – his specific gravity was no different from anybody else's and the good Yefim Nikitich Smolich taught him to swim. 'I came to love that man,' Babel says in one of the very few of his sentences over which no slightest irony plays, 'with the love that only a boy suffering from hysteria and headaches can feel for a real man.'

The story is called 'Awakening' and it commemorates the boy's first effort of creation. It is to Nikitich that he shows the tragedy he has composed and it is the old man who observes that the boy has talent but no knowledge of nature and undertakes to teach him how to tell one tree or one plant from another. This ignorance of the natural world – Babel refers to it again in his autobiographical sketch – was a Jewish handicap to be overcome. It was not an extravagance of Jewish self-consciousness that led him to make the generalization – Maurice Samuel remarks in *The World of Sholom Aleichem* that in the Yiddish vocabulary of the Jews of eastern Europe there are but two flower names (rose, violet) and no names for wild birds.

When it was possible to do so, Babel left his family and Odessa to live the precarious life, especially precarious for a Jew, of a Russian artist and intellectual. He went to Kiev and then, in 1915, he ventured to St Petersburg without a residence certificate. He was twenty-one. He lived in a cellar on Pushkin Street, and wrote stories which were everywhere refused until Gorky took him up and in 1916 published in his magazine two of Babel's stories. To Gorky, Babel said, he was indebted for everything. But Gorky became of the opinion that Babel's first stories were successful only by accident; he advised the young man to abandon the career of literature and to go 'among the people'. Babel served in the Tsar's army on the Rumanian front; after the Revolution he was for a time a member of the Cheka; he went on grain-collecting expeditions in 1918; he fought with the northern army against Yudenich. In 1920 he was with Budyonny in Poland, twenty-six years old, having seen much, having endured much, yet demanding initiation, submitting himself to the test.

The test, it is important to note, is not that of courage. Babel's affinity with Stephen Crane and Hemingway is close in many respects, of which not the least important is his feeling for his boyhood and for the drama of the boy's initiation into manhood. But the question that Babel puts to himself is not that which means so much to the two American writers; he does not ask whether he will be able to meet danger with honour. This he seems to know he can do. Rather, the test is of his power of direct and immediate, and violent, action – not whether he can endure being killed but whether he can endure killing. In the story 'After the Battle' a Cossack comrade is enraged against him not because, in the recent engagement, he had hung back, but because he had ridden with an unloaded revolver. The story ends with the narrator imploring fate to 'grant me the simplest of proficiencies – the ability to kill my fellow-men.'

The necessity for submitting to the test is very deeply rooted in Babel's psychic life. This becomes readily apparent when we read the whole of Babel's canon and perceive the manifest connexion between certain of the incidents of *Red Cavalry* and those of the stories of the Odessa boyhood. In the

story 'My First Goose' the newcomer to the brigade is snubbe
by the brilliant Cossack commander because he is a man with
spectacles on his nose, an intellectual. 'Not a life for the
brainy type here,' says the quartermaster who carries his
trunk to his billet. 'But you go and mess up a lady, and a
good lady too, and you'll have the boys patting you on the
back . . .' The five new comrades in the billet make it quite
clear that he is an outsider and unwanted, they begin at once
to bully and haze him. Yet by one action he overcomes their
hostility to him and his spectacles. He asks the old landlady
for food and she puts him off; whereupon he kills the woman's
goose in a particularly brutal manner, and, picking it up on
the point of a sword, thrusts it at the woman and orders her
to cook it. Now the crisis is passed; the price of community
has been paid. The group of five re-forms itself to become a
group of six. All is decent and composed in the conduct of
the men. There is a general political discussion, then sleep.
'We slept, all six of us, beneath a wooden roof that let in the
stars, warming one another, our legs intermingled. I dreamed:
and in my dreams I saw women. But my heart, stained with
bloodshed, grated and brimmed over.' We inevitably read
this story in the light of Babel's two connected stories of the
1905 pogrom, 'The Story of My Dovecot' and 'First Love',
recalling the scene in which the crippled cigarette vendor,
whom all the children loved, crushes the boy's newly-bought
and long-desired pigeon and flings it in his face. Later the
pigeon's blood and entrails are washed from the boy's cheek
by the young Russian woman who is sheltering the Babel
family and whom the boy adores. It is after her caress that the
boy sees his father on his knees before the Cossack captain;
the story ends with his capitulation to nervous illness. And
now again a bird has been brutally killed, now again the
killing is linked with sexuality, but now it is not his bird but
another's, now he is not passive but active.

Yet no amount of understanding of the psychological gensis of the act of killing the goose makes it easy for us to judge it as anything more than a very ugly brutality. It is not easy for us – and it is not easy for Babel. Not easy, but we must make the effort to comprehend that for Babel it is not violence in itself that is at issue in his relation to the Cossacks, but something else, some quality with which violence does indeed go along, but which is not in itself merely violent. This quality, whatever it is to be called, is of the greatest importance in Babel's conception of himself as an intellectual and an artist, in his conception of himself as a Jew.

It is, after all, not violence and brutality that make the Cossacks what they are. This is not the first violence and brutality that Babel has known – when it comes to violence and brutality a Western reader can scarcely have, unless he sets himself to acquire it, an adequate idea of their place in the life of Eastern Europe. The impulse to violence, as we have learned, seems indigenous in all mankind. Among certain groups the impulse is far more freely licensed than among others. Americans are aware and ashamed of the actuality or potentiality of violence in their own culture, but it is nothing to that of the East of Europe; the people for whom the mass impalings and the knout are part of their memory of the exercise of authority over them have their own appropriate ways of expressing their rage. As compared with what the knife, or the home-made pike, or the boot can do, the revolver is an instrument of delicate amenity and tender mercy – this, indeed, is the point of one of Babel's stories. Godfrey Blunden's description of the method of execution used by the Ukrainian peasant bands is scarcely to be read. Nor is it only in combat that the tradition of ferocious violence appears, as is suggested by the long Russian concern with wife-beating as a national problem.

The point I would make is that the Cossacks were not exceptional for their violence. It was not their violence in itself that evoked Tolstoy's admiration. Nor is it what fascinated Babel. Rather he is drawn by what the violence goes along with, the boldness, the passionateness, the simplicity and directness – and the grace. Thus the story 'My First Goose' opens with a description of the masculine charm of the brigade commander Savitsky. His male grace is celebrated in a shower of epithets – we hear of the 'beauty of his giant's body', of the decorated chest 'cleaving the hut as a standard cleaves the sky', of 'the iron and flower of that youthfulness', of his long legs, which were 'like girls sheathed to the neck in shining riding boots'. Only the openness of the admiration and envy – which constitutes, also, a qualifying irony – keeps the description from seeming sexually perverse. It is remarkably *not* perverse; it is as 'healthy' as a boy's love of his hero of the moment. And Savitsky's grace is a real thing. Babel is not ready to destroy it by any of the means that are so ready to the hand of the intellectual confronted by this kind of power and charm; he does not diminish the glory he perceives by confronting it with the pathos of human creatures less physically glorious, having more, or a higher, moral appeal because they are weaker and because they suffer. The possibility of this grace is part of what Babel saw in the Cossacks.

It is much the same thing that D. H. Lawrence was drawn by in his imagination of archaic cultures and personalities and of the ruthlessness, even the cruelty, that attended their grace. It is what Yeats had in mind in his love of 'the old disturbed exalted life, the old splendour'. It is what even the gentle Forster represents in the brilliant scene in *Where Angels Fear to Tread* in which Gino, the embodiment of male grace, tortures Stephen by twisting his broken arm. This fantasy of personal, animal grace, this glory of conscienceless self-assertion, of sensual freedom, haunts our culture. It speaks to something in us that we fear, and rightly fear, yet it speaks to us.

Babel never for a moment forgets what the actualities of this savage glory are. In the story 'The Brigade Commander' he speaks of the triumph of a young man in his first command.

Kolesnikov in his moment of victory had the 'masterful indifference of a Tartar Khan', and Babel, observing him with genuine pleasure, goes on to say that he was conscious of the training of other famous leaders of horse, and mentions 'the captivating Savitsky' and 'the headstrong Pavlichenko'. The captivating Savitsky we have met. The headstrong Pavlichenko appears in a story of his own; this story is his own account of his peasant origin, of the insults received from his aristocratic landlord, of how when the Revolution came, he had wiped out the insult. 'Then I stamped on my master Nikitinsky; trampled on him for an hour or maybe more. And in that time I got to know life through and through. With shooting ... you only get rid of a chap. Shooting's letting him off, and too damn easy for yourself. With shooting you'll never get at the soul, to where it is in a fellow and how it shows itself. But I don't spare myself, and I've more than once trampled an enemy for over an hour. You see, I want to get to know what life really is . . .' This is all too *raffiné* – we are inclined, I think, to forget Pavlichenko and to be a little revolted by Babel. Let us suppose, however, that he is setting down the truth as he heard it; let us suppose too that he has it in mind not to spare himself – this is part, and a terrible part, of the actuality of the Cossack directness and immediacy, this is what goes along with the grace and charm.*

In our effort to understand Babel's complex involvement with the Cossack ethos we must be aware of the powerful and obsessive significance that violence has for the intellectual. Violence is, of course, the contradiction of the intellectual's

---

* The celebration of the Cossack ethos gave no satisfaction to General Budyonny, who, when some of Babel's *Red Cavalry* stories appeared in a magazine before their publication in a volume, attacked Babel furiously and with a large display of literary pretentiousness, for the cultural corruption and political ignorance which, he claimed, the stories displayed. Budyonny conceived the stories to constitute a slander on the Cossacks.

characteristic enterprise of rationality. Yet at the same time it is the very image of that enterprise. This may seem a strange thing to say. Since Plato we have set violence and reason over against each other in reciprocal negation. Yet it is Plato who can tell us why there is affinity between violence and the intellectual life. In the most famous of the Platonic myths, the men of the Cave are seated facing the interior wall of the Cave, and they are chained by their necks so that it is impossible for them to turn their heads. They can face in but one direction, they can see nothing but the shadows that are cast on the wall by the fire behind them. A man comes to them who has somehow freed himself and gone into the world outside the Cave. He brings them news of the light of the sun; he tells them that there are things to be seen which are real, that what they see on the wall is but shadows. Plato says that the men chained in the Cave will not believe this news. They will insist that it is not possible, that the shadows are the only reality. But suppose they do believe the news! Then how violent they will become against their chains as they struggle to free themselves so that they may perceive what they believe is there to be perceived. They will think of violence as part of their bitter effort to know what is real. To grasp, to seize – to *apprehend*, as we say – reality from out of the deep dark cave of the mind – this is indeed a very violent action.

The artist in our time is perhaps more overtly concerned with the apprehension of reality than the philosopher is, and the image of violence seems often an appropriate way of representing the nature of his creation. 'The language of poetry naturally falls in with the language of power,' says Hazlitt in his lecture on *Coriolanus* and goes on to speak in several brilliant passages of 'the logic of the imagination and the passions' which makes them partisan with representations of proud strength. Hazlitt carries his generalization beyond the warrant of literary fact, yet all that he says is pertinent to

Babel, who almost always speaks of art in the language of force. The unexpectedness which he takes to be the essence of art is that of a surprise attack. He speaks of the manoeuvres of prose, of 'the army of words, . . . the army in which all kinds of weapons may be brought into play'. In one of his most remarkable stories, 'Di Grasso', he describes the performance of a banal play given by an Italian troupe in Odessa; all is dreariness until in the third act the hero sees his betrothed in converse with the villainous seducer, and, leaping miraculously, with the power of levitation of a Nijinsky or a panther, he soars across the stage, falls upon the villain and tears out his enemy's throat with his teeth. This leap makes the fortune of the Italian company with the exigent Odessa audience; this leap, we are given to understand, is art. And as the story continues, Babel is explicit – if also ironic – in what he demonstrates of the moral effect that may be produced by this virtuosity and power, of what it implies of human pride and freedom.

The spectacles on his nose were for Babel of the first importance in his conception of himself. He was a man to whom the perception of the world outside the Cave came late and had to be apprehended, by strength and speed, against the parental or cultural interdiction, the Jewish interdiction; it was as if every beautiful violent phrase that was to spring upon reality was a protest against his childhood. The violence of the Revolution, its sudden leap, was cognate with this feral passion for perception – to an artist the Revolution might well have seemed the rending not only of the social but of the perceptual chains, those that held men's gaze upon the shadows on the wall; it may have seemed the rush of men from the darkness of the cave into the light of reality. Something of this is suggested in a finely wrought story 'Line and Colour' – like other stories of the time of Babel's sojourn in France in the early thirties, it was written in French – in which Kerensky is represented as defending his myopia, refusing to wear glasses, because, as he argues very charmingly, there is so much that myopia protects him from seeing, and imagination and benign illusion are thus given a larger licence. But at a great meeting in the first days of the Revolution he cannot perceive the disposition of the crowd and the story ends with Trotsky coming to the rostrum and saying in his implacable voice, 'Comrades!'

But when we have followed Babel into the depths of his experience of violence, when we have imagined something of what is meant in his psychic life and in the developing conception of his art, we must be no less aware of his experience of the principle that stands opposed to the Cossack principle.

We can scarcely fail to see that when in the stories of *Red Cavalry* Babel submits the ethos of the intellectual to the criticism of the Cossack ethos, he intends a criticism of his own ethos not merely as an intellectual but as a Jew. It is always as an intellectual, never as a Jew, that he is denounced by his Cossack comrades, but we know that he has either suppressed, for political reasons, the denunciations of him as a Jew that were actually made, or, if none were actually made, that he has in his heart supposed that they were made. These criticisms of the Jewish ethos, as he embodies it, Babel believes to have no small weight. When he implores fate to grant him the simplest of proficiencies, the ability to kill his fellow-man, we are likely to take this as nothing but an irony, and as an ironic assertion of the superiority of his moral instincts. But it is only in part an irony. There comes a moment when he should kill a fellow-man. In 'The Death of Dolgushov', a comrade lies propped against a tree; he cannot be moved, inevitably he must die, for his entrails are hanging out; he must be left behind and he asks for a bullet in his head so that the Poles will not 'play their dirty tricks' on him. It is the narrator whom he asks for the *coup de grâce*, but the narrator flees and sends a friend, who, when he has done what had to be done, turns on the 'sensitive' man in a fury of rage and disgust: 'You bastards in spectacles have about as much pity for us as a cat has for a mouse.' Or again, the narrator has incurred the enmity of a comrade through no actual fault – no moral fault – of his own, merely through having been assigned a mount that the other man passionately loved, and riding it badly so that it developed saddle galls. Now the horse has been returned, but the man does not forgive him, and the narrator asks a superior officer to compound the quarrel. He is rebuffed. 'You're trying to live without enemies,' he is told. 'That's all you think about, not having enemies.' It comes at us with momentous force. This time we are not misled into supposing that Babel intends irony and a covert praise of his pacific soul; we know that in this epiphany of his refusal to accept enmity he means to speak adversely of himself in his Jewish character.

But his Jewish character is not the same as the Jewish character of the Jews of Poland. To these Jews he comes with all the presuppositions of an acculturated Jew of Russia, which were not much different from the suppositions of an acculturated Jew of Germany. He is repelled by the conditions of their life; he sees them as physically uncouth and warped; many of them seem to him to move 'monkey-fashion'. Sometimes he affects a wondering alienation from them, as when he speaks of 'the occult crockery that the Jews use only once a year at Eastertime'. His complexity and irony being what they are, the Jews of Poland are made to justify the rejection of the Jews among whom he was reared and the wealthy assimilated Jews of Petersburg. 'The image of the stout and jovial Jews of the South, bubbling like cheap wine, takes shape in my memory, in sharp contrast to the bitter scorn inherent in these long bony backs, these tragic yellow beards.' Yet the Jews of Poland are more than a stick with which Babel beats his own Jewish past. They come to exist for him as a spiritual fact of consummate value.

Almost in the degree that Babel is concerned with violence in the stories of *Red Cavalry*, he is concerned with spirituality. It is not only Jewish spirituality that draws him. A considerable number of the stories have to do with churches, and although they do indeed often express the anticlerical feeling expectable in the revolutionary circumstances, the play of Babel's irony permits him to respond in a positive way to the aura of religion. 'The breath of an invisible order of things,' he says in one story, 'glimmered beneath the crumbling ruin of the priest's house, and its soothing seduction unmanned me.' He is captivated by the ecclesiastical painter Pan Apolek, he who created ecclesiastical scandals by using the publicans and sinners of the little towns as the models for his saints and virgins. Yet it is chiefly the Jews who speak to him of the life beyond violence, and even Pan Apolek's 'heretical and intoxicating brush' had achieved its masterpiece in his Christ of the Berest-echko church, 'the most extraordinary image of God I had ever seen in my life,' a curly-headed Jew, a bearded figure in a Polish great-coat of orange, barefooted with torn and bleeding mouth, running from an angry mob with a hand raised to ward off a blow.

Hazlitt, in the passage to which I have referred, speaking of the 'logic of the imagination and the passions', says that we are naturally drawn to the representation of what is strong and proud and feral. Actually that is not so: we are, rather, drawn to the representation of what is real. It was reality that Babel found in the Jews of the Polish provinces. 'In these passionate, anguish-chiselled features there is no fat, no warm pulsing of blood. The Jews of Volhynia and Galicia move jerkily, in an uncontrolled and uncouth way; but their capacity for suffering is full of a sombre greatness, and their unvoiced contempt for the Polish gentry unbounded.'

Here was the counter-image to the captivating Savitsky, the image of the denial of the pride of the glory of the flesh to which, early or late, every artist comes, to which he cannot come in full sincerity unless he can also make full affirmation of the glory. Here too is the image of art that is counter to Di Grasso's leap, to the language in arms – the image of the artist's suffering, patience, uncouthness, and scorn.

If Babel's experience with the Cossacks may be understood as having reference to the boy's relation to his father, his experience of the Jews of Poland has, we cannot but feel, a maternal reference. To the one Babel responds as a boy, to the other as a child. In the story 'Gedali' he speaks with open sentimentality of his melancholy on the eves of Sabbaths – 'On those evenings my child's heart was rocked like a little ship upon enchanted waves. O the rotted Talmuds of my childhood! O the dense melancholy of memories.' And when he has found a Jew, it is one who speaks to him in this fashion: '. . . All is mortal. Only the mother is destined to immortality. And when the mother is no longer living, she leaves a memory which none yet has dared to sully. The memory of the mother nourishes in us a compassion that is like the ocean, and the measureless ocean feeds the rivers that dissect the universe.'

He has sought Gedali in his gutted curiosity-shop ('Where was your kindly shade that evening, Dickens?') to ask for 'a Jewish glass of tea, and a little of that pensioned-off God in a glass of tea'. He does not, that evening, get what he asks for; what he does get is a discourse on revolution, on the impossibility of a revolution made in blood, on the International that is never to be realized, the International of the good.

It was no doubt the easier for Babel to respond to the spiritual life of the Jews of Poland because it was a life coming to its end and having about it the terrible strong pathos of its death. He makes no pretence that it could ever claim him for its own. But it established itself in his heart as an image, beside the image of the other life that also could not claim him, the Cossack life. The opposition of these two images

made his art – but it was not a dialectic that his Russia could
permit.

LIONEL TRILLING